MW00440398

Street Games

◄ An Eric Myrieckes Novel ►

 BLACK PEARL BOOKS PUBLISHING
www.BlackPearlBooks.com

This book is a work of fiction. Names, characters, places and incidents are products of the author's imagination or are used fictitiously. Any resemblance to actual events or locales or persons living or dead, is entirely coincidental.

Street Games

An Eric Myrieckes Novel

Published By:

BLACK PEARL BOOKS INC.
3653-F FLAKES MILL ROAD – PMB 306
ATLANTA, GA 30034
404-735-3553

Copyright 2005 © Eric Myrieckes

All rights reserved. No part of this book may be reproduced in any form or by any means without the prior written consent of the Publisher, excerpting brief quotes used in reviews.

All Black Pearl Books titles, imprints and distributed lines are available at special quantity discounts for bulk purchases for sales promotion, premiums, fund raising, educational or institutional use.

Special book excerpts or customized printings can also be created to fit specific needs. For details, write to Black Pearl Books: Attention Senior Publisher, 3653-F Flakes Mill Road, PMB-306, Atlanta, Georgia 30034 or visit website: www. BlackPearlBooks. com

FOR DISTRIBUTOR INFO & BULK ORDERING

Contact: **Black Pearl Books, Inc.**
                3653-F Flakes Mill Road
                PMB 306
                Atlanta, Georgia 30034
                404-735-3553

Discount Book-Club Orders via website:
www. BlackPearlBooks. com

ISBN: 0-9766007-4-9   LCCN: 2005932351

Publication Date: September 2005

ACKNOWLEDGEMENTS

Thanks to my remarkable sons, Eric Jr., Rashaad and Rasheed. You guys are phenomenal. The three of you motivate my every thought. All that I do is for the benefit of you. Through you little men, I discover the inspiration to keep on keeping on when I don't have strength to go an inch farther.

Ms. Lisa M. Abril, you're my heart, my reason... an intricate piece to my puzzle. To tell you that I love you is simply not enough. Mami, yo espero que tu no tengas miedo a la altura, porque vamos a ver lo que hay en la cima. Thank you for your constant encouragement in my endeavors. With you life is sweeter, deeper, happier—better.

I extend my deepest gratitude to the following family and friends who've been supportive:

Grandma Mary Williams, I have so much appreciation for the love and faith you have in me. Walter Williams Sr., my tough-ass granddad. Thank you for demanding me to be the example of what I want to see in the world. Because of you, I'm headed in the right direction.

To my parents, Linda Myrieckes and Billy Williams Sr. – who taught me to set my goals high. Thank you both in abundance for the gift of life you have given me. Look at me, I'm an author now!

Author Cordless Sims, if it weren't for you, I wouldn't know diddly about the craft. To have you as an example of work ethics and craftsmanship is an honor.

The "Unknown Silence" (Yeslin Escobar), you find a way to bug the hell out of me, but your friendship is unmatchable. You've been there from word one and knew that I would make it. Thank you. By far, you've been the most interesting and impelling person throughout this writing process.

The real 21 (SVS), your insight and taking the time to read sample chapters is appreciated. Creating history with you has been an unforgettable experience. You'll always have a friend in me, homie.

To all of my past and present novel writing students, thank you for posing such tough and challenging questions. You all keep me sharp in my knowledge and application of the craft of writing. See you in class!

Auntie Net, my favorite. Thank you for having the eyes to see my literary dreams and sending me to school for journalism and freelance writing. I told you it would pay off.

The best thanks of all goes out to those that left me for dead, to those that took their costumes off and revealed their true selves, to those that grin in my face while they secretly anticipate my failure. You know who you are, just as I know. You only push me to live, stimulate my growth, fuel my ambitions to succeed against the odds. By all means, keep it up, you're doing a great job.

DEDICATION

"Street Games" is dedicated to the lasting memory of:

Daisy B. Williams

Ida Britt

Teresa Robinson

Ramone Perry

Stephen Holmes

Street Games

◀ **An Eric Myrieckes Novel** ▶

 BLACK PEARL BOOKS PUBLISHING
www.BlackPearlBooks.com

PROLOGUE

A K-9 barked and scratched with vigor at the side of one of many pinball machines positioned throughout the immaculate finished-basement.

Jayme Johanson rewarded the shepherd with long strokes. "You found something, huh, boy? Good boy."

A huge man with massive hands and a smoldering Cuban cigar stuck in his mouth crossed the room to see what set off the shepherd's senses. "I hope this mutt found what we came for."

She shifted her green eyes at the solid man. "It'll be nice to retire before I'm thirty." She climbed beneath the arcade game and pulled off the false bottom.

Bundles of banned money fell to a well-polished hardwood floor.

"Ding! Ding! Ding!" Smoke rings floated away from the huge man's thick lips. "This is the best pinball game I've ever played." He took out a two-way radio and spoke into it. "Get down here, Nester. The cash cow is in the basement." He watched loads money drop out of every machine Jayme removed the bottom from. "I wish Curlew was still around to get a piece of this action."

"Damnit, would you stop mentioning Curlew, it pisses me off every time I think about his murder." She slid the zipper of her bag open.

"This isn't even the beginning of what I have in store for Lamont. He fucked up when he killed one of ours." The huge man began to fill his nylon sack with money.

Moments later Nester came down the stairs with a plastic container of gasoline swinging at his side. "I'll be damned. I'm getting used to this. I knew we didn't bring enough bags to load all this up."

Jayme smiled. "Stuff your freaking tighty-whities if you have to. We're not leaving one dime. People like Lamont don't deserve to have money like this."

Ten minutes passed and the trio headed toward the stairs with their nylon sacks packed to the hilt.

Nester tossed the empty gasoline container on an oversized billiard table. "Let's get out of this place. I have Cleveland and the Browns." He followed Jayme to the first floor. "Pennsylvania is calling me."

The huge man took a long draw on his cigar then thumped it across the drenched room. "That's for Curlew."

The room went up in flames.

CHAPTER ONE
Limbo

There is only one thing on this earth that dominates me. The things I have done to secure it have embarrassed the devil. The filth that smudges it fuels my ambition to hoard it. The texture of it...the texture excites an unbending hard on. But the things I'm gonna do with it will convert my atheist mother into a believer. I rubbed six Benjamin Franklin's between my brown fingers. "Murdock, money has a hold on me. I can't get enough of it."

"Who isn't attached to loot in some twisted way?" Murdock tossed his ball cap on the table beside an in-house phone. "I'm jealously in love with it myself, cousin. Why else would I murder for it?"

"What's your reason for loving these evil-ass pieces of green paper with pictures of dead racists on it?" I sat the money in front of Murdock. "What's so special about this shit that prompts you to kill?"

The DJ's raspy voice boomed through the sound system. "The roof, the roof, the roof is on fire!" Sweaty and scantily dressed bodies on the dance floor responded with, "We don't need no water let the motherfucker burn. Burn motherfucker burn!"

Murdock focused back on me. "I'm in love with it for the same reasons everybody loves it, I'll just go to the extreme to get it. Cash gives me power and advantage. I can buy all kinds of shit with it. Shit that puts a stupid-ass Kool-Aid grin on my face. Your possession ain't too much different."

"Different?" I turned to my friend. "I'm hypnotized by the might of dollar for an entirely different reason. You know how fucked up it was for me and my sister growing up. Nobody else in my family is gonna experience life like we did. Adams is gonna be a household name. I'm gonna be the one to create a legacy for my family. Crackers been doing it for years. They still passing down old-money made off slavery. You got to respect crackers though, 'cause they smart. They be thinking on the lines of what their great, great, great grandkids can buy." I put my hand on Murdock's shoulder and looked him in the eyes. "Crackers ain't no smarter than me." I leaned in closer. "When I die in these streets, at least sixty of my generation is gonna be straight. I put that on everything that means anything."

"You talking about Rockefeller paper, Limbo." Murdock fingered the brim of his hat. He was in deep thought. "Do you know how many kilos we'd have to sell to see that type of cash?"

"Yup, that's why I won't stop hustling until I see it." I took a brief trip to the future and thought about my unborn grand babies. "But I feel like I'm running out of time, Dock."

"Man, what you talking--? "

"Here you guys go." Amber came to my private table on the second floor, which overlooked the entire club. She placed a bottle of Cristal in front of me.

Me and Murdock looked at her as if she had lost her damn mind.

"Amby, what's the meaning of this?" I smoothed down my goatee. "Limbo, don't you even trip and call yourself going off on me. I just work here remember? Trip on the white biddy at the bar."

Me and Murdock went to the banister and looked down at the bar. A blonde with hair past her shoulders, who looked as if she was one of Hugh Heffner's Playmates, raised her champagne flute. I nodded. She lit the room with her gorgeous smile.

"Hold up, Amber." Murdock stepped to her. "Let me holler at you."

"About what, Murdock?" They crossed the velvet rope and headed for the stairs.

"What you got in mind tonight?"

"Going to sleep and not with you. Maybe...don't you have a woman at home? Look, we've been through this script a thousand times. I might let you audition for a starring role in my movie when you're free from obligation. I'm too much woman for you anyway Murdock."

"Amber, why does it always got to be the run-around with you? Me and my woman ain't even together for real. We have one of those, fuck you, but ain't gonna leave you relationships. I don't want to hurt her--"

"Boy pah-leeze."

Murdock followed Amber down stairs into the crowded club. I picked up the phone and called the bar.

Hershel picked up before the first ring was finished. "I knew you'd be calling me in less than two minutes, but Amber wouldn't bet me."

"What's up with the blonde and the bottle?"

"I don't know, she's a newcomer though. I told her that you or Murdock didn't indulge, but she insisted. Something isn't right I tell you. This one is so pretty I can't stand to look at her. She hurts an old mans eyes. She must be the devil."

I could feel her watching me. I scanned the room from my seat and there she was staring from a dark corner. "She's just feeling me, Hershel. She's not the devil."

"Then she'll due to the real one gets here."

"You see Murdock?"

"Yeah, he's trying to get a sniff of Amber's goodies."

"Tell him it's time to shake the place. I'm calling it a night." I needed food, sex, and sleep… and I needed it in that order.

Big-mouth, Nina, from Prospect Projects, told me that a stick-up crew from Pittsburgh showed up at Brother's place tonight. They dropped a few hundred dollars on the pool table, asked a few who's doing what questions then rolled out. I checked my rearview mirror to make sure I wasn't being followed by anyone other than Murdock. At 4:39 in the morning, my Range Rover and Murdock's Q45 were the only vehicles on Scalp Avenue.

As I pulled away from a traffic light, I though about how I used to have dreams of heaven. Now I'm living in hell and its good to me. If you had to deal with the elements that consume my nights, you would want a home-cooked meal, a good shot of pussy, and sleep too. Life is like a bad dream only you don't awake from it, sleep is the only temporary relief. Me and Murdock came to Johnstown two years ago and locked it down. I looked over at the tote bag, worn from years of lugging bulky money, sitting on my passenger's seat and

4

smiled. Sixty-four thousand from a Friday's collection is a good days pay. I was up five grand from last Friday's take.

The parking garage came into view, Murdock flashed his high beams, drove around me and entered the garage first to make sure that me or the money wasn't about to be ambushed. I respect Murdock's "Better safe than sorry" philosophy, but no one knew how we drove here each morning, switched cars and left out an underground exit headed to our respective homes. Murdock's in the sumptuous Richland Mines in the opulent Windbar. We practiced this routine religiously to mislead someone who was plotting a jack move or worse. The whole goal was to minimize the chance of leading the jackers to our homes and putting our families lives in danger.

Nary a minute had passed when I pulled into the garage to find Murdock sitting of the hood of his car with a Ruger in hand. I parked beside him and between the rest of our fleet of cars. I grabbed the tote bag and hopped out. "Who was the white broad that sent us the bottle of Cris?" That question had been on my mind since we left Club Everyday People.

"Don't sweat the small stuff. Miss something for a change." Murdock tucked the gun in his khakis. He kept his attire gangster. Corn rolls, Dickies, wife beater T's, a ball cap broke ninety degrees to the left—today it was the Cleveland Indians. Daily he broadcasts his signature style, the untied Timberland boots.

"How could I? She wanted to be noticed. Besides, when I start missing little shit, Blake will decorate both our wrists with iron bracelets."

"Four-one-one told me that Ms. Blondy transferred here from North Carolina State to finish her last year of college at U.P.J. She's putting in some intern hours at Lee Hospital.

Four-one-one is the nickname that everyone calls big-mouth Nina. "Damn that girl be knowing the business, she should be a news anchor."

"What makes you ask? You don't do the white girl thing." Murdock looked at me sideways. "If Elixir's evil ass even thought you imagined fucking with a snow bunny, she'll tear the hick-ass town up."

Murdock knew that I had everything I wanted at home. My relationship with my wife is monogamous, for the most part. Any messing around was consensual. We'd have a ménage a trois with different women from around the world that Elixir carefully chose from the Internet. Although, she never invited a white woman into our bedroom because of her deep-rooted hatred. "Murdock, you know I don't get down like that. I don't need to fuck around on my woman, we fuck around together. This new face got a name?"

"Rhapsody."

Rhapsody? That's different, I thought.

Murdock nodded, still looking at me sideways.

"I like the way this broad held up her champagne glass when we scoped the room to see who sent the bottle, but it was strange the way she stared at me after Amber delivered the Cris' to our table. The more I think about it, it felt like she was studying me instead of checking me out. You feel me?"

"Nah, Cuz, your mind playing tricks on you."

"I hollered at Hershel before we left and he told me that he told the broad that we didn't drink, but she insisted on sending the bottle anyway."

"Hershel sells liquor for a living. That was a three-hundred dollar sale. Do you really thing that greedy-ass Hershel would insist that she didn't? You know that thirsty niggah ain't turning no money down . . . besides it ain't no stranger than the rest of them gold-digging bitches that be staring and watching, but too scared to step because they know Elixir will get in their ass."

Murdock definitely had a point.

"Limbo, you got to tell Elixir to take the press off these hoes. She fucking up my extra-curriculum pussy. I'm an advocate of slanging dick on the regular basis to as many hoes as I can. On Grip, cousin, I don't see that faithful bullshit."

I smiled. Elixir had made it difficult for Murdock to get his funky off. What did he expect? Murdock is Elixir's first cousin and Elixir is Avonte's best friend, which is Murdock's baby mamma. Since Avonte couldn't handle Murdock's adulterous ways, Elixir had her back.

"Relax, Limbo, you're making something out of nothing. The bottle of Cris' was just a gesture to show that the tack head had class. She can separate real players from the lames when they are in her presence. It also tells me that that bad-ass white girl has heart. I'm sure somebody put her up on game about your maniac wife, but she wasn't afraid to step. I take that to mean she's trying to set the ass out."

"I have to agree with you."

"About what?"

"She is the finest pink toe I've ever seen. It don't make logical sense how pretty she is." We gave each other a pound then Murdock asked me how he should handle the situation with Black Mike.

"How much is missing?" I sat the moneybag down.

"Not much, seven thousand. He ain't smoking, so he's down right sneak thieving. I started to crack his shit, playing on my intelligence. Feeding me some bullshit that our packages were short."

"Were they?" I pissed him off.

"Limbo." Murdock had an annoyed look on his face. "I don't know whether I'm supposed to take that as disrespect or disrespect."

"On Grip, Homey." I threw up our neighborhood sign. "Ain't no disrespect. I just wanna make sure Black Mike gets dealt with justly. If I have him punished for something on our

7

part, it will breed animosity and hatred to those on the outside looking in. It will also send the wrong message to the rest of our workers. The wrong type of fear will have motherfuckers on the inside of our camp working to destroy us on the low."

"The niggah is tapping the packages." He bounced his head in rhythm with his words.

"Where is he now?" I couldn't wait to get home.

"In the trunk of that broken down Mazda in the back yard of the dope spot."

"Break all of that niggah's fingers. Bust him back down to block status. Let Dollar run the spot, he's been looking to climb the corporate ladder. Make sure Black Mike knows that he has one week to get my money up . . . ." I shook my head. I used to think Black Mike had potential, but now I'm disappointed. I'm sure the fool weighed the consequences of stealing from me. The extremities between getting away with it or getting caught. ". . . I wonder what he thought I would do if he was caught, and Murdock, just so we send the right message, when his cast come off, take him somewhere, and blow his dream maker out."

After Murdock and me talked for a few more minutes, I tossed the tote bag on the back seat of my Lexus 400 LS and told him to page me the time the sun went to sleep. He hopped in his BMW 750 IL and threw up our hood with his fingers. I was finally going home.

Food. Sex. Sleep.

I popped in my bootlegged CD of Kool and the Gang's Summer Madness – the instrumental version. It blended well with this hot Summer-morning night. The street ahead of me was dark and long. It seems like the more eager I am to get home, the longer it took. This is a familiar feeling. I felt this way on my last prison bid. The closer my release date came, the further away it was. The last mile in any destination is always the longest. The clock on the console read 5:10 am. Another ten minutes and I would be pulling my plate from the microwave, having pornographic thoughts with Elixir's name written all over them.

Lately, Elixir had been complaining about the hours I kept. It wasn't that she didn't understand the hustle, she had just out-grown it. I remember when she was the Bonnie to my Clyde, when she was more supportive of my occupation, when she enjoyed the fringe benefits. Now her conversations and mannerism towards me is of didactic nature. She says she'd rather have an average man with an average life, than to have the luxuries and worries that come with my current life. She and my mother share the same fear. The phone call that breaks them from a troublesome sleep, informing them that another family has been torn apart due to death or jail. Elixir is willing to trade everything we have in exchange for a welfare check, a project apartment, having me at home when she closes her eyes at night and opens them the next morning, knowing that I'm safe, and her and the children won't be abandoned.

Time definitely changes people. In 1990, when we were eighteen, Elixir would carry my guns in her purse and my drugs stuffed in her twat while we crossed state lines because her record was flawless. Eight years, triplet sons, two prison bids later, she wanted something for the first time that I couldn't give her -- an average man, with an average life. I'm no better than a crack head, an alcoholic, a prostitute, or a trick. I have a habit too -- moving kilos of cocaine.

My first carnal need had been met. My baby handled her business in the kitchen. Candy yams, New York Strip Steak, Collard greens, corn-on-the-cob, sweet macaroni and cheese, and buttery sweet rolls were waiting on me when I got home. I threw down. Now I was ready to have my second carnal need met. Sex.

My sons looked so innocent while they were sleeping. Looks are deceiving because my boys are bad as hell. Elixir always said that they got it honest. I refilled their humidifier, as I do every morning, to keep their asthma from acting up, and kissed their tiny foreheads. After I checked on the boys, I stood in the doorway of our bedroom watching Elixir in her sleep for a few moments. The house was so quiet I could hear the therapeutic hum of the children's humidifier. She lay there on top of the sheets in her see-through blue bra and panty set with these cute little animal-printed footies. Her chest rose and fell with ease. Her tender nipples were taut and hard. My dick damn near tore through my pants. By the time I undressed and climbed into bed the head of my dick had swollen up like a mushroom. I traced her anatomy with the tip of my finger. Sensing that she could rest better, now that I was home, Elixir smiled in her sleep.

God I love this woman, I thought to myself. I kissed her and outlined her lips with my tongue until her eyes popped open. When she focused on me with her beautiful brown eyes, I said, "Good morning."

She threw her arms around me and pulled me into her space. "I had a dream --

I put my finger across her lips. "Shhh." I wasn't in the mood to talk. I wanted to twist our souls up. I kissed her deeply. Our tongues probed each other's mouths. I slid my hand inside her panties. She was wet, warm, and excited. I could feel her heart race as she squirmed under my touch.

Every time we made love it was like our first time over and over again. Each time we screwed, I fell in love with her more than I was yesterday. She gapped her legs open. I pushed two fingers inside her throbbing pussy. I slid down between her thighs and pulled her panties to the side.

"Mmmm, that's what I like," she whispered, pulling her legs up and palming the back of my head.

10

I took a deep whiff then stuck my tongue in her dewy flesh. She squealed when my tongue touched her pussy. She shoved her hips at my face while telling me how much she loves me. Her panties were sopping wet. My dick was so tight it was about to explode.

She lifted her hips. "Are you ready to take them off? Please take them off." She respects my panty fetish. I need to see her in panties and pull them off myself. When she helped me wiggle the panties past her ass, she pulled a leg out and parted her legs like the Red Sea. Her pussy was shiny with juice. She was so wet the juice dripped from the crack of her ass, soaking our sheets. I couldn't do nothing but rub my whole face in it. She went into a passion frenzy when I licked from her asshole to her clit with long, flat manipulative strokes. When I finished giving her head, she ordered me to, "Stand up!"

Elixir's wet tongue flicked at the tip of my mushroom. A shiver sliced through me. My dick jumped with excitement from her every kiss. When the pre-come formed on my head, she glossed her full lips with it. She licked me like I was a melting ice cream cone; she wasn't letting any of me go to waste. She put my head in her mouth, teasing me.

I balled my toes up. Although she was teasing, it felt good. "Stop playing."

She gripped my ass cheeks and pulled as much of me into her face as she could, pushing my mushroom into the crown of her throat. I couldn't take it anymore. "Turn over, ass up."

"What are you going to do to me? She asked in a mischievous tone while assuming the position.

"What do you want me to do?" I rubbed my mushroom against her wet hole.

"Hit it like it's the last time you're gonna get it."

I entered her, holding on to my headboard and using it to slam myself deep and hard into her warmth. She thrust her hips back against me for maximum penetration. My nuts bounced against her pear-shaped ass with each brawny long-dick stroke. Elixir was always appreciative of an early morning fuck. We screwed until we both had leg-shaking orgasms. We collapsed on the bed into each other's arms. She laid her head on my chest. I threw my dreads over her shoulder, covering her back. Elixir's body was covered in a thin sweat that made her smooth cocoa butter skin shine in the partial darkness.

There was muffled laughter. Elixir immediately covered up. We looked up and our boys were peaking around the doorway pointing.

"Get y'all little asses in the bed." I used my daddy-means- business voice. They scurried down the hall.

She sucked her teeth. "Bad butts. How long you think they been standing there?"

I shrugged.

I wasn't experiencing my temporary relief from life's bad dream a good twenty minutes before the ringing phone shook me awake. I looked at the caller ID.

Unavailable? How is my phone ringing while it's reading unavailable? I questioned myself and the reliability of the phone package we bought. I picked up but didn't say anything. I was tired, the bed was calling me, and I wasn't in the mood.

"Lamont Adams?"

I immediately caught the belligerent voice. A cold feeling ran through my gut. "Cop, why the fuck you sweating me at my home? How -- It's too early in the morning for your bullshit." The nerve of this motherfucking disrespectful Detective Blake, calling me where I rest. He had been harassing me in the streets, pulling me over every chance he got. Inviting himself to a seat at my private tables in the clubs I frequent. Spreading meaningless photos of me and Murdock across the table while we were in known drug areas. We couldn't get around that. Damn near everywhere-Black folks

12

live is a "known drug area." Blake had even used this psychological maneuver a time or two, while I was out with Elixir. Planting the seed of fear in her mind, causing her to worry herself sick and me at the same time. Detective Blake had just broken the rules. He brought a situation that was supposed to be handled in the streets to my home. It was at this moment that I decided Detective Blake had to be dealt with. "Dig this Blake, if you ain't gonna arrest me, then stay the hell off my dick."

Elixir was wide-eyed and all ears.

"It's 6:55," Blake said, "in ten minutes, we'll be kicking your fucking door in on a drug warrant. I'm going to personally put of pair of cuffs on you. But not until me and my boys point guns at your family. I hope that little love doll lying beside you is naked when we cuff her -- "

I looked over at Elixir, she was newborn naked except for the animal-printed footies. My blood was starting to thicken. I covered the phone and told Elixir to put something on. A piece of fawn colored hair cascaded down the left side of her face. She gave me a knowing look through those beautiful brown eyes. I put the phone back to my ear and Blake was still talking.

" . . . I'm sure I can trump up some charges to inconvenience your wife for the next thirty days or more. That leaves us with your sluggers. I'm going to go out of my way to make sure they see their drug dealing daddy ride away in a police car. We're even going to have the lights flashing for you. I would love to take care of your boys while you and your wife enjoy the accommodations in my county jail, but I'll be busy cleaning more scum off my streets. I guess that means I don't have time to baby-sit. I'm going to stick their black asses in temporary child custody services before your fingerprint ink dries. That'll be a hell of an experience, don't you think?"

I could almost see Detective Blake sneering at me on the other end of the phone. His anomalous pale face and those beady eyes. I'm a rational thinker and I have an exceptional quality of performing well under pressure. I lined him up to reveal his true intentions. In my best poker voice, I asked the quarrelsome cop, why he would expose his hand and tell me what card he was going to play.

"Because, Limbo, I'm a gambling man. I'm willing to bet you'd rather have me play a different suit."

CHAPTER TWO

Detective Robert Blake's posture was crooked, just enough to cause him to be arrogant. Although his posture was bent, he was wiry in his movements, sinewy in his actions. He stood in the old train station's parking lot, next to his Pontiac 6000, sipping Espresso through a straw. Ever since the now forty-year-old detective was a child, he wished that he could drink without the use of a straw . . . like normal people. He hated that his abnormality caused women to be repulsed by the freak in him. He had a cleft lip and a deep crevice where his nose should have been. It looked like he shoved a double barrel shotgun in his mouth, pushed the trigger with a big toe, and lived through the aftereffect. His clothing reflected his world view. Supermarket sneakers, threadbare jeans, and a coffee stained T-shirt that read: Dreams are like rainbows, only fools chase them.

The homeless used the old train station's parking lot as their place of residence. There were cardboard tents, shopping carts, smoldering barrels, and trash scattered everywhere. The surrounding neighborhood had done so much complaining about the strong urine stench that it forced the city to place several transportable bathroom stalls throughout the lot. As Detective Blake looked at the bums, he thought, this was almost my life.

A bag lady hobbled, dragging her right foot, as she pushed her trash ridden shopping cart through the lot. She stopped every few feet to chug down some malt liquor and to shout vulgarities. The ramblings between the piercing vulgarities were incomprehensible. She wandered aimlessly from one end of the lot to the other, showing an uncanny interest in Blake's Pontiac 6000.

"How does it feel to finally get the chance to put them size thirteen's on Limbo's neck?" Agent Curlew joined Blake at the rear of the car as the bag lady hobbled away.

Blake looked down at his sneakers and attempted his version of a smile. "I can't wait to see the look on his face when sees you." Just then a royal blue Mustang pulled into the lot, playing loud, trunk rattling offensive music.

CHAPTER THREE
Limbo

There would be retribution for the threats Blake made against my family. There's a time and place for everything. Today wasn't the right time, the train station, definitely, wasn't the right place. Too many potential witnesses . . . but just in case things got thick, Murdock was on point with his better safe than sorry philosophy. He would beat me to the train station by twenty minutes.

I know that Blake would hit me with the interrogative verbiage, but I had no idea what he would question me about or what he thought he had on me. Through deductive reasoning I kept trying to figure out why Blake wanted to meet with me at the old, abandoned train station. I could only come up with one answer.

He wanted his palms greased.

When I turned onto the road leading to the train station, I hit five-nine on my cellular speed dial. Murdock picked up on the first ring. "What up, Cuz?"

"Ain't shit," "What's cracking with the set up?"

"Nothing major. I can handle this situation by myself. A niggah close enough to the pigs to chop they asses down. I been feigning to get rid of Blake. This'll give me a chance to try out Goldie Mack."

"Easy, Loc. They? How many is they?"

"Just chill and be my eyes. I'm unarmed -- "

"I thought you told me that the faggot said he wouldn't arrest you if you met with him."

"He did." I was getting closer to the train station.

"Then strap up, niggah!"

"Blake ain't shaking hands right. If he does have something on me, I don't want a gun case on top of it."

"On everything Cuz, I'mma keep him honest. He said you ain't going to jail then you ain't going, homey. Goldie gonna pay your bond today.

"On Grip, Murdock, you're gonna get your chance to scrap but we'll pick the backyard to knuckle up in. The ball is in Blake's court. Let's see how he dribbles."

"If he fouls, Goldie gonna go off."

There was no point in trying to talk sense into Murdock. Once he set his mind on something, it was carved in stone. He'd been that way for as long as I could remember. Even when we were shorties -- straight gang banging -- the O.G.'s couldn't handle him. Murdock was going to put in work regardless of what shot the O.G's called. He often said, "Limbo, I respect the old homies, but nar one of 'em bet' not get in my way, 'cause I'mma have to see them, too."

I have no problem with leaving I.D.'s hanging off toes, but I'm not a senseless killer. In the same token, I wouldn't be using any sense if I left witnesses behind. Certain situations

18

left me in the purgatory. This was one of them. On any given day the parking lot could be occupied by ten to fifteen vagabonds. For the homeless sake, I hoped Detective Blake didn't foul out. I told Murdock to keep our call connected so that he could stay on top of the business. I put N.W.A.'s Fuck the Police in the CD player and dropped the top on my five-point-O. I pulled into the train station with the arrogance of a rich street niggah.

As I drove through the lot it reminded me of some pictures, from a National Geographic, of a third world country. Everyone was moving in slow motion. Behind the tattered clothing and desolate faces of the homeless, I saw their eyes. In the language of their eyes was desperation and pain. Neglect and abandonment. Hunger and failing health. Hatred and confusion. Broken spirits and broken dreams. And they have the nerve to call America "The Land of Opportunity." In the language of their eyes, I saw everything contradictory to opportunity. The further I drove into the lot, the more it deteriorated. Variations of skin didn't matter here. The homeless all had the same color -- dirty.

When I parked, Ice Cube was screaming at the top of his lungs from my stereo, ". . . fuck that shit, 'cause I ain't the one, for a stupid motherfucker with a badge and a gun to be beating' on and thrown in jail. We can go toe-to-toe in the middle of a cell." Blake was leaning against the trunk of his Pontiac with his arms crossed. I was parked directly behind him but on the other side of the lot, pointed in the same direction as his car. I could see the back of someone's head, sitting in his passenger's seat. With my cell phone in hand, I went over to Blake.

"Limbo, I'm glad that you found time . . . how do you people say it? . . . to bust it up with me." He offered me his hand with a hideous smirk.

The bullshit begins. I stared at his hairy hand like it had piss on it. "On the drive down here, I kept thinking how are we going to talk face-to-face when all you got is a head with a hole in it?" I struck a nerve. I watched every ounce of strength that he had go south.

"Fuck! Fuck! Fuck the Police!

Blake looked past me to my car. With a sorry attempt to refortify himself, he said, "While you were doing all that thinking, a smart fellow like yourself didn't forget to think about terroristic threats on a law official did you?"

He would have to come better than that. "The first amendment wasn't a suggestion was it?" I never stopped checking out the head of some guy sitting in the front seat of Blake's car.

After we went a few more rounds exchanging mental jabs, Blake knocked on the trunk. The passenger door opened and I was delivered a blow beneath the belt . . . and it hurt.

Time stood still as I scanned the Rolodex of my mind. I remember this Klansman now standing beside Blake, smiling a shit-eating grin at me. The first and last time I had seen this man was a month ago. He was in my crack house crawling on the linoleum floor searching for crumbs of crack that he hoped fell from the kitchen table. His lips were chapped. He looked exhausted as if he'd been on a cocaine binge for days, and was too weak to find the strength to let go. I'm twenty-six. Beneath exhaustion he looked to be about the same age.

"Black Mike, get that dude off the floor," I said, handing him a paper bag with nine ounces in it. "He's part of the reason we live good. You gotta take care of him like he's taking care of us. That ain't good." I pointed to the man who was now tasting -- God only knows what -- he found on the floor.

"Limbo, I ain't forcing that broke motherfucker to chase ghosts." Black Mike gave me a look like he couldn't care less.

"What you think be going through motherfuckers heads like that -- " I looked at the man under the table. " -- When they come down?

20

Black Mike shrugged.

"They remember who looked out for them when they were down and out, and who didn't. The ones who did, their loyalty is stronger than man's best friend. The others, like you, that carry them fucked up, they think devious shit to do to you. Shit like rob you or set you up with stick-up boys or the law. Your customer becomes your enemy. What I did next was for business, but more for Black Mike's education. It was my job as head niggah in charge of this operation to make sure that Black Mike understood the importance of his role towards my goal -- money. I took an ounce from the paper and broke a nice piece off. I went into the kitchen and liberated the pitiful man from ran-down linoleum.

"Thanks," he said through a dry, broken voice.

He pulled some crumpled bills from his pocket, "Here take it. I appreciate -- "

"Lying, motherfucker. I thought you was broke? Black Mike snapped, stepping forward.

I gave Black Mike a look that both quieted and weakened him. "I would've told you the same thing if you left me feining. Pay attention little niggah. From now on I'm gonna charge you for this game." I broke off another chunk, gave it to the man, took the crumpled bills, and passed them to Black Mike. "Hit me on my hip when you get me right."

I gave the cracker some crack, took the chump change, and gave it to Black Mike. Now this short man dressed for a typical summer day, stood in front of me with a shit-eating grin. His head was oblong just as I remembered. His eyebrows were connected and he had one of those Scandinavian ski slope noses. Today he has a new feature that I will remember for the rest of my life. A chain hung from his stubby neck with a badge attached to it.

"Looks like you're drowning," Blake said in his patent detective voice, "jump in the car, and let me throw you a life jacket."

He had hit it on the nose, I was feeling seasick. I forced down the bile in my throat. Blake pat searched me before I climbed in his back seat.

"There's no need for me to introduce you to Federal Agent Curlew. It's obvious you were acquainted well enough with him to sell him eleven grams of crack cocaine, a schedule two narcotic." Blake took a sip from his straw. Coffee dripped from his chin to his denominational T-shirt. He started reading from a surveillance report. "On Friday, the first of May, 1998, at approximately 3:30 AM. Lamont Adams -- also known as Limbo -- entered the residence at 1438 Franklin Street where D.E.A. Agent Sean Curlew was operating undercover. Adams gave a paper bag to and had a conversation with Mike Patterson -- also known as Black Mike -- before entering the kitchen and offering Agent Curlew a marble size piece of crack cocaine. Moments later Adams exchanged a similar sized piece of cocaine with Agent Curlew for forty-three dollars of marked U.S. currency." Blake looked at me through the rearview mirror. "Should I continue or would you prefer to hear the tape-recording of the transaction?"

"With your record" Agent Curlew shifted his weight and reached over the seat, sitting a pair of handcuffs beside me and a form with my name and alias, age, social security number, and D.O.B. on it. "This infraction will put you away for no less than eight years."

I took a furtive look at my cell phone trying to picture the expression on Murdock's face as he listened to this bullshit. I couldn't quite picture the expression, but I did read his mind when my display screen went from caller connected to caller disconnected. Blake had fouled out. I watched Blake through the mirror. When I looked at him closely, I could see that one of his eyes were lower than the other. His face was twisted in such a way it made me think his breath stinks.

He caught me staring and said, "I want you to think of me as Harry . . . Harry Houdini that is."

A few scornful sarcastic thoughts came to mind, but I kept my cool. "Oh yeah, Frank -- Frankenstein that is -- why is that?

"Because I can make this little incident disappear."

I looked out the window into the decadence of the lot. "Shit like eleven grams don't magically disappear. So how do you plan on pulling that one off?"

Did he really just ask me that? I tried to figure out if Blake and his crony thought that I was a pussy dressed in thug clothes. I guess he thought my locks were a fashion statement. I'm a real dread. A rebel. My shit represents defiance towards the law. "You sick sons of bitches. You want me to get on the stand and point a finger at the people who trust me?"

"It's a small price to pay -- "Agent Curlew craned his compact neck looking past the headrest at me. "To make eight years go away. Give me a few good busts that'll get me my promotion . . . and it's possible that you'll get a license to hustle."

"Hell, it's possible I might shift thunder." I looked into the third world again at some bag lady pushing a cart, cursing about her living conditions, I would assume. "You crooked motherfuckers are attacking my integrity."

"While at the same time, Blake fired back through the hideousness in his face, "trying to maintain the strength of your character. We're the real gangsters -- we don't go to jail. Come aboard and you won't go either." The double cross was blatant in his voice.

"If I don't?"

The automatic locks made a blunt click. There were no back seat door handles, just an empty hole where the lock should have been.

"Then save me the trouble and cuff yourself, while I read you your rights." Agent Curlew motioned to the handcuffs next to me. "Make sure they're tight."

They had me confused with the weak. My death would come before my dishonor. I went into deductive reasoning mode. There was a long silence between us. The gaps were filled by the cursing bag lady.

"Do your wife and sons a service, help yourself. Let us help you help yourself." An image of Elixir popped in my head at Curlew's mention of my family. Her warm brown eyes sitting beneath those long eyelashes. The butterfly shaped birthmark right below her panty line. Her loving smile that set off her adorable dimples. Her caring touch that kept me running home. Those dainty outfits she wears, defining her sexuality. There was a lineage of beautiful black women in her family and it hadn't skipped her generation. I was amazed at how such a tiny woman (5'6", 115 pounds) could carry such a heavy load. Then after some time, I realized that strength isn't measured in size, but by one's determination. Only Elixir could calm this roaring lion inside me.

Reasoning . . . deducting . . . .

"Sign the paper, Limbo" Curlew urged me, breaking me from my private thoughts.

Deductive reasoning mode switched over to my conflict resolution skills. "A license, huh? I'm down." Hearing myself say that didn't feel right. Another flash popped in my head. Elixir and I, in our parenting endeavor, had to speak with our children about the implications -- both good and bad -- of tattle telling. After an incident in their kindergarten class.

The locks clicked again. Looking at Blake, Curlew tapped his Casio. I assumed that he was reminding Blake that they had other things to do and a time frame to do it in.

"Sign the form." Curlew demanded. He was too anxious to toss me a pen. "Your signature makes the deal official. Then we'll have the charge dismissed.

"I ain't signing shit. My word made the deal official. If that ain't good enough for you then do what you gotta do."

Agent Curlew was up for a full fledge debate, but Blake stopped him before he got started. "Okay fine. Here's my pager number. I'll be out of town on other business until next Thursday. I want you to page me every day until then, keep my ear to the street. We'll put together a sting when I come back. Pop your cherry. You'll do good, you look like a natural."

Motherfucker trying to clown me. "I ain't no actor like your boy Curlew." Blake and Curlew found humor in that comment. When they were through with their laugh, Curlew got out and opened my door. As I was climbing out Blake stopped me. He told me that the first time I failed to call him, he would have me arrested in the manner he described on the phone.

"Yeah all right, it's all good," I walked away not bothering to look back. Then I heard him say . . .

"Limbo, it's great to finally be working with you."

Making my way across the lot to my car, I crossed paths with the cursing bag lady. She had her head down so far in the shopping cart it made it impossible to see her face. From the looks of it, she had on every stitch of clothing she owned. I could tell she was wearing a wig because of the way the hair set on her head. The shopping cart was packed with aluminum cans, engine parts, PVC piping, and some out-dated newspapers. There was no telling what else was beneath the rubble. I looked down at her feet and saw Murdock's signature, the untied Timberland boots.

"Machine in motion. What that Grip like, cuz?" Murdock lifted up a newspaper, revealing a Mack 10 with an extended clip -- Goldie.

I reached into my pocket and handed him some money, to make it look good. Nine times out of ten Blake and Curlew were watching. "Murder, murder, murder, homeboy . . . and tell them pigs a niggahs name is Limbo not Uncle Sambo." I always had poor conflict resolution skills.

Johnston, PA is one of those towns where every Black person knows every other Black person. Everyone waves to everyone in passing. Damn near the majority of Blacks here are family, leaving very little room for love. The relationship that could be had, are still intact or have been tried. That left the Black community with three options: Brothers screwed white girls, sisters screwed out-of-towners: the other option -- incest. Downtown Johnstown is no more than two miles of narrow lanes and squat brown buildings. This place is so small, if I tried hard enough. I could throw a rock from one township to the next. This is why Murdock and me lived in neighboring counties. Can't shit where you rest at. A brother like me from a large city, who has a difficult time recalling names, Johnstown is like a corrective penance. Actually, I hate this one-horse town. It ain't slick enough. It's a good place to raise my children. I love the money and being treated like a celebrity, but I wouldn't miss it one bit.

On my way home I spoke with Jerry Vidya, my lawyer. I instructed him to sell my Windbar home, along with my interest in the exotic aquarium shop, Fish Scales. After I told him that I wanted the proceeds from Fish Scales to be divided amongst the homeless down at the old train station, he said, "You're a lot of things, Limbo, but all around you're a good person."

I reached the point where Bedford Street turned into Scalp Avenue, "We call that keeping it gangster. I fuck with you 'cause you keep it gangster."

"Thank you," Jerry said. "Well then you keep on keeping it gangster and you'll go far."

"Until the day I die." My pager vibrated against my hip. The display screen read 187. Murdock handled his business. I told Jerry to log the time of our conversation in his files. Then we said our good-byes and I called Elixir.

"What's up Baby? She tried to disguise her worry.

"You know the drill, it's time to bounce, Slim."

26

She let out a deep breath. I couldn't tell if it was a sigh of relief or frustration.

"How long before you get here?" She asked with much attitude. I quickly found out it was the latter -- frustration.

"I have to switch cars first. Twenty, twenty-five minutes."

When I pulled into my in-house garage, there were five pre-packed suitcases sitting by the door that led to the kitchen. One for each of us. Along with the suitcases were two fireproof strong boxes. One contained my children's' baby book, immunization records, medical history, birth certificates, and S.S. cards, bonds and certificates of deposits. In the other were several car titles, the deed to our home and summer cottage, life insurance policies, passports, spare keys, credit cards, and checkbooks. All I had to do was hit my stash and we were out. Since we were going to be on the road for a while, and would need room for the boys, I switched the Mustang with the LX 470.

I was loading the trunk space when Elixir came marching my sons through the door. The look on her face told me that I wasn't getting any pussy any time soon.

"Limbo, understand what I'm about to say."

I was right, she's mad.

"This is it. I have to do what's best for these boys. I love you with my everything. Been in love with you since we were kids. But this will be the only time that I'll uproot these children.

"What's uproot, Mommy? We both looked at our son, Latrel. The garage started to have a draining feel to it.

"Not now," she said, "Y'all get in the car."

"I got the window." Lamont pulled Latrel's ear.

"You always get a window." Lontrel scurried to the car first. His brothers followed.

"If you want to keep selling drugs then you go right ahead. But the next time you leave us for any reason concerning drugs or because of drugs, I'm taking the boys and we're leaving you. Them boys count on you for everything. They need you in their lives consistently. The sad part is that don't even really know what money is." Her hands were on her hips now. Her head was moving from side to side. "You think they'd rather have you or some money?"

I got ready to stand up for myself and rationalize, but Elixir threw up her hand as if she was stopping traffic.

"I'm not finished. Don't none of this shit mean anything if we don't have you here to share it with us. As long as you sell that crap, you can't promise us shit worth taking to the bank. That you're coming home tonight. That you'll be alive tomorrow. That we're going to the fucking zoo. A stable family not shit! I can teach them everything but how to be a man. That's your job and you need to take the necessary precautions to teach them." A single tear ran down her face.

I stood there with the jackass look on my face.

"And what about me?" She asked. "I'm not old and dried up. I'm still young and fine. You want another niggah laying up fucking me and raising your sons?" She punched me in the chest. "Huh, niggah, is that what you want? 'Cause that's exactly what's gonna happen if you leave me again. Do not try me."

Ouch that hurt! Not the punch, but the implication. Elixir was now pointing a finger in my face. "I don't want to look out my kitchen window to see some broom pushing, burger-flipping motherfucker playing football with my sons. I will if you force me to, Limbo. I wanna look out the window and see your stupid ass, that's why I married you. I'm not doing another prison sentence with you. I'm not buying my clothes to fit visiting room regulations. Nor will I be sweating the phone waiting for the caller I.D. to say unavailable, and I'm damn sure not going to be hanging out by the mailbox waiting for the mailman to run, hoping he has a letter from you again. You wanna talk to me? Then make sure you can do it without an ink pen or a collect call."

Elixir had definitely said a mouthful. She struck every nerve ending in my body, making me feel raw. And she had every right to want a stable life. My first thought was, shouldn't I just get out the dope game and give her my half on stability? She and three spitting images of me were what I cared most about in this world. I had just reached a few million dollars in cash. I could fall and be all right. She was still standing there in her sassy stance, boring a hole through me with those powerful brown eyes. Then my second thought hit me. A few million dollars ain't shit. I could think about a few things and spend that.

After Elixir told me off, she kissed me as if she hadn't verbally assaulted me. I was too stunned to kiss her back.

"Now that we have an understanding." Elixir held me around the waist, looking in my eyes. "I don't know where you're taking us, but I will follow your lead. I will stick by you. I just ask that you stick by us. I will follow you to the end of the earth if you make the right decision. Now let's go, 'cause I'm hungry."

I had no idea what decision I would make. I can't abandon my dreams, but I did know where I would lead my family to. Cleveland.

CHAPTER FOUR

Detective Blake handed Curlew a few hundred dollars for the bet he lost. They had put Limbo in a compromising position. But Blake never thought in a million years that Limbo would agree to snitch.

"Don't ever go against me." Curlew adjusted the sun-visor mirror to watch Limbo cross the parking lot. "Throw some Buck Rogers numbers at them, and people like him will sell their mothers out."

Blake shook his head. "Something isn't right. I've been having this eerie feeling ever since my feet hit the floor this morning. The same feeling I had, the day my father died in the line of duty." Blake was now watching Limbo through the rear-view mirror. "Looks like our boy has a heart for the homeless." Curlew watched Limbo give money to the bag lady.

"Here it is you have a common street punk that poisons people for a living giving his money to some bum, that'll probably buy drugs with it anyway." Blake turned to Curlew. "Does that make sense to you?"

Limbo exchanged a few words with the bag lady then drove away. She stuffed the money in her pocket then hobbled with her shopping cart towards Blake's car. She was right behind the car when the reverse lights came on. She stood in the path shouting vulgarities.

Curlew leaned out of the window flashing his badge. "Lady move out of the way!"

The command fell on deaf ears. She stood there.

"Give her a few dollars," Blake said, putting the car back in park. "That's all she wants."

"Weren't you the one that just asked me how much sense does that make?" Curlew reached over and hit the horn.

"We're not drug dealers, just do it, would you already! I'd give it to her myself, but I gave you all the money I had until I stop by the credit union."

Curlew sighed then hung a five-dollar bill out the window. Still cursing the lady started toward the money. When she reached Curlew's window the Mack 10 was already in her hand. Before reflex instructed Blake or Curlew to think about drawing their weapons, machine gun fire ripped through the car. Forty-five slugs passed through metal and flesh. When the five-dollar bill reached the lot's pavement both lawmen were dead.

Murdock disappeared into the lot's interior.

CHAPTER FIVE

Limbo

June 2000

The winding road that led to the Cambria County Prison was bumpy. Being tossed around in the back seat of an extradition van bound by handcuffs and shackles was not how I planned to spend my sons' seventh birthdays. This journey from Ohio back to the drab Johnstown on a drug warrant began two weeks ago.

For as long as I live, I'll never forget those rotten ghetto ass kids that got me hemmed up. It was like the warrant miraculously popped out of the true blue sky. Just the day before my arrest I had my private investigator, Jack Spencer, run my name through the system. I was clean, like I had been for the last twenty-three months. I was at my home girl, Kesha's, apartment in Willow Arms playing cards.

"Come on 'round this corner, I'mma show you how tight a sista's card game is," Kesha said to Murdock, slapping a Queen of Spades to the table. "Next time ask a bitch if you can bid six. Set that shit." She raked the cards off the table. A smoldering blunt hung in the corner of her mouth, as she talked shit. "I hope you niggahs brang your bank roll in, 'cause you left your Spade's game in the car."

"Run it back." Murdock snapped. He snatched the deck and started shuffling. He was frustrated. Kesha always put Murdock in a rough abrasive mood when she took our money and ran her garbage mouth while she did it.

"You no-game-having-trick-babies, know how to count." She took two hundred and fifty dollars of the five hundred-dollar pot. "A sista loves taking ya'lls money. Put it up and I'm gonna count it up. I do this shit for a living and I ain't taking no lunch breaks." She passed the blunt to her partner, Chickenbone. The word in the hood was that Kesha was putting statutory rape game down on Chickenbone. The homeboy Chickenbone offered Murdock the blunt he had just rolled. It was obvious that Chickenbone had no idea that we didn't get high. Murdock shook his head. Kesha tried to stop Chickenbone when he turned to me.

I checked the young homey off the top. "Lil Cuz, I know you're new on Hoova turf, so I'mma give you a pass this time. You just got a stripe disrespecting Limbo." I hit my chest for emphasis. "I'm gonna let you keep it as long as you never do it again. I don't put nothing in my body I can get rich off of. Don't miss the jewel." Our felonious homeboy, C-Mack, from the Dirty South rolled in the spot. "Kesha, whose baby daddy you fucking this week? I been trying to reach and touch the hood for the last hour. Stop dodging his woman and put the phone back on the hook."

"I done told them goddam kids about playing on my fucking phone. One of y'all take'em home with you when you go, before I strap them in a car and pull a Susan Smith. I'm

34

taking all y'all on the Maury show anyway to see which one of you deadbeats is which one of my babies' daddy." She stormed off to the children's' room. When Kesha was out of earshot, we shared a common laugh. We all hoped that nar one of them bad-ass kids was ours. I had only the thirteen and fourteen year olds to worry about. Kesha was breaking me off when I was a juvenile, too. I was thirteen in "85." She was twenty-two. She had a baby every year after that until "96" and from what Murdock and C-Mack told me, the poonani was still top shelf and tight as virgin pussy.

For the next five minutes all we could hear was . . . It wasn't me playing on the phone, Mommy, one child said.

You had something to do with it. Whack! Whack! Whack!

Get me last, Ma another child shouted.

I'm gonna make sure I get you next! Whack! Whack! Whack! Another child this, another child that. Whack! Whack! Whack!

I felt for them.

"She's fucking y'all kids up." Chickenbone blew smoke rings.

"That ain't anything." C-Mack gave emphasis to his words with his hands. "My old girl put hands on me; combinations and jabs off the hook." He demonstrated a series of punches.

"You down south niggahs been getting the beat down since slavery." Murdock shuffled the cards.

"You already know."

Whack! Whack! Whack!

We were all laughing and cracking jokes about ass whoopings when someone knocked on the door with urgency. The collective laughter froze. We knew it wasn't a homey because they would have walked right in. I slid the safety off my Glock and aimed it at the door from underneath the card table.

Chickenbone went into the back where Kesha was still beating the kids. Murdock sat his .45 on the table and covered it with his Houston Rockets ball cap. C-Mack sat up on the counter, putting his twin 380's in the sink at arms reach.

When they knocked again, we all nodded to each other and then Murdock told whoever it was to come in.

The police walked in.

One white cop, the other Black. Kesha came in the room huffing and puffing with a leather strap in hand. "What y'all want?" She stood on defense.

I have to admit the whole episode looked fucked up. The belt. Crying kids. Thick marijuana smoke. Tattooed tears. Blue bandanas. The expression of thugsters. I held my nine steady because I wasn't sure how this would play out.

"There were two nine-one-one hang-up calls from this address." The white cop started.

"Our dispatcher tried several times to return the calls but kept getting a busy signal." The Black cop eyed us. He was looking real edgy. While Kesha explained what happened to the cops, I managed to slip my gun under the cushion beneath me. C-Mack went and stood by Kesha, keeping the cops on that side of the apartment. Murdock didn't move and Chickenbone leaned against the threshold of the hallway, leading to the bedrooms. To make an even longer story short, they ended up running our names because of a mixture of marijuana and minors. Everyone else was clean -- thanks to their aliases. Normally, I would have used alias too, but since Spencer told me that I had no warrants, I was proud to give them my government name. The rest is pretty much evident.

After leaving Cleveland County Jail and traveling through four different states swapping prisoners of every criminal facet and spending five tiresome nights in different county jails, I was glad Kesha kicked them kids' asses the way she did.

I walked into the unit. The electronic sally port door clicked behind me to remind me of where I was -- again. The unit had a collective stressed-out feel to it. Every set of strange and familiar eyes in the place stopped what they were doing to stare at me as I went to the C.O.'s desk with my bedroll. I scanned the room for telltale signs of the big-mouth's jaw I would have to break. I have to set and example and let these cats know that I ain't to be fucked with. I heard a familiar voice call my name. When I turned around Dollar was standing on the top tier. He came down to me. We shook hands and embraced.

"Long time no see," Dollar said. "It's good to see you, but not under these circumstances."

"You know how this shit goes." I could tell that Dollar had been locked up for a good minute because he was on swollen. His thick neck was erect between his massive shoulders, making his head look too small. The all-around even haircut didn't even help. His broad chest made the top of his T-shirt snug. A set of huge forearms hung to the side of his five-foot-none frame. "What you been doing pushing up the whole jail?"

"That's what real niggahs do when they're in the joint. Get muscles and tattoos." He showed me his stomach artwork that enhanced his six-pack. "Besides, I'm trying to catch up with you."

"You still got a whole lot of work to do player." I flexed my pecks. "What's the low-down in J-town?" We started walking to the cell the C.O. assigned me.

"When you bounced the hood was on depression status. The money wasn't moving. Nobody had any coke to make it dance, until a posse from the Burg came through. That didn't last long, though, they're all in here now, too."

Dollar sat on my toilet and brought me up to speed on the loop while I made my bunk.

"You know they found that niggah Black Mike with his think box busted and all his fingers broke."

"Get the fuck outta here." I looked at him like he was lying.

"On everything. They think them Hill niggahs did it." That was good to know. I shook my head. "That's fucked up." Mentally, I was laughing. We talked for close to two hours and I tried to call Elixir, but I didn't get an answer at home or on her cell phone. I called my lawyer, Jerry, and made arrangements for an attorney-client visit. Then I showered and called it a night.

Only a week had passed and I had begun to add on to the collective stress. Jerry informed me that I was looking at eight years and that bail would be denied because I'm a flight risk. The cops had questioned me about the murders of Detective Blake and Agent Curlew. I told them, "I was on the phone with my lawyer discussing the sale of my home. Ain't that right, Jerry?"

Jerry flipped his briefcase open. "Yes, I have the documentation of the call right here. My client was being billed for that consultation at the exact same time of the murders."

Homicide Detective Fruita leaned in across the interrogation table so close to me that I could feel the in and out of his Doublemint breath against my face. "Why is it that every time we questioned you about a murder, you're on the phone, out to lunch, on the golf course, or with your lawyer in his office? He turned slightly to Jerry for a reaction.

"That question was for me right? I wanted to look in his eyes.

38

He turned back to me. This time his nose was almost touching mine.

"Have you ever entertained the concept of coincidence?", I asked.

... None of this I was bothered by. I was tripping because I still hadn't talked to my wife. She wouldn't even return Murdock's calls. All that my mother kept saying was, "Give her some time."

Time for what?, I thought. Now I'm dialing my house back to back.

"That all you gonna do, dawg, is hold the phone up?" A hustler from Pittsburgh's Homewood section questioned.

I mumbled purposely. Hoping that he would jump out there.

"Speak up, niggah!" He jumped.

I mumbled even lower. He moved closer to me in an effort to hear what I was saying.

"Stop wasting your time." He was now in my firing range. "Sport coat got -- "

Ummph! I hit that niggah so hard, he dropped to his knees then went out. I was trying to tell him that I had a top notch fight game, he just couldn't hear me. My mother doesn't have Golden Gloves trophies sitting on her mantelpiece because they're a part of the décor. I thought. I was still holding the phone, looking down at the dude when the C.O. rushed over to me.

When Dollar came back from his visit, I was caged in my cell under a forty-eight hour lock down. Watching the day room from this angle frustrated me. I needed to use that dam phone.

Dollar walked up to the bars, stuck his fist inside, and gave me a pound. "How long you got?"

"Forty-eight. I tried to tell that funny built C.O. that the lame just passed out, but he wasn't having it. Fuck it though, the time don't stop." I stared at the phone thinking about Elixir and my sons.

"They said when you dropped ole boy, he was laying at your feet shaking and shit."

"Dollar." Some young dude was walking toward my cell. "Let me get a soup. Two for one, I gotcha store day."

"Let me finish hollering at my boy. I'll be up there in a minute. That's all you need?"

"Got some nachos?"

"I got whatever you need as long as you got your money right."

That's why I fucked with Dollar. Selling drugs don't make a hustler. It's easy, anybody can do it. But everybody ain't all-around hustlers like Dollar. "I see you still in everything but a casket."

"The hustle don't stop, and when I do lay up in that casket, I got something to sell they ass on the other side, too."

There was a commotion at a spades table. This guy named James was ranting and raving about what he was going to do to his partner he reneged while money was involved.

"How can a niggah with one tooth be tough?", Dollar looked at me and waited for my response.

"It ain't no secret he's been getting hit in the mouth his whole life. He shouldn't have that tooth left, for as many people he's set up. . . these lames sit around here playing cards, chit-chatting with the niggahs, basically, telling him they shit is cool." The way they were over there smiling and laughing while James talked tough pissed me off. I squeezed the bars so hard I could feel my pulse in my hands. "These snitches break-up families and have real niggahs like me doing their time. How the fuck can you wear a wire on your homeboy? Your homey you grew up with or the same niggah that put you on your feet?"

Dollar shrugged, looking down at the concrete floor. I didn't like the message his body communicated.

"Do you know how many mamma's sit in the back of the courtroom and die inside, because of niggahs like him? And these cats running around here skinning and grinning with this motherfucker." I looked Dollar in his face because he was part of the problem. "You Johnstown niggahs is one of a kind, homeboy. In my hood we kill our unwanted and useless."

"What's up? Let me get you out of this shit before you stress all the way out and wind up in the pill line," Dollar said, changing the subject. "I got this fly little homey that wants to see you.

"I'm cool." Elixir was on my mind. "I'm having enough problems with pop up visits and unsolicited fan mail from these knuckle head broads now, trying to wreck a niggahs home for some dick and a pair of shoes."

"Unless you want to be locked up along with Mr. Adams," the C.O. yelled from behind his desk. "I suggest that you step away from that cell, Mr. Nelson."

Dollar looked at the C.O. then at me. "He like screaming niggahs whole names across the unit and nit picking all day long. Like its gonna get him a fatter pay check. These C.O.'s be sweating minor shit. They don't understand that the jail will run itself smoothly if they let it. He could play solitary on the computer for eight hours and still get paid the same thing. I'll holler at you, Limbo." We gave each other a pound and he walked away.

The next time I saw Dollar it was after shift change. I was doing push-ups when he walked up and sat my mail between the bars.

"Who wrote me?" I asked to see if he had been eye hustling my return addresses. I wanted to know what his angle was.

"I don't know." He had a bewildered expression.

41

I wanted to laugh, but instead I fixed my face with stern grit. Best he learns now before he goes to the penitentiary and does that dumb shit and gets his whole head knocked off. I shrugged. "Since when did we start getting each other's mail?"

"I figured -- "

"I fucks with you, Dollar, but I don't fuck nar one of you niggahs in here tough enough to be finger fucking my mail. Don't let that shit happen again. Let the police do his job." I stared him in his eyes until he surrendered and looked away. Pussy. Snatching my mail from the bars, I sat on my bunk. "I'll holler at you, homeboy."

"Damn, Cuz, it's like that?

"Niggah! You ain't my cousin. You don't know me." I jumped up from my bunk. "I said, I'll holler at you." I couldn't hold it any longer. I laughed when Dollar walked away with his tail tucked between his legs.

I went through my mail. There were letters from Murdock, two tennis shoe chasers, one I vaguely remembered. A letter from Elixir and a letter from an attorney's office in Cleveland. Of course, I opened my wife's letter first.

Dear Lamont:

I know this letter has found you greeting each day with motivation of a champion. The children and I are fine. I'm sure you're wondering why you haven't been able to contact me. I was advised by my lawyer, Curtis Morrison.

I looked at the mail again. The return address from the attorney read: The Law Office of Attorney C. Morrison .....

. . . to have limited communication with you until the divorce papers were finished. Your son, Lontrel, came in the house the day after you were arrested with the fuzzy stuff from a dandelion. You remember the stuff we used to blow and make wishes? He asked me if he made a wish would it come true. I told him that it would if he really believed in what he wished for. We went back outside, later, so he could release his fuzzy into the air. When I asked my baby what did he wish for, he said it was for you to come back home. I burst into tears because you can't make my baby's wish come true. Can you? Limbo, you're a good man. A provider, accountable and committed. But you're missing the main ingredient -- responsibility. I gave you an ultimatum, the streets, or us. You made the wrong choice and that's when I divorced you in my mind. I knew it was only a matter of time before the inevitable happened. Thank God it wasn't your death! Your arrest and my son's unfulfilled wish made our divorce official. Everything the streets give you is superficial. What I gave you was real. I asked you not to test me. Now its my full responsibility to do what's best for our children. Space isn't hard to find Limbo. Eventually I know -- because of this "street life" you so desperately chase -- you'll thank me for giving you your space. I love you, but for the sake of our children, right now, I need my space.

Ms. Elixir Adams Raymond.

I was ill. I lay in my cage for days neglecting myself. I even had a hard time licking my wounds. I tried to stay focused, but my sight was set on sleeping the pain away. My eyes flicked open every once in a while, but I saw nothing but haze. That tiny voice between my ears kept allowing me to hear my son tell his mother, "I wished for my Daddy to come home."

In the days that I stayed in that state of being, I realized one thing: Anything that you cannot let go of when it outgrows you, possesses you. Divorce papers couldn't free me from Elixir.

CHAPTER SIX

Limbo

It took a month before the swelling on Dollar's pride went down. After that we became tight. It was obvious that I had made my point crystal clear about the mail situation because he never touched mine again. In fact, recently, I overheard him checking someone for fondling his. Into the fifth month of my abduction, my captors decided that today would be my sentencing day. I sat watching the clock waiting for it to strike one. I hated the idea of a fat, silver-head, redneck sitting behind a mahogany desk playing God. The Judges didn't know me, other that what their misinformed criminal report says. What gives them the qualifications to determine my fate?

That ever familiar sound from the sally port door clicked and interrupted my private thoughts. What I saw come through the door was the different extremes of winner and loser. James, the snitch, came in the unit grinning his one tooth smile. Talking loudly about the judge gave him time served. The truth was more like somebody else was serving his time. If that's what it takes to be a winner than count me amongst the losers.

A Hispanic guy came through the door behind James. He was staring at his feet with his shoulders slumped over. He looked as if suicide was easier than the sentence the judge had passed down. Win, lose, or draw. I refused to come back in here looking sick like Pappi.

I sat in disgust as the deputy sheriffs drove me back from the courthouse up that windy, bumpy road that led to Cambria County Prison -- my new home. This time the torturous bumps had no effect on me. I was numb. I couldn't believe this shit. The district attorney botched the case and could only recommend that I serve seventeen months -- county time -- as opposed to the eight-year mandatory state sentence he was formally enforcing. As I was leaving the courtroom the D.A. gave me a look that amounted to hatred. "I'll get you the next time Mr. Adams," his voiced painted with hostility.

"Like I got you this time?" Displaying a little bitterness of my own.

"Humph!" He snapped with his nose turned up and arms crossed, looking like a bitch.

You'll have better luck holding your breath." I readjusted my nuts, giving him a good idea of how far they hung.

Seventeen Months? I shut down shop, sold off my property, moved my family across state lines, and all I got was seventeen months county time. Don't get it twisted. I'm not complaining about the dime but damn. As the jail came into view, I made up my mind. This minor set back would be the catalyst to my major come back. My grandmother always told me that in every adversity -- mine being the loss of my family, living in this big ass room with a gang of lames for another twelve months -- there is a seed of equivalent benefit . . . I wondered what mine would be.

I finally gave into Dollar's persistent attempts to take into the visiting room and meet his girlfriend's friend. Besides I had grown tired of looking at hard legs all day long. I could use the female persuasion to ease my mind right about now. I had grown tired of replacing a woman with artificial stimulation from strokes of my hand. There's no telling how many of my babies are swimming in this jail's drain.

CHAPTER SEVEN

Rhapsody

Well, Well, Well, . . . Limbo decided to meet me. I know exactly what to do to keep him interested in seeing me. I thought, as I stood in front of my closet.

From my ensemble, I chose a classy but revealing two-piece cream and blue outfit. The short skin tight skirt highlighted my oval backside. If Limbo pays close enough attention, he can get a peak at my satin panties when I cross and uncross my legs. Which I will be sure to do a few times. My fitted silk top exposed my bare midriff that I splashed with glitter. If I really want a man and want to keep his attention, I wore a silk top on our first encounter. Something about the silk against my skin kept my nipples hard. If he was just some clown that I really didn't want to be bothered with, I wore a different fabric that didn't make me erect. My open toe heels did nothing but compliment the outfit. I looked at the clock on my dresser and realized that I was running late. I grabbed my credentials, threw on a pair of Chanel frames, and ran out the door.

Cambria County Prison from my home is a thirty-minute drive. If I showed up more that twenty minutes late, I can forget about visiting Limbo today. Checking my watch again, it was 6:01, and I hadn't been in the car for five minutes. I was pushing it. I put Kenny G in the CD player, dropped my Volvo into fifth gear, and put my foot on the gas. Silhouette is the best song in the world to listen to while on the expressway. I swear, the song hadn't even played one full time before a State Trooper snared me with his speed trap. Now I have to admit I was over the limit, but I wasn't driving that fast. I'll never make it, I thought as I pulled onto the shoulder, took my registration out of the glove compartment, and rolled down the window.

"Where are in a rush to, little lady?" He flashed his light in the car. I watched his gaze go from my face to my belly piercing, to my silky thighs.

"I'm running late for an appointment at the county jail -- " I read his name tag as the other cars zoomed by "Officer Ragen, how fast was I going?" I handed him my credentials and registration.

"Seventy in a fifty."

I guess I was going a little too fast. Officer Ragen looked at my credentials and asked in an unbelieving tone, "Federal Bureau of Investigations?"

"D.E.A. Jayme Johanson. I'm working undercover and as I told you, I'm running late." I passed him my business card. "If you could extend me your professional courtesy, I'd really appreciate it if you would send the ticket to me in the mail. I really must be going." I couldn't express really enough.

"You mean you're on a mission as we speak?" He turned from a no-nonsense officer of the law to an excited jovial man. Mission? This jerk has seen too many spy movies.

50

"Undercover work, yes"

He gave me a mischievous smile. "What time do you have to be at your checkpoint?"

I took in a deep breath and sighed loudly, hoping he would get the point. "By six-twenty."

He looked at his watch. "That gives you eleven minutes to get there, little lady. How about you extend me your professional courtesy; let me join your mission -- off the record of course -- and I'll escort you to the county jail."

"Deal." I took back the jerk.

"I hope you can drive this thing, little lady." He patted the roof of my car. "Follow me and you'll make your appointment." When Officer Regan walked away I heard him giggle and say, "I've been waiting for this moment my whole life. I'm working with the Feds. Wait 'till the wife learns about this."

"Asshole."

I made it to the county jail just in the nick of time. I signed in and was escorted to the visiting room. Dollar and my girlfriend Keri were already seated. I winked at Keri and mouthed the words "thank you" to Dollar. I wondered what juicy information Dollar had this week. As I watched Keri and Dollar interact, I couldn't help but to think that Dollar could have done well in the Bureau. But with his criminal history, informant would have to do.

Limbo came into the visiting room and I stood up and waved. Now seeing him for the first time I a lighted area, I couldn't help but notice that he is a very handsome man. The mug shots we have on him does him a disservice. His jet black locks laying against peanut-butter skin, framing his mature face could have gotten him on the cover of an Ebony magazine. He moved in my direction with a powerful set of legs with the grace of a well-conditioned athlete. Why is the ideal man of a girl's dreams either a criminal or gay? I swear this man makes a worn jail uniform look like a Brioni suit. On a professional level, I'm here to do my job. On a personal level, that's a whole different ball game. I'm going to enjoy reading Limbo's cover story.

When I agreed to meet this woman I had no idea what to expect. I definitely didn't expect her to be the finest female in the room. "Hey, what's up?" I'm Limbo." We shook hands. "It's nice to meet you." I could tell that she was a hairy woman because of the blond fuzz on her stomach.

"Francine. Likewise." She flashed a wide smile. The way she looked at me was intense. I could tell that she was high maintenance when I peeped the exotic Bvlgare ring, watch, bracelet, and necklace set.

"The road leading to this place is terrible." She sat down in the chair across from me. "How are you doing?"

"I'm cool. Sensi by Armani right?"

Her wide pretty smile lit the visiting room. "A man that knows his fragrances. I'm impressed."

"You must think I bite." I patted the chair next to me.

"Not at all I'm the one who bites. I sat here so that I can get a good look at you. Look for the full of shit signs." She leaned back in her chair and crossed her legs.

I damn near choked when she did that. "My full of shit signs aren't that obvious where you can see them with the naked eye," I managed to say.

"I'm going to the vending machine for a Sprite. Would you like anything?"

"Nah. I'm Cool."

Vanilla eye candy started towards the machines with the confidence of a runway model. She walked on foot in front of the other with an alluring sway. Her ass wasn't flat according to popular belief. It was the exact opposite. Nice and round. In her switch, she had some rheumatic cadence. She knew I was watching along with the rest of the visiting room. I noticed Dollar's girl rolling her eyes at the show Francine was putting on. Her ass in that tight skirt went, "Your left, your left, your left, right, left!" Her hair style was kind of fly. A blond, feathered corporate America cut that enhanced her beauty and amplified her baby-shit green eyes.

When she came back, she handed me a Ginseng Tea. "You look like a ginseng man. Don't be bashful, it has to better than what they're giving you back there."

It was my favorite but I wasn't going to tell her that. Instead I thanked her.

"Limbo, you don't remember me do you?"

I gave her a perplexed look. "Am I supposed to?", my eyebrow raised with curiosity.

"Ninety-eight. Everyday People . . . I sent a bottle of Cristal to your table."

She started to look familiar. "That was you? Dollar told me your name is Francine. The girl from that night name was . . . something sexy."

"Rhapsody." It's my middle name. Everyone calls me it."

"Yeah, that's right Rhapsody. And you had longer-"

"I cut it." She ran her fingers through her hair. "You like it?"

She was fishing for a compliment. I wasn't going to yank her chain. "I never got the chance to thank you that night."

Rhapsody looked down at the floor for a moment and then back at me. "I'm optimistic that you will once you're out of this place." She hesitated then added, "I don't have to worry about what'serface coming in here showing out do I?" She uncrossed her legs.

When she did that I started to have pornographic thoughts of fucking her with those high heels on. When I focused back on Rhapsody, she was still waiting on her answer. "Nah, no need to worry about Elixir."

"You said that like it hurt -- "

It did.

" -- I apologize if I caused you to have ill feelings."

My face turned serious. She stared at me, but I said nothing. There was silence as I returned her gaze. "What's up, Rhapsody?" Why are you interested in me?"

"Why not?"

"Look at you, you're pretty enough to have any man you want. Your jewelry speaks volumes. A woman like you ain't trying to holler at nobody in jail unless you was fucking with them before they came in, so what's the deal?

She grabbed her Sprite. "Do you want me to go?"

"Not before you answer my question."

She hesitated for a moment as if to gather her thoughts. There was silence again as Rhapsody and I stared at each other. Finally she let out a deep breath and said, "I'll start by saying thank you for the compliment. For the record, "I've been interested in you way before you landed yourself in this place." She paused as her face took on an embarassed expression. "That night I sent you the bottle of Cristal, I knew you and your friend didn't drink. The bartender told me. I did that to let you know I'm interested. I'm barely making ends meet. I couldn't afford that bottle. It's not my fault that you dropped off the face of the earth and just so happened when you re-appeared, you're in jail, and this gave me the opportunity to show you that I'm still interested." She looked at me for a long time, then said, "Excuse me if I have offended you in any way . . . and as far as my jewelry goes, my father was a jeweler and I was his only little girl. Since you need an explanation, my father gave me a lot of expensive jewelry before he and my mother passed away."

"Rhapsody, I apologize. I didn't know . . . also I'm flattered that you went through so much trouble to le me know that you're digging me. Let's rewind this a little bit."

She gave me an intriguing look. "How far are we going back?"

I extended my hand. "What's up Precious? They call me Limbo."

She smiled her infectious, wide smile and took my hand. Over the next hour and a half we swapped thoughts on world views, money matters, politics, and religion. She told me that she was studying psychology and behavioral science. She says she is obsessed with the way people think and how they behave under different circumstances. She asked me to describe my favorite body of water in three words.

"I thought for a moment while staring in her shitty-green eyes. "Warm, wet and tight."

"That's really interesting to know, Limbo." She grinned.

"Why does that interest you? I couldn't keep my eyes off the nipple print in her blouse. She explained to me that you can question a person about one thing, but actually, their answer reveals a personal part of themselves.

"So what did I really just give you the answer to?"

"How sex feels to you."

"Stop playing. Get the hell outta here. Say word."

"Seriously. Limbo, you've told me so much about yourself tonight, through similar questions, but I'm going to keep that on the low, low." She gave me one of those lip curling expressions that autographed femininity. We mentally sparred, enjoying each other's company and laughter until the C.O. announced that visitation was over.

She stood to leave. Rhapsody took a step closer to me. "I really enjoyed our visit."

"I had a good time myself." Looking down from my six foot height, I sized Rhapsody up to be about five-five, a hundred-sixteen pounds, 32-24-34.

"This doesn't have to be the last time." She touched my lock. "If that's all right with you."

"I'm spoiled."

"So am I."

"Don't start nothing you can't finish."

"After these twelve months are up, we can really get started," her tone was littered with mischief.

"I guess we'll see each other soon then." I reached out to shake her tiny hand again.

She reached and hugged me instead, whispering in my ear, "I thought you could use one of these."

Rhapsody's slender body felt so good wrapped in my arms

The innocence she radiated made me want to protect her . . never let her go. I'm always fortunate enough to attract the good girls. "I'll call you in an hour to make sure you made it home safe." I let her go because I had to. "You better bounce before the C.O. starts tripping."

"That old snaggle tooth lady better not say anything. She'll make me go off in here."

"You sound like you got some Black in you."

"Uh um . . . never have. But I will when you come home."

I watched her as she turned and smiled then waved at me before she disappeared through the visiting room doors.

It was after eight when I was done being stripped searched and had made it back to the unit. I noticed that Rhapsody's scent, Sensi, had clung to me when I plopped down in the chair next to the phone. It's always the weirdest things about a woman that really turns me on. Rhapsody . . . the way she curled her lips did it for me. I picked up the phone and called my homeboy.

"P.I. Spencer," he said in his abrasive voice.

"What's cracking, Spence?"

"Limbo. Why haven't you called anyone in the last few days? Everybody has been waiting to hear from you. Jerry, me, Murdock, and your wife."

"I don't have a wife." My words conveyed no emotion.

"Well you need to call Elixir at -- "

"I talked to her and the boys the other day. Why, what up?"

"Just call her at your Aunt Jean's house. I'll let Elixir break the news to you."

My heart skipped a few beats. "Is every one all right?"

"They're fine. Just call her."

"All right. Check this out. I need to find some skeletons in the closet." Spence put me on hold while he said something to his secretary and grabbed a pen. I don't know how Spence does it but he could dig a piece of dirt out of the Virgin Mary's pussy if she isn't as clean as she claims to be. I'm sure that's why he's Cleveland's most sought after Private Investigator.

"Gimme what you got." Abrasive vocal cord.

"Female, Anglo Saxon. Francine Rhapsody Parrish, born in seventy-six. She's from Portage Pennsylvania by the way of Charlotte, North Carolina."

"What's up with the pink toe?"

"I've know Spence long enough to know that his emphasis said, Niggah, I know you ain't fucking with a white bitch!" He just posed the question with some diplomacy. I told him that I wasn't sure yet.

"Well is that all you have on her?"

"Yeah."

"Gimme until tomorrow on this, in the meantime call home."

"It's on." I hung up and called my Aunt's house. Why is Elixir kicking it at my Aunt's house anyway? My son, Lamont answered.

"What's up, little man?" It felt good to hear my son's voice.

"Nothing."

"You taking care of your mother and brothers for me?"

"Yup," he made the "P" in Yup make a popping sound. "You owe me some money, daddy."

"Do you know all ten of the words I told you to look up?"

"Yup." Popping sound again.

"Spell succubus, tell what part of speech and what it means."

He started to spell the word. "S-U-C-C...umm. . .U-B-U-S."

"I told you, you're not the best speller in the world. Tell me the rest."

"It's a plural noun and it means a demon that takes the form of a female and has sex with sleeping men."

"Don't tell your mother I gave you that word. Subterfuge."

He spelled it then said, "It's a noun that means a plan or trick to escape something unpleasant."

"Next week we're going to the T section of the dictionary. I'll have your big cousin Murdock drop your money off."

"Okay . . . Daddy."

"What up little man?"

"When you come home are you going to buy us a new house?"

"Lamont, the one you're living in is new. Don't you like it?"

"I'm not talking about that one. I did like it, but it burnt down the other night."

58

My world started spinning at an alarming rate. I was holding for dear life then all of a sudden it slammed on the brakes and flung me off. "Burnt down?" Then I heard Elixir in the background ask Lamont who he was talking to.

"My Daddy."

"Give me the phone," she said, "go outside and play with your brothers until dinner is ready."

"I love you, Daddy."

In the fourteen years that I've been intimate with Elixir, I've come to know her like the back of my hand. There was signs of distress in her voice.

"I hold you responsible for this." Her words were choppy. According to my understanding of her, tears would be forming now. "And I want to know what you're going to do about it?"

Anxiety slapped me in the face and left me with a troubled mind. I pleaded for the remedy to my illness. "Please tell me that my pinball machines are safe."

"You heard your son!" She hissed. "What part of burnt down don't you understand, the burnt or the down? You're worried about them stupid-ass pinball machines, when you need to be worried about where your kids' and I are going to live at and about putting some clothes on our backs." She sniffled. "We lost everything." From the sound of it, the tears were free flowing like the Nile.

"Calm down, Elixir." I went into rational thinking, deductive reasoning and conflict resolution mode all at the same time. "Let me think a minute."

"Think about what, Baller? You've been using money to solve your problems. You have plenty of it to fix this one with. I'm ready to go, your aunt is already getting on my nerves. We need a place to stay!"

"Y'all gonna have to chill for a minute."

"Why?"

I'm glad we wasn't face-to-face. "Because . . .", I hesitated, not believing what I was about to say.

"Because of what, Lamont?"

"My hustle was stashed in them pinball machines." There I had said it, still trying to convince myself the money was gone. The same way I earned three and a half million, I lost it -- up in smoke. Now I knew what it felt like to be a millionaire one day and dead broke the next.

"Hell nah. I am not feeling you at all right now. I didn't mind giving up everything we had for us to have a family. Now we don't have shit but the clothes on our backs and we still don't have a family. I blame you! I followed you down here and walked away from everything that meant anything. Look where you lead me. A responsible man would have my back right now. I swear, Limbo, I'll never forgive you for this. That's my word!"

"Shut the fuck up and stop bitching." We were both quiet for a moment. "I'll take care of it, I always do don't I?" I knew this wasn't the time, and I don't know what the divorce papers implied, but I checked the status on my position on the sly anyway. "When I come home, I'm gonna make everything right and we're going to be all right."

"There's no doubt in my mind that you'll make everything right, but you're not coming home to me." She banged the phone in my ear. With that I knew where I stood.

"Hey, Limbo," this skinny dude said. "You know where the broom is at?" He stood there looking at me holding the mop.

"Niggah, I'm a hustler." I barked then added, "I look like a motherfucking orderly to you?" I went to my cell to get Murdock's new cell phone number. Murdock picked up on the second ring.

"Yeah," he said with a grunt.

"Yo Cuz, situation critical."

"Homey, that shit ain't nothing. It's a motherfucking blessing your family wasn't in the house."

"Tell the homey we gonna hold him down, he already know it's all love. The whole hood gonna support." I heard C-Mack say in the background.

"Did you hear your locced-out homeboy?"

"Yeah, tell that niggah I said what's up. Where y'all at?

"We're in the hoo–ride about to hit Kinsman. Them P. Stone Bloods off a hundred sixteenth, hit our hood last night, filled Cha-Cha with hot-balls and booked him for a quarter brick. Cha-Cha is going to live, but my homey is paralyzed."

The hoo-ride is a custom made assault vehicle. On the inside, the door panels are stripped down to the metal. There are several retractable flaps in the re-enforced metal. -- in various locations --- just big enough for a fully automatic weapon to push through it. While the flaps were closed, they were undetectable to the eye on the outside, unless you knew what you were looking for. The middle section of the back seat has a crawl space big enough for an average-sized man to lay from the back seat into the trunk – in order to use the M-60 mounted on a tripod. The license plate is on a retractable system, too. It would lay down giving the shooter a clear visual of any target that may be in pursuit.

On the outside, the four-door Delta 88 was an average looking car with limousine tinted, bulletproof window, and a modified turbo engine. Instead of alerting our enemy during a drive-by, speeding through their hood, hanging out of car windows with automatics, if we manned each flap, we could simply drive through at a normal rate where the enemy was off-guard and kill everything moving. The beauty of the hoo-ride is that it left a crime scene, clean. All the ejected shell casings stayed inside the car.

Knowing what Murdock was going to say next, I cut him off.

"Don't show your hand, I'm on a jail phone."

"Niggah, fuck them phones! We finna put in work."

"He already know, it's left to death." I heard C-Mack say.

Murdock said something to C-Mack that I couldn't make out. There was a brief quiet then Murdock said to me, "Homey, that's fucked up about your crib. The only thing that stood up against the fire was two fireproof strong boxes."

"There go them fools," C-Mack said.

"Hold on, Cuz." Murdock put the phone down, but I could hear everything going on.

"They're on your side," C-Mack said. "Go down to the gas station, turn around and come back up the street so I can give these fools what they want." I heard their 455 engine purr an intermittent murmur.

"Put your percussion phones on," Murdock advised.

"I already know."

A few more seconds passed and C-Mack said, "Time to make these fools TV celebrities."

"Tat! Tat! Tat! The gun fire was piercing. I couldn't keep count but I know over a hundred rounds had been fired in about a minute's time. The tires screeched and the 455 changed from purr to an angry roar.

"That was for the homey Cha-Cha," C-Mack said with enthusiasm in his tone.

"We got a Cutlass on our ass," Murdock said, "Get it off!"

I heard some ruffling. I assumed it was C-Mack climbing into the back seat. Next there was a series of "Booms." An M-60 has a distinctive sound when it goes off. I could only think of one thing while I listened to the M-60 bark. I'm glad it was them following the Delta and not me.

"Time for another paint job." Murdock picked up the phone.

The hoo-ride had been painted fifteen different times that I could remember. I wondered what color paint it would get this time. "Murdock, I need you to get my family a place."

"Done. I know you're salty about your crib, homey. Everything gonna be all right. Don't stress it."

"I ain't stressing." I lied.

"Niggah stop fronting, I know you better that you know yourself. Your voice is a dead give away."

"Lace Elixir up. Clothes, furnishings, everything."

"I got you," Murdock said. "The crib is on me, but your girl got dope man taste, so the lace up is on you."

"I'm fucked up in the game. My whole hustle went up with the house."

"Hell nah. Put that on something."

"On the hoove, Cuz. But I'm gonna bounce back in a major way. You down for another picnic?"

"Ain't no question. We been eating together. We ain't gonna stop grubbing 'till one of our caskets drop. Niggah, I put that on the hood.

CHAPTER EIGHT

Rhapsody

Keri and I decided on getting a bite to eat after we left the county jail. There was a slight disagreement on where we should eat. I won, as usual, and she followed me to Olive Garden.

"What will you be having this evening?" A scrawny waiter asked while replacing our ice waters with Pina Coladas. His uniform looked like it was a size too big. We ordered and shared information for our field reports while we waited.

"Dollar said some dealers from Harrisburg came into town last week." Keri sipped her Pina Colada. Her amber eyes twinkled with the dining room lighting. Her soft lips left a pink lipstick print on the rim of her glass. Her body was thin and sleek and, at time, she was cuter than others. It depended on how she wore her natural red hair. Today, it was up in a bun with a curly lock dangling on either side of her dollish face. Real cute.

She continued, "This Harrisburg crew is staying with a ..." She pulled a paper from her purse and read to herself the information written on it. ". . . a black female who goes by the name of Mocha."

The name rung bells. I knew that name, and a face to match it was within my grasp . . . then it dawned on me. "Mocha, Jessica Stevens. Before you transferred here from west bumfuck, the DEA was investigating Mocha. The only thing solid we learned about her is that she -- basically -- runs a hotel."

"Hotel?" Keri gave me her valley girl confused expression.

"Yeah, a hoe and tell. Drug dealers come from out of town and usually stay at Mocha's house until they are familiar with the area. She screws them before they have the chance to screw every other lonely girl in this town. The dealers support her marijuana habit and give her money towards her household. And reliable sources tell us that she provides the dealers with the necessary who's who and who's doing what information in order for them to distribute their drugs."

"Good name, hoe and tell," Keri said. We both laughed.

The scrawny waiter returned with my seafood platter and Keri's lobster and crab meat special. She ate off of my plate and I nibbled off of hers. I asked her, why did someone else's food always taste better than your own. She just shrugged with her mouth full. We ate in silence for a while. I was thinking about that fine man I had just left. Too bad he was an assignment and I couldn't keep him forever. That's right, Jayme, my inner voice whispered.

In between bites, Keri said, "I'll pull the file on Jessica 'Mochas' Stevens, when I get to headquarters on Monday. So what's the four-one-one on the notorious Limbo". She dipped crab meat in the hot butter.

"He's private."

"That has never been a problem for you before."   Her look was suspicious.

I finished chewing my food before speaking.   "He's different from the others . . . very careful, observant, attentive, and smart."   When Keri looked across the table at me, I stared down in my plate so she couldn't read the message I felt was written on my face.   I hated that Lamont Adams was an assignment because I found myself enchanted by him and attracted to him.   His crooked smile made him adorable.   The last time a man was able to make my panties wet just because he was in my presence, I was a naïve high school girl losing the battle against acne.   I shifted my gaze from the platter to my hand bag -- where my wet panties were now tucked away.   I couldn't wait until our next visit.   With time he'd let down his guard and open up to me.   From the moment I laid eyes on Limbo, I knew that -- given an opportunity -- I would open up to him.

". . .Jayme! Jayme, did you hear anything I said?"

I'm glad that Keri interrupted my reverie because I was turning into a naïve school girl again.   "No, what did you say?" And don't use my name, stay in character."

"Never mind."   She rolled her eyes.   "You want to fuck him don't you? Look at you, dammit. You think I can't see?"

Keri is an expert at reading people, especially me. I was only fooling myself thinking that I could fool her. "It's not like that."

"Then what the hell is it like?"   Her jealousy was bubbling. I could feel her amber eyes boring a hole straight through me.

"I just think he's cute."

"Geeze, Rhapsody -- "   She dropped the fork into the plate and pushed it away from her.   " -- the last time you just thought somebody was cute, I came home early and found the pizza delivery boy in our bed with his dick in your mouth. And I do mean boy." She was yelling now.

Other patrons were now staring. Despite my embarrassment, I called after her as she hurried toward the exit. Every opportunity that presented itself to Keri for throwing the pizza guy in my face, she did. I had been on several sexual adventures with other women in my sexual life, but Keri is the first that I've grown to love and attempted to have a monogamous relationship with. To let the truth be told, I made a mistake in my decision.

Trial and error has shown me that I'm not strictly a lesbian, but I am bi-curious. Nature just didn't program her with the right equipment to satisfy my womanly cravings Keri had very right not to trust me -- hell, I don't even trust me -- but her childish outburst and tantrums in public were uncalled for, unattractive, and turning me off in a major way. Her jaded behavior was not helping to repair what little relationship we did have left. I let off a deep sigh and went after her. The garbage I put myself through. She was in her car hugging the steering wheel, crying.

She is so pathetic, I thought as I climbed in the passenger seat. "What is wrong with you?" Pointedly. Her eyeliner had run and turned her cute face into a sad clown's mask. Instinctively, I reached out to wipe away the mixture of tears and Cover girl, but she withdrew from me. "Keri, this isn't about Limbo being attractive, so what is it really about?

"Don't give me your motherly tone." She hissed. "You know what it's about. I want you to myself. I want us to have a normal relationship."

"I hate to be the bearer of bad news. Wake up, Keri. A same-sex relationship is not normal." I framed the word "normal" with a quoting finger gesture. "Our relationship can be so much better if you take all the demands off of it. Learn to go with the flow. Your jealousy is turning me sour."

68

While I was giving Keri a piece of my mind, she had an squinting look on her face.

She didn't pull away when I rubbed her thigh. "I need variety in my life and a strap-on doesn't give me the variety I need. I love you and what we have, but I haven't given up on men. I will not castrate myself so don't cause friction by trying to force me to." I was on a roll, might as well go the distance, I told myself. "I knew that you were on your way home while I was with the pizza guy . . . and his name is Arick, by the way. I was hoping that you'd be spontaneous and join us. Do you have any idea of how excited I was imaging how much fun we all would have once you came home?"

All she said was, "Get the fuck out of my car!"

"For you to be thirty years-old, your behavior is so childish. If your goal is to run me away then you're barking up the right tree." I leaned over, kissed her cheek, ran my finger over her crotch and got out. Before I shut the door, I paused. "Don't wait up."

It was two-something in the morning when I finally stumbled through the door. Keri was sitting on the sofa in the dark with her legs pulled up to her chest, staring at a fuzzy TV screen. This bitch is fatal. I wasn't up for a fight. I kicked my heels off, sat my keys and hand bag on the aquarium stand and headed to the bathroom to shower. The water felt so good pelting against my skin. My coochie awoke from a deep sleep as I rubbed a bar of Mango, oatmeal soap between my legs. I ran my middle finger between my silky fold and circled my clitoris. "Umm!" Every time I taste my pussy slick fingers, I get a libidinal jolt. Tonight the warm water in combination with Hennessey intensified the sexual current. I pushed my finger back between my folds in search of the opening to my dick-starved coochie and suddenly the shower door flung open. Startled, I gasped, dropped the soap and put my hand over my racing heart.

"You two-dollar whore. You insist on fucking around on me. Why Jayme?"

Keri stood there with my panties in her hand looking as if she had crossed the border line of insanity.

"I can't believe you violated my privacy. The nerve of you. What the hell were you doing going through my purse?"

"You were just going to come in here and wash his scent off then climb in the bed with me?" She picked up my skirt and blouse off the floor and started sniffing them. "It's that easy for you. What's his name?

"You're sick." Now I was pissed. "You've lost it. And don't you ever go through my shit again without my permission."

"Where were you Jayme? She laughed a little to herself. It sounded deranged. She hit herself against the forehead. "Oops, forgive me, Rhapsody."

She had gone completely bonkers, I thought. "Get the hell out of here! You have your panties in a bunch and I'm not in the mood for your bullshit, Keri. I'm tired and I need to get cleaned up so I can go to sleep."

"At least I have my panties on to get in a bunch." She threw my panties into the shower at my feet. "You're such a slut. How many times do I have to ask where were you at?"

"I'm not going to be too many more of your whores and sluts. You're starting to piss me off and you're going to wind up getting fucked up. It doesn't make a difference where I was. You already have it fixed in your mind that I was out screwing around. I don't have the breath to be wasting trying to convince you otherwise. Now put my shit down and get the hell out of here before we get into an altercation that will not be to your advantage. Trust me."

I just knew we were about to fight when she stepped so close to the shower that the water bouncing off my body splashed her face and sweat outfit.

70

She looked at me for a long moment, becoming wetter by the second. She frowned. "No, you cheating little tramp, trust me. This is far from over with." She inspected my clothing once more, dropped them and flushed the toilet on her way out.

"Ahhh!" I yelled as the hot water burned my skin.

From the bedroom I could hear Keri knocking things around and between the bumps and bangs she was saying, "I invested all my time into this bitch and this all the thanks I get." Bump! Bump! Bump! "She must be crazy to think she can do me any kind of way. I'll show you crazy, bitch!"

If this was a prelude to the behavior I would have to put up with when I come home from drinking and dancing, then I don't want Keri in my house when I come home any more. I walked to the bedroom and it looked like an earthquake hit it. Clothes were thrown everywhere. My nightstand lamps were on the floor. The drawers were left open like someone packed in a hurry. There were no clothes left on hangers in the closet. The empty hangers were still swaying on the pole. My shoes were scattered everywhere. I picked up a mismatched short and shirt and slipped into it. Surprisingly, the rest of the house was as calm as an eye of a storm, with the exception of the front door standing wide open. I went to the door in time enough to see Keri speeding off in the night with no headlights on.

I pushed the box of sex toys onto the floor, with everything else, and climbed into bed.

CHAPTER NINE

Limbo

"Top Tier standing count. Lights on, on your feet, this is your six a.m. standing count! The C.O. shouted.

Of course I was on point. Up and dressed since five-thirty. Ain't no telling who might have been looking to get stripes off a niggah. One thing is for certain, it wouldn't be an easy win, cant get caught sleeping when the doors crack

"C.O. Bruce, my celly having chest pains, I think he's having a heart attack." Someone called out from below me.

The C.O. responded, "Tell your celly he will not interfere with my count. He will be on his feet when I come through. He is not even permitted to have a heart attack on my shift."

The whole unit started rattling their cell doors and making satirical remarks . . .

" . . . Stand this dick in your mouth . . ."

". . .You faggot muthafucka, get that man some help."

". . .Count these nuts, bitch . . ."

". . . Fuck you cop! Get the nurse in here. . ."

When the count cleared the dude with chest pains was carried to the nurse's station. I went to the phone.

"P.I. Spencer."

"What's cracking, Spence?"

"You sound like you're in high spirits for a man who just lost a three hundred thousand dollar home."

"Don't be fooled by the voice, I lost a whole lot more than that. . . insurance will cover the house and I'll cover the rest when I get out. What's up with them skeletons?"

"There are none. Francine Rhapsody Parrish. . . she checks out. Twenty-six year-old college student majoring in psychology. Born in Maine, grew up in North Carolina then moved to Portage, P.A. as a young adult. There's not even a parking ticket credited to her. The thing that does come up in the system is that her parents were killed on a hi-jacked plane four years ago over in Sierra Leone, her father was a jeweler who apparently was trying to buy blood diamonds."

Dollar signs popped in my mind. "She's worth a little something then."

"Worth about as much as a penny with a hole in it. Her old man was in debt and had just filed a Chapter-9 before he died. He didn't have anything to leave behind."

"Thanks Spence, its breakfast time around this place. I'll hit you back later in the week."

"Peace."

"It's on."

After a terrible breakfast of some shit I couldn't identify, I went up Dollar's cell. He was laid back on his bunk browsing through a Hustler magazine.

"I didn't know you were into fien mags, homey."

Dollar sat up and swung his feet around to the floor. "I'mma keep it real with you gangster. I love me some paper pussy. It's all a niggah can get in here."

A red headed white boy stuck his head in Dollar's cell. "Yo, Dollar, Damante died."

We both looked at Redhead. Dollar frowned. "Stop jinxing a niggah like that."

"Who is Damante?" I asked.

"Baby D," they both said at the same time.

Redhead stepped further into the cell. "His chest pains were real. Word is, he had a slight heart attack in the cell and a massive one in the nurse's office. A guard said that he would have lived if they had got him to the nurse sooner."

"How the fuck does a young brother have a heart attack?" Dollar tossed the magazine on his locker.

"Just like an old one." Redhead fired back.

"This jail shit is serious." I sat down next to Dollar on his bunk. These motherfuckers don't give a shit about us. They'll let a niggah die. Man, its fucked up Baby D didn't get to go home. Now his soul is stuck in jail forever. Fuck this jail shit! On everything I love, it's going down in the streets before I come back to this bitch."

Redhead gave me a pound. "I feel you, dawg."

Dollar shot the basketball into the hoop. "When you gonna see Rhapsody again?"

"This weekend. Why, what's up?" I tossed the ball to check it. "Your girl coming ain't she?"

"I don't know," I can't get in touch with her. I tried calling her last night and this morning." He slowed the dribble down while he spoke. "That bitch, Rhapsody, slung that ass in the visiting room yesterday like her pussy is the ill nah-nah. That comeback pussy. When you get done, pass that ass off so I can fuck." He shot again and missed.

I snatched the rebound and scored. "No broad I kick it with will fuck with you after I'm done. Don't take it personal, but we different type niggahs. How you gonna turn me on to a broad then tell me you wanna fuck her? You straight up grimy." I dunked the ball. Ok, niggah. Your ball game is just like you. Some shit."

"I didn't know that you was a rest haven for hoes. I thought it was bro's before hoes?"

I sat down on the ball in the middle of the indoor court and wiped the sweat away from my forehead. "On the real, though, I ain't on no shit like that. I'm going home to my family. Rhapsody is just something to do until I touch down. You go home next month, try your hand. She's fair game. I hope your hoe game ain't nothing like your ball game." We started towards the unit. "I will tell you this though, if I did ever decide to beat the pussy up, it's a wrap."

CHAPTER TEN
Rhapsody

A man wielding a hand gun appeared in a storefront window. I aimed my glock and hit the target with four slugs as I walked through the insurgency training center city. An old lady with a broom popped up in a doorway. I pointed my weapon at the plywood figure. When I realized that there wasn't a potential threat, I withdrew my weapon. Someone to my right yelled out, "help." I spun to the voice and dropped to a knee and fired one shot into the head of the man figure holding a knife to a cashier's throat. When I heard movement to my left, I tucked and rolled and landed on my belly. It was only figures of children who had popped up on a porch.

"Drop the gun, and stand up slowly." The voice was behind me. "I don't want to hurt you. Do it . . . now!"

I pushed my glock out in front to me. As I eased to my feet, I unholstered the 380 strapped to my ankle.

"Slow, "the voice commanded. "Now kick the gun away then turn around and face me."

I complied, keeping the tiny gun concealed at my side. Ten feet away from me was a business man figure, carrying a briefcase. Standing behind him was a bad guy with a gun.

"Put your hands where I can see them" the computer voice said.

I dropped flat on my butt, firing two shots between the legs of the business man and into the knees of the bad guy. I countered those shots by lying horizontal with the ground and ripping off two more slugs into the bad guy's face.

There were claps in the distance, mixed with a few whistles. The director of the obstacle course came over the loud speaker. "Johanson, congratulations, you just broke your own record. One minute and thirty-eight seconds. Nine discharges, seven vital entries, two crippling shots, and no injuries to civilians. Keep up the good work and you'll take the Hostage Rescue Team's firing trophy home for the fourth year in a row."

I smiled and waved at the smoked observation glass, where the head honchos sat in air conditioning, manipulating the computer. They tried their best to make me look like an ass in what they considered a masculine event.

I started counting in my head when Stewart of A.T.F. came up with a lidded bucket and shook my hand. I wondered what was in that bucket.

"Nice job, Jayme." He sat the bucket down. "I was wondering if you could give me some private shooting lessons. I want you to help me fire this thing." Stewart grabbed his crotch, and humped at the air.

Asshole. "You broke a new record today, too."

He tilted his ugly head in an inquisitive manner. "How's that?"

"It only took you four seconds to make a complete ass out of yourself. You should check into it, I'm positive that you qualify for the genius book."

The rest of Stewart's male chauvinist encouragers laughed at him.

"You think you're such a good shot, huh?" Stewart smirked, passing me his Glock 10, handle first. "It's easy to hit a target that's standing still. Let's see how well you do with something moving. There are eight rounds in the clip. Show us how good you really are." He picked the bucket up. "No one since "92" has gotten more than six on record." He turned the bucket upside down and pulled the lid off. A gray mass fell to the ground and scattered in every direction.

Instinctively, since I'm right-handed, I dropped to my left knee to get closer to my target, simultaneously I released Stewart's glock and unholstered my own. I immediately remember that I only had seven shots left. The muzzle became my eyes. We were done. After the second kill I realized that they were mice. The human eyes react better to motion than any set of eyes, other than an owl's. So it didn't immediately register that my targets were mice. When I was done firing the seven shots, six carcasses lay in the distance. *Damn, I missed one*, I thought. I got ready to stand up until I got a glimpse of motion about sixteen feet away. I picked up Stewart's Glock and ripped off two shots at the two mice scurrying along the fake storefront still searching for shelter. They were counted amongst the dead when I stood up. "Put that on record."

I walked away, leaving Stewart dumbfounded. I hate mice. I wouldn't be so hard on the guys, if the hadn't made a bet on who would get me drunk and fuck me first. I was certain that I would see Keri here today, since she hadn't been home in two days. Oh well, it's not like she hadn't called herself running away before. She'll come around when she gets the chip off her shoulder.

Just as I reached my car someone started calling me. Tabetha from the Record's Department was running on the asphalt. By the time she reached me, she was out of breath, bent over, with a hand on one knee trying to catch her wind.

"Now you see why cigarettes are the number one cause of death?" I shook my head at the state nicotine had her in.

"Girl, I keep telling myself I need to quit." She gulped air between huffs and puffs. "Here." She passed me a manila folder, finally standing straight up. "It's the file on Jessica Stephens that Keri wanted to look over. How long is she going to be out on a leave of absence anyhow?

"Leave of absence?" I must have had a perplexed look on my face because Tabetha asked, "You didn't know? I just figured you would have because she's your roommate."

"I haven't seen Keri in . . . since the other day." I really wondered what was on her mind. She's vanished twice in our year together.

Tabetha looked down at the folder. "I guess I'd better hold onto this."

"Wise choice." I knew that Tabetha was a talker and would ramble on forever about nothing. So I nipped it in bud before she got started. "Well, Tab, I'm running late. I have an appointment at the salon and a tanning session I must keep."

"Some girls have all the luck." She strolled off. There was still time to kill before visitation at the jail started. I stopped by the gym for some kick boxing and a quick yoga session, then I went home and showered. I slipped into a pretty Dolce and Cabana pant outfit, D.G. sandals, and a matching apple cap. I looked good, felt good, and had been waiting on this day all week.

"My seed of equivalent benefit," Limbo whispered into my ear as he hugged me in his muscular arms.

"What do you mean by that?"

"My grandmother always told me that in every adversity there is -- "

"A seed of equivalent benefit." I finished his sentence then asked, "And you feel like I'm yours?"

"I don't ever say anything I don't mean. I expect the same thing from you in return." He held my hands and stepped back, taking me all in. "What's up though? You look good today."

"Are you trying to say that I didn't look good before?"

"Nope, I'm just acknowledging a beautiful woman."

I was flattered. "Chivalry will get you where you want to go." I smiled from ear to ear.

"Thanks for putting me up on game."

I handed him a Ginseng tea. He told me that it was his favorite.

"Wow! That's a coincidence." I lied. I knew every important detail about Lamont Adams that would make it easy for me to get into his life.

"Thank you for the card, but you didn't have to send me the money. I'm all right, Baby Girl."

I put my hand on his thigh. "Fifteen dollars is all I could afford. I just want to help in anyway I can."

He turned to me and put his hand on top of mine. "I'm feeling that, but I'm good. Keep your money for yourself."

"It's settled then." I threaded my fingers with his. "I'll send what I can when I can."

I guess Limbo saw that there was no use in trying to convince me to do otherwise and figured that changing the subject would be his best option.

"Why your girl, Keri, didn't come see my boy?"

I was in the moment with Limbo and enjoying every second of it. Keri was the furthest person from my mind until he mentioned her. Why had she taken a leave of absence? Why did she think her asinine shenanigans would prove? And most importantly where is she? I sighed and looked down at my toes as I wiggled them. It was a habit I'd formed when I was being dishonest. "Keri isn't really my girl like that. We're just roommates, and to be gut-honest if I could afford a better place and a friendlier environment, I wouldn't be staying in Keri's house. Denny's doesn't pay me anything. So I'm forced to put up with sometimey behavior. She's a modern day Sybil. Sometimes she's a total bitch and the rest of the time she's a bitch. The whole chemistry of my day changes when I get in that house. The stress is showing itself in my grades. She is really driving me nuts. I'm not used to walking on eggshells and tip-toeing around people's foul moods."

"Shit, where I'm from, we believe in curing our headaches. Sounds to me like you need to pack your shit and bounce."

"Don't let the jewelry and the clothing fool you. I just take real good care of what I have, but my parent's left me financially castrated. I have no other family. Denny's is part time, so I alternate between paying my school fees and my portion on Keri's rent and utilities." I was really wiggling my toes now.

"Now don't you think it makes more sense that you keep your money and not send it to me? He had a stern fatherly look that demanded an explanation.

Just like a misbehaved child, I began to explain, "Most guys go through so many women in search of that down chick. The ride or die type, that they lose focus of what they want in a woman and can't recognize her when she's sitting right beside you . . . holding your hand." I squeezed his hand. "I'm not exactly sure what it is about you, but from the club, I knew that I was willing to hold you down. When I have, I want to share it with you. When I don't have, I'll share what I do have with you. When the phone hung up last night, it was then I realized that when you're smiling, I want to be the cause of it. If you're down, I want to sex you up to lift you up. My intuition doesn't lie to me, so I depend on it, Limbo, to guide me in matters of the heart. You gave me good vibes and I want you to make me keep feeling them." It kind of scared me to see that my toes weren't wiggling. He sipped his tea and we sat in quiet for what seemed like forever. I wondered what was on his mind. From our phone conversations, I could tell that there was still remnant of emotional pain from his wife divorcing him. So I had done either one of two things: pushed too soon or pushed at just the right time. I was just about to suggest that we share a pizza when he spoke up.

"You make a brother feel like a king. Keep lacing me up with those pretty words and I might let you put the feminine touch on my kingdom."

I had to use his line on him. "Thanks for putting me up on game."

"You catch on quick."

I kissed his cheek. "Keep schooling me."

CHAPTER ELEVEN
Limbo

Through my cell window I watched Summer change into Fall. Fall moved into Winter and Winter slid into Spring. It's strange how things work themselves out. At the beginning, Rhapsody was just somebody to pass time with. Now I couldn't see her not being in my life. She had done what no other had. She kicked-in the visiting room doors every visiting day. She made me look like a celebrity at mail call. It was after midnight. I turned up the volume on the radio, kicked back on my bunk and read her letter.

My Ghetto Superstar:

I thought that fingerprints could only be left on material things. So how is it that yours are on my soul? I was just laying here gazing at your picture and wondered if you were a poem, what you say to me. All I know is that your power is so strong that it ties my essence in knots and only the breath of God can untie me. Just laying here in my bed, all alone, thinking about you, writing to you makes me feel as if there is a little hummingbird inside my chest flapping its wings . . .I wish you could put your hand on my heart and feel how fast it beats for you. You are the only man that has ever been capable of doing me like this. Please don't stop. Ever

> *Rhapsody*

Ten dollar money order enclosed.

No sooner than I finished reading her letter the radio disc jockey announced, "This is the Quiet Storm with another love dedication, for lovers only. We have Rhapsody on our love line tonight. Caller go ahead."

"I want to dedicate Piece of My Love by Guy to my friend Limbo."

"Where is he tonight?"

"Away . . . doing time."

"Sounds like he's more than a friend."

"I want him to be."

"Is there anything you would like to say to Limbo tonight?"

"Yes." There was a pause. "Limbo, every time we talk, right before the phone warns me that it's time to say good-bye, my heart beats to a faster pace. I have even noticed the moistness of my palms; the dryness of my mouth. I don't want us to be disconnected without me telling you that I love you. I've been wanting to tell you that for sometime now and when the phone hangs up and I haven't, I feel empty and plain inside. If tomorrow came and there was no us, then I would like the rest of my life in regret because I didn't say what I needed to when I had the chance. I love you, Limbo."

"Player, you got yourself a keeper. This jam goes out to you. Guy, A Piece Of My Love."

There was whistling and bar rattling. My next door neighbor yelled through the vent, "Limbo, I admire your work. You're my hero, my niggah."

She was real smooth. I had to respect her game, but what I was attracted by most was her persistence. She wouldn't stop until she won. I definitely had a soldier in my corner. I kept it on the hush-hush because I like her drive. To keep it gangster though, she had won months ago. Tonight, Rhapsody went the extra mile.

CHAPTER TWELVE

The night was young in Cleveland and filled with the urine stench of the project. Murdock, C-Mack, and Chickenbone were hanging out on the block shooting the breeze, while the young hustlers, working the grave-yard shift, earned their living sell crack rock.

C-Mack scanned the hustlers with his keen, raven eyes. Females from around the Hoova often referred to C-Mack as a "Pretty black niggah." He was every bit of six-foot-four and light on his feet. At twenty-eight, a lot of violence laid in his wake. Limbo had been noted for saying, "That's a dangerous brother. Look dangerous up in the dictionary and I bet you'll find a picture of C-Mack.

C-Mack used a boar bristle brush to brush his waves while looking at the hustlers. These niggahs lucky they homeys, he thought.

Murdock ran his hand over his goatee. "Back in the day when I was getting my grind on, I used to be out this bitch four and five days straight in the same clothes getting my money. Ain't shit changed but the people and the time. These little cats used to riding big wheels, now look at them." Murdock tapped Chickenbone. "I'mma tell you something, though, homey." He paused for effect. "Limbo is a stone cold hustler. Straight up, the niggahs gets his grind on. It's just in him. We were fourteen when his mother sent him to the store with ten dollars to buy some milk and shit. The niggah bought a ten dollar double up from that pimpish cat, Manny Cool. When Limbo went home that night he had a car load of groceries. A month and a half later, he turned a few crumbs into eight kilos. The home-boy ain't looked back since."

Chickenbone passed C-Mack a forty-ounce. He guzzled down the remainder of the Malt liquor. "Dig this, I'm feeling the homey's success story, Cuz. But I ain't have time for the bump and grind. Too much work involved, ya dig. Hustlers are my number one vics. I'd pick one of them niggahs out and lay in the cut on him. When he finished clocking for the day, I'd rob his bitch ass." C-Mack threw the empty bottle to the ground. "When I went broke, I'd rob me another one. That's my M.O. to this day."

I heard about you, Cuz," Chickenbone said, "when I was going to school, they used to tell ghost stories about you around the lunch table. The said you were always watching the streets from the shadows. You went from hood to hood sticking niggahs up. You was so cold with it, they said you would take the money and leave the dope. Then tell niggahs that you'd be back for the rest of your money when they finished selling the shit. When I first started hustling, all it took was for someone to say they saw you and the block would clear out."

Murdock looked at C-Mack then to Chickenbone. "Why you think the homey ain't in Tennessee no more?"

"You already know," C-Mack cut in, still brushing his waves "I ran outta niggahs to rob." They all laughed while giving each other pounds.

"When ya'll gonna let me roll with y'all?" Chickenbone asked.

"Those that are chosen chose themselves, youngster." Murdock turned away from Chickenbone, and pointed out a rail thin man walking towards them.

Straight Shooter had been in the hood for what seemed like forever. He was your worse type of fien. He would . . .do anything to get high.

"What ya'll working with?" Straight Shooter looked bugged-eyed. His lips were so chapped they looked as if they would break and bleed any minute. He dug in his pockets, making fists inside his filthy jeans. He kept looking around like he was being followed.

"Niggah, what you working with?" C-Mack patted his pockets, feeling something long and narrow. "Pull your pockets inside out."

Straight Shooter did as he was told. His glass crack pipe fell to the dirt. "I . . .I got some information. I need a fifty, but I'll take a twenty piece for it, though." He picked up his pipe. "I know who set Cha-Cha up."

C-Mack hit Straight Shooter with a body shot then countered with a six-inch hook that sent Straight Shooter to never-never land. C-Mack was the nicest in his hood with his hands. And he loved to use them. He had went all the way to the National Boxing Circuit and tried out for the Junior Olympics team -- made it, then quit. "Too much work involved, ya dig?"

"Drag his nasty ass in the alley." C-Mack turned to leave. Murdock had his Timberland on Straight Shooter's chest.

"Where you going, Cuz?"

"The niggahs playing with the business, I want that info. He want a twenty, I'm gonna cop him a stone." C-Mack went up the block and had a young hustler give him a rock while Chickenbone dragged Straight Shooter into the alley by the scruff of his shirt.

The sensation was warm and soothing. Straight Shooter thought that he was in a nice hot shower. Which the last time he had taken one was a little over a year ago. As he came to, he could hear laughter and somebody coaxing him to. "Wake up, niggah.". He reached up to turn the shower off and realized that he wasn't in a shower. Three steady streams of urine pelted his face. He shook as if he were a wet dog coming out of the rain. All he said, while being pissed on was, "I charge ten dollars a head for this."

Murdock aimed his stream at Straight Shooter's mouth while he was quoting prices. When Murdock found his target, he yelled, "Bull's-eye."

Straight Shooter spat the golden liquid out.

"Niggah, don't you ever come in Hoova hood talking about you know the business, but you ain't setting it out unless you get broke off. You amongst gangsters. Niggah, come correct out the gate, then let us show our appreciation. You understand?"

"I do." Straight Shooter wiped his face with his sleeve.

C-Mack held out his hand. A rock sat in the center of it. "This is what you want right here. Tell us what we need to know."

"It was that evil motherfucker from Rolling Sixties. The one with mix match eyes."

"Siberian." Murdock looked down at the filthy crack fien.

Straighter Shooter nodded. "Yeah, that's him. Siberian."

"Ummph! Chickenbone kicked him in the ribs. "How you know?"

Straight Shooter coughed, holding his side. "I was in Cliffview turning tricks and I overheard Siberian talking to his cousin, one of them P. Stone Bloods, outside the window. Siberian was telling his cousin where he could find Cha-Cha and how much work he had. They even talked about the split everybody was getting after the jack went down. Siberian even told his cousin that he had a hit he wanted him to do that would cause an all-out war in the streets between the Crips and the Bloods."

Murdock, C-Mack, and Chickenbone exchanged glances. Murdock already knew who Siberian's cousin was, but he wanted to know if Straight Shooter knew. The answer would give credibility to Straight Shooter's story and explain a lot of unexplained street beefs, robberies, and murders over the years. "What's Siberian's cousin name?"

"I can't think of it. It's the drugs, man."

Chickenbone kicked him again. "Think of it niggah."

Straight Shooter moaned in pain. "He called him Demoe."

Murdock made a gun with his fingers and shot it. "You just signed Siberian's and Demoe's death certificates."

"Should've done that in the first place." C-Mack gave him the rock. Straight Shooter stood to leave.

"Niggah, go on and smoke that right now." C-Mack stopped him. "Cause I'm about to kill you. The same way you came with the business on them niggahs, you'll go with the business on us."

"Come on ya'll stop tripping. I let ya'll piss on me for free."

"Shut the fuck up." Chickenbone snapped.

C-Mack pulled out a big .44. "You better get your last blast before I blast that ass."

Murdock made sure a bullet was in the chamber of his 9mm. Chickenbone thumbed the safety off of his 357.

Straight Shooter knew from the look in their eyes that this was "all she wrote." He stuffed the whole rock in the top of his pipe. He knew that the dope circulating on this block was grade A. It only took a small piece to make his ears ring. Armed with that knowledge, his plan was to hit that big rock so hard that it would pop his heart before the bullets tore through him.

He looked past the Bic flame at the three grim reapers that were once young jitter bugs. Two of which he watched grow into monsters. He put the flame to his pipe and sucked greedily as the rock sizzled. His eyes looked crossed as he watched the thick white smoke rush through the pipe into his lungs. He became numb. His ears rang as he prayed to his crack God, Scotty, to beam him up.

Bam! Bam! Bam! "Motherfucker, hold that! C-Mack stood over Straight Shooter when he hit the ground. They all watched him gasp for air as the crack smoke escaped from the holes in his chest. C-Mack pressed the .44 against Straight Shooter's forehead and put him out of his pathetic misery.

CHAPTER THIRTEEN

Rhapsody

"Have a seat, Johanson." A Cuban Cohiba hung in the corner of his mouth.

I always feel like a misbehaved teen in some principal's office when I'm called into the Special Agent in Command Headquarters. On this side of SAC Thurston's desk. I'm nervous and uneasy. I think it has something to do with his powerful demeanor. Six-foot-four, three hundred-twelve pounds -- solid. A waxed, bald, tailored suit man with skin close to the color of a foggy dawn.

"I'm pulling you off the Lamont Adams' case. It's been ten months and I'm not seeing any signs of progress. I'm beginning to believe that we torched his house and arranged seventeen months jail time for nothing." He closed the blinds on the window facing the office area for privacy. "I even intercept any mail Lamont Adams' wife tries to send him. There is no reason for you not to be connected to this guy, Johanson. It's all been laid out for you."

I crinkled my nose. "Pulling me?" I had to calm myself and adjust my voice a few notches. "It wasn't for nothing, Thurston. Lamont is broke, we're three million dollars richer because of him. Do you actually think that a well connected man like Adams is going to stay bankrupt? We're in this together, like it or not. You can't pull me off this case."

I'm the SAC goddammit! Why the hell can't I? He rolled that stinky cigar from one side of his mouth to the other.

"Because...I've invested more that my time. There are slews of money that we stand to make off Adams. Besides, he confided in me last night about his future drug activities. Be patient, SAC, it's just a matter of time." I lied, and my heels are too tight to wiggle my toes. Limbo and I haven't chatted about anything other than life. In fact, when I'm with Limbo, I try my best to forget I'm operating undercover. You can't forget Jayme, I won't allow that, my voice reminded.

"Time is all Internal Affairs needs to find out what we've been doing. Adams is the last one, Johanson." He leaned forward on his desk. "What you got?"

I kicked off my shoes to give my feet freedom to move. "When he gets out—"

"June eleventh. Thurston swiveled his chair around to face a wall calendar.

"Correct. He's going to run another drug ring in Cambria."

"How do you fit into this scenario?"

"He asked me to move in with him. I have to cross the line to get his complete trust." Toes wiggling.

"I don't know about that, Johanson, deep cover has its pros and cons. Don't forget about what Adams had done to Agent Curlew."

"I'm not incompetent like Curlew was. I can handle it. Adams' crimes will pay us dividends, partner. It will be our office responsible for bringing him down. I'll probably get a metal."

"If anyone can make it happen you can."

"A walk in the park. Men are defenseless against the power of a woman."

Thurston steepled his huge hands. "I'm giving you four months from the time Lamont Adams strolls out of jail to find out where he's stashing his money. And to put him back in jail with no hopes of ever seeing the streets again." Thurston glanced at his calendar once more. "You have to get away from Adams for a few days in August."

"Why?"

"The Bureau in West Virginia is investigating a dealer by the name of Jerico Winston and his female accomplice, Sprinkle. They're moving a lot of cocaine and weapons, the locals aren't too happy about it." Thurston flipped through a manila envelope. "The boys in West Virginia have an informant who's connected to their racket. By August the informant will have a door open for you and Tara to walk through. I need you to make a buy."

"How come one of the other Drug Enforcement Agents can't make the buy? I need to concentrate on our meal ticket."

"Because you're the best agent for the job. It's not open for discussion. Have you eaten lunch?"

"No." I slipped my shoes back on.

"I know this soul food place that cooks a mean lunch dish. You wanna get a bite?"

"Thurston, I'm going to sit this one out. I have a few errands to run while I'm here in Altoona. I can't seem to find the time to take care of them in Johnstown playing the insatiable Rhapsody."

He smiled at me. "Okay, I'll catch you the next go-round. Hell, I might even buy you a restaurant. You heard from Mayweather? How is she?"

"Haven't heard from Keri since she took leave." I walked out of the SAC's office, closing the door behind me. I can care less if I ever hear from Keri again.

What is Limbo doing to me? Or what have I done to me? I pondered the questions around on the way to my car. How could I be so stupid, fabricating a story for Thurston just so I can stay connected to the man of my dreams a little longer? Limbo is entirely too smart and careful to discuss anything illegal with me. It's not his style. Even if he had, at this point, I'm not too sure what I'd do with the information. This whole arrangement meant more to me than stealing more of Limbo's money or putting him in jail, it's personal. You're not Rhapsody, Jayme, Don't screw this up.

"Don't you start." I put the car in drive and drove away.

We kissed deeply when he came into the visiting room. Our tongues explored each other' mouths meticulously. The first time we kissed it was magical. The sensation in my nerve endings was nothing less than electrical. And now...now our lips were locked in fiery passion, causing me to feel that same current. He palmed my ass, alternating between rubs and squeezes. He held my face as we sunk deeper into the kiss.

"Mr. Adams," a voice came from the intercom system. "You're not in a hotel."

He waved in a surrendering manner at the 'eye in the sky'.

"Your 'wicks' are getting so long," I said as we took our seats.

He ran his hand down the length of his lock hanging in the center of his stomach. "You think so, huh? I ain't never heard nobody call them wicks. I like that."

98

"I like you boo." I was being silly. "You're my baby. Tell Mama what you like."

He looked at me and I could tell that his mind was animating something. He smiled his infamous crooked smile. "I like women who…" He whispered the rest in my ear.

I got a hot flash as his candy breath pulsated against my ear. When he took his tongue out, I opened my eyes and said, "I like women too."

"Cool. I knew you was a freak." He adjusted the bulge in his pants. We're gonna do big things."

"A freak? You don't give me no credit. You're going to be surprised at that I am. I have a satiation for kinky sex."

"Why am I only good for a piece of your love then? What's going on in your life that you can't tell a niggah about?"

"I was wondering if you heard my dedication."

"Loud and clear."

"Then you heard the part where the song says 'please hush, no questions asked."

"You got that. The way you let me know you love me, made me feel…exceptional. You blew a niggahs head up. When did you fall in love? He looked me directly in they eyes. His gaze held me.

"I didn't. When you fall into something, nine times out of ten, you get hurt. I walked into love with you, Limbo. I don't know exactly when it happened, but I awoke one morning and I had arrived." Sitting here with Limbo, it was amazing. I haven't felt this way in years. The world was full of people, but he's the only person in my world. Everyone in the visiting room was invisible to me until commotion broke out.

"Mutherfucker, how you gon' call yourself playing on me from jail? A black, baby doll cute, thick hip girl with jet black hair down back, yelled standing over this brown-skinned bald headed guy. "Who the fuck is this bitch, Shakir? Who the fuck is she? She pointed at the girl who had just walked up.

Shakir was caught off guard and his stunned expression proved it.

Thick hips turned to the equally cute, toffee skinned petite girl with brown hair almost as long as her and asked, "Bitch who is you? What the fuck you coming up in here visiting my man for?"

"I'm the bitch that's about to beat your ass."

The cat fight was on. The little petite girl was all over Thick Hips. They rolled, kicked, scratched, and swung wildly at each other. The smaller girl ripped Thick Hip's halter top off. Her ample breast flipped and flopped as she tried to strike the smaller girl to no avail.

Petite had a fistful of Thick Hip's long hair in one hand while she landed blows with the other. "Should ...kept...your fly...mouth...shut. We could have been ladylike about this."

The panic alarm went off. Several guards rushed into the visiting room. It took three of them to pull the petite girl off of Thick Hips. Six guards ushered the inmates out of the visiting room as another three took control of the altercation.

Limbo waved to me before he went through the door. I mouthed the words, "I love you" to him.

The following day it had been thunder storming for a good portion. The National Weather Advisory broadcasted a tornado watch for Cambria County and its surrounding areas. The high winds pushed my car around with ease as I headed to the jail Mother Nature couldn't have acted up at more opportune time.

For months now, Limbo has been under the impression that Keri is the roommate from Hell, and that my financial woes made it impossible for me to make other living arrangement. Which was a blatant lie because I hadn't seen Keri since the first time I visited him. Furthermore, Keri lives in my home. Female manipulation, plus a staged conflict equals out to persuade the unconsciously concerned party to dance to your music. I learned that from the best who had ever

100

done it. Stefino Denero, of the Young and the Restless. Psychology in rare form.

So far, I was getting the response I anticipated. Limbo stood in front of me, scanning me for the second time. I followed his confused gaze from my Reeboks to my soaked Tommy jeans to my equally damp Hilfiger pull-over.

"I thought that I was the one in jail. What's your reason for coming up here embarrassing me, wearing the same clothes you had on yesterday? What's up with that?"

I sighed and broke eye contact, focusing a tan spec in the floor tile. "I'm sorry...but I—", I forced a tear out. My toes were wiggling a mile a minute and I hadn't even begun with my lie.

Limbo sat down beside me and stroked my back. "What's with the tears? Are you all right?"

"Keri and I had it out last night. I was fed up and couldn't bite my tongue anymore." The tears were dripping from my cheeks now. "She...kicked me out. I had to sleep in my car last night. I'm screwed, I went by her house this morning, and all of my things were thrown on the front porch. She wouldn't reimburse for my portion of this month's rent. I don't have any idea what I'm going to do. I started sobbing.

Still rubbing my back, he asked me where my things were at now.

"Piled in my car."

Limbo cupped my chin in his hand and lifted my head. "I can't have my girl sleeping in a car. It's raining like a mother out there. Where's your cell phone?

His girl? "In the car," I said with a whine.

"There's a Western Union by the Courthouse. Go there and wait for me to call you." He wiped my tears away. "Gimme twenty minutes." He walked away.

CHAPTER FOURTEEN

Limbo

"Damn Cuz, what she do, suck your dick in the visiting room? That bitch better have boss head." Murdock said.

"Nah homeboy, she held me down this whole bid. She's a rider, so I'm gonna hold her down. It's only right. Plus it's beneficial for the move we're gon' make." My plan to move three hundred bricks was flawless.

"I feel you. I'm a go hit her now, then she can snatch up the other half by one o'clock tomorrow."

"Bet."

"It's on."

I went to my cage to take a leak then came back and called Rhapsody.

"Hello." She sounded stressed.

"Where are you?"

"In the parking lot of Western Union."

"Check it, the password is succubus. I had five grand wired to you. Go to a hotel tonight. Tomorrow, I want you to find us a place, somewhere in Richland. At one o'clock tomorrow, pick up another five, same password. Ten grand should be enough to get a crib up and running." I could her sniffling as thunder cracked. "Baby Girl, you don't have to cry, I got you...Rhapsody."

"Yes."

"I do trust in you, Limbo."

"I have to go. I'll call you in the morning. These motherfuckers is locking us down because of the tornado watch."

"They'll lock you in a cell if it's a tornado?"

"Fucked up ain't it? I'm never coming back. I gotta go."

"Limbo."

"What's up?"

"Thank you...I love you."

"I know."

As the storm conquered the night, I read a novel called Beat the Cross by this slick talking cat named Cordless. I already knocked down Jerry Blackshear's 'Legit Baller'. I was seriously considering throwing a few dollars into the publishing industry.

A few years from now, I could see these street books blowing up like the rap game did. The thunder roared then a few seconds later the power went out. "Damn!" I shouted in frustration. My man Rick was just about to fuck the knucklehead Christine.

Dollar had left a few months back, with no one to kick it with, I spend the rest of my time reading. Now that I think about it, somebody should write a book about me. All they had to do was edit my P.S.I.

I'll never forget June 11th. I was being released, and Timothy McVeigh was being executed by lethal injection. I was drawn to the TV on my way to the sally port door. The prison officials from Terri Hut read McVeigh's last words. The poem Invetus:

"Out of the night that covers me. Black as the pit from pole-to-pole. I thank whatever Gods maybe for my unconquerable soul. In full clutch of circumstance, I have not winced nor cried aloud. Under the bludgeoning of chance my head is bloody but unbowed. Beyond this place of wrath and tears looms the honor of the shade, and yet the menace of the years finds...and shall find me unfrail. It matters not how straight the gate, how changed with punishment the scroll. I am the master of my fate, the captain of my soul."

"I feel you dawg." I headed to the door. "I don't give a fuck either."

The C.O. grabbed my arm. "Hey, Mr. Adams, I just started my own construction company. I have a job for you if you want it." He offered me his business card.

"Ergophobia." Yanking my arm away from this crumb-snatcher. It was obvious he didn't know what the hell I was talking about from the expression on his face. "Look it up, you dumb motherfucker."

By the time I was processed out, the sun was beaming. Rhapsody ran to me and jumped in my arms. She wrapped her thin legs around me and made love to my tongue.

CHAPTER FIFTEEN

Rhapsody

He held me in his arms. I could feel his stiffening cock pressing against my desperate coochie. "I'm so glad you're home."

"You ain't the only one."

I climbed down and looked at the cock print in the pants of his warm up outfit. "Looks like Charlie needs some attention too."

"Charlie? Why you call my man Charlie? Why not something more suitable like Big Boy?"

I laughed and lead him by the hand to my car. "Your package came yesterday."

"What was in it?" He raised a brow at me while I dodged the pot holes in this raggedy road.

Did he suspect me of snooping through his belongs? You didn't ask me to open it."

He approved of my response, his crooked smile told me so.

"I saw Dollar last night at Everyday People. He had the nerve to try to take me to the hotel. Can you believe that? He even got belligerent because I told him he was dead wrong for trying to go behind your back."

"Did he put his hands on you?"

"Pssh, I wish he would have."

"Then don't hold it against him, he don't know no better. Dollar had threatened to blow my cover if I didn't give him some. I'm not going to let the alcohol be his excuse. Last night Dollar became my enemy. If I could have arrested him, he would be in jail. I had to get my enemy before he got me. "You know the word is that Dollar isn't right."

"What you mean ain't right?" He reached over and moved the lock of hair covering my eye. I'm assuming he did it to get a good look at my face while I explained. "They're saying he's a snitch. You remember that big case in Lancaster?"

"Yeah, Kingpen Nipsey. His whole crew got hit with the RICO. Nipsey's jeweler and car dealer ended up doing some time too."

"Well word is, Dollar's the reason them guys received life sentences. This guy named Twan put him on front street. Ran it down in front of everybody. Dollar didn't even put up a fight."

"I know Twan that sounds just like him too. Why didn't you tell me this before?"

I turned off the main road bringing the car to a snails pace. "I just found out about it after he showed out on me last night."

Limbo shifted his eyes in both directions. "What are we going down by the old mill for?

108

I was feeling naughty. I licked my lips to advertise my mood. "No use in waiting until we get home. Show me why I shouldn't call him Charlie." It wasn't long after I parked that his cock in my hand stroking it. He was only semi-hard and he was huge.

"Don't play with it. Suck it. "He guided my head into his lap. "You been talking shit for a year now. Back it up with your tough ass."

His swelling cock made a slapping sound against my forehead as he hit and taunted me with it.

"Put your mouth on it." He rubbed his cock-head on the wet junction of my lips then slapped it against my face again.

I licked him from his wrinkled balls to the head, covering him with my saliva. I took him in my mouth, working him slow at first, showing him that I'm a pro. Long deliberate slow pushes and pulls. Slurps, tight auctions, throat vibrations, spit and umms. Then I switched the style up, once I put my neck into it. He grunted when I spun his head around in my mouth, then deep throated him, taking as much of his cock as I could.

"Aarrgh." He growled, getting rough with me, mulling my hair tight in his fist, pushing my head down on him faster and faster. When Limbo started to thrust his hips, fucking my face, I think my gag reflex turned him on.

He pulled me up by my hair to look at him. "You wanna fell this dick don't you?"

I drooled a long thread of spit, stretching from his cock-head to my lips. My chin was glazed and soaking wet. "Please give it to me, don't make me beg." I was so horny, I wanted to be treated like the trashiest slut alive.

"Get out of the car. I'mma give you what you want."

He pulled his muscle shirt off and threw it in the dirt. No trespassing signs were nailed to trees, in broad daylight, in a wooded area, on the side of a dirt road Limbo had his pants gathered at the ankles and me... I had on only my Nikes. He sat me on the roof of my Volvo with ease. My coochie and his face was eye-to-eye. My arousal dripped onto the driver's window. He spread my twat open and flicked his tongue against my love button. I pulled the hood back so Limbo could get it all. When I wrapped my legs around his neck, he pulled at my labia with his teeth. I almost squirted in his face when he stuck his finger in my tight asshole. I'm one of those rare women who ejaculates when I come, but my orgasms are limited to anal stimulation. Limbo pushed his finger in my pooper knuckle deep in rhythm with his licking and sucking until I started chirping at the top of my lungs, "You're going to make me come dammit. That's it...just like that...I'm come...coming. God yes I'm coming!" A bomb went off between my legs, come shot in Limbo's face. He was surprised by my ability. He licked my juices from his lips and smiled.

Limbo bent me over the hood, the engine was still warm. He rubbed his cock against my agonized clit then force fed me. I bucked my hips in sync with his thirsty humps.

"Rougher...I...I like it rough." He was so wide and long inside of me, I wanted more. "Wet, warm, and tight like your favorite body of water right?"

He answered with a grunt.

"Rougher, Big Daddy."

Limbo wrapped a hand tight around my neck. With the other hand, he tugged at my hair forcing me to look at the No trespassing signs. He rammed my hot womanly depths until he filled me with his creamy fluid. He stayed inside me for a few more spermy strokes.

We drove into our gated community's entrance. "I know we talked about this before, but now that you're a free man, Big Daddy, what are you going to do?

"I still haven't made my mind yet. But I have been thinking about opening a chain of sports bars and then get into publishing. Street fiction is gonna blow up, mark my words.

I could see that Limbo wasn't pleased with what I had done to the house.

"It's empty," he said with his arms spread, spinning in a circle of nothingness.

I held him around the waist. "Ten thousand dollars is not a lot of money, Big daddy." The way he had my coochie aching, Limbo earned the name Big Daddy. "After I took care of rent and a double security deposit there was only three thousand left. That was barely enough to furnish the bedroom. Come, let me show it to you."

The bedroom …the setting was perfect. I created a calm relaxing place. The Lux Versace bed was separate from the rest of the room by a thin sheer curtain cascading down from the canopy top. It gave the room a lived-in vibe. I hadn't slept here, yet. I associated this room with sex. Dark curtains hung from the windows to block out the world. This room was our personal space it reflects my sensuality. Along the walls were five, five foot oil burners. In here we could shed our names and inhibitions along with our clothes and be ourselves…be as wild as we want to be.

Limbo looked through a digital camcorder, mounted on a tripod, focused on the bed. Hi shifted his eye from the eyepiece to me.

I shrugged. "A lot of sexy things are going to happen in here. And I'm not going to hurt my knees while they're happening."

He followed my gaze to the fluffy white carpet.

I lit an oil burner. "Your package is in the closet."

Limbo looked in the box then at me in awe.

"Not that one, the other one." I closed my box of sex toys. "We'll play with this stuff soon enough."

"You a stone-cold freak. I swear you learn something new about a person every day." He took his package and sat it on the stereo stand.

"What do you want to do first, Big daddy?"

"Take a bath. Then throw this warm-up suit away."

"Why?" It was in perfect condition and he looked good in it.

"'Cause I went to jail in it."

CHAPTER SIXTEEN

Murdock and C-Mack was un-affected by the outward display of hatred directed towards them. The pool hall was crowded. Cigarette smoke and cold stares filled the room. There had been bad blood between the Hoover Crips and Rolling Sixties Crips for years not. There is a thin fabric that kept these vicious gangs from destroying each other in the ghettos of Cleveland—Limbo.

They approached the back of the pool hall. A stocky young man dressed in a Carhart outfit, Converse sneakers, with braids dangling at his shoulders guarded the entrance to a private room. Over the door a sign written in black letter read: The Gangsters Den.

"Who you wanna see?" The stocky guy exchanged hard looks with C-Mack and Murdock.

"Cut the games, Danny DeVito. You who we wanna see. If you didn't, we would've been stopped long before we made it back here." Murdock said. "Go get that niggah, Siberian, and tell him he got company."

C-Mack stared at the sign. "We should sue these motherfuckers for false advertisement, Dock. Ain't no gangsters den behind that door unless we in it."

Murdock pounded his clenched fish onto C-Mack's. "You giving him too much." Their laughter stopped when Stocky attempted to do his job.

"Alright, I know ya'll strapped. Give me the gats and I'll take you to Siberian."

"Damn, little nomey." C-Mack shook his head in disgust. "This how they giving you the game over here. Listen here, Pimping, they fucking up your cripping. I usually rob niggahs for game, but since I'm feeling real generous, I'm gonna lace your shoes up. Gangsters." He paused for effect. "Gangsters don't give their guns up, Cuz."

Inside the Gangster's Den, a little bit of everything was going on under the dim light. A thick hip chocolate sister with a flat stomach and nice tits danced nude to Trina's The Baddest Bitch. She was grinding her body against a pole in the middle of the room. She made eye contact with Murdock, dropped low, then bent over and put her palms on the mirrored floor. When the sister stood up, she was holding her ankles. The meaty vagina poked out like a fist.

"Thickness is my weakness." Murdock winked and she smile.

A group of men clad in work pants and T-shirts huddled in a semi-circle, shooting dice.

"...Niggah, you betting with him? Watch both they faces when I eight," he said to the rest of the group.

"You talking slick. Bet another hundred you don't eight." The hustler doing the side betting challenged.

114

"Put up," the dice roller said.

They both threw money on the floor. One man stood on the money. The dice skipped across the hard wood and…landed on eight.

"Damn this niggah luck!"

A black jack game was going in another corner at a table with a spotlight suspended over it. Murdock and C-Mack found Siberian in the back of the huge room sitting on a couch with his head rolled back, arms stretched out on the back of the couch with a TV remote in his grip. There was an average looking, well proportioned, red-bone wearing a dental floss G-string between his legs performing heart stopping fellatio.

"Umm, baby, you got boss head." When Siberian rolled his head forward and opened his mix-matched eyes, Murdock and C-Mack was standing there. Siberian focused his attention on the Red-bone. He watched her polish his knob for a few more moments while running his fingers through her permed hair. "Star, I have company you can finish up later."

She licked him one more time—a slow—from his wrinkled scrotum to the head of his penis. She then tucked his member inside his jeans and zipped them.

"Bring me a bottled-water for Murdock and ahh…bring a bottle of Yac for Crip Mack." Siberian waved her off.

"I'm chasing that with Corona, little mama." C-Mack slapped her ass. They all watched it jiggle, as she strutted away clicking her heels against the floor.

"You Hoova boys is out of bounds, ain't you" Siberian pointed the remote at a large screen that hung overhead. He looked at them through one brown eye and a white eye that made appear to be blind on the left side.

"Limbo called a meeting of the minds, Murdock said, as he and C-Mack sat on a couch facing Siberian.

Siberian scowled at the mention of Limbo's name. He hated Limbo on the low, he only put up with Limbo because he had to. Siberian felt that he should have been appointed regional commander of the Ohio Crip families and not Limbo. Siberian could never understand how Limbo utilized his influence on the streets, earned so much love from the streets, and instilled so much fear in the streets. Deep down, Siberian wished that he was Limbo. When the last regional commander, Strife, was murdered, the rest of the Crip heads voted Limbo successor. Since then, Siberian put his plan into affect. He had been cahoots with his first cousin, Demoe -- with inside information on Crip activities. Demoe would use the knowledge to rob and murder, keeping the gang war full throttle. When things went totally hay wire and it appeared as if Limbo's wasn't capable of holding the position of commander. Siberian would step in and end the wars, earning the head's respect and vote.

Siberian cleared his lungs. "What Limbo want to talk about that's important enough for the minds to meet? His tone showed no emotions as he browsed through cable channels.

"Breaking bread," C-Mack said between sips of cognac.

"The mention of money captured Siberian's attention. He dropped the remote on his lap, leaned in closer, and asked, "How much bread?"

Murdock shrugged a shoulder and twitched his lip. "Seven digits, Condo by the lake change?"

Siberian thought of his cousin Demoe. "When and where?

Outside the pool hall, Murdock's cell phone rang. "I know this is that Vet hoe from the other night. Bitch been blowing me up since I dropped her nothing-ass off."

"Cuz, you know how them knuckle heads get when they dick dizzy. Let me answer that motherfucker."

Murdock passed him the phone.

C-Mack pressed the send button then rapped the words, "Suck a niggahs dick, or make a niggah rich."

CHAPTER SEVENTEEN
Limbo

I soaked in the tub an hour before Rhapsody came in the bathroom. She took a wash cloth from the rack and began to lather it.

"What you doing, woman?"

"Washing my man up." She kneeled down beside the tub and started washing me. "Who'd ever think that I'd have my own brown Chippendale." She rinsed the lather from my chest.

Elixir never washed me. I could get used to this.

"Do you have any plans?" She started humming.

"Not until tomorrow." I stood up so she could get the private parts of me. "Why, what plans you got?"

"Let's go out to eat."

"How about you cook for me. I like home-cooked meals."

"No go. I can't cook a lick." She took another rag and wiped my face then kissed me.

"Not even a little?"

"Burn up a pot of water." She kneeled to wet the face rag again. Big Daddy hung in her face as I stood there with my fist on my waist, looking down at her. Rhapsody made me feel like a Pharaoh being prepared for a royal feast. When she was finished, she led me to the bedroom. She told me to lay down then climbed on the bed with me. After closing the opening in the sheer curtain, she squeezed lotion in the center of my chest. She rubbed me down in silence while staring into my eyes. She smiled when Big Daddy started to swell.

"You like that, huh?"

She nodded then tried to jerk babies out of me. She started at my nuts. She licked my sack then sucked one nut at a time. What she did next, at first, I wasn't sure if I was supposed to enjoy it or feel violated. Her wet tongue lapped at my asshole. I jumped then grabbed her head.

"Relax, Big Daddy," she said, easing a pillow beneath me.

I was still holding the top of her head when she licked me there again. And again. I hesitated when she tried to push my legs back, but her tongue felt so good I wanted her to have more access. I always thought it was supposed to be the other way around, but now it was my feet in the air. Minutes later, I was holding my own legs back while Rhapsody kissed my ass and jerked me off. Her hands were well lubricated from lotion.

"Tell me when you're going to come," she said, not missing a beat.

Maybe I was bugging out, but it felt like Rhapsody was using her tongue to spell out Limbo, I love across my ass. Her mouth was wet and…hot. I stayed in the buck until I said, "I'm 'bout…I'm about to come!"

She put me in her mouth forming a tight seal with her lips. Rhapsody sucked me hard and fast. She moved up and down my dick…while twisting her head.

I balled up my toes and stiffened my legs when I erupted. "Oh shit!…oh shit!, girl" My entire body was shaking as she drunk my load. That was the best orgasm I ever had.

She wiped the corner of her mouth with the back of a hand. "That's how much I love you."

I was trying to bring my breath back to a normal pace. "You're a cold-blooded freak."

"You don't have much room to talk. Don't forget it was your legs over my shoulders."

"You got that little bit." I had already made up my mind to give Rhapsody a fair shake. She had never done nothing to me other than show me love. I can't let that go un-rewarded. I knew that she had freak potential from my evaluation of our months of conversation. But after that move, I was locked in for the long haul. Fuck Elixir.

Inside the package Murdock sent me was four outfits, cell phone and pager, twenty thousand in cash, a pistol, and a Teflon vest. I just threw on some jeans and a hooded sweat top and was stuffing the .45 magnum in my front waist band when Rhapsody came back into the room.

"What do you need that for?"

"What was it you told me a while back…'hush, no questions asked. That was it right?"

"As you would say, you got that."

"I love a fast learner," I put five grand up and gave Rhapsody the rest. "Get us some furniture in here and stretch that further than one room."

"After we ate at Ladbrooks, I had Rhapsody drive me

through the city. I had to peep the lay to see what adjustments needed to be made in order for my plan to work.

"Is there some particular reason why we're driving around like this? She stared at me waiting for the traffic light to change.

"Just feels good to be liberated. Pull over here for a minute."

She parked in front of Brother's Place. I stepped out the car for privacy and dialed Murdock. Someone picked up on the fourth ring.

"Suck a niggahs dick or make a niggah rich."

"I'm gonna get your wild-ass rich, but you have to get one of these hood rats to suck your dick. What's cracking, Cuz?"

"Ain't shit. How was the white meat? C-Mack said. "Is the pussy any good?"

I looked through the windshield at Rhapsody, she blew me a kiss. "Good as a motherfucker, Cuz. She tossing salads and some more shit."

"She freaking like that. Tell her to plug me in with one of her nasty friends. I'll get a kick out of farting in one of them hoes faces."

We both laughed then I said, "Niggah, you crazy."

"You already know."

"What does the attendance meeting look like?"

"It's all to the good. We were just leaving Siberian's grimy-ass. He'll be on deck tomorrow."

"We're gonna handle that little situation the old fashion way." Strife would finally rest in peace.

"I'm a religious fanatic of the old fashion way, Cuz."

The next day it was time to execute the first part of my plan. I stood in the dining room of Murdock's log cabin. The posh cabin was located in a wooded area on the out skirts of

Johnstown. The two men sitting at the huge table waited for me to speak. C-Mack was posted in the corner closet to Trigger, from Insane-Crips. Murdock stood to the left of where Siberian was seated. I was at the head of the table drumming my fingers on the back of a chair. "Gangsters, I have called us together for the purpose of inviting you men to a picnic. A picnic that will unite our hoods and feed us good at the same time."

"Limbo, I don't know about us eating together." Trigger shifted his weight to get more comfortable. "Getting money together can go either way. Draw our hoods closer together or force them further apart."

"That's true." Murdock spun his ball cap to the left. "But the only way it can divide us is if someone 's intention is to keep us at odds with each other. If that's the intention of any Crip here today then speak up."

Every man in the room exchanged glances.

Siberian broke the silence. "We've come a long way from out right killing each other, but there's still room for progress. I'm with anything that'll keep us growing. What's the specs on this picnic?"

Everyone's attention turned to me. "It's a gold mine about an hour away from here. In this spot that I speak of, the crack game is as sweet as I've ever seen it. You can knock down sixty keys a month with the right crew."

"Sixty?" Siberian rocked back on two chair legs. "Sounds like a diamond mine."

"Dig that," Trigger said. What you got in mind, Limbo?"

"The lay out is sweet. A four Housing Project set up. Me and Murdock worked it once using a crew of locals. The way I have it figured is we run a six month operation. Slam three hundred keys and be done with it. Everyone here will walk away rich men."

"What does that work out to be over six months." Trigger is a stone-cold hustler, among other things, but he's a little slow with numbers.

"Fifty-two kilos a month. Thirteen a week." C-Mack said from his post in the corner.

They hung onto my every word. "As it stands there's no real competition, so we can walk right in and set up shop. Bricks go for forty, but we're gonna move them fast at twenty-eight on the weight side. I get them my connect for fourteen thousand and four cent."

"You can drop a bird for forty? Them '88 prices," Trigger said.

"Not in Johnstown." Murdock took the floor. "Ounces go for two grand. Stone-for-stone, you make thirty-nine hundred back. Body slam a key on the break down tip, pitching from a crack house, and you come up on a hundred thirty-sic grand, counting the short money."

"Which reminds me -- " I could see C-Mack was getting antsy. " -- each project has at least two full-fledge crack houses. Anything you make over your package from a crack house in whatever project you're assigned to is yours to keep. Another thing, if anyone outside the crew we put together gets in the way of one penny of this eight point four million dollar split, I want them smashed the old fashion way. No mercy."

Murdock smiled.

I continued. "Everyone here today will go with a paycheck of no less than two point one million at the end of six months...Your bonuses and your payroll is strictly on how you put your hustle down. My suggestion is that you use the crack house to your advantage. It can cover all expenses and benefits."

Trigger was counting on his fingers. "Two point one." More finger counting. "That's a four way split...it's five of us in here."

Siberian raised a brow. "And what you mean by smashing niggahs the old fashion way?"

I smiled. "I'm glad you volunteered -- "

"'Cause niggah, you just got elected!" Murdock pressed a mini nine to the back of Siberian's head and squeezed the trigger.

"Ain't nothing like the back of the head...the old fashion way," C-Mack said as Siberian's brains oozed onto the oak table, polished to a blinding gloss.

I turned to Trigger. "Does that clear up your concerns about the split?"

C-Mack went to Siberian and lifted what was left of his head. "In case you still listening, we're gonna find your co-defendant, Demoe, and send his ass to the crypt keeper too." C-Mack, let go of his head. It made a dull thud when it wrecked against the oak.

"You motherfuckers is crazy!" Trigger couldn't take his eyes off Siberian.

"No!" I barked "We just dead serious about killing niggahs who keep us at odds with each other. The very niggah responsible for Strife's death and every other problem we've had in the past."

Murdock threw up Crip killer. C-Mack came behind him and tossed up Blood killers.

"That's how the Hoova Crips groove." I threw up Everybody killer. "You niggahs trying to eat or what?"

Trigger stuck out his big fist. "Machine in motion."

I followed suit. "Machine in motion."

"Cripping is an all day demonstration with me." C-Mack put his clenched hand on mine. "Machine in motion."

"Machine in motion, cousins." Murdock added his fist to the pile. "Now let's get this motherfucker moving, we got six months."

With Siberian's body anchored to the bottom of Johnstown's dam, and a team of professional street pharmacists in place, it was time to make arrangements to bring the cocaine in by the truck loads. It was eight in the morning when I walked into Cedric's car dealership. Cedrick was standing at an automatic coffee maker, with his back turned to me.

I leaned against a used Pontiac. My jersey did nothing to protect me from the air-conditioner.

"Long time no see old friend"

"Hot dammit. I was hoping you came by to see me." He was shaking my hand now. "Things are about to change around here."

Cedrick was a middle-age, white man with high cheek bones and a prominent chin. But he's as crooked as a broke finger. He came from a family of organized criminals. A quasi con-man but all business. Specs of gray littered his hair and he had put on a few pounds since we last did business, but overall, he was still a woman magnet.

"Let's talk dollars, Ced."

"Now you're speaking a language I'm familiar with." He loosened the bow in his Bugs Bunny printed tie then led into his office that was colder than the showroom.

I anchored myself in a leather chair facing his desk. "I need you to bring the product down the highway, just like old times." Knowing that Ced' comes from the get over on everybody, all of the time, school of thought, I was prepared to pay him twenty grand each run and a little powder for his personal use. The key to ruffling Ced's feathers is you have to let him think he's winning at his game. "I'll pay you ten G's a run plus traveling expenses.

He arched his pointy fingers over a desk calendar. "There's a lot of risk involved pulling my car trailer up the interstate. It's not like it used to be."

Bullshit. He could run and down the highway hauling cars on that big-ass truck and never get stopped with a dealers tag.

He made a hand gesture toward the showroom. "I could lose everything I have here. "I'm sure you're stuffing more than ten thousand dollars worth of drugs in those cars. That just isn't enough for me to go to prison for."

"Fifteen a run, and we'll call it a done deal."

"I can't consider starting my rig up for fifteen, Limbo. That doesn't cover my monthly bills."

"How much will it cost to start your rig up?"

He began with the dramatics, running a hand through his hair. Letting deep sights escape his mouth while looking into the distance, as if what he said would actually hurt him."

Another long drawn-out sigh.

"Limbo, I'm killing myself here. I'll bring it in for you for a kilo a trip...I'll tell you what, I'll cover my own traveling costs."

The fool had just conned himself and saved me fifty-one hundred in the process. "Damn, Ced' that's steep!" I was quiet for a moment. We both listened to the hiss of the air-conditioner as he watched me contort my face in thought. "If you wasn't my man and I didn't really need you...man...you got that. Done deal?"

He jumped up and shook my hand. "Sure, done deal." He showed his pearly whites.

CHAPTER EIGHTEEN
Rhapsody

I was sitting in the middle of the living room floor tearing the bubble wrapping from the DVD player when Limbo came through the front door. "You just missed the furniture delivery guys."

He sat on the sofa and ran his hand across the soft leather. "Nice."

"It'll due. You have to put the kitchen set together. The coffee and end tables will be delivered tomorrow and the washer and dryer on Friday." I was reading the installment instruction for the DVD while Big Daddy surveyed the house. He seemed pleased.

"You put this together?" He opened the glass door of the entertainment stand.

"No." I removed a tress of hair from my face that was getting on my last nerve. "The delivery guys did."

He pulled me up from the floor. "Come on, let's go have some fun. I'll help you with this later."

"Where are we going?" I looked down at my faded U.P.J. sweats. "I'm not going anywhere dressed like this."

"You'll see when we get there. If you're not comfortable in that then go change, but what you have on is cool."

I slipped on some Nike Air Max, Polo jeans and matching shirt. Now I felt comfortable enough to go out in public.

"I'm not going in there." We were in the huge parking lot of a paint gun arena.

"It's only paint." He kissed my forehead as a father would daughter to convince her that there wasn't any monsters under the bed. "And it washes out."

"Big Daddy I don't like guns. Can't we go skating or something?

He took the keys out of the ignition. "We're gonna have fun. Come on," he said shutting the door behind him.

I took a deep breath and followed him inside.

"Welcome to Patty's Paint Blast," the attendant greeted us. Her red shoulder-length hair reminded me of Keri. She handed us release from any liability forms to sign. "Today is our traditional theme day. Today's theme is cops and robbers. If you would give the gentleman at the costume window your sizes, he'll issue you your costumes and safety gear. The ladies' locker room is to the left, men's to the right."

This is just freaking great.

"I'm not putting on a cop get-up." Limbo went to the window.

Just great Jayme.

Talk about irony, for the first time in my life I felt awkward in uniform. I was positive that this wasn't Limbo's

128

way of telling me that my cover was blown, but this was too close for comfort. The playing field was almost identical to the fed's training alley. Limbo came into the arena ready for battle. He wore a black burglar suit, protective eye gear, and a black scarf around his locks.

"We're gonna have to get you one of these outfits so you can play dress up for me at home." He patted my ass. "I'm into role playing."

Great! This whole scenario had over played itself. "I really don't want to play this stupid game, Big Daddy. I'd much rather be skating or horseback riding."

"I got a horse you can ride later. But now we're gonna have a paint gun fight." He pointed the gun at me. "what you scared I'm gonna win?"

I was uncomfortable have a gun trained on me. From the ruthless look carved in Limbo's face, I could tell that other people had been on this same side of his gun...His face was the last ever saw.

His dangerous face shifted back to its alter-ego, boyish and innocent. "Baby Girl, I promise to take it light on you."

"Fine. Let's get it over with."

As I eased deeper into the obstacle course, I assessed all of its nooks and crannies. Limbo could be hiding anywhere. From psychoanalyzing Limbo's complex personality, I knew he wouldn't hide in the obvious. Where ever he was, I could feel the black of his eyes on me. I went into a zone that blocked the non-relevant out. I focused on one person -- the burglar. I knew the taste of his scent. The way his hundred eight-five pound body sounded beneath the steps of his boots. I knew that he got a thrill that he likened to an orgasm, from seeing the frightened expression on his kills face. He would try to shoot me at point-black range.

Deep into the labyrinth of false fronts and cardboard buildings, his masculine scent became stronger. Just like the plywood figures at the training course, I knew he would soon spring up. IO heard him laugh…then the patter of feet running away from me. The laugh…it was no longer warm and loving, but cynical and cold. In a hurry I followed the laughter of the running burglar. I reached for my walkie-talkie to give my partner the suspect's location and call in for more back-up, but soon I realized that I had no radio. I was alone in this paint-spattered, cardboard city.

I entered a make-shift alley way. No longer could I hear the suspect, but he's here. The smell of aggression was thick. There were three aluminum garbage barrels lining the buildings and two doors that promised to plop me in a different part of this maze. He's behind the door to your left, Jayme. The voice in my head warned. The door knob was warm. Yes, yes, he's here, Jayme. I twist the know slow. Suddenly a lid flew off a garbage can on my left. A burglar popped out like a Jack-in-the-box with his gun pointed at me.

I lifted the heft of my gun. "Freeze, drop the weapon! Do it now!"

Then I heard it …

The distinct sound of a mechanical trigger springing back into position. A paint ball grazed my shoulder as I walked the burglar down. With eight pulls of my trigger, I took eight steps toward him. He was hit will all kill shots. The burglar stared at me as if I were crazy, standing over him with a gun pointed at his head.

Limbo swayed my gun away from his face, removed the paint covered glasses and examined the multi-color paint globs around the heart area of his costume. Climbing out of the garbage can, he looked at me with confusion. "Let's go, I don't want to play no more." He wiped the paint from his forehead and stalked toward the men's locker room.

We ended up going to Johnstown's tourist attraction, the Inclined Plane. It's the world's steepest vehicular incline. The motor at the top pulls two 38-ton trolley cars up a 71.9% grade hillside. The only thing that I disliked about the journey from bottom to top was the time it took to get there. Not only was it the world's steepest, I like to think of it as the world's slowest rollercoaster. But the restaurant at the top was worth the ride.

Since Limbo wouldn't drink with me over dinner, I absorbed enough Mai Tai's for the both of us. I was feeling good and tipsy. The breeze brushing across my face was warm and clean at this altitude. Looking down on the town from the observation deck is a fascinating experience, especially with the influence of liquor.

"Come her." I pulled Limbo into my arms. We kissed like high school sweethearts on prom night. I felt like royalty standing on top of this world with him. You can't keep him forever, Jayme. You just can't.

"Where did you learn to shoot like that?" He rubbed my arm. His touch...firm yet gentle to the point it gave me goose bumps.

"My father taught me. He could handle a gun well. I've e been shooting since I was a little girl.. I..." I lost my train of thought.

"It hurts you to talk about your parents?" He tucked his index fingers in my waist line and pulled me closer.

I laid my head on his chest staring into the skyline. "I'm alright, sometimes I just wish that it was me on that plane and not them."

"I feel your pain, but I can't really relate. I haven't lost anyone in my family that I'm close to like that. I can't imagine losing my old girl."

No he didn't. "Old girl?' I bet your mother would kick your butt if she heard you call her a terrible name like that." My phone rang. "Excuse me, Big Daddy. People always call at the wrong time. Don't they?"

"It'll be like that." He lurched off toward the souvenir shop.

I flipped my phone open. "Hello."

"I thought you were going to call me back yesterday, Jayme."

"I'm doing fine, father, and what have you been up to today?"

"Nothing. I was doing fine until your mother decided to fix her horrible tuna casserole."

"You're the one who sits there and eats it with a this-is-my-favorite-dish smile on your face. You should tell mom that you don't like it. Goodness gracious, what's so hard about that, Father" I could see Limbo talking to the cashier inside the small shop.

"Jayme, you know that I can't hurt Magy's feelings, she puts so much pride in her food."

"Well then enjoy it and keep your complaints to yourself. Father, I really can't talk right now. I'm sorry I'm busy. Working busy."

"I just want you to know that Thanksgiving dinner is at your Aunt Shelly's this year. I know how you feel about the bitch, Jayme, but I don't think no one hates the cunt more than I do. Since I got a head start, I figured you could use one too. Take these next few months and come up with a full-proof bullshit repellant strategy."

"Thanks." Just what the hell I need. "I'm not up for Aunt Shelly's decorous behavior this year. It's sickening to see her act that way, she grew up on a pig farm like the rest of mom's sib -- "I noticed that Limbo wasn't inside the shop. There was no mistake about it, he was standing behind me. The warmth of his breath was tickling my neck hairs. Busted. Had he heard me say Mom? My father was saying something on the other end, but I cut him off. "Okay, I have to go now. Tell Magy I love her." I hung up and Limbo caressed the small of my back. I was penned between his lean body and the observation deck railing.

He planted a soft peck behind my ear. "Who's Magy?"

132

"My best friend, Keke's mom." Toes came alive and started moving like worms inside my shoes. "The panorama is beautiful from up here. It's almost like you can see into forever."

"You like this huh?" Limbo pushed his crotch against my rear end.

"Yup. The view is pretty, but I like that too." I pushed back.

"I can show you something even prettier." He made a call from his cell phone. An hour later we were sitting in a nearby park on a set of swings. I scraped my feet slightly against the ground while we talked. Limbo said something so stupid about Monica Lewinsky giving Bill Clinton a blow job that I laughed tears in my eyes. Through my blurred vision, I saw a hot air balloon set down on the baseball diamond. "Wow, I've never saw one up close before. It's...so big and neat."

"Why do white people talk like that? It's so big and neat?" He over emphasized the way white folks talk. I didn't sound like that, did I?

"Come on, Baby Girl, let's go check it out."

CHAPTER NINETEEN
Limbo

Rhapsody's excitement grew as we approached the balloon. She took on the silly expression of a kid on Christmas. I winked at Boss Hogg, he gave me a furtive nod. I met Boss Hog years back. Him and ten other balloonists were in the mall's parking lot preparing for lift off. Only it turned out that Boss Hog wasn't going anywhere. He hadn't paid his registration fee to the Aeronautical Federation and he was banned from entering Flood city's seventh annual ballooning competition. After talking with him a few minutes, I offered to pay the fee if he would take me and Elixir up sometime. I've been up hundreds of times since then.

"Excuse me. Ah, we don't mean to disturb you, but my lady like your balloon. She wanted to get a closer look if you don't mind?"

Boss Hog appraised Rhapsody's beauty. "Not at all." He was priming the balloon.

Rhapsody circled the gondola (basket) staring at the vibrant blue and orange fabric in awe. "It's gigantic, Big Daddy. It's like looking up at a skyscraper. I wish we brought a camera. Gosh it's so pretty."

"Pretty?" Boss Hog tossed a rope over the gondola. "The beauty of a balloon isn't when it's sitting on the ground. You experience the true beauty when you're in the air."

Rhapsody squeezed my hand. "I'm sure you do."

We had her. "How much will it cost for you to take me and the lady for a spin?"

Boss Hog tugged at a lever to release some hot air out of the top. "Normally...I would accept your money, but I'm afraid that I'm tired. I'm going to call it a day?"

"No problem." I tugged at Rhapsody's hand, leading her away. Her focus never left the balloon.

"I said, "I'm calling it a day." Boss Hog announced. "You can take the lady up yourself if you think you can handle it."

"Yeah, right, that's absurd!" Rhapsody shifted her gaze to Boss Hog.

"What, you don't think I can handle it" The thought of us floating through the sky without a pilot rattled her sense of fear.

She snatched her hand away from mine. "I'm saying it's ridiculously unreasonable for logical thinking people to consider jumping inside this thing – -" She motioned to the balloon like Vanna White presents a letter on the Wheel of Fortune. "..like operating it is second nature. We don't the first thing about ballooning." She turned her scorn on Boss Hog. "And you -- "

I traced the contour of her lips with my thumb. "You'd be surprised by what I know. You don't trust me?"

"No! Not with my life. Are you crazy?"

"Trust the man." Boss Hog interrupted.

"You stay out of this."

I removed the hair covering her ear and whispered. "You put your life in my hands a long time ago. Your life is safe with me, trust me." I climbed in the gondola. Rhapsody watched in disbelief as I checked the fuel gauge, wind gauge, and altimeter. Boss Hog shook my hand and left. He climbed into a Ram truck that pulled up shortly after we landed. I closed the hot-air release vent and gassed the balloon. It jerked up, hovering over the dirt. I reached out my hand. "Are you coming?"

She crossed her arms and pulled them tight across her chest, displaying the defiance of a small child. "You are insane."

"No, I'm sane. I'm just living in a crazy world." I reached out to her again.

She sighed. "Limbo, you better know what you're doing. This isn't too bright at all." She stretched out to meet my hand.

I gassed the balloon, making a seven foot gap between us.

"I'm already skeptical about going up in this thing with you. Keep playing, it's nothing for me to change my mind." She did that thing with her lips that had a way of turning me on.

"I'm just fucking with your, cry baby." I opened the hot-air release vent. The balloon floated back down, helped Rhapsody in, then lifted off.

The two-way radio came to life when the altimeter read 512 feet.

"Limbo, we driving north east, we have a good visual on you. At about fifteen hundred feet there's a stream of wind that'll float you to the door step of heaven." Boss Hog spoke to me from his truck. "Boss Hog, I been trying to get to heaven my whole life. So far ballooning is the closest thing I know to being in the presence of God. It feels good to be riding in the wind again."

Boss Hog's wife, Tammy, got on the radio. "Hey man. It's good to have you back. I'm good and rested, got me a nice hot cup of mud, so I'll be chasing you punctilious land. When do I get to meet this woman responsible for you pulling your balloon out?"

I looked at Rhapsody, she shrugged.

"Friday is cool with me, Tammy."

"Man that's three days away. Be at my house tomorrow at seven, bring your appetites."

Boss Hog got back on. "Safe ballooning, my friend, see you when you bring her down."

Rhapsody was looking over the gondola at the land mass when I said, "I told you that I could show you something prettier." I put my arms around her small waist and stuck a hand inside the front of her jeans. I rested my chin on her shoulder, while looking at my small piece of the world.

"What did she mean by chasing us until we land? Why don't they stay at the park and wait on us?

"Because there's no telling where we might land. I'm good but not as good as Boss Hog. He can pick a location and land there, I still need any open field I can get." I pushed two fingers past the elastic of her thong. "You don't see a steering wheel do you? Up here you're at the mercy of the wind."

"Why did you put me through that? You arranged this with your friend from the start."

"To see if you trust me."

"You're crazy, you know that?"

"I'm not the one who climbed in this big-ass balloon with someone I wasn't sure could fly it."

She looked over her shoulder at me, realizing I had a point.

138

"So this is what it feels like to be a bird? She said more like a statement than a question.

"Among other things. This is how God sees us from his vantage point. Up here makes everything down there insignificant."

"This is beautiful, Limbo. It's so quiet here, I can hear my heart beat.

"The only thing I'm ever conscious of while I'm drifting is the wind.

We reached the air pocket that Boss Hog told me about. The sky was in every direction. I radioed Boss Hogg. "I'm riding the wind for about an hour."

"Sounds like suckie suckie time to me." The radio cracked back.

"Me last long time." We all laughed. I turned the radio off.

Rhapsody was touring each side of the gondola, inspecting each of the views. "The symmetry of land is amazing."

"Tell me how you see it."

She was quiet for a minute while she stared at the scenery. "It's like mother natures quilt work...patch work. You can see all the colors of summer. See look. " She pointed. "Right there, it's the hay fields of gold, and ...and on this side it's the green tree tops and manicured golf courses. She was excited as she experienced the appeal of Earth. She let me to another view. "The plowed fields is...is rich and so black. Look at the way the sun reflects off the water. It looks like a lake of diamonds. You can even see the manipulation of nature. When you look this way." She pointed again. "The land hasn't list its virginity. Seems like a pair of shoes have never touched it. But over there." She motioned to town. "The rows of houses, buildings, and roads are stacked on top of each other. Then when you look away from town, the view gives you a good picture of the way it was. Being up here does make you feel you're in heaven."

I lifted her hair and licked the back of her neck. "Let's give new meaning to the Mile High Club. Have you had an orgasm in heaven?"

Her body shuttered as if she imagined the feeling. She turned to face me and met my tongue with hers. I gripped her round ass while I caressed a honeydew tit. By the time I lifted her T-shirt and sucked on her tight nipples, her milky skin was covered with goose bumps. We floated and floated. She unbuttoned my jeans and tugged at my dick, rubbing the growing head on her navel while sucking my bottom lip. Ten minutes later we were naked floating toward the warmth of the sun. I stood in the middle of the gondola with my dick buried in Rhapsody's wet pussy. Her fingers were threaded behind my neck. Her thin legs were wrapped around my waist. She eased up and down my steel pole, our bodies humped in harmony like poetry.

"Ssss!" Her moan was as quiet as the wind. "Big Daddy, your cock feels so good."

I steadied my gaze on hoer baby-shit green eyes. "Show me how good it feels to you." She arched her back and took as much of my road that would fit.

"Don't disappoint me. I know it feels better to you than that."

She did her best to take me again. Dancing on my pole, she rolled her creamy hips in a slow grind. But failed to consume the whole of me.

I rammed her wetness, trying to force my dick to fit.

"Ooooh, ooh, oooh!" She pulled back to ease the pressure.

I urged her on. Best she gets broke in now. "Don't hold back, Rhapsody. Gimme the pussy, make it fit. You can do it." I hit it again.

"Oh God, Limbo...not so hard."

"Take it then. Gimme all this pussy." I squeezed her cherry-shape ass cheeks tight, pulling her down fast against my hip thrust. I was trying my best to gut her.

"Ahh...oooh." A lone tear ran down her face. "Big Daddy, it...hurts but feels so good." She went into a passion frenzy. She forced herself to meet the tip of my pounding jackhammer.

"Tell me you like it hard." I licked her throat then bit her pink nipple.

"Ssss, God yes. Harder dammit! You can have it all, take this pussy away from me. I love your Black-ass so much."

I did just that. Took it away. For the next ten minutes, I beat the pussy up, gouging out a groove. She bucked against me biting her bottom lip with a tear of stained face. I sucked on her neck and smacked her ass. I love to feel the female flesh wiggle.

"Spank me...spank me like you want. Spank me hard, Big Daddy."

Now I'm slapping her ass between deep penetration. "You deserve to get dicked like this...don't you?"

"Give it to me good, Daddy. I deserve for you to fuck me in my ass. Please make me come."

I held her teary gaze steady. "Ask me again for what you want." I'm digging good, pulling her down onto me by her shoulders.

"I want to...come." Her voice was pleading. "Fuck me up the ass."

The wind blew across my bare ass when she said that. I damn blew my top in her warm hole. I sat her down then bent her over the gondola. We drifted through a cool cloud. The moisture from the cloud left our skin wet. I licked the wetness gathered on the small of her back. I rubbed her drenched pussy then smeared the sloppy juice on her ass hole. Her milky ass looked so good from this position, I bit a cheek leaving my teeth print behind then pushed into her slow. She was tight here, but more receptive.

"Big Daddy, slow…go slow for me." She held a flat palm against my thigh in an effort to control my thrust.

I talked to her while I moved a few inches in her duke-chute.

"Sex is about variety. Sometimes I have to fuck you. It's good for your attitude." I spelled "Limbo" across her ass with my middle finger. "And sometimes…I'm gonna make love to you."

Her tits swung in mid-air. "She held onto the gondola and leveled her gaze on me over her shoulder. "What are you doing to me now, Big Daddy?"

"Filling your request to be fucked" I pushed another two inches in her. Her hole relaxed then I picked up the pace. By the time I slid in another three inches Rhapsody was squealing.

"You're stretching me! Oh, my freaking, God. You're stretching me…you're going to…make me faint. I love you so much…ooh, I love your black ass, Limbo." Her titties were bouncing around now. She stood straight up with me when I gave her the last inch. I fucked Rhapsody in the ass, nibbling on her ear while I fingered her. We came together while floating into heaven.

A day later we were backing out of Boss Hog and Tammy's driveway after a fried chicken dinner and Tammy's subtle interview of Rhapsody. My phone rang, it was Tammy.

"Don't say nothing just listen."

I looked at Boss Hog and Tammy's front door. "Cool."

"If you don't do nothing else, get rid of that white bitch, she's cancer. She's more trouble than she's worth. You can't see that she's a photo copy, because she got you blinded by beauty and booty. Believe me when I tell you, you're cracker girlfriend ain't right." Tammy hung up.

I looked over at Rhapsody and she blew me a kiss followed her million dollar smile.

"I like your friends. Tammy is a mess. We should hang out them more often."

Tammy wants to see me back with Elixir. Naturally, she'll be against Rhapsody read into her wrong. I dismissed Tammy and made a mental note to keep Rhapsody away from Tammy. "Yeah. We can kick it with them. That'll be cool"

Friday night, the line was long outside of Everyday People. It stretched around the corner to Prospect Street. Onlookers watched as me, Murdock, C-Mack, and Trigger parked the chromed out Hummer and bypassed the line.

The bouncer working the door, gave this thick redbone her ID and purse back. He glanced up and noticed us. "My main man, Limbo." He pound his clenched fist onto mine. "I heard you was back. Things haven't been the same since you left, but I know that gonna change now." He touched fist with Murdock and the rest of the homies. "Hershel's inside. He'll be glad to see you and Murdock."

"It's good to see you, Bear, but I'd enjoy this reunion more knowing that you're back on the team."

"Limbo, as much as you did for me and my little league team, you know I'm gonna hold you down. Ain't no question about that."

"Same as before, no guns in the club but the ones I bring?

Bear nodded.

"How many did you let in tonight?" Murdock rolled his head from side to side to relieve tension in his neck.

"Two guns and four honies carrying switchblades."

"Yo, Bear, what's the fucking hold up? A niggah trying to get his groove on." Someone yelled from the line.

"Shut the fuck up and wait or you'll be grooving your shallow ass somewhere else." Bear barked.

I passed Bear an envelope with a few grand stuffed in it. "Get rid of the guns and knives." I pointed to the envelope. "That paycheck will keep you for awhile."

The club was packed with wall-to-wall tennis shoe chasers wearing close to nothing. Flashing strobe lights in combination with rap music made the atmosphere hypnotic. The spot was jumping. The bass deafening. On the dance floor, sweaty skin pulsated to the pounding beat.

"Booties covered in Coogie." Trigger rubbed his hands together like he was about to get into mischief. "I'm gonna have a field day in this punk-ass town. I'm fucking all these hoes."

C-Mack shoved Trigger. "Niggah, hoes don't fuck with you. You still waking up with crack fien pussy...by force not choice."

"Damn, Cuz, you must play professional basketball 'cause you got a hell of a crossover."

"I'm just fucking with you, homey." C-Mack threw an arm around Trigger's shoulder. "But you do be waking up with crack fiens."

We all laughed as we cut a path across the dance floor. A few dudes that had hustled for me acknowledged my presence by waving bottles of Moet and Cristal in the air.

The sexual innuendos I received by the time I reached the bar was crazy. A fine chocolate flavored sister named Trina, turned her back to her dance partner and winked at me. She licked her full lips while freaking herself down. The she massaged her inner thigh, wide hips, chest, and blew me a kiss caused a chain reaction to win my attention. Yani hugged me then kissed my cheek. She raked her fingers through my locks. "You're looking good enough to..." She stared at me with penetrating brown eyes while wiping the lip stick off my face with a napkin. "You make me horny. Call me tonight and it's going down." She put the lipstick stained napkin in my hand. It had her phone number on it.

"How are you, Limbo?" A pretty petite girl asked.

Who are you? It didn't matter that I didn't know her, because she still hugged and pinched my ass.

"Save me a dance. " Her voice was smooth and sexy.

"I don't dance, little Mama."

"Neither do I, standing up." She walked away, her ass bounced with every step.

If Rhapsody didn't act right, I was definitely going to find out how well that sister dances.

Hershel stood behind the bar smiling as we approached. His hairline had receded some and he had acquired crows feet around his walnut shaped eyes the color of mud since I had seen him last. His smile widened, his even white teeth was a blatant contrast to his charcoal skin.

I reached my hand across the mirror-top counter. "How you doing old timer?"

"I must be alright, ain't thought about suicide in a whole ten minutes." He took his small hand back.

C-Mack laughed. "I like this dude already. Let me get a bottle of Yac."

"Coming right up." Hershel focused on me while shaking Murdock's hand. "I see you brought the D.O. double G out with you."

"You know I gotta take this niggah out. If I don't he'll start shitting on the floor and tearing up shoes."

"It's good to see you both." Hershel walked away and came back with C-Mack's liquor. "I'll fill up your private bar in the morning."

I introduced Trigger and C-Mack to Hershel.

"I haven't opened the upstairs since you left." Hershel passed me a key that opened the back door that led to the private upstairs area. "It didn't seem right to have anyone up there but you. Come on, it's just like you left it."

He unlocked a door that opened to a long flight of stairs. At the top was a large room with a glass balcony that overlooked the entire club. Leather sofas hugged the walls. A moon shaped table faced the dance floor. Like Hershel said, the room was like we left it. Pool balls scattered across the pool table. Sitting beside the in-house telephone was the bottle of Cristal Rhapsody sent us a few years back.

Trigger and C-Mack were getting their drink on while me and Murdock pointed out familiar faces.

Trigger refilled his glass. "Who is sexy tan-skin sister sitting down there with that mean looking chick?"

"Over there." Murdock pointed to two of the finest sisters in the joint.

"Yeah." Trigger licked his lip. "What's up with them?"

"The lighter one is Steph, she's cool people, but she ain't been right since her brother was murdered. The other cutty -- "

"I'm not sure why, but I cut Murdock off. "That's Andrea, she's not having it. A niggah ain't getting no rhythm from her evil ass. You got to be church going, career niggah to get a piece of that so forget about it."

Murdock tapped me on the shoulder. "Look."

We all looked in the direction of his pointed finger. Yani twisted and grated her bodacious body in the middle of the dance floor. She sucked on her finger and stared at me. The only thing she was missing was an elevated stage, a pole, a tiny G-string and dollars stuffed in her crotch.

"Cuz, she trying to go." C-Mack pulled out a pack of Swisher Sweets. "Let's take her for a ride on the Amtrack."

"I'm good. I'm not fucking with Yani. I don't know what she been doing, but every niggah she fucked tried to commit suicide when she bounced. I don't want no pussy that good."

"The homey keeping it gangster," Murdock said. "She fuck niggahs minds up like Prince does them hoes."

146

Trigger was talking on the phone in hushed tones. I already knew that he was connected to the ladies room but I asked anyway. "Who you talking to?"

Trigger covered the mouthpiece. "My new woman and she don't smoke dope."

C-Mack shook his head. "You really is burned the fuck out."

We all took turns listening to a female masturbate while being coached by another voice.

"We need to be down in the bathroom," Trigger said.

"You motherfucking right." C-Mack gave him a pound.

"What's up, fellows?" The voice came from behind us.

Murdock dropped the phone and snatched the gun from his waist. Trigger and C-Mack turned with their guns pointed at the voice.

"Goddam, Limbo! Tell your peeps I'm cool peoples." Dollar raised his hands. His eyes told on him Dollar was scared as hell.

"Pussy"

"Nah, niggah, I hear foul things about you."

Trigger cocked the hammer on his .38. "What kind of foul shit you hear about this faggot, Limbo?"

"Easy loc…" I stepped closer to Trigger. "This niggah is a rat-ass niggah. Be cool or we'll be in jail by morning."

Dollar stretched his arms in a pleading gesture. "What you talking about, Limbo?"

Humph! C-Mack caught Dollar with a blow to the eye. "I hate you snitching motherfuckers."

Dollar dropped to the padded floor. He put a hand on his swelling eye. "This is how it is, Limbo? We 'posed to be cool. I'm the one who hooked you up with your woman and this the thanks I get."

The clubbers could tell that there was some sort of commotion going on, but it was hard for them to get a good look from the way my private room was positioned above them.

Trigger's face lit up with pure excitement. I had to end this before Trigger got an inch in his finger.

"Not once have you tried to straighten the charge. You raggedy-ass rat, make your head get small."

Dollar looked puzzled as he stood on his feet.

I glanced at Murdock then back to Dollar. "Oh, you don't know how to make your head small? Somebody tell this snitch how to shrink his shit."

Everyone pointed to the exit sign.

"Vacate the premises before I punch in your shit again." C-Mack rolled his sleeve up. "Niggah bounce."

We all watched from the balcony as Dollar made his way across the dance floor. He looked back at us when he got close to the door.

I waved him on. "It ain't working yet." Not that he could her me.

After Dollar left the building, C-Mack was opening and closing his fist as if he were working the pain out. "Big as your boys head is, he'll make it to the end of the block before it starts to shrink."

Trigger laughed. "The way you him, he's gonna wake up in the morning looking like Spud McKenzie. You lucky we was here to save you though. If we wasn't, that niggah woulda got up and beat your tough ass."

"Yeah right." C-Mack clenched his fist. "I might still slam the soul outta his hot ass the next time I see him."

I called downstairs to Hershel and told him never let anyone upstairs without my permission.

"If ya'll didn't have the line tied up with them pissy-tail girls in the bathroom, you would have known he was on his way up."

"It's cool, Hershel, just don't let it happen again. Next time, wait until you can get through." I hung up and gathered everyone the table. "The first shipment is coming in tonight. All of our prices stay the same. This way we don't compete with each other. Bring in two-fifty for a quarter ounce, and twenty-eight for the whole kilo. This is love what these niggah is used to paying. For every kilo you get, I need twenty-eight back in order to have our paychecks right in six months. No shorts. Use the crack houses to your advantage because all of your expenses is on you: your workers, living arrangements and whatever you do that requires money is your responsibility." I turned to Trigger. "We all know how you like to trick, but don't sweat it, Cuz, crack house money will buy more pussy that you can fuck. Murdock, gimme your hat."

I put four folded slips of paper inside the hat and passed to C-Mack. "Everybody take one. Whatever project you get is yours for the next six months."

C-Mack unfolded his paper. "Cooperdale."

"Solomen." Who the fuck named a project Solomen?" Trigger asked, looking at his paper.

Murdock balled his paper up. "I'm holding down Oakhurst."

I handed Murdock his hat. "That leaves me with Prospect Projects."

CHAPTER TWENTY

Rhapsody

Limbo had been home from jail for only a month now and I had grown to love life as the imposter, Rhapsody. Stop it Jayme, you can't have him. I looked around at the life Rhapsody had built for herself. The life-size wall pictures of her and Limbo, the wall-to-wall carpeting, the 72 inch screen TV and exotic aquarium. I sat here in her living room and became angry while debating with the annoying voice in my head. Who was I angry with Rhapsody or me? She everything in a man that I always dreamed of. Someone who found new ways everyday to make her feel loved. A man that constantly made her feel like the Queen of Queens. She had fallen in love with the man I want to spend the rest of my life with. You can't have him, Jayme. You have to destroy Limbo and Rhapsody. Now do your job.

"Would you shut the hell up?" I picked up the disposable camera, went upstairs and pushed the heavy reinforced steel door open. I took pictures of every phone number Limbo had written down. By the time I was done there were pictures of the closet safe, four fully automatic weapons, the steel doors, about eight thousand in cash in another ten thousand in food stamps, and a digital scale. Unbeknownst to Limbo, our computer was set up to record all incoming an out going calls. I downloaded a month's accumulation of conversations onto a flash drive then hid it inside my cyber skin dildo. Good job, Jayme. You deserve a treat.

Holding the synthetic cock made me moist. My coochie was still sore from the way Limbo put it on me last night. But I couldn't resist the urge to rub it between my legs. I untied my drawstring PJ's and they dropped to the floor. Thank God I was already pantiless. I turned on the camcorder and sat on the edge of a chair in front of it. I lubricated the cock with my mouth before I pushed it inside me. I freed my breast from the sports bra that caged them. The rod sliding inside of me felt extra good. It's something being filmed and watching myself in the digital screen that intensified masturbation. I had just started caressing my tight nipples when the door bell rang. "Shit" Limbo had forbidden for anyone to know where we lived. He even had the mail go to a post office box. So it had be U.P.S. delivering the mink bed quilt. I hurried and got myself together then went to the door. "Who is it?"

"Delivery ma, ma'am."

When I opened the door a guy was standing there with a dozen of red roses and gift box wrapped in gold. I gasped and laid my hands on my heart.

"Are you Rhapsody?"

"Limbos says that you are very special to him. The time that the two of you has spent together is only the beginning of forever." He gave me the roses and gift. I told him Thank you

152

then went to close the door so I could read the card tucked inside the bundle.

"Excuse me, Ms. Rhapsody, that's not it. I have twelve more dozen for you. A dozen for each month you and Limbo have known each other. I also have a long stem rose to say thank you for the bottle of Cristal you gave him the first time he saw you."

I cried like a baby as the man ran back and forth filling our living room with different color roses. As I held the door open, one of my many nosey neighbors said, "Honey, he loves you. Hold onto him, never let go."

You can't keep him

Limbo has never told me that he loves me, but he shows me he does. My neighbor is right, I do need to find a way to hold onto my man. Forget that freaking voice trapped in my head. I took the card from the flowers.

We're going to play a game called Limbo says. Ready? Limbo says open your gift now.

Inside the box was an Oscar de la Renta form fitting mini chemise with bows at the shoulders and long tasseled ties. The material was pink silk. There was a pair of pink ankle-strap high heels and a matching handbag. First I laughed then I shouted, "My God, I love this man." When I held up a pair of tailored made silk thongs with Limbo's name embroidered across the front in diamond chips. Inside the purse was a bottle of Pasha by Catier and two envelopes marked open first and open second. I was bubbling with excitement as I followed his instructions.

Limbo says, you have twenty minutes to get dressed then open the second envelope.

The clock on the wall read 9:42 am. I was dressed by ten. Limbo says, you have twenty minutes to get the mail from our post office box.

I jumped in my Volvo and drove to the post office. When

I opened the box there was a strip of pictures of us having sex inside the picture booth in the mall. I smiled and remembered the day. When we stepped inside of the booth there was a small group of shoppers staring at the pictures falling out of the slot.

Limbo picked up our pictures then looked at the group. "Yo, they arrest people for being peeping toms."

I laughed again, glanced at the pictures once more, and took an envelope out. Limbo says, on Mian Street, there is a shop next door to Subway and between the music store. You have twenty minutes to walk through the door.

On the drive downtown, I couldn't figure out for the life of me what was next door to the Subway that I'd been in a million times. I parked about a block away, fed a hungry parking meter, then turned my feet in the direction of Subway.

Pedestrian thought I was a nut case when I shouted, "Oh, my God." Each time I read the sign Ida's Jewelry. I took control of my bearings and went inside. A husky, dark man locked the door behind me and hung the closed sign up.

An impeccably dressed, beautiful tan woman with a round face greeted me.

"It's a pleasure to meet you, Rhapsody. I'm Ida and that's my husband Jimmy."

Ida took my hand. "If you follow me this way, we have a special showcase arranged for you."

"For me?"

"Yes, honey. Limbo wants you to choose a necklace, bracelet and earring set from the selection. Something to go with this pretty outfit."

All of the lights in the store went out and my showcase lit up -- keeping me focused on the delicate pearls that lay beneath the glass. Ida sat a vanity mirror on the counter and asked me which one I wanted to try first.

"That one."

"Good choice." Mrs. Ida removed the pearls. "Natural black is every ladies desire, but remember ...your aim is to match...your outfit."

I laid the pearls against my skin and fell in love with the reflection in the mirror. By the time I was done trying on the different necklaces, I chose the natural pink set with teardrop earrings.

On my way out the door, Mrs. Ida handed me an envelope but didn't let go of it when I reached for it. "You're special to Limbo. He's close to me and Jimmy's heart. So don't let us down by hurting him. I'll come looking for you myself if you do. Ain't that right, Jimmy?"

Jimmy nodded. "I'll be the one doing the driving."

"I won't, Mrs. Ida." I lowered my head. I felt as guilty as O.J. looked on trial. "Limbo is very special to me, too."

Ida and Jimmy both watched Rhapsody cross Main Street.

"Jimmy, how much gas you got in the Buick?"

"About a quarter tank. Why?"

"Fill it up, she's gonna break his spirits."

"You must have been reading my mind."

Ida turned to Jimmy. "As long as we've been together...your thoughts are my thoughts."

My eyes had watered by the time I opened the envelope.

Limbo says come across the street for brunch.

I looked across the street and in the restaurant window there was a sign advertising brunch specials. At some point in life there comes a time when people experience what it truly takes to make them happy. And come to find out, it's not the type of person or particular status or material thing that we groom ourselves to have, or educate ourselves to achieve. It's the exact opposite that brings fulfillment. The unexpected.

It makes me think that everything I've done up until today was in vain. Limbo is my opposite. My parents raised me to marry an educated white man, firmly established in his career. Limbo is far from white. He's street smart, foulmouthed, intelligent, high school drop-out. I took an oath to uphold this country's constitution. Limbo is a drug dealer, who hates everything this country stands for, and lives according to his own constitution, yet it is him who fills me up and enhances the quality of my life. It is Limbo that gives my purpose new meaning. I want to love Limbo absolutely, because he is my defining element. I realized this starting at a brunch special for lovers sign

So what you feel that way. He'll never accept you for who are, Jayme.

"Yes he will." I mumbled, then crossed the street.

A tall olive complexioned hostess greeted me. "Good morning, Ms. Rhapsody. We've been expecting you. Your table is this way."

The restaurant had a sexy feel to it. Miles Davis played at a low volume. The flame of scented candles flickered in the breeze of slow spinning ceiling fans. Couples laughed and giggled with one another while feeding each other fruit.

I sat at a secluded table drinking Kiwi juice when I opened the envelope with a blue ribbon tied to it that I found on my seat.

Straight up, I never thought that we would make it this far. If someone could have convinced me that kicking it with a white woman was erotic as the experience you introduced me to, I would have added creamer to my coffee a long time ago…Limbo says look up.

My heart skipped a few beats when I saw Limbo coming across the room with a cup of coffee an d a bottle of creamer. He looked good in his tan linen pants and vest. His white collarless button down matched his gator belt and shoes. He

156

wore a tan head crown over his locks. The precision line on his beard and the diamond necklace had my baby looking good.

He sat down across from me. "You're sexy when you're dressed like that."

"Thank -- "

"Limbo didn't say to speak." He stirred his steamy liquid then sipped it. "Rhapsody, you mean a lot to me. When I was on lock down and needed a friend, it was you that came to me. You a rider and I respect the soldier in you. Where I'm from, friendship and loyalty is everything. Your friendship hasn't done nothing but grow stronger since you came into my life. My sons dig your style, so it's all to the good." He looked down into the darkness of his cup. "Limbo say move closer."

He kissed me with so much feeling while stroking my face with a powerful hand. The silk chemise had my nipples rock hard. I still had my lips puckered when my eyes fluttered open to find Limbo smiling at me. I wish he would kiss me again.

"I -- "

"The game is called" Limbo says. I didn't say to do anything but to come across the street for brunch. I am ready to get my grub on. Limbo says, "Take your thong off".

"Take my thong off? What?", I laughed at my nervousness, but I knew that I heard him right.

His peanut butter face turned serious. "Limbo says un-ass the panties."

My nervousness still tried to disguise itself as a laugh. I looked around at the other couples caught up in the moment the decided to enjoy the moment, too. Limbo nodded his head when I dropped my undies on to an empty saucer.

"Limbo says open your legs -- wide."

"Like this?" I know he can't see from that side of the table, but I'm sure he has a pretty good idea of haw far I spread them apart.

157

"Just like that." He disappeared under the long tablecloth. I thought he was joking until he tongue-kissed me on my coochie. I gripped both sides of the table when he started French kissing my lips down there as passionate as he had the ones on my face.

I became religious when he took me with a finger and rhymatic licks. Squirming in the seat, I blurted out, "God, I love you." A few couples gazed in my direction then went back to what they were doing. "I love you so much."

A waiter came to our table. He zoomed in on my thong.

I tried to squeeze Limbo's head between my thighs to keep him still what at the same time turning the plate over on my thong.

Limbo pried my legs apart.

"Miss, are you ready to order?"

Limbo flicked his wet tongue against my clit then nibbled on my inner lip with his teeth.

"Umm…God, yes. Yes dammit."

The waiter raised his brow.

Limbo sucked me.

"Yes, Big daddy." I made a goo-goo face at the waiter. "Yesss…I want to order. No, no, not yet."

He gave me a flirtatious smile in return. "Can I bring you a fresh glass of Kiwi juice?"

"Yes, give it to me… I mean no, no thank you."

The waiter left, Limbo was attentive to the sounds of my purrs. He matched each cat call with the perfect lick and suck. I think it was the combination of mixed emotions and Limbo's tongue, but for the first time in my life, I came without having anal sex. I came hard and heavy when I squirted come in Limbo's face.

He cleaned my love juices from his face with a napkin. "Let's go, Baby Girl."

"I thought we were going to eat?"

"I did. I'm going to feed you in paradise."

CHAPTER TWENTY-ONE
Limbo

Outside the restaurant, there was a stretch limousine waiting on us.

"This is too much, Limbo. No one has ever done anything remotely near any of this for me. Thank you doesn't express my gratitude."

Thank me later, the day hasn't even started." I rubbed her round butt when she bent over to get in the limo. The limo's interior was plush. A TV and a DVD player hung above a wrap-around mini bar. On the mahogany counter top, fixed professionally inside a wicker basket, was fresh fruit -- everything from grapes to cantaloupes.

She asked me where we were going.

"Limbos says be quiet, put this on." I tossed her a blindfold. I sat across from Rhapsody.

"We're playing that again." She tied the black cloth on.

The limo started to its destination. I closed the partition for privacy and pulled her tiny thong from my vest pocket. "Limbo says show me your pussy." I sniffed the intoxicating fabric. Rhapsody jerked the silky chemise up around her stomach and gapped her legs open.

I like what I saw. The hoop earring attached to her delicate fold. The pinkness, that is sure to please me, of her wet crease. Rhapsody's pussy is pretty -- a sight to see. The golden patch of hair was neat and trimmed. But the lips...the lips were bald as a baby's ass. Her thick nipples looked like two pudgy fingers poking through the Indian silk. "Spread it open."

She didn't flinch a muscle. "You didn't say Limbo says. Se I listen sometimes."

Smart ass. "I didn't say open your mouth either. Limbo says open it, let me see it."

She pulled her knees to her chest, reached around her thighs, and stretched her pussy apart -- total pinkness.

I scooted to the edge of my seat then slipped my "fuck you" finger inside her.

She pulled in a breath, out cam a low hum. Her pussy gripped me, it tugged on my finger.

"Limbo says open your mouth."

She flicked her tongue at the air. "Feed me, Big Daddy."

I stuck the fuck-finger in her mouth. She sucked it slow. The bottom of her heels wee now planted on my chest. A deformed monster grew inside my pants. I pushed my finger inside the warmth of her hole again and instructed her to open her mouth. This time Rhapsody licked her lips before flicking her tongue in my direction. I cast my gaze down at the diamond encrusted thong in my hand and stuck the crotch in her mouth.

"Limbo says don't let them fall out or the game is over."

I sat back on the seat. The limo picked up speed.

Rhapsody was eager for my next command. She squirmed her bare ass against the soft leather, causing it to sweat from skin contact. She was more than sexy blindfolded, holding the thong in her teeth with her slit covered in sex juice.

I could smell her sweet wetness. "Play with that thang, girl, make it sing to Big Daddy."

The sexual energy was intense. She kicked her heels off and cocked one leg on the seat. With the other foot, she found my stiffy. She rolled her clit between her manicured finger tips as she massaged me with a foot.

"Fuck yourself...Limbo says."

Rhapsody heard the chatter of my zipper when I unleashed the retarded monster.

"Umm", the moan was muffled. She pushed two fingers in and out her hole fast. I was cool, calm and collected massaging myself, watching her get off. Until her pussy started sounding like a soapy dish rag. I told her that I like when she does this for me and I asked her if she could make me like it more.

She nodded.

I gave her two grapes to see what she would do with them. She pushed them inside her heat, played with her clit for a moment, then popped them out with her PC muscle. The grapes rocketed to my side of the limo. My dick was swoll to the point where I thought my skin would break. "Here, work this for me, Baby Girl." I gave her a banana.

She felt the erect fruit to identify it and was happy to peel it. The banana slide inside her with ease. She bit down hard on her thong as she fed the banana to her split. Rhapsody took the foamy fruit out and fed it to me.

I couldn't take it anymore. I ran my tongue along the bottom of her foot then sucked each toe. Then I found myself on my knees rubbing my dick up and down her gash. "I'm feeling you, Baby Girl."

It's me and you for the long haul. We're gonna do big things together, but don't ever cross me."

She gasped for air when I worked my way in her depths. Her pussy made me feel like I was in a sauna. I slow grinded the poonani, played with nipples through the silk, and kissed her neck for the first ten minutes. But the next ten, I had her knees pinned to her shoulders. My big black gators were braced against the seat behind me. I buried myself in the pussy. "This what the fuck I'm talking about."

It felt like a little man was inside her pussy playing tug-of-war with my dick head. It tugged and pulled me in more. "You feel so good girl. I gotta keep you on a dick diet." I started hitting it in a rocking motion, pushing off the seat behind me.

Rhapsody went from erotic moans, to a panter, to something close to a feline cry, the muffled words of…"Come inside me."

I was already on the brink of eruption so I pushed until I filled her hole with white love.

She let the thong go, which was cool with me because my mission was complete. A liver of sweat trickled from beneath the blindfold. Rhapsody reached for the blinder.

I grabbed her hand. "I didn't say take that off."

"I have to clean myself up."

"Don't worry about it, Baby Girl, I got you." I took a cloth from the mini-bar and wet it. She jumped when the ice-cold cloth came in contact with her love oven. I cleaned her pinkness with the guidance of her hand, then cleaned myself. Rhapsody was slipping into her thong when the chauffer buzzed the rear phone.

I threw the cloth in a waste paper basket. "Hello."

"Mr. Adams, we'll be arriving at the air strip within five minutes. Your lawyer is also on the line requesting that he has a word with you if you are not indisposed."

"Nah, it's cool put him through."

A few clicks were followed by: "How's it going, Limbo?"

"What's up, Jerry?"

"I just wanted to say enjoy yourself. You can stay longer if you like. I don't need the bird back until tomorrow."

"Thanks...but I'm good, I'll be back in the early am. I have a few things I need to take care of in the morning.

The chauffeur opened the door and guided Rhapsody out.

I followed. I took her blindfold off and Rhapsody saw Jerry's Lear jet.

"I know you're not about to tell me that you can fly this, too." She turned to me with her hands on her hips. "I'm not going for it."

"Yes, you would. I didn't tell you I could operate my balloon, but you went for it. Don't trip, there's a pilot, I can't fly this thing."

"You chartered a jet for us?"

"It belongs to a friend of mine. I got mad love in this town."

"It's obvious. Where are we going?" She started up the steps. I didn't bring anything."

"You don't need anything where we're going."

"And where is that?"

"I already told you, Paradise."

We landed in the Grand Bahamas at the Nassau International Airport. A staff of gorgeous Bahamian women was waiting on us with Bahama Mamas and lobster and shrimp shish kabobs.

"Virgin for Mr. Adams." The prettier of the three said, passing me a drink. Her smile was as warm as the blaring sun.

"And the Island's finest rum for Ms. Parrish." She did a slight curtsy after giving Rhapsody her drink. Every time I come here I'm greeted like this, the hospitality and peacefulness made me want to relocate. Paradise Island and hot-air ballooning is everything I picture my dreams of heaven to be.

We left the airport in another limo. Before we crossed the bridge into Paradise, I stopped on Bay Street and bought a platter of conch. It's a dull, chewy shell fish, but it's -- "

"So good." Rhapsody took another bite. "Limbo, I can't believe you arranged all of this. Thank you for what has turned out to be the best day of my life."

"Don't sweat it. Baby Girl. I just want to see you smile."

Rhapsody squeezed her eyes shut like she was trying to get something out of her head.

I touched her. "What's wrong?"

"Nothing. It's just my inner voice, it irritates me sometimes."

"Tell it to shut up."

"I do, but it's unruly."

Paradise Island's, Ocean Club resort is situated on countless acres of manicured lush lawns, bordered by miles of beach. We stood on the resort's open-air patio overlooking the beach. The sky was bright and littered with gliding parasail. The crystal clear water was make-shift playground for buzzing jet skis. The packaged merriment of frolicking booties in tiny bikinis crowded the beach. Ass everywhere! But at night…white sand would be truly private.

Rhapsody squinted into the sunshine. "This really is paradise. I can't believe people try to capture all this beauty on a post card."

"The beach is what Paradise Island is all about." I was checking out this onyx-black island girl with an unbelievable body. "I come here to be by myself. I can kick my shoes off here and relax, I even dance a little bit here."

"Dance?" Rhapsody took her eyes off the same sister I was checking out then cast her gaze on me. "You told me that you don't know how to dance."

"Nah, Baby Girl, I told you I don't dance. Not in clubs anyway. Over here, the only thing that exists is right now. I can let my guard down and enjoy life 'cause I don't constantly have to watch my back."

"You're a sweetie pie, you know that?

"Don't be fooled." I kissed her forehead. "Let's go, I wanna show you something."

"No, let's get bathing suits and have fun in the water."

"We'll come back tonight. It'll be so empty this beach will seem like it's ours alone." I led her away.

Rhapsody stared down in the excited wonder at the jaded ocean floor. We toured the island's surrounding water in a glass bottom boat. An hour later we were dining at the Dun restaurant under candle light as the sun set in the Caribbean.

I ate a spoonful of fruit salad. "When it comes to picking your mate, you have to choose someone you trust with your life. The way I figure out who I can trust, I always ask myself if I was in a circus swinging high on a trapeze who would I have enough trust and confidence in this person to catch me from the other trapeze." I paused, memories came rushing back. I turned and caught the last of the sun's orange disappear behind the horizon. Me and Elixir watched this same view. "I never thought anyone would be on the other trapeze except…I trust you to catch me."

The sparkle in Rhapsody's eyes disappeared. Her pretty face took on a poignant expression.

"There are some things that you don't know about me. Things that I should tell you."

"Rhapsody, I don't dwell on past shit. Nothing you did in the before me means anything to me. You just came off your period last week that rules out that you were born a man. It ain't like you the police, so I don't care about nothing else. I go by what I see and feel now."

She met my gaze again. For a moment, I thought that I saw a stranger trapped behind her baby-shit green eyes trying to escape.

She laid a hand on top of mine. "What do you see, Mr. Adams?"

"I told you, a woman that I trust to hold me down. A woman who won't make my times get rough, and a woman I can count on to go through hell with me if times do get rough."

She squeezed my hand. A tear dripped from her chin into her cleavage. "I love you."

"I know."

After dinner we went to an outdoor concert and danced as the songstress, Anita Baker sang her heart out. By midnight we were walking along the quiet beach barefoot. I had my pants rolled up to my calves. The breeze pushing off the ocean was salty, refreshing, and relaxing. There's nothing better than strolling beneath the stars with a gorgeous woman while the ocean laps at your feet.

"Rhapsody says make love to me."

"How many women do you know can say they've been fucked in heaven and made love to in paradise?

She smiled and pulled her dress off.

CHAPTER TWENTY-TWO

· Earlier, that same day, while Limbo waddled in surpassing delight on a tropical island, two men arrived in Johnstown to capitalize on the city's drug trade. They were sent by their boss to prepare for the take over.

"You looking good, Ma, namean? What's your name? Amir a well shaped, cinnamon colored girl who was watching him and his comrade shoot pool.

She blushed and showed off her deep dimples. "Nina. What's yours?

"Amir." He shook her hand. "That's my partner, Silk."

Silk winked and set the table for a game of nine balls. "What's the haps around here? It seems slow."

"It's what you make it, depends on what you guys are trying to get into. Where yins from?" Nina directed her question to Amir, whom she found to be attractive. He was tall and dark, which was right up her alley. Although handsome wasn't a criteria of hers, she thought that Amir was cute.

"Yins? What you mean by that?" Silk stopped what he was doing.

"That's our way of saying ya'll."

"I done heard it all." Amir chalked a pool stick. We're from Philly, little Mama. We're trying to get into you and one of your girls." He passed Nina his cell phone. "Call one of your girlfriends for Silk and we can kick it."

"Sounds like a winner to me." Nina blushed again. She programmed her phone number in Amir's speed dial then called her first cousin, Mocha.

"Your dime, my time, holler." Mocha was charged up with beer and Xanax.

"What are you doing, girl?"

"The same thing I was doing when we hung up twenty minutes ago, getting my high on and you're about to blow it."

"Girl, I'm at Brother's Place and there are two fine brothers up here from Philly. They trying to holler."

Dollar signs dangled in front of Mocha's hazel eyes. "They hustlers?"

"Think so, but I don't know yet."

"Aren't you the one the call four-one-one? The hell you mean you don't know, what kind of whip they driving?"

"A Benz wagon, with chrome rims."

"Hustlers. Yins come and pick me up."

"Okay, we'll leave when they finish shooting pool."

"Nina."

"Huh?"

"Come straight here. Don't let nobody stick their fangs in them before you get here. Can you handle that?"

"Chill out, I got this."

"Yins hurry up!"

"Girl, don't trip. I'm on my way."

A half an hour later they were at Mocha's clapboard house filling each other out. An hour after that, Nina and Amir played the touch game on the love seat, while the mattress in the bedroom above them screamed out in protest from Silk and Mocha's bump and grind.

Between Nina's big mouth and Mocha's open doors, Amir and Silk had the information they need to make their crew's transition easy and a place to stay until they made their move.

"Them Cleveland boys got this place on lock, huh, shorty? Amir rubbed Nina's solid thighs."

"They're doing their thing. Anything that's sold is theirs, whoever sell it work's for them.

"That about to change, namean?" He unbuttoned her blouse. "Can you hook me up with them?"

The bed upstairs was yelping loude4 now.

Nina pulled at his belt. "You need to talk to Limbo. He plays the back, but everybody knows he's the man."

He kissed her neck. "Can you make it happen?"

"I don't get into stuff like that, but Limbo has a private room in Everyday People. He's there almost every night."

Amir traced her nipple with his tongue.

Nina let out a soft groan as she unzipped his pants. "Do you have a rubber?"

"Let's bounce, Awk," Silk suggested, then threw back a shot of Seagram-7. "Limbo ain't showing up tonight, it's going on two. I'm trying to know that hoe, Mocha off again, namean?"

Amir combed through his thick beard. "I follow you, but let's chill a little longer. Ain't shit else to do, fuck them hoes. We can leave with one of these other hoochies." He pointed to a group of beautiful women gathered around Hershel's bar staring at them.

"Nah, Awk, let's twist Mocha and Nina out first." Silk flashed a small bag of ecstasy pills. "A few of these and the gang bang is going down, I wanna fuck Nina and try out her dick sucking lips anyway."

"I'm with that."

Just then Limbo, C-Mack, and Murdock appeared at the glass balcony high above the club.

CHAPTER TWENTY-THREE

Limbo

Me and Rhapsody made it back to J-town by a quarter to one in the morning. The chauffeur ushered me to my car. I kissed Rhapsody and ordered the driver to take my baby home. I watched the limo's taillights vanish in the night then called Murdock.

"What's cracking, Cuz?" he asked, then laughed.

I pulled away from the curb. "Same thing I wanna know, it's your world. I'm just trying to breathe a little air. Where you at?"

"On the grind, fucking with this niggah C-Mack. Listening to his crazy-as stories about his pimping uncle Pap."

I told him that I was coming to pick them up. We needed to talk numbers.

"I'll call Trigger and have him meet us there." Murdock said.

"Cool."

Thursday's are usually slow for Hershel. There were only a few cars in the parking lot. There was one car that stood out. A Mercedes Station Wagon. The car interested me because it was a 2002 model and it is still 2001. We parked behind Everyday People and used my private entrance.

When we got inside, out of habit and ego, we went and stood on the balcony to peep scenery and, of course, to be seen. The club was naked as the parking lot suggested. But there were strangers below us, peeping us out. One dude was a red niggah with nappy hair and a sharp line up. I could tell that he was taller than the other guy, despite the fact that he's slouched in his chair sipping a Heineken. The other guy had a dirty-rotten look etched in his face. He continuously combed through his thick beard.

"You know the peons with the reckless eyeballs." C-Mack spun the pinky ring on his finger. "I'm about due to knock somebody into 2010."

"They ain't from around here." Murdock leveled his gaze on the strangers.

"Philly boys, " I said. "Philadelphia plates on the wagon outside."

"What kinda time you think these guys on?" Murdock leaned on the banister refusing to look away first.

"I say we find out." I pulled out my cell phone.

"Everyday People, Hershel speaking, how can I help you?"

"What's up old timer?"

"Slow night."

"Send up a bottle for C-Mack and a bottle of Moet for my guests."

"I didn't know you were her, what guests?

174

"You see the two dudes seated by the DJ's booth?"

"Yeah, they've been here since midnight. I've never seen them before, I don't forget faces."

"Tell them that I would like for them to join me."

Hershel agreed, but told me that he gets a bad vibe from the strangers.

"I feel it, too"

Hershel went to the strangers table and, exchanged a few words, pointed in my direction, then escorted them to the stairs.

The dark-skinned scoundrel with the beard cleared the steps first. His diamond Allah emblem bounced off his chest in sync with his hop. The taller red dude was right behind him twirling a Mercedes key ring on a pinky finger.

The DJ spun a record where Biggie Smalls defined the meaning of beef.

C-Mack and Murdock frisked both men. C-Mack was rough with the red dud, kicking his feet apart and forcing him to the wall.

"I thought we wee invited up here because ya'll wanted us to feel like we're at home." Hiss afro comb fell to the floor when Murdock removed the dude's wallet and threw it on the table in front of me.

"I can't enjoy myself if I don't feel comfortable." I read he driver's license from the first billfold Aron Shaffer then the other Demetrius Baler. "Make yourselves comfortable." I motioned for them to sit.

Hershel came and served drinks, eyed the men suspiciously then left. C-Mack sat down beside me. I slid the wallets across the table, minus the ID's. I examined their photos once more. "Aron, that's your name right? What bring you two Philly players to J-town?"

"Call me Amir, namean. And this is my partner Silk. It's

funny you should ask that question, Limbo, because we were sent here to find you."

Me, Murdock, and C-Mack exchanged glances. I motioned to Murdock. He came over and I whispered in his ear while giving him their ID's. "Have Spence run these names. Keep their addresses and social security numbers on file incase we have to touch these niggahs families. Tell the homey, we need what we can get tonight." I thought for a moment, while looking across the table at the strangers who knew me, but didn't have a clue that they were. "Call Ghetto, have him come down here and make sure the Benz stays in the lot tonight.   After he handles that, have him meet us at Chore Boy's house." Murdock went to the other side of the room to make the calls, I focused on my guest.

Amir fiddled with a hair in his beard. "You must be C-Mack, I saw you box a couple of years back. Heard a lot of things about you."

"Believe them."   DC-Mack nursed his drink while maintaining eye contact.

"Why is it that you know so much about us and we don't know shit about you?" I wasn't feeling this dude or the quiet one.

"Because it's my business to know, I've done my homework. I know that your and your partners, Murdock over there, Trigger whose not here for some reason, and the junior Olympic boxing champ got the drug game holed up. You're making major moves with all four projects on lock. See we --

"Niggah, who is you?" And who is this we that you're referring to?" I removed a lock that hung in my face.

Biggie Smalls hit a punch line. "Beef is when I see you, you guaranteed to be in I.C.U."

I learned a long time ago that there is no such thing as coincidence. Everything happens for a reason, including the DJ playing this song. I couldn't help but to think that this conversation would eventually lead to beef.

Silk just sat there twirling the key ring on his finger, like it was a compulsive behavior, his psychotic niche.

Amir laughed. "I don't see the need to reintroduce myself. I represent a cartel outta Philly. My boss is a fair man, a lot more even-handed than myself. It's a business practice if his -- out of respect -- that I give my best effort in trying to establish a business relationship with our competitors, before we move our team in and set up shop.

"Set up shop?" C-Mack clenched his fist without a conscious try. "You got me fucked up. He turned to me. "Who we got on deck in black Arabia?"

"I hate to disappoint you Crip Mack." Silk found his voice. "We don't tolerate gangs in Philly."

"Cripping is across the nation." Trigger cleared the steps.

"You must be trigger happy Trigger with the schizophrenic finger." Amir offered a hand to Trigger.

The homey looked at me. "Who is this niggah, Cuz?" Trigger gave me and C-Mack a pound.

"I don't know." C-Mack started to get up. "But I'm about to punch this niggah in his mouth."

"Easy, Loc." I grabbed C-Mack's arm. "Your guess is as good as mine, Trig' but I think we was just getting to the part where Amir here -- " I identified Amir by nodding in his direction. " -- makes us a business proposition. Speak your peace, we're all listening.

Them damn keys had just about ruined my nerves. C-Mack's cool was eager to leave the building.

Amir refilled his glass sand slid the Moet to Silk. "My boss is offering you fifty grand a month for the next year in exchange for two of the project complexes. We want to move in as peacefully as possible with as little blood shed...as possible. This place is small, but it's big enough for us all to get money."

Silk leaned forward. "And to sweeten the pot. I know we can give you prices on whole ones less than what you're paying now." Keys again.

"Throw a number at me." Murdock joined us.

Amir drained his glass again. "Eleven flat."

"Straight come up." C-Mack steadied his gaze on Murdock.

"Sound like something to you, homey?"

"I'm feeling that, plus the fifty stacks a month, we can't lose. Speak on it, Trigger."

"They say all money ain't good money, but I say free money is easy money. Ya'll just ain't offering enough free money. Limbo, what you think about these niggahs business proposal?"

Amir and Silk's whole demeanor had changed listening to the homey's feed back. Who was I to rob them of here fifteen minutes of fame. I needed a few more minutes for Ghetto to handle his business. "Shit, we stand to come up all the way around the board fucking with these dudes. So, Amir, how does your boss suggest that we keep the peace once I accept your offer?"

"You know, the standard protocol." Silk never looked up, he never stopped spinning those keys. "We all sit down and set up boundaries for your crew and ours. Along with a fair game zone."

"Fair game zone, huh? More like a gray area." I drummed my fingers. "An advertisement area where our workers and your workers hustle together, competing for size and price with the intentions of pushing customers to shop within a specific boundary. I like that, commercial, underground marketing.

The keys stopped. "It's also important that we agree not to let anyone else come in and disturb this network, fuck up the income."

Amir took over again. In that respect, it doesn't make a difference whose lines have been crossed, we'll come together to protect our business interest."

"Ya'll be kidding me right? This is a fucking joke, who put you up to this?" I started laughing, then we all laughed at them so hard that Amir went from cordial to cold and angry. I thought about how Rhapsody always throws one of my lines back at me and decided I'd throw Amir's back at him. "It's funny you should say that, because me and my partners have already made a solid agreement."

"And what's that?" Amir gritted his teeth.

"To smash niggahs like you," Murdock answered, "who tried to step on our toes, fucking with our income."

C-Mack smiled. "The old fashion way."

Trigger's 40 Glock was in hand.

I continued as Amir's face took on another expression. "I respect that you tried to work this out like players, but nobody will dictate what I can and can't do, or what your punk-ass boss thinks that I should do in a spot that I got on lock. That's crazy, hell, fuck nah, we can't come to an agreement."

C-Mack took his bottle of cognac to the head. "And if clown niggahs or your boss's actions go any further that this conversation, we gonna be on Crip gangster shit."

Amir ran his comb through his beard and focused his vicious eyes on me. "Just 'cause you shitting in these woods don't make you a bear, player."

"Nah, it don't but it do make these my motherfucking woods. If you're not a believer, then you and your partner will wind up shitted on. Your stay safe pass expires when you leave this room. Get caught out of pocket, we're gonna bury you in the woods."

Murdock went to Amir and Silk's side of the table. "Mrs. Gordon, down at the morgue, does good work. She'll make you look like you're still alive."

179

Silk stood up, "It doesn't look like we're gonna come to a peaceful agreement. Sadiq, my boss, doesn't take this stale mate to well."

Amir got up," Our offer no longer stands, we'll make other arrangements."

Just what the fuck I needed.

After I locked up, me and the homies piled inside Mack's Hummer. We drove to at a snails pace past the club's parking lot. Amir and Silk examined their crippled car in disbelief. The windows were shattered. Tires flat, headlights absent, tail-lights AWOL.

They watched us as we crept by.

Murdock made a gun with his hand and shot it at Amir.

"See, Cuz," C-Mack put his foot on the gas. "This why I don't get down with the dope game. Too much unnecessary bullshit involved with it. Here it is, I'm running my own spot, I don't even move this like this. I rob niggahs. Stick up boys are different from all other hustlers. Our intent is to kill or be killed if a situation arises. We was 'posed to give it to them from the word go."

"You're rolling with this operation because you love your hood." I told him to turn left at the next corner.

"You already know, I got mad love for you too, homey."

Trigger shuffled through a CD case. "Don't trip C-Mack. You just gotta understand a dope man's logic. With us, we deal with drama a little more polished than stick-up boys. See, you'll just pop off right then and there if that's what it takes to walk away with the money. Where as us," Trigger banged on his chest. "We can't go out in a blaze of glory and make the spot hot. If we did that, we'd never get paid. But when the paper is threatened, we plot to eliminate the threat without any attention being drawn that'll be bad for business."

180

"Well put, Trig. That's good 'G' right there." I turned in the seat. "Murdock, what did the homey Spence come up with?"

"The boy Amir is a gangster. He beat a murder case in '98.' He was on trial again last year for kidnapping a big dope boy and girl. Killed the broad in front of the niggah. Amir forced the cat to take him to the stash, but the dude got away in the process and went to the police. The first day of trial, the dude was found dead in his hotel room, with police protection. With nobody to point the finger at Amir, he walked. Get this, though, he's been arrested twelve times for picking up prostitutes.

"He got a thing for prostitutes, huh?" I stroked my mustache.

Murdock nodded.

"What's the business with the addresses and ID's?" C-Mack hit the left blinker. "And what's the business on quiet, red niggah?"

Murdock went on. "Spence said both addresses are bogus, he needs a little more time to cross reference the social numbers with the driver license numbers. Demetrius Baker, Silk, been in and out of the joint for drug trafficking. Did some Fed time, too. I'm thinking if their boss sent a gun, he sent a thorough hustler. Which means they've probably having the same conversation we're having."

C-Mack parked. "They're on top of their game, they know everything about us. Makes me wonder what else they know."

"Why we stop at Chore Boy's crib?" Trigger asked, looking at the rundown house.

CHAPTER TWENTY-FOUR

"Call them knuckle heads and have them pick us up." Amir ordered. He stood over the Mercedes, furious at the sight of the once brand-new car. The car belonged to Silk, but Amir was the angriest because they were disrespected. They watched the money green Hummer eased by them.

The men exchanged mean mugs.

Murdock pointed a finger gun at Amir and pulled the trigger.

That was all it took for Amir to make a vow. "I'm a have fun splitting these niggahs wigs."

The Hummers tail lights faded into the night.

"They don't get down, then we lay 'em down, namean?

"I know what your mean, Amir, but we gots to come correct with these dudes. They ain't no slouches." Silk palmed his cell phone. "I'm willing to bet that they're plotting on us right, Limbo is a smart hustler, a thinker. The only reason it wasn't drama tonight is because Limbo is keeping things quiet for business. If we stick around they're coming."

"Then we get them before they get us, you know how this shit go. Sadiq wants to put his hand in this spot, we're gonna a make it happen." Amir watched a train carrying steel pass under a bridge.

Silk made the call to his boss.

"A salaam slyakim." Sadiq's voice was drugged with sleep.

"Walaykim salaam." Silk leaned on what was left of his car.

"Everything kosher?'

"Nah, Awk, he's not willing to do business with us."

"I'm counting on you. Don't let me down. Your success depends on my extending my reach."

"Sadiq, I've never failed on you and I don't plan to. These guys been around, they mean business. It's gonna take some force."

Sadiq laughed. "They said Limbo wasn't a push over. How much force?"

"At least thirty soldiers. We're gonna check some things out around here. I'm a have my car towed home, then I'll be back in a day or so."

"Towed?"

"Yeah, that was their way of welcoming us to town."

"Silk, I've been grooming you long time. You know how things work. Most importantly, you're my number one bread winner. I think it's time for you to see some real money. Get me inside Johnstown and I'll bring you all the way in. You'll understand the meaning of big time as my right-hand man."

"I'll be able to claim my position soon."

"I knew I could count on you."

Sadiq gave Silk the fuel he needed to realize his street dreams. Silk always imagined himself on top. He had done well moving up in the ranks to captain. He was never satisfied with that title or the ghetto-superstar status that came with it. Captain just wasn't high enough. Silk looked in the nigh air at the smoke rising from a steel mill in the distance. He was finally about to see how high the top really was.

CHAPTER TWENTY-FIVE

Limbo

Chore Boy's tattered house is situated high on a hill overlooking Everyday People's parking lot. We were all huddled around the living room window watching Amir and Silk. Ghetto, the young buck responsible for giving the Benz a makeover, was upstairs blowing Chore Boy's wife back out for a piece of crack.

"Chore Boy, go upstairs and tell Ghetto to wrap it up, I need to holler at him." I like Chore Boy, he didn't ask questions or protest, he was obedient. He would beg, roll over, play dead, stand on his hind legs, and sit where he was told. The only thing Chore Boy is concerned about is his treat.

"I was hoping that we'd have a smooth run."

"Limbo, you of all people know that nothing goes as planned." Murdock said

"That's why we have to smash these cats real smooth and quiet."

A black Maxima with customized plates that read 'Nina 411' pulled into the lot below us.

I watched. "If we don't we're gonna have a street war on our hands."

Trigger nudged Murdock. "Ain't that the big mouth girl's car with the fat ass?"

"Yup." Murdock nodded. "Now we know why they know so much about us."

"Nah," Trigger said, "diarrhea mouth might of told them some shit, but they came here with knowledge about us and how we putting it down."

I agreed.

"I feel that , too," C-Mack scratched his head.

A dark girl climbed out of Nina's passenger seat. C-Mack asked who she was.

"The neighborhood hoe," Murdock put his foot on the windowsill and leaned forward. "Mocha"

"These lames is trick niggahs." C-Mack smiled.

I could damn near see C-Mack's brain clicking. "Yeah, and we're gonna offer them a piece of pussy and trick them outta their lives."

Murdock must have read my mind, "Kesha?"

"The best who ever done it, " Trigger said.

"Don't admire my work, break me the fuck off." Ghetto gave us dap.

We all like Ghetto because he was rowdy and wore his name like a badge of honor. He had a Karl Kani shirt thrown over his shoulder. His jeans hung so far of his ass that they revealed the works fuck you written in bold letters across the back of his boxers. He is so skinny that I can see his heart beat through his bird chest. He even had to pull his belt to the last hole, which did no good because he still had to constantly pull is pants up.

Murdock and C-Mack had a particular interest in him, because they said that Ghetto was Crip material. I peeled him off a few hundreds.

"Fuck is this? This all I'm worth?" He put the money in his pocket. "You niggahs about to make my try ya'lls chins. I think I can get a easy win, it's only four of yins against all of me." He beat on his chest. "Seems even to me."

C-Mack smushed him. "Get your weight, Ghetto." He passed Ghetto a blunt. "Let's get blinded off the haze, blaze up."

Trigger ruffled the top of his braided head. "When you catch up t0 the size of your hear, niggahs better duck, you gonna be a motherfucker."

"Shit, they better duck now." Ghetto lit the blunt then took an envelope from his deep pockets and gave it to me. "After I finish smoking up Mack's weed, I'm gonna try you, Trig'. I know I can get you." He jumped up and ruffled Trigger back on the head. They kept clowning with each other while I went through the envelope.

They enjoyed their smoke session, and I watched Amir and Silk ride away with Big Mouth and Mocha.

"What you got there?" Murdock joined me at the window.

"Ghetto is thorough." I passed the envelope to Murdock so he could draw his own conclusion.

Murdock nodded. "I told you that young niggah is Crip material. C-Mack, come peep this out."

C-Mack went over the contents. "Trigger, who putting it down in Philly?"

Trigger passed the blunt to Ghetto. "Uzi and Ronny live up there doing big things with Left To Death records." Smoke was coming out his nose as he spoke.

"Uzi from Back Street or Big Uzi from Tray Deuce?" C-Mack asked.

"Tray Deuce." Trigger blazed up a Black and Mild cigar.

"Oh, the homey murder-for-hire, a straight head buster." C-Mack gave the envelope back.

"Well now we have a solid address where Uzi can bust a few heads." When I was coming up I used to get my ass kicked for bad grades. Silk's little girls grades were honors, but the report would definitely get her family in a heap of trouble.

From time to time, I would go home and eat Rhapsody out in her sleep. I admit I'm strung out, but so is she. Her breathing pattern changed while I sucked on her. Six minutes is the longest I've ever went without waking her up. I always woke up the second Rhapsody put her lips on Big Daddy. This was a game of ours. This morning my tongue game was either sloppy or top notch, she was awake in under three minutes.

I turned over late in the afternoon to find Rhapsody slipping her little body into a pair of low rider jeans. "Where you going?"

"Grocery store. I'm going to fix you a meal fit for champions."

"Bring me back the special from Cocoa's Soul Food. No pork."

"You don't trust my cooking? Hands on her hips.

"Nope. I wanna eat not get sick. Tell Cocoa to give me a cream-cheese pie." I turned over to get a few more minutes of sleep when she hit me with a pillow.

CHAPTER TWENTY-SIX
Rhapsody

I awoke bright and early with my head on Limbo's chest. The beat of his heart thumped in my ear as I focused on the lump inside his briefs. It's moments like this that made me envious of Rhapsody. If I told him the truth about everything, would he hate me? Couldn't we put our heads together and work this situation out so that he could cheat going back to prison? Could he ever forgive me and accept my love for what it s? Real. He'll kill you, Jayme, or die trying.

I got up and started doing house work in my delicates. Cleaning always helped me to calm a troubled mind. But I felt a sense of real freedom and unconditionally comfortable doing chores in my panties and bra. I had been cleaning and re-cleaning between the kitchen and laundry room for hours before I came up with the solution to my problem. I came to the conclusion that being true to love is the only thing important. Everything else is insignificant with out it. Now that I had real love in my life, for the first time, I was going to be true to it. Whatever the outcome.

I hadn't turned in any of the data or recordings I had gathered on Limbo's criminal activities, so he's safe in that respect. I stood in front of a floor-to-ceiling mirror, in our living room and confronted both women staring back at me. "Here it is, like it or not, Jayme. We're going to help Thurston out with the West Virginia thing then we're turning our badge and gun in."

"You can't do this, we worked our whole life -- "

"Shut up, I'm running things now. Rhapsody, we're going to come clean with Limbo once Jayme quits. He'll have to know that our love is sincere after you quit, despite your lies."

He'll never believe you, don't throw everything away on a hope.

"I said shut the hell up." I cracked the mirror with a broom handle. "This is how it is. No more lies -- period."

The distorted image didn't have trouble finding a voice.

What about Limbo's money that you and Thurston stole?

I walked away.

Don't you abandon me!

I kept going.

Don't turn your back on me! Jayme, do here me talking to you?

"Not anymore." I never looked back. "And don't bother me while I'm ignoring you." My plan was perfect. Nothing else could possibly go wrong between now and then.

My cell phone rang.

It scared the hell out of me. I stuck the broom in the broom closet and took the phone from its charger. "Hello."

"Rhapsody, I'm glad that I caught you."

Hr voice gave me the creeps.

"We need to talk," she said.

My skin turned pale and cold.

I was at my wits end. Limbo asked me where I was going as I threw on a pair of jeans and a blouse. Grocery shopping was the first thing that came to mind. Just that fast I broke a promise. I lied to Limbo again. He made a snide remark about me cooking when I told him I had plans of fixing him something to eat. I whacked with a scented throw pillow and left.

Out of all times, why had she chose to come back now? There's no way that she could possibly think that we're suppose to pick up where we left off. I turned onto my street. Something about it looked different. It seemed ...something about the trees had changed. I parked in my driveway behind her Saab.

I watched with skepticism as she climbed from her car. She had put on a few pounds that made her look...good. Her fiery-red hair was done up in a french bun. She had on a tank top, torn to make it a half shirt, that she wore over low waist jeans, her red thong raised above the jeans waistline. At first I thought I was seeing things, but the closer she came to my car the more visible a gold belly chain with a Jayme charm attached to it became.

I got out of my car. "Hell must've frozen over. So what brings you to town, Keri?"

She visibly withered at the thick insinuation of my voice. "I'm not good for a hug or kiss? This isn't the greeting I anticipated after being away for so long."

"What did you really expect, Keri?" I thought about the deranged look on her face the last time I saw her standing in front of the shower smelling my clothes like she had completely lost it. "We didn't exactly go our separate ways on good terms or don't you remember?"

She hugged me and packed me on the mouth. "I missed you. I apologize for my behavior. Can we go inside and talk. I would have let myself in, but you changed the locks." She smelled explosive like expensive perfume. One I couldn't call by name.

"You left me or did you forget that, too? Not one single call, a fuck-you-go-to-hell letter, an E-mail, nothing in over a year. Seriously, what did you expect, Keri? But what I really wan to know is what you expect now that you've popped up on my doorstep like nothing ever happened?"

"I don't want to fight with the one person I love more than life itself." She spoke with the innocence of a toddler. She took my hand. "But I would like to sit down and have a grown-up conversation with you."

I had been away from home long enough for dust to gather on the wood surfaces throughout the house. I looked around and realized that this life, in a sense, was jail. I had built a life according to what my parents had planned for me. I was only successful at following their script, living up to other people's standards and expectations. My whole motivation, for as long as I can remember, revolves around pleasing others. What about what I want? What about the things that makes me happy? Rhapsody's life gave me contentment. The longer I stood there in my living room processing my life, the more I wanted it to be a par of the past.

"Is something wrong? Thurston said you haven't been yourself lately." Keri sat on the love seat. "You look like you seen a ghost or something."

"No, I'm fine. You want to talk, so talk."

"You're right...I left to evaluate myself, did some soul searching. I understand now that I let my jealousy get way out of hand. I was looking for ways to validate my insecurities through you." The coolness of the room caused her nipples to harden, pushing them against her torn T-shirt. "All of my relationships before you were based on jealousy, anger, and

194

fear. So that's what I understood a relationship to be. When you showed me the exact opposite, I panicked because, at the time, I thought a relationship had to be angry, possessive, and all those negative things. I sound crazy, don't I?"

"Sounds like you've recognized and understand some of your shortcomings."

"The first step to correcting them is to recognize."

I sat beside her. "You sound good and you look good, too."

"It's the new air I was breathing while I was away."

"You've come back to stay?"

"With you, yes."

"Keri, let's not go jumping the gun here. I'm not ready"

"Jayme, Rhapsody, listen to me. I've leaned from my mistakes. I love you and I need to be in your life. Friends with sexual benefits. No demands, it's not all about me. I'm willing to have an open relationship with you. If that's what it takes to be a part of you. I know the value of what we had, and I'll be broke if I don't have you again."

My intuition was screaming trouble, but what came out of my mouth was, "Prove it."

"How? I'll do anything."

Keri was on her way to our Easy Storage bin to get her things that I had packed away. She had my extra keys so she was straight. I was now in line ordering Limbo's food when my phone rang. I switched to voice mail because I needed time to think. Think Keri in the Limp, Rhapsody equation. I'm so compulsive. Here I go again trying to please everyone. I just pray that I walk away from this with my man in tow.

All the way home I rehearsed my lines. *'Limbo, I have something to tell you. I think you should sit down.'* Nah, that sounded phone and entirely too clichéd. The people in the car beside mine stared at me like they had never saw anyone talk to them self. The light changed. *'I don't know where to begin.*

I'm not who you think I am.' Didn't like the sounds of that either. *'Limbo, you know that I would never do anything to hurt you, right?'* I tried bluntness for sound. *'I work for the Feds. I was supposed to set you up, but I fell in love with you.'* I tested several lines by the time I got home to find that Limbo had left. My cell phone rang again as I put his food in the microwave.

"Hello."

"Johanson." Thurston's voice sounded like a bull horn.

"Yes, your majesty."

"Didn't Keri tell you that I said to get in touch with me? Why haven't you returned my calls?"

"When you're undercover, you can't talk to the Feds when you want to. You talk when the opportunity, presents itself."

"Well, I know this is the perfect opportunity, because Adams just left ten minutes ago. We have a unit tailing him."

I could tell that he had that stinking cigar in his mouth. "You have somebody watching me watch him?"

"From time to time. Go to your PC, I'm sending you something."

"Okay." I climbed the stairs and logged on. "I'm in the system." Four people popped on the screen. Three of them had profiles.

"Achoo!" Boomed through the phone.

"Bless you." I studied the screen. "Summer colds are the worst."

"Allergies. In the pictures is Sprinkle, Jerico, James Lee, and someone intelligence hasn't identified. In this file you'll find everything Intel has on the West Virginia case to date. Study it, you have a few more days before you and Tara go down there."

"Thurston, I've been thinking --

196

"I'll do all the thinking, Johanson. Fill me in our situation, and email me a report on Adams by Monday for legitimacy. Adams has been out of jail a month and the drug activity in Johnstown has increased by ninety percent, and I don't have a single summary of what you've learned. I need something to report to my boss." Thurston hung up.

I checked my messages, there was one from Limbo.

"I love you, too, his message started, "I had to make a run with the homies…something came up. I'm gonna pick you up around nine tonight. I want you to check this spot, Chocolate City, out with me. I'm thinking of buying it, and turning it into a sports bar…"

CHAPTER TWENTY-SEVEN

Keri

There is no way in the world I'm going to play second fiddle to some stupid drug-dealing nigger. Jayme belongs to me and that's the way it'll always be. I can't figure out for the life of me why she can't figure that out. What I feel for her is beyond love. Jayme is playing live-in, taking that filthy black dick, and collecting a pension for it at the same time. She's out being the perfect girlfriend while I'm forced to waddle in a pile of her stale, dirty laundry, staring at a blank ceiling that resembled the last year of my life. Blank.

I tried on every pair of Jayme's soiled panties in hopes of glimpsing her inner most thoughts. The menstrual stained pair that clung to me now brought back the fondest memories. The pain was intense, but worth it. I rubbed the crotch of her underwear against my clean-shaven vagina until I brushed burned my love lips. Now her DNA would be a part of me forever.

A whistling tea pot called me to my love potion. I took my time navigating my way into the kitchen, I looked at every inch of the house in great detail through Jayme's blue contact. This was a different experience that excited me. I was finally able to see life as she saw it, through her eyes.

In the half bathroom's wastepaper basket, I found exactly what I needed to make Jayme's essence a part of my own. I took the sanitary napkin and placed it in my tea cup, the one a picture of us on the side. As the napkin marinated in the hot water, the aroma rising from the steamy cup was beautiful. Persuasive enough…to compel me to love her harder. I drank the warm liquid with her panties stretched tight across my ass. I wore a grove in the wood floor as I thought. Thought of how I would have her all to myself once Limbo was out of the picture, one way or another. I laughed and laughed ass the maneuver formed in my head.

"It's a classic," I said to the image of Jayme on my cup. "If I can't beat you then I'll join you -- for now." I shattered the cup against the cast iron stove. "Only for now."

CHAPTER TWENTY-EIGHT

Limbo

Murdock and C-Mack was lounging in our private room when I arrived at Everyday People. The club was empty at this time of morning.

Murdock pointed the remote at a TV monitor flush against the furthest wall. "We have a problem." The one-eyed monster came to life. On the bottom of the screen was the letters REW. He pressed the play button once the tape had stopped rewinding. "What's this?" I glanced at them both.

C-Mack made a sour face after he threw back a shot of cognac.

"Watch it, Cuz."

The local anchorwoman appeared on the tube, *"This is Channel Seven's breaking news at seven. Good evening, I'm Althea Hinton, reporting live from Cedrick's Dealer ship in Moxam. Mr.*

Cedrick Newman, thirty-two, son of former mayor, Andrew Newman, was found dead this evening in his office along with a suicide note by his secretary, Amber Stevens. Ms. Stevens describes the finding as an unbelievable gruesome bloody mess." Althea turned the mic to the weeping lady. The minicam's light flooded Amber's face. *"Did Mr. Newman show any warning signs that he was suicidal?"*

"Not at all, Cedrick was very professional. His attitude was one to copy. He never seemed to get upset by things that would upset most folks. I've never even know the man to have a headache."

"Were you aware that he had a drug habit?"

"He partied at holiday office parties, but I couldn't confirm that Cedrick had any type of habit. The drugs and hem killing himself doesn't fit his character, he was so full of life."

"You believe that it was foul play involved?" Althea thrust the mic in Amber's face once more.

"I don't believe this was a suicide. I told the police…"

The minicam followed as she moved closer to the showcase doors. The paramedics wheeled Cedrick's body through the double doors. Amber covered her mouth and wept as the stuffed body bag rolled by her. Spectators stood behind yellow police tape.

"The authorities haven't ruled out foul play, but nothing has been determined at this time. An update on this story will air on our nightly news segment. This is Althea Hinton on Seven at Seven. Back to you Anthony."

"Thank you Althea. In other news…"

I asked, where was that taped.

"That's yesterday's news." C-Mack brushed marijuana ashes from his shirt. "I had this little chicken head tape the fight for me yesterday while I was taking care of the business. I didn't watch it until about an hour ago, and that when I hit ya'll up."

My whole operation was going to fall apart without a sure way to bring the drugs in, now that Ced' eighy-sixed or whatever the fuck happened to him.

"The dope getting short." Murdock was taking his braids out, "Next week we won't have a crumb of coke. The boy Silk left on the Greyhound this morning, and Amir came through all the projects this morning in a rental. Eye hustling."

The Notorious B.I.G was dead-ass when he started screaming 'more money more problems'. It was easy to set up shop in this spot because the town was in a crisis. The hustlers were doing good see an ounce a couple times a week. That's why the prices were sky-high, and the rocks were the size of the shit I blew off the table when I used to bag it. We were saviors when we came through with the mighty-white and flooded the spot. Just when the money was good, and the operation was running smooth, problems popped up like the chicken pox. The Philly boys. My runner, and to top it off, the steel mills went on strike. The bulk of my paper came from the mills.

On my way down her to meet up with the homies, I drove past two of the four mills. Each time I witnessed the same thing, hundreds of demonstrators bucking their jobs. They protested their jobs with angry slurs, group songs, and picket signs that read: *We will not work until we receive better health benefits and lower taxes.*

I don't give a fuck about their gripes. I wanted them to take their crying asses back to work so me and my crew can get paid. If things kept taking their own course, going against my plan, this would end up being much longer than a six-month operation.

"Niggah, come back to earth with us." C-Mack sucked in a cloud of smoke.

"I was thinking."

"That's what worries me." Murdock put a hand on my shoulder. "When you get that look, that mind of yours is thinking some crazy shit."

"Ain't no question." C-Mack crushed out his blunt.

"Fifty kilos, our records, and the federal sentencing guide lines will put us behind bars for life."

"I didn't say anything about us mulling it, Murdock."

"You were thinking it, though."

"You motherfucking right he was." C-Mack gave Murdock a pound.

"What's the deal with Kesha?" I directed the question to Murdock.

"Home girl will be here in the morning."

"Solution one," I said, "C-Mack what's cracking with murder-for-hire?"

"I shot the business at the homey last night. Fifty stacks a body. He said our headache will be gone within three days of taking the job. He put that on the neighborhood."

"Solution number two. Give the homey a job."

C-Mack threw his hands up. "Hold up, our mule ate a bullet. We got the Philly pussies that wants to funnel some work through here, and break us off at bottom of the barrel prices. We ain't talking about making the trip. Let's take their money, let them open shop then rob and kill them niggahs. They gonna die anyway, might as well get something out of it. Their work can hold us down until we figure out how to make our own move."

Murdock scratched his head. "Stick up kid to your heart, but that ain't the move, homey."

"Yeah, Mack." I leaned against the pool table. "Them cats is gonna be problems period rather we give them our blessing or mot. If we allow them to do business they're gonna bring a crew with them."

"Then instead of having two problems to get rid of nice and quiet, we'll have a whole crew on our hands" Murdock unraveled a braid.

I was quiet for a moment. We don't need a street war. Beef and getting money don't mix, Mack, it's one or the other. That's a slick lick if we was sticking and moving, just sliding through you know. But that ain't the mission we on. The best thing to do is give Uzi the go-ahead and peel them cats' caps. We can't afford to let this problem bother us no longer than we have to."

"Run your house, Cuz." C-Mack leaned back, balancing the chair on two legs with his hands threaded behind his head.

"Whose gonna make the re-up run?"

I told them that I could get the product here while the weather is still nice, but once it changed, we would have to make other arrangements.

"What the fuck does the weather have to do with anything?" C-Mack put the chair down on all fours and looked at me.

Murdock sat down in the couch and let out a sigh. This niggah is crazy, C-Mack."

Murdock knew what I had in mind. The more I thought about it, the more I knew it would work. Boss Hog was down with just about anything. Why hadn't I thought of this before? I turned to Mack, "You got to have good weather to fly a hot-air balloon."

"Who you know with a hot-air balloon?"

Night covered the town like a warm comforter. Downtown's office lights sparkled in the darkness. We pulled in the club's parking lot a few minutes after nine.

Rhapsody fixed her lipstick in a tiny vanity mirror. "Gimme some, Big Daddy." She puckered her pouty lips. We shared an intimate kiss then went inside.

It was early, the place wasn't packed but it wasn't empty either. I nodded at a few people and gave dap to others, as me and Baby Girl found our seats. Rhapsody removed her leather jacket to reveal a form fitting shirt over a pair of skin tight jeans that laced up on the side. I peeped the cats checking out Rhapsody's hourglass figure. It was cool with me. It let me know that I have something worth having when other cats broke their necks to see her. As long as they didn't disrespect, though. The music was thumping. Musiq Soulchild sung about going through the ups and downs and joys and hurts of love. Couples slow-danced while Trina and her girls danced with each other. When Trina noticed that I was with my baby, she gave a hateful look then rolled her eyes. She whispered to her girls, but I paid no mind.

Rhapsody surveyed the club from front to back. "So this is the place you wan to buy?"

"Thinking about it." I flagged a waitress. "What you think about it?"

"A little remodeling to fit a sport bar theme, and you'll have something here."

The waitress came to our table. "Hey, Limbo, what can I get for you?"

"What's up, Kim?" I nodded toward Rhapsody. "Bring the lady whatever she wants."

"I'll have an orgasm with a cherry on top." Rhapsody never bothered to look up.

Kim went to fill the order.

"Picture this," I said. "Over there, where the dance floor is, I'll have the monitors for sports events, and right -- "

"All these beautiful sisters around here that's been trying to get with you form day one," Trina said with her hands on her baby-making hips, popping her chewing gum. "Soon as Elixir is outta the picture, you choose the same enemy that hung our grandfathers from sycamore trees to seep with.

206

Limbo you ain't shit! She said in the same tone as a racist might use to deliver scornful words you dirty nigger.

"Don't start no shit in here, Trina." She knew I meant business. The last time she talked shit, I let Elixir tap that ass.

Trina's girls gathered around. Rhapsody wasn't threatened, she took her rings off and pulled earrings out.

Trina looked at Rhapsody and rolled her eyes. "Bitch please."

She turned to me. "You like black jelly beans?"

Her girls were sucking their teeth and gritting on Rhapsody now. I figured if I answered her question, she would take her girls and kick rocks before she pissed me off. I told her no.

"Why?"

"They're nasty and they leave a nasty taste in my mouth."

"To a black woman -- a real woman -- a white skank with our men taste just like a black jelly beans in our mouths."

"Nasty!" they all said at the same time.

"brother's really is sorry and trifling. The first thing a niggah with some money does is get a white bitch. What the fuck was the point of getting some money to give it back to them?" The taller of the girls slapped hands with the pudgy girl of the bunch.

" 'Cause he still a slave and don't even know it." Pudgy shook her head in disgust.

"She'll bring him down, they've been doing it for centuries." Another girl said.

"All right, ya'll beat it. Get the fuck away from here with this bullshit."

Trina's ignorant ass ignored me. "You got a lot of nerve bringing this dusty-ass, dirty-foot tramp in here, showcasing your trailer trash. Didn't you read the sign out front? It says

Chocolate City not Cracker County." She switched her hateful gaze to Rhapsody. "Just so both ya'll know."

"Fuck it, beat her ass for G.P. Trina", the tall girl said.

Rhapsody finished tying her ponytail and pushed her jewelry towards me. "And what am I supposed to be doing while she tries to kick my white ass? Rhapsody downed her orgasm and stood up.

"Oh, this bitch thinks she's bad." Another girl said.

Rhapsody stepped to Trina. "See, it's not about black or white…"

Trina's expression changed, not knowing Rhapsody had heart. I didn't know either, until now.

"…it's about holding your man down. First sign of trouble and you sensitive hoes is complaining and fucking your man's friend. Then you heifer's use your prehistoric sex as a weapon, act like you're too good to suck a dick. I understand why Black men desert ya'll for women like me. Now are we going to keep insulting each other with this racial dumb shit, or are we going to fight?" Rhapsody rolled her sleeves up. "You can get some next on G.P. since you want somebody to beat my ass."

Too-tall looked away.

I was enjoying the exchange. Under different circumstances, I wouldn't mind seeing them throw down. I stepped between them. "Ain't nobody kicking nobody's ass unless it's me. Trina, take your drama-queen butt somewhere and chill out. You stay in some bullshit."

Rhapsody attempted to have me move. "Nah, Bid Daddy, don't save this dizzy hoe. She popped her gums strong, let's see if she can back it up."

"Dirty foot, you want a piece of me?" Trina said, over my shoulder. "You lucky he did stop me from getting knee deep in your nothing ass. You can damn sure get what you looking for."

"This ain't about me being white, it's about you wanting to fuck my man. You're kind of sexy. Limbo, bring this bitch home so we can both fuck her."

"No she didn't." The pudgy girl put her hands on her hips.

I don't know what it was, but it seemed like Trina was considering it.

"Come on, Rhapsody. We out before this shit get hectic in here." I turned around to grab her leather from the chair when she kissed me and caressed my crotch in front of the growing crowd. Then she gave me this freaky lick across my lips.

"Trina," Rhapsody paused. "We can all fuck or you and I can fight. It don't make any difference. I'll win either way, because in the end, this'll still be my man."

With that said, Rhapsody led me out to the parking lot by my hand.

There was a pair of thongs under my windshield wipers. Attached to the crotch was a note that read: *Next time, I want you to take my panties off. Love, Yani.*

Rhapsody shook her head. "Dope man groupies."

I pointed the car in the direction of my home.

"Big Daddy, I don't want to be home by myself tonight."

"I'll be back in an hour after I drop you off."

"Promise."

I laughed noncommittally.

"An hour, Lamont."

"Where'd Lamont come from?"

"That's because I'm serious. I'm going to have a bitch fit if you're a no show."

"I said I'll be there, Baby Girl."

Fifteen minutes later, I watched Rhapsody walk through our front door. I went to make arrangements with Boss Hog to bring the next shipment in.

I knew there was no way that I would make it back in a hour. It was four hours alter when I stuck my key in the front door. Rhapsody had to be upset, because the downstairs was pitch-black. Usually she'd be stretched out across the couch asleep, but swore up and down she was awake and waiting. The water was running in the upstairs bathroom, Rhapsody must be taking one of her midnight beauty baths. I noticed the smell of lavender and the flicker of candle flames bounced off the staircase wall. I climbed the flight to get in the tub with her, but was shocked Rhapsody laying spread eagle on a sheet of plastic atop our bed. She was naked, not counting the crotchless panties She's a bonafide freak so I wasn't surprised by the sight before me.

The toilet flushed.

That's what bothered me. I shot Rhapsody a look that amounted to violence. "Who the fuck is in my house?" I took out my 9mm and put one in the chamber. I knew that I was feeling Rhapsody, but a crime of passion, I never imagined. I had made up my mind to murder this bitch and the motherfucker in my bathroom. No one was allowed to come in my house or have knowledge of the Bat Cave's whereabouts. Not only did she break the rules, she disrespected me to the fullest. My ego got involved. I couldn't stop thinking about how she had been giving that prize pussy away. Deep down, I knew I couldn't trust her. My face tightened. I turned to the bathroom door. "Come the fuck outta there." Rhapsody didn't seem to care that I was turning into a demon.

She made a low moan. "Big Daddy," her voice was just above a whisper. She arched her back and squeezed baby oil all over her body.

In my mind I was bugging out, here I was calculating my get away after the double murder I was about to commit, and

Rhapsody had her porn face on. She bit her bottom lip then stuck a black dildo in her twat and motioned for me to come to her with her free hand.

The bathroom door swung open.

Keri leaned against the door frame. Her red hair matched her red vixen outfit. The next thing I zoomed in on was the life-like strop-on that had me out matched. Then it was her pointy, pinkish brown nipples the size of thimbles that sat above a cherry push-up bra. She was too sexy and petite standing there with her fuck-me pumps, fishnet stockings and garter.

Keri bat her lashes and closed the space between us. "It's nice to see you again." She reached for my nine and clicked the safety on. "What are you going to do with this? Her accent suggested that she's from the south.

I couldn't believe it when she bent over and sucked on the barrel of my gun. A tattoo of a unicorn stretched from the swell of her ass to the center of her back. My other gun woke up. I know it was about to go down. The sound of Rhapsody fucking herself behind me, and the sight of this well-formed bombshell in front of me had uninhibited sex written all over it. No wonder they couldn't get along when they lived together, they were fucking the whole time.

Keri stood on her tippy-toes to kiss me. She sucked on my tongue hard. She looked at me attentively through amber eyes. "Let's get started, we have a long night ahead of us."

I rubbed on her ass on the way to the bed where Rhapsody was waiting. The red light on the camcorder indicated that we were being filmed. Rhapsody sighed and took a deep breath when she pulled the dildo out and stuck it in Keri's mouth. Baby Girl's melons swelled each time she filled her lungs with air. Keri was bent over the bed chasing the dildo with her tongue as Rhapsody teased her. While they were playing cat and mouse, Keri reached back and fondled my zipper. Rhapsody smiled when I started to undress.

Keri now had her tongue in Rhapsody's rose-pink pussy. I climbed on the slippery bed and hung Big Daddy over Rhapsody's painted lips. The inside of her mouth was an inferno. It was erotic to see her lips slid on Big Daddy while she got her pussy ate. Seeing a pretty set of lips on my dick is the best sight in the world.

Keri looked up from her meal, but didn't fail to roll her thumb against Rhapsody's clit. "Save me some, Rhapsody, I want to suck on it, too."

I was grinding my hips, holding Rhapsody's head steady using her mouth like a pussy. I kept the rhythm when I focused on Keri. "It's enough for you to get some." I turned back and a portion of Big Daddy disappeared in Rhapsody's mouth.

Rhapsody had proven to be the perfect hybrid woman. She's a lady in the daylight, a soldier when it's time to fight, and a freak at night. She had no problem fulfilling the ultimate male fantasy, because threesomes were a fantasy of hers, too. I didn't know what made me more horny, Rhapsody's aromatherapy oil burners or the scent of all this moist pussy. I pulled out of Rhapsody's mouth and stood behind Keri. It was a hell of a sight and a contrast to see a rubber dick swinging between Keri's legs and a meaty twat at the same time. She was doing her job eating Rhapsody's pussy because Baby Girl was squirming in combination with ooohs, aaahs, and sssh.

I'm stroking myself looking at Keri's ass and red-haired twat while she did her thing between Rhapsody's legs. I got so excited watching them, a dose of precome leaked onto the carpet.

Rhapsody moaned then gasped for air. "Are you going to give it her, Big Daddy?"

"Somebody put something in me!" Keri looked back at me.

I already had plans of taking Keri to nirvana, but I had to taster her red petals first. I reached between her thighs and rubbed her wet flesh. Keri let out a soft moan. I licked the juice she left on my fingers.

"Do it now, Limbo. Please." Keri wagged her tail at me.

I spread her sweet twat and found her thick clit with my tongue. I paid close attention to Keri when I flicked my tongue against her.'

She let me know when I licked a place she liked. "Oooh, right there."

Rhapsody said. "God, yes."

I nibbled on Keri.

"Put your mouth on me," Keri whispered between pants. "Lick me, put your tongue deep in me."

Keri ate Rhapsody and I gobbled her.

Keri put her head down, arching her back causing her ass to poke up more. She parted her twat and I mean it opened wide. "Punish me. Drive me like I was an old stick shift. I want to feel your balls slam against my ass."

Big Daddy pushed into the tightest, little pussy I ever felt. All I could think of was, 'Oh, shit look what I'm doing'.

"Dammit, switch gears!" Keri barked. "Harder. Just…a…harder, Limbo."

I paced myself.

Rhapsody sucked the dildo while her pussy got sucked, and she never took her eyes off me while I broke Keri off, doggy style. It started to get good to me as I drove from first to fifth gear.

Keri couldn't give rhapsody's thirsty pussy the attention it deserved because I had my foot on the gas pedal. I was hitting so hard the unicorn was galloping across Keri's back. Rhapsody did the next best thing as far as I'm concerned. She climbed beneath Keri -- in the sixty-nine position -- and licked me and Keri in the same rhythm that we fucked. Our sex juices covered her face.

"Arrgh!" my nuts were getting heavy. I wanted to hold it, but I know I was going to erupt. "Arrgh..."

"Come inside me," Keri said, "Spank me while you fill me up."

I smacked her bare flesh about four times while I filled her tight pussy. Rhapsody made the moment intense with my balls in her mouth.

It was crazy, it was them on them. Rhapsody's titties made a slapping sound as she bounced up and down on the strap-on.

It was them on me. Rhapsody sat on my face while Keri took Big Daddy for a ride. They French kissed the whole time.

It was me on them. Rhapsody was sliding up and down the strap-on again. "Make me come, Big Daddy. Give it to me."

I spit on her asshole then pushed my way inside. Me and Keri had Rhapsody sandwiched, gang banging her internally.

Rhapsody usually found the Holy Ghost during sex, "Oh, God yes," she said over and over. After Rhapsody ejaculated on my thigh, I was read to let loose for the second time. They were kissing when I announced that I was about to come.

"Don't waste it in my ass, I want to drink you."

I pulled and knelt in front of their faces. Rhapsody took me in her mouth. As soon as she put her pretty lips on me, I filled her mouth with semen. I came so heavy and hard, I almost collapsed. Rhapsody shared my load with Keri when they kissed. I shot the rest of what I had on their faces.

I woke up the next morning with two beautiful women and the smell of pussy on my face. Couldn't nobody tell me shit. A cool morning breeze pushed through the window, bellowing the sheer curtain around my bed clad with lesbians. I took the video cassette from the camcorder, stick it in the downstairs VCR, and relieved the whole experience again.

Boss Hog's two-way radio squawked to life as the balloon was being driven by the momentum of the wind.

"HC 59, this is Air Traffic Control at Cuyahoga Tower. Do you read?"

"Roger, Cuyahoga Tower, this is HC 59, go ahead,

"We have some traffic coming in at two-thousand feet," the controller said. "I need you to drop to nine-hundred feet, clear the way a little.

"Roger that." Boss Hog opened the hot-air vent and watched the altimeter gauge decline. "HC 59, dropping from eighteen-hundred feet to nine."

"HC 59, you should have a visual."

Boss Hog could see the twin-engine plane flying above him to his right. "Copy that, Cuyahoga Tower."

"HC 59, you'll be leaving our airspace and we'll be handing you off to Allegheny County In approximately six minutes. Allegheny Tower will pick you up in route. Safe ballooning."

"Over and out," Boss Hog looked to the crate of cocaine sitting at the bottom of the gondola and smile. It's only a matter of time now.

CHAPTER TWENTY-NINE

With Boss Hog's help, Limbo had managed to bring his next drug shipment within city limits with no problem. In the week that had passed, there was still the matter of Silk and Amir that ate at his being.

Limbo gazed through the windshield as he waited. He started the car when Ghetto came out of the house and made his way up the block.

Ghetto pulled his pants up to his waist and plopped his frail self in the passenger's seat. "You called good money, the niggah laid up with Nina and Mocha?

"Good looking." Limbo eased away from the curb.

"That ain't it, though."

"What you mean?" Limbo pushed a 2Pac CD into the disk player.

"Who got your back?" Ghetto pounded on his chest. "Say I'm the man."

"Not now with the bull, Ghetto, you know you my little man."

"Thought so, niggah." He tossed a sandwich bag of crack cocaine on Limbo's lap.

"The fuck! You know I don't ride like this." Limbo pulled onto a side street, cracked his car door and let the drugs fall to the pavement and kept rolling.

2Pac was in the background raping about how he came to bring the pain.

"Relax, my niggah. You the one who sent me up in them hoes' crib to see what was happening."

"You got that from Amir?"

"Yup."

"How'd you pull that off?"

"I went in there fronting to Mocha about how I was tired of fucking with you, 'cause you wasn't doing me right. I told her I was on some renegade shit, and that I was trying to get some work that wasn't yours. I hated on you hard."

Limbo looked at Ghetto through the corner of his eye. "Where was Amir?"

"Sitting right there, sucking it up. The slow-ass niggah fed right into it. He asked me…"

"What you trying to get, youngster?"

"Half ounce." Ghetto sized him up. He would have bet his bank roll that he could take this chump.

"What you know about hustling?"

"What you know about minding your business, if you ain't got what I'm looking for?" Ghetto turned to Mocha. "Mocha, what's up with this niggah with the afro on his face?"

"He good people." She busied stuffing marijuana into a bong.

"Chill youngster, you got a lot of spunk. It's all on the level, namean?" He went to the bottom of the stairs and yelled up, "Nina, bring me my bag."

A minute later, Nina cam downstairs in a skimpy nightgown, with a small draw-string bag. "Hey cutie pie." She pinched Ghetto's cheek and passed Amir the bag.

"You think I'm cute?"

"Sure do."

"Then when you gonna give me some pussy? My doggy style is on one million."

"Boy, you so mannish, you need to quit."

"Come on," Amir said, "let me holler at you in the kitchen."

Ghetto sat at the table watching Amir weigh on a digital scale.

"I'm gonna fuck with you, youngster." Amir turned the scale around so Ghetto could read the weight. " 'Cause I like your flow and we both dislike Limbo."

"Yeah, that niggah foul. If I had my own army, I'd bust his head and take over this shit."

"Don't worry, youngster, your thoughts are already in the making."

"That says twenty-nine grams." Ghetto counted his money.

"I'm fronting you one."

Limbo pulled into the projects. "You just earned your place in our hood."

Ghetto's face lit up. "Straight up, Limbo. I'm a Crip?"

"A motherfucking Hoova Crip, Cuz." Limbo gave Ghetto his neighborhood's hand-shake. "What else did Amir say?"

"To find out everything I can about you and the homies. He stressed about finding out where everybody is resting. He gave me his cell phone and pager number and told me to hit him when I was done with the package so he could give me a big eighth. Oh, yeah, he said he was going out tonight."

"Where to?"

"Your spot. Everyday People."

Kesha lounged in a hotel suite, living it up at Limbo's expense. She was happy to get the long needed break from her children, but, honestly, she was bored out of her mind. She had been wandering the hotel's grounds and surfing cable for a week now. She prayed for some excitement to break up the monotony. She picked up the phone on several occasions to contact C-Mack, knowing that he would stop by to scratch her itch. Kesha stared at the phone for the millionth time and decided against it, like she had the rest.

Kesha had real feelings for C-Mack. Every time they had sex, it jumbled Kesha's emotions. C-Mack was unaware of Kesha's sensitivity toward him. He thought it was the same for her as it was for him. As easy as C-Mack came, he was leaving until she called on him again. The relationship arena wasn't his type of hype.

Kesha understood the importance of staying inside the hotel and not allowing the locals to get familiar with a new face. She had to make a grand entrance at just the right time. She sighed and gazed at a shopping mall from hr floor-to-ceiling window. Enough is enough. What's a little shopping going to do? The mall is right across the street. She'd be back before she was missed.

Kesha dressed and was on her way out the door when the phone rang. "I knew it too much like right." She sat her purse on a nearby table, kicked her shoes off and answered.

"What's cracking, Cuz?" Limbo asked.

"Not a motherfucking thin. Why you ask me that retarded-ass question? You tell me what's suppose to be cracking, cooped up in a room all by yourself. I can't even watch a decent fuck flick."

220

"Damn, why you biting my head off for?"

"I'm bored."

"Relax, homey, you get to come out and play tonight."

Philadelphia's Keely Street is positioned in a quiet middle-class neighborhood. Silk moved his high-school sweetheart and eleven-year daughter to the area, two years ago, after he moved up in rank with Sadiq's drug cartel.

The killer had scanned and surveyed the inner workings of the street for three days. The killer had Silk's family's routine down to a science. He knew every possible escape route from the street, he even knew the times of the day old-man Smith took his cocker spaniel out to piss. The killer loomed in the darkness of a garage watching Silk's house. Tonight he would strike.

"Right foot blue." The electronic Twister game announced.

Tia, Silk's better half, slid her leg over her daughter's back and through Silk's legs.

"Ooh, mommy, you got your butt in my face."

Tia and Silk laughed.

"Left hand yellow."

Egypt, the little girl, had some trouble knotted between her parents, but she managed to put her tiny hand on the yellow circle.

"Left foot green," the Twister voice said.

"It's your turn, Daddy."

"The green one is way over there." Silk looked between his legs. "How in the world am I supposed to get my foot over there?"

"You can do it, baby." Tia's voice has always inspired Silk.

Silk shifted his weight so that his arms were supporting his and Tia's weight. He struggled not to pinch Egypt between his knees and the dotted floor.

"Daddy, you are my superhero, you're almost there."

Silk couldn't hold the combined weight any longer while stretching to the green dot. They fell on the dotted canvas in laughter and love. They were having the time of their lives, as they do every Thursday evening -- family night, when Silk's in town. They laid there in each others arms, until Silk started to tickle them.

Egypt laughed and laughed under Silk's delicate touch.

Tia jumped on Silk's back. "Run, Egypt, girl run!"

Egypt bolted to the other side of the room like a bat-out-of-hell.

Silk flipped Tia over and pinned her on her back. "I should tickle you until you pee on yourself."

"And you know you won't be getting any nookie before you leave."

Silk looked at his daughter, who was plastered with a smile. "Cover your ears, Egypt."

She plugged her ears.

He switched his gaze to the pretty dark-skinned woman beneath him. "You can't go a whole week without getting a dose of this dick," he whispered.

"So I lied. Kiss me."

He helped Tia up. After the kiss, he tickled her anyway. They all sat down on the couch together.

Tia played with Silk's ear lobes. "How long do you think you'll be in Johnston?"

"Johnstown. I don't know, but it shouldn't be as long as the last spot we was in."

"I hope not, Daddy. You still gonna come home every weekend?"

"Promise, princess." He kissed his daughter's forehead. "You know I wouldn't miss a weekend away from you and your mother. Ya'll my favorite girls, namean?"

"Baby." Tia caressed his neck. "You forget about the pizza."

"Shit!" Silk jumped up. Let me go get it." He grabbed his car keys.

"Daddy, when is your job taking you to Johnston?

"Johnstown, Egypt."

"In the morning," Tia told her.

Silk stepped out the door.

The street light cut into the garage, splitting the darkness in two. The killer seemed fascinated by the light. He pushed his thick hand into the light and examined it as if he never seen it before. He then pulled it into the darkness and then the light again.

The hand game to an abrupt stop when Silk came out of the house and left in a rental car. The killer hadn't expected Silk to leave, but he figured this was the time to make his move.

He would be waiting with Silk came back.

He moved foreword with apt mastery as he left the dark confines. He was dressed according to his mission -- all black. He crept up the cobblestone walkway that let to Silk's front door with nonchalance. He knocked on the door.

It's time.

Egypt was reading a Sayta Nile short story to Tia when the knock echoed their ears.

"It's your father. He left his house keys, take them to him." Tia pointed to a set of keys on the bookshelf. "He always does that when he drives a rental."

Egypt skipped to the front door and pulled it open.

"Da -- "

The killer bullied his way in with a silenced 9mm Sig in his hand. He grabbed Egypt and clamped a hand over the child's mouth. He led her into the living room to her mother.

Fear man-handled Tia when she saw the menacing man smothering Egypt's mouth. The sight of the gun pointed at her daughter's head power drove her heart into shock. Tia's eyes went liquid as she watched Egypt's tears drip from the killer's hand. She would never forget him. His skin was the color of hell's ashes. He was as wide as a WWF wrestling champion. He had three long braids hanging from his chin.

Tia dropped the book and leapt to her feet. "Don't hurt my baby." She was sobbing. "For Allah's sake, don't hurt her."

"Sit down, don't make me tell you again." The shrill of his voice was unnerving.

Tia sat on the edge of a cushion.

The killer whispered to Egypt, "I want you to be a good little girl and go sit with your mother."

Tia cried and held her arms out as Egypt came to her.

He allowed them to hug for a moment before he spoke again.

"This is -- "

"We don't have any money here." Tia's vision was blurred with tears.

"Don't you ever fucking interrupt while I'm talking. I'm not interested in your money."

Tia looked at him with pure horror. What does he want then? Please, Allah, don't let this man rape my baby, let him just have me, she prayed.

The shrill of his voice halted her petition to Allah.

"I want you to do what a woman is supposed to be doing at this time of day."

"What should I be doing, mister?"

"Get your motherfucking, prissy-ass in the kitchen and fix me something to eat. I can't watch both of ya'll, so I'm gonna trust you to be by yourself in there. IF you do anything stupid like fuck with that wall phone above the blender or run out the back door, Egypt will pay for your actions with her life. But if you spit in my food, you, your daughter and everybody on your mother, Regina's side of the family will pay for your actions with their lives. Now do what you were told, put some loving in it, be creative. A lot of people are counting on you.

Tia hugged Egypt and went into the kitchen.

"Are you going to kill us? Egypt never looked in his direction.

The killer took the phone off the hook then pulled the hooded sweat shirt from his bald head. "Some things are better left unsaid."

"Promise me that you won't let me die without knowing your name."

He was thrown by what Egypt had requested. There was no fear left in her young eyes.

"When is your father coming back?"

"He's not ... not until next week."

"I guess we're going to have a long wait." He fiddled with a small electronic device he picked up from the coffee table.

"Left foot blue," the killer grinned.

Silk parked in his driveway and noticed that his front door was partially open. He thought nothing of it. "I left my keys anyway," he mumbled. He stuffed a buffalo wing in his mouth and went inside.

"Egypt, guess what daddy has for...you. What the fuck!"

The killer grinned at Egypt. "Wasn't a long wait after all!"

He turned the gun on Silk.

Silk dropped the buffalo-wings and pizza box. "Man, I'll take you to the money. I don't want any problems."

"You already have one and money won't fix it. I hope you don't think this is a novel or a movie and I'm gonna take forever killing you. I hate it when they do that."

"Where's my -- ?"

The first bullet tore through Silk's chest cavity. His eyes widened as the force slammed him into a wall. He looked at the hole gushing blood and tried to stop it.

"Daddy!" Egypt was on her feet.

"Right foot yellow."

"Sit down", he pointed the gun at her.

"God, no," Tia called out from the threshold of the kitchen. She watched Silk holding his hand to his chest with blood oozing through his fingers. His wedding band was covered with a red mess.

"Bitch, is my food done? Let me have to tell you again and Egypt gets it." He turned back to Silk and put a bullet though his head.

Silk's head banged against the wall. He slid down the wall and stopped in the sitting position. A blood smear colored his path.

Egypt turned away from her father's corpse and watched her mother shrink into the kitchen.

Tia came back into the room a few minutes later crying. The plate she carried shook in her trembling hands.

"Sit it over there," he said, "and you do the same. Don't take this personal. Tia, I tried to leave you and Egypt outta this. It's sad that ya'll don't have a life outside of Silk's convention. Should've gotten out more and you and your daughter could been spared. You might not believe this, but I waited for days trying to catch Silk alone. Both ya'll turn around, on your knees."

"Can't you let us go?" Egypt was done crying.

Tia couldn't stop the tears. "I promise we won't say anything about you. I'll say we came home and found him dead." She looked at Silk. "Just let me and my baby live."

"That's the way I planned this, it should have been that way. On your knees, my food is getting cold."

Egypt had assumed the executioners position and was staring at the floral design on the couch. After some hesitation and gaining the needed strength from her daughter, Tia made it to he knees.

The killer put the gun to the back of Tia's head and blew a large portion of her brains out.

Egypt squeezed her eyes shut.

Tia slumped forward on the couch. Her blood soiled the cushion.

Egypt opened her eyes and looked at her mother then glanced at her father. She turned to the killer. "What's your name?

He was thrown a curve ball again. "They call me Uzi. Why you wanna know my name?"

"When I come to hell looking for you, I want to know who to ask for." The tone of Egypt's voice and the slow rhythm she spoke in shook Uzi.

He pointed the gun at her.

She pushed her head against the barrel, closed her eyes, and told her parents she loved them.

Uzi pulled the trigger. When Egypt's head exploded, it left a crimson mess. Her body hunched beside her mother's. They both looked as if the were making salat.

"Left foot red."

Uzi took his plate into the kitchen and ate.

CHAPTER THIRTY

Thursday night, ladies night, women took advantage of free admission and drinks until midnight. Women showed up to Everyday People by the dozens. Electrifying music poured from the interior into the streets. C-Mack parked the Hummer on a side street.

Kesha was opening the car door when C-Mack grabbed her arm. "Hold up, home girl, what's the business with the silent treatment?"

"You noticed." She shrugged.

"Why wouldn't I?"

Another shrug. "You never notice nothing else."

"Let me get a hit of what you smoking on. What the hell is you talking about, girl?"

"All you see me as is your home girl, huh?"

"How else am I 'posessed to see you?"

"See." She clenched the door handle. "Just forget it."

C-Mack let her take a few steps before he rolled the window down. "I smoke too much weed to read your mind. I don't know what you tripping on, homey, but if you got something to say, then spill."

"Fuck it, Mack."

"You remember what -- "

"I know what the fuck the niggah look like." She turned to leave. She looked as if her feelings had been wounded.

"Kesha!"

"Be safe, right?" She didn't look back.

"Yeah, be safe." He didn't know what was bugging Kesha. It must be that time of month. He watched her bend the corner. Bitches.

All eyes were on Kesha. She wore a full-body jean suit that clung to every part of her bodacious body. The dark denim showed off her over developed breast and the basketballs in her back pocket in great detail. She was built like a 70's Coke Cola bottle. Her rich skin was the color of toast.

There were scattered whispers through the club. Guys wanted to know who Kesha was with. The females wanted to know where she came from and when she was going back.

Kesha noticed Amir on the first browse of the room. How hard is it to spot a dark brother with a beard as thick as Bin Ladens?

She wiped a micro-braid away from her face. "A shot of rum." Kesha's mind drifted to C-Mack. "Make that a double." She eased onto the bar stool. "And a Corona with a squirt of lemon."

Hershel was mesmerized by Kesha's full lips.

While Hershel fixed her drink, she spun the seat around to face the club. Kesha made eye contact with ·the curious. She enjoyed the attention. It was validation that she still had it. If she wasn't taking of things for Limbo, she would use the needed attention to have fun.

Kesha maintained eye contact with Amir. He smiled; she winked.

"Here you go Ms. Lady." Hershel sat the drinks on the bar.

"Thank you."

"New around these parts?"

"No, I don't get out much."

"I'm Hershel, and you are?" He stuck his hand out.

" I like the sound of Ms. Lady."

"Ms. Lady, seeing that you don't get out much, let me show you a good time. My relief will be here in an hour."

The club went ballistic when the DJ played Black Rob's Whoa. Bodies flocked to the dance floor.

Kesha threw back the rum and banged the glass on the counter. "That's my song." She sat a ten dollar bill down, picked up her Corona and went to the dance floor.

She bobbed and twirled and shook and gyrated her amazing body to the beat.

Patrons were chanting, "Like whoa, like whoa."

Kesha beckoned Amir to join her with the wag of a finger and wanton eyes.

Thinking with the wrong head, he couldn't resist the invitation. Amir wasn't big on dancing, but he had a few things he wanted to say to Kesha.

She sipped Corona and slipped a hand around Amir's neck. "I was wondering how long you were gonna let me dance by myself. What's your name, soldier?" Kesha was loose in the trunk. Her ass performed like a belly dancer when she got in groove with Black Rob.

"Amir, Ma. Why don't you come to my table and kick it with me after this song."

"You must have left your girl in the house. What's a good looking brother like you doing by yourself?"

"I'm not from around here, Ma. But I'm solo, a woman gotta bring a lot to the table for me to call her my girl, namean?"

"Self proclaimed player."

Amir watched Kesha's lips move when she spoke.

"I wouldn't call it that, " he said.

"Then straighten it."

"Choosey...what's your name, Ma?

"Lady"

Amir led Kesha to his table. "So where's your man, baby sitting?"

"Don't have kids, but he's away at football camp. He plays for the Steelers. Carlos Hendrick -- tight end." She saw the disappointment in Amir's wooly face. "That don't stop me from doing me, though."

"How about we get a bottle, then get somewhere?"

"Depends"

"On"

"Can you fit a Magnum? I'm not with having my time wasted."

"Like a scuba diving suit."

"I don't do rooms."

Amir took her hand and stroked it while he talked. "Where you wanna go, Ma? I'm not familiar with Johnstown, namean."

I'm not either, but we can go to my summer home. It's a cozy cottage about thirty minutes from here."

"Your crib, the same crib you share with Carlos?"

"Let me find out, a big boy like you is scared. He's playing in Dallas in the morning. He won't be home for another two weeks. You can stay the weekend if you can stand the heat."

He traced her hand. "I can't believe he left all this woman alone."

"Am I still alone?", she batted her fake lashes.

"Nah, Ma, not tonight. Let me get us something to go."

"Get Hennessey Timeless."

"You like that."

Kesha glossed her lips. "Straight out the bottle."

Kesha was destined to get the last nail in Amir's proverbial coffin.

Limbo, C-Mack, and Trigger watched the exchange between Kesha and Amir from the nest high above the club.

Amir passed some girl his phone number on he way to the bar.

"Why Kesha rolling her eyes at us like that?" Murdock chalked a pool stick. "Which one of ya'll pissed her off?"

"I don't know," C-Mack said. "She spased on me a while ago. Talking in riddles with her foul ass."

"You know she going through it. She snapped on me today too, Limbo turned to Murdock. "Nine ball, a hundred dollars a game, twenty dollars a shot."

"That's a bet all day long."

Trigger kept his eye on Kesha and Amir. "They're leaving."

They all watched Amir escort Kesha out of Everyday People with his hand around her small waist.

Limbo blasted the cue ball with a pool stick. "A pretty face, big ass and a smile, will fuck you around every time."

CHAPTER THIRTY-ONE

Keri

"What are you going to do then?" Jayme and I were spooning on the sofa watching a rerun of 106 and Park. I got a kick out of studying the heathens. Shows like this made it easy for me to mingle with them.

"I don't freaking know, built I have to leave tomorrow." She had that whine in her voice that confirmed she was worried.

"What time is Limbo coming home?"

"Don't know that either. He's bound to stroll in here at three, four in the morning. I'm glad he's been letting you stay with us a few nights. I spend so much time in this house alone."

I put my arms around her waist and pulled her closer to me. "You're going to West V with Tara right?"

A sigh. "Yeah."

"Then tell him that you're going to hang out with her all day tomorrow doing girl stuff, stay the night at her house."

She told me that would probably work, but she just hadn't been away from the asshole for that long of a time. "It will work." I told her. "You're here most of the time by yourself anyway. Don't have a bitch fit, he'll be happy that you got a breath of fresh air. If it'll make you feel any better, I'll cover for you. Just get your tail back here the day after tomorrow before he makes it home."

Jayme turned to face me and kissed my nose. "You've changed so much. It's like a new person, Keri."

"I want to be a part of your life, so I'm going with the flow because I love you."

"We can talk about anything, can't we?" She stroked my face.

Of course, I told her. We should be honest about everything.

"I want to tell you something."

I felt her belly, "Don't tell me that you're -- "

"God, no. We have been going at it like rabbits, though."

"Then what is it?"

"I'm in over my head, Keri. I'm really in love with Limbo."

"That's obvious. Have you told Tara that?"

"No." She detected my growing irritation. "I'm in love with you, too."

"Don't tell anyone else what you just told me. The Bureau will put you I therapy when this is allover, if you can't handle it. I'll definitely be there for you." I thought for a moment. "You have enough concrete information to put him away. Get out now before you become emotionally ruined."

"That's the thing, I don't want out. I don't want this to ever be over. We can all be happy together like we are now."

"Are you crazy, Jayme? You can't be Rhapsody forever. This had to end."

"No it doesn't. I'm not planning on being Rhapsody. I made up my mind to come clean with him. I have a plan to keep Limbo out of jail."

"What! Do you really think he's going to accept you once he finds out you're an agent? Geeze, Jayme use your head."

"I'm leaving the Bureau. I'm not sure what will happen when I tell him, but I know beyond a shadow of a doubt that Limbo loves me. That should count for something. Watch this." She picked up the phone.

I picked up my vitamin bottle and took my last pill. "Who are you calling?"

"Our man." Jayme pecked me on the lips.

CHAPTER THIRTY-TWO
Limbo

C-Mack eased the Hummer along a narrow dirt road. There was only three feet visibility without head lights on. Murdock's summer cottage was in the dense wooded area. C-Mack used the cottage's living room light as a guide post.

"Trigger," I said, "when we pop this niggahs top, take Kesha back to the hotel while we get rid of the body."

"It's on." He sucked on a Newport.

"It's only a matter of time now." Murdock rubbed his hands together.

"On the hood, homey," C-Mack said to no one in particular. "If I was minutes away from death, I wouldn't complain after getting a piece of pussy like Kesha's."

"On the low, you know she's feeling you." Murdock said.

"Stop fronting." C-Mack waved him off. "Where'd that come from?"

"A blind man could've told you that. As slick as you are, don't tell me you ain't peeped that shit a long time ago." My phone rang.

"Hello."

"Hi, Big Daddy."

"What you know good, Baby Girl?"

"That it's me and you until the world blow up. I was just sitting here with Keri thinking of you, and wondering if you was thinking of me, too."

"All the time."

The Hummer rolled to a stop.

"I love you," she said.

"I know."

"Keri wants to say hi."

"Hey, mister man." Her voice is crazy attractive. "We were talking about what we're going to do to you when you come home. We even drew straws to see who gets to do it first."

I was going to tear her ass muscle loose. I couldn't wait to get home. "Who won?."

The homies was in my mouth, they could hear the conversation on the other end in the hushed car.

"It won't be any fun if I told you. The sooner you come home, the sooner you'll find out what we have under our skirts."

"We already took our skirts off," Rhapsody yelled from the background.

C-Mack tapped and pointed. I glanced at the cottage as the living room lights went out. A few seconds later the bedroom light came on.'

"I'll be there later." I hung up.

240

"You let another white bitch know where the bat cave is, and we don't even know where you stay. You slipping, Cuz. You better leave hem white hoes alone." C-Mack climbed out the car first. The back door swung open and out came Trigger and Murdock.

Trigger pulled a sweat shirt over his Teflon vest. "It's bad enough you got one, but two is bound to be trouble."

"Stop hating," I said. "If the shoe was on the other foot, ya'll would be blowing their backs, too?

"Nah, I'm feeling the homies." Murdock pushed a clip in his Glock. "Grandma always told us that a trust worthy cracker is a dead cracker."

CHAPTER THIRTY-THREE

Amir unzipped the long zipper on Kesha's jean suit. Her C cups were thankful to be released from the denim prison. Her charcoal areolas were the size of silver dollars, the nipples stood up like cigarette butts in an ash tray.

Amir ran his tongue from her breast to her navel. He didn't mind the stretch marks that seemed to crawl across her stomach. He was more concerned with the prize that awaited him beneath the indigo thong.

Stretch Marks!

Amir sat up. "I thought you didn't have kids."

"I don't. I was pregnant before, but...I lost my baby. We're not doing it on my couch, let's go upstairs."

Kesha put on one of Murdock's Body & Soul CD's in the stereo.

"That's a little loud, Ma, namean?"

"I want to hear it in my bedroom. The music makes me hot."

"Turn it up some more then."

"Stop playing boy. Hit that light switch and come on."

Kesha tossed her big butt form side-to-side as she climbed the stairs.

Amir smiled and followed.

They tugged and pulled at each other's clothes until they were naked. The music was crystal clear. H-

H-Town sang about getting freaky with you.

Kesha pushed Amir to the bed. "Let me ride it."

Amir was eye level with her nappy patch. I know you not gonna leave me hanging, I'm trying to see what your head game is like."

It's boss. Be patient, baby. We got all night." She rolled a condom down his shaft and climbed atop him.

With an assortment of pistols, the four gang members climbed the stairs. They stood in the dark hallway watching Kesha bounce on Amir. She put on an Oscar winning performance.

Limbo nodded to his partners and they crept into the room.

"Now your black ass know what good pussy." She dug her nails into Amir's chest, bucking against his chiseled body. Out of everyone who entered the room, she felt C-Mack's presence. She made up her mind then and there, that she would never compromise her sex again.

Amir's eyes were clamped shut.

"Don't you over dose on me, this pussy has been know to stall hearts."

Amir was enjoying every minute of it. He held on the reigns of her wide hips.

"Look at me when I'm fucking you. Let me know it's good to you."

You heard the lady motherfucker. "Limbo aimed a .38 at Amir's face.

"What the -- "

"No screaming," Murdock said. "It won't do any good."

Amir pushed Kesha off him and recoiled in horror. On one side of the bed was Murdock and C-Mack. On the other side, Limbo and Trigger. He was trapped in the middle. If looks could kill, Kesha would have died twice.

"You filthy, slimy bitch!"

She ignored him, slipping into her clothes. "Ya'll could've let me get my shit off."

"Go downstairs and wait."

"Fuck you, Mack, I hope you enjoyed the show." Kesha turned the bottle of Hennessy up and left the room.

Trigger went through Amir's clothes, after stuffing a sack of lime-green marijuana in hi own picket, he threw Amir the pants.

"Man, this doesn't even have to be like this. It ain't that series." Amir's gangster was evaporating like it was saliva on hot asphalt. "Let's work this out."

"Put something on." Limbo delivered the words with a serene calm.

"Please, man, let me make it, namean? Give a niggah a pass. We can -- "

Trigger clubbed Amir atop his head with a closed hand. "Shut up, put the pants on."

"I swear, it don't have to be like this." Amir scooted into the jeans. "I can get shit. Money, drugs -- lots of drugs."

"Yu had your chance to cop a plea." C-Mack grinned. "But you had to a tough niggah and take this situation to trail. I dig it, though."

"If it'll do you nag good, your partner, Silk and his family."

Limbo glanced at his Iceman watch. "Checked out of Hotel Life, and hour ago." He sat on the bed's edge. "Personally, I don't feel that nobody else should be forced to give up their ghost."

"Just tell me what to do. Anything, man, I swear." Amir dropped his head. "Fuck what you heard, I don't wanna die."

"Maybe you shouldn't have left your gun in your car. Then you could have tried your hand, and we wouldn't have to listen to you beg." Limbo tossed Amir's cell phone at his rusty feet. "Get the motherfucker on the line that sent you down here to fuck with my paper."

Amir looked at Limbo then the other products of public housing. He sighed with grief and dialed the number.

"As salaam alakunm" Amir said in the phone.

"Wa laykum as asalaam," Sadiq said. "Everything is in motion. Silk and the men are laving here in the morning."

"No, Awk, Silk is a stinking memory. Call it off or they're gonna kill me, too."

Limbo held his hand out. "Let me talk."

Feeling a fraction of relief, Amir passed the phone.

"Thank you, you've been cooperative." Limbo shot Amir in the face, then put a pillow over his face and drove two more .38 slugs home.

"The last two bullet was for inconveniencing me," Limbo spoke with clarity into the phone. "How many more of yours has to have a permanent change of address before you get the point? I touched Silk in his home. If you take this any further, I'll hit you where you rest."

Sadiq laughed. "I don't take threats lightly. Amir was a good man. I admire your chess game, Lamont Adams."

"I would hope so, Samuel Fleming."

Another laugh. "You've proven yourself to be a worthy competitor. Bodies in garbage bags isn't good for business."

"We agree on something."

"If you ever come to Philadelphia, I'll personally see to it that you'll leave with a neck tie."

"The feeling is mutual. Us northern boys are traditional. I like to call it old fashion. It's a dome call waiting for you this end and, Your boy Amir seems to be enjoying his."

"See you around, Limbo."

"For your sake, I hope not."

CHAPTER THIRTY-FOUR
Keri

Birds were chirping when I left Jayme curled up in bed. Limbo hadn't made it home by the time I decided to leave. That was to my liking, I was able to spend quality time with Jayme alone. How much longer does she expect me to watch such filth pound away at her love muscle while I pretend to enjoy it, participate in it? I backed out the driveway with a bit to eat in mind and some other things.

I cannot believe that Jayme had the gall to tell me that she's in love with a parasite. She left me no choice but to correct her frame of mind, set right her wrongs. Jayme has never asked my permission to love anyone other than me. Something must be done -- soon.

Gas marts were the only thing open for business this time of morning. I found a bagel with cream cheese in the cooler section. I picked up the Tribune Democrat to pass some time with the daily paper. I dislike going to our house without Jayme to fill the empty spaces. Disliked it with a vengeance. The thought of being without Jayme made my skin craw. Trust me it's all my fault, only if I hadn't left her for so long. Oh, I know what to do. Yes, that's exactly what I have to do. I should have thought of it sooner. Kill Limbo. Yes, kill him to say my Jayme.

I had just finished pumping my gas and was leaving the gas mart when a black Volvo blew by me going in the opposite direction, Jayme's Volvo. If I had gone with my first thought, I'd be at home playing dress up in Jayme's cloths. I'd never had this opportunity to follow her.

Jayme turned off Eisenhower Boulevard into an Easy Mini Storage. She rented a unit there and stored miscellaneous items and old furniture. I was just here a week ago getting some things of mine that she had packed while…I was away at that dreadful place. I should have never left my Jayme alone to fend for her self. I picked up my journal and penned myself a reminder to never leave her again. I watched her from a shopping plaza's parking lot while I nibbled on my bagel.

Jayme lugged a box from her back seat and unlocked the unit. She looked around as if her sixth sense warned her that she was being watched. What could she be storing coming from Limbo's at this time of morning? I touched the chain hanging from the ignition. On the ring was a key to unit 9672. My nosey nature made me want to know what is in that box. There's no telling what Jayme is up to. I have to protect her, even from herself. I rambled through my purse for my vitamin bottle, but found it empty.

CHAPTER THIRTY-FIVE
Rhapsody

Tara was sleeping peacefully in the passenger's seat with a strange smile on her face. I can still taste the residue of her toffee skin like it was yesterday. Her breast rose and fell beneath a tiny urban tee. I honestly miss the reaction her stubby nipples gave me when I fondled her soft cups. I used to pretend that her succulent cunt was a chocolate tootsie pop. We met, seven years ago, at the academy. Tara gets credit for turning me out, so to speak.

She's my first woman-on-woman experience. The encounter transpired from a dare. Never looked back. Ultimately, Tara and I decided that making-out would destroy our beautiful friendship. I wish...I wouldn't mind having another lick at the center of her tootsie pop.

"Tara, girl, wake up. We're here."

She stirred for a moment, yawned then lifted her onyx lashes. "Whootie...West Virginia. Damn, Jayme" A pause. "Could've let me rest a few minutes more. You love to cock block."

"What are you talking about?"

Alicia Keys' Falling seeped from the radio. It made me think of Big Daddy. The video concept, visiting her guy in jail, fit Limbo and I. I'm glad Keri has my back, because I'm positive he'd flip out in a few hours when comes home to find that I still haven't returned from the hair dresser and shopping.

"Why ask a question then ignore me? She sucked her teeth.

"Thinking," I said. "What was it you said?"

"My dream, Jayme. This fine brother had me bent, nev4er mind. You cheated me, it ain't cool to wake people up." She crossed her arms in a pouting manner.

I laughed too hard.

It was after midnight when we checked into our suite and crossed the boundaries of sleep.

I awoke to a piercing pounding on the door. Whoever it is doesn't the implication of a Do Not Disturb Sign. Tara rolled out of bed the same time I did. She took her 380 from beneath a pillow and forced it in the back of her coochie cutter shorts.

On the other side of the peep hole stood our confidential informant, Chad Hobbs, and the objective, Phoebe. I glanced at my watch 5:11 am. What in the hell are they doing here this early? I checked to see how tart my breath was before I opened the door. Oh, well.

Chad had a spooked look on his hard face. I could tell that he'd been smoking crack all-night by his twisted mouth. His once white eyeballs now an eternal beige with threads of strained red. He towered over the gorgeous woman standing beside him.

"It's the caterers, somebody order baked chicken?" Her asymmetrical earrings dangled from cushiony lobes. Hun dun hair draped over a shoulder covering one breast. Her white skin roasted to a well prepared almond hue from the sun's inferno or a tanning salon. The hallway's track lighting reflected off her glossy lips -- full lips. Our surveillance photos stole from her beauty.

Another teeth sucker. "Well? Invite us in."

"Excuse me, it takes a minute for my brain to register when I'm rudely awakened from my sleep."

Phoebe chuckled as they brushed past me.

"There's my favorite cousin." Chad rushed over to Tara and gave her a hug that nearly knocked them both over. He stepped back shaking his head while looking at her coochie shorts. "You looking good, cousin." He pulled her in again.

She and I knew that he just wanted to touch her. Tara told me of his advances, how he literally groped her with his eyes, making her uncomfortable when she drove down last week to meet him and to familiarize herself with the particulars of this case. I bumped the door closed with my butt and locked it. Sprinkle stood to James Lee's left.

Tara peeled out of his embrace. "What are you doing her so early?"

He jerked his head toward Sprinkle. "I told you how my girl Sprinkle is, she makes her own rules, goes by her own schedule."

From where I stood, I could see that Sprinkle wasn't built bad at all. The arch and curve of her lower back filled the J Blaze jeans nice. "I have a hard time following rules myself." I loaded my weapon. The sound of a 9mm cylinder sliding back is an attention grabber. Its infrared beam broke the dim lit suite in two.

They turned to face me.

"If I was either f you, I'd be doing my damnest to pull the paint off the ceiling."

They raised their hands. James Lee's blood in his inky skin went on vacation, leaving him a dull bright. His mouth was agape in disbelief.

The "try me" look engraved in my face convinced him to believe it.

Sprinkle's smoky-gray eyes smoldered with anger. Tara even looked at me in surprise. If Sprinkle wanted to make things up as she went along, then I would freestyle, too.

"Rhapsody, what are you doing?" Tara stood between the couple. This is my family, he's good people. It's all god."

"That's right, Tara, you're his cousin, but his only family goes by the name cocaine, This is called self preservation, if I were you, I'd strongly consider it. Don't trust any who doesn't stick to a plan when there's big money involved."

Tara surrendered with a puff of air.

I went on now hat she was with me. "Now get with the program, Tara, and pat them down. Be careful with this one." I lad the beam on Sprinkle. "She might have something up her sleeve."

"Ya'll, bitches on some other shit," Sprinkle enunciated each syllable. "James, what the hell is up with your peeps? She glared at him. "You wasting your time if you trying to pull a jack move, we didn't come prepared."

"Just chill." Tara took a .45 from beneath James's leather. She found a short 357 resting quietly in a holster beneath Sprinkle's summer jacket.

"Now let play find the wire. Strip" I aimed the menacing red light James's zipper. "Be quick about it."

"Fuck that shit!" Sprinkle delivered her words clear with grave deliberation. "I'm not taking off a damn thing."

James Lee already unbuttoned his jeans.

Sprinkle slapped his arm. "You follow every command except mines. Grow some motherfucking nuts."

"You're going to get naked one way or the other. Either you'll do it by your own hands, or the coroner will do it by his."

"Listen to her," Tara said, "she's serious. We all stand the chance to get a little richer one our trust issues are resolved."

"Whether I'm asshole naked or wearing three minks, you still have to prove to me your business is worth my time." She sucked her almost perfect teeth. "What makes you think you'd kill me and leave this room alive?"

"I'll try my luck."

Chad's boxers fell o n the heap of his clothes.

Phoebe's face flushed with indignation. She glared at him with rage. "Soft ass."

• "It's not often I'm butt-ass in a hotel room with three sexy women, then like little cousin says, walk away with major paper."

My patience wore thin. "Three...two..."

A gorgeous redhead strutted down an aisle of Rite Aid, hurrying to the pharmacist's counter. "I'm picking up a prescription Kimberly Mayweather."

The old white man yawned and closed the register. "Just a minute."

He went to the "M" section of his prescriptions ready for pick up. "Kimberly, Kimberly." He read through an assortment of names, over the rim of his glasses, as he shuffled through the bagged narcotics. "Nothing for a Kimberly Mayweather."

"What do you mean there's nothing? She banged her fist on the counter top. "Check it again, dammit! I need that prescription, I know it's here."

The tired pharmacist shot a furtive glance in the direction of the security guard who wasn't paying attention a usual. "When did you put your prescription in?"

"The computer places my order every two weeks like clockwork." She motioned him toward the bagged narcotics with the flick of a hand. "Check it…Kimberly Mayweather and take the molasses out your ass."

From the look etched in this woman's face, her tone, and the aggressiveness that she's struggling to contain. The pharmacist was overjoyed to be on the opposite side of the counter. "Our computer system has been down over a week ma'am. I'll take another look but I doubt it's here. Kimberly with a 'K'?"

She clenched the vitamin bottle in her sweaty palm. She tightened her lips forming a small circle, her teeth grind together, her penciled-on eyebrows bunched together. "How the hell else do spell Kimberly?"

"Calm down ma'am, I don't have a problem looking once more." He rambled through the bags.

Nothing.

"Goddammit! I don't believe this shit." She stormed toward the exit knocking merchandise from the shelves.

Phoebe and Chad stood naked. I left their clothes on the bathroom floor with the shower and sinks running. "Just in case the Feds booby trapped your clothes with listening devices. Now they can't eavesdrop." It's what I've always done to stay informed of criminal activity.

Chad rocked back on the balls of his crusty heels to check out Phoebe's butt. "Damn, girl, I didn't know you were strapped like that. No wonder Trent's crazy about you."

A spasm of irritation crossed her face. "Don't ever disrespect me again," she growled the words out between clenched teeth.

Tara had empathy for Phoebe and gave them both bed sheets to cover themselves. I didn't care about Phoebe's attitude, she needed to know that I wasn't a push over. Now that my presences had been established, I just wanted to set the stage for the buy so I could go home to Limbo. Still pushing my hand a little further, I balanced an empty Sprite can on the doorknob. If someone as much as sneezed on the door from the hall, the can would clatter against the marble floor. On the twentieth floor I wasn't worried about no one coming through a window. "Now that we're on equal playing ground, I feel much better. Tara, if that can falls, it's a jack move. Shoot your cousin in the head first. I'll handle this one."

Phoebe's eyes raked the room. Her lips pursed with suppressed fury. She didn't enjoy the element of surprise being reversed at all. She brought it on herself. I respect game and her effort of trying to unravel me, though.

Phoebe adjusted the sheet around her immature breast. "You put on a good show, Rhapsody. You just better not be the law."

"Lawless." Tara plopped on the bed with Chad's 45. trained on him. "For auntie's sake, Chad, I hope this isn't a deadly game you're playing."

Chad kept his eyes plastered to the Sprite can, like he was willing it to stay in place. "Stop with the shenanigans, Tara. You know I don't roll like that. I smoke a little dope, but I ain't scandalous. Talk, hold hands, give each other beauty tips, or whatever it is ya'll have to do to get this in motion, because if I ain't about to get some pussy, I'm gonna be needing my clothes back -- pronto, no telling what I might do when this thing grows up."

"Shut up!" Phoebe and I said at the same time in a ragged burst.

"All of this is uncalled for." Phoebe bit her bottom lip, exposing a dime-thin gap in her teeth. "If there wasn't some level of trust, none of us would have agreed to meet in the first place." Now she sucked her teeth with nerve. "I was in the neighborhood and decided to drop by."

"For what?"

Our meeting isn't supposed to take place for another sis hours." My gun was getting heavy. I switched it to my other hand.

Chad watched the Sprite can.

"Change of plans," she said.

"Is there something wrong with the phone? Tara never turned away from Chad.

"I don't know, is it?" Phoebe sucked her teeth again.

"Stop fucking around and let's take care of business so I can be on my way." I tucked a tress of hair behind my ear. "What kind of change?"

"It's like this." Phoebe focused on me. "If you're in a rush then leave. I ain't pressed, I'm doing you a favor. We'll talk tonight at nine. Dinner. You had you fun, get my clothes so I can go."

Tara emptied Chad's gun and gave it back. "Chad, you didn't say we were going to turn this into an outing. We can't stick around here we have other business to take care of."

"Ya'll act like that's my problem." Phoebe went into the bathroom and returned with their clothes. "Tonight at nine or no deal. That's the way it is."

Tara let out a deep breath like she had been defeated. "Where are we meeting for dinner?"

Phoebe fought with the jeans to pull them on. "We'll be in touch."

I locked the door behind them then flopped down beside Tara. "Tara, I have to be back at home way before nine. Try last night. Look at this." I showed her my cell phone, it had five messages from Limbo on it. "Limbo isn't going to accept this from me. How am I supposed to explain pulling a disappearing act, and on top of that not answering my phone? Damn! Damn! Damn! I stomped the floor with each expletive.

"Phoebe thinks we need her to score. After that stunt you just pulled, she really ain't trying to feel what we have to do. You just played her, now she's gonna drag us through the shit."

I laid back on the comforter exhaling. "You don't understand, Tara. This is out of the ordinary for -- "

"Child, I know the case back home is important, but so is this one. You can handle Limbo."

"You're missing the point." Little did she know, I couldn't even handle me let alone somebody else. I wasn't trying to destroy Limbo, I was planning a way to come clean. Pretending I'm David Copperfield didn't help matters. Why am I stressing? Keri has me covered.

"Don't blow a gasket." Tara laid back, too. We both stared at the stucco ceiling. "Everything will work itself out, Jayme. How about we find a yellow pages and find us somewhere to get our wigs busted. We've got ourselves a dinner date."

The night was tender and the air was comfortably warm. Phoebe called our room ten minutes ago and told us to come down to the lobby. No sooner than we stepped out of the elevator a Navigator Limousine glided to a stop outside the lobby doors. Chad stepped out the back, inviting us to join them with a wave of his hand. He was dressed to a tee. I almost didn't believe he was the same man from this morning.

I eased down he long seat and scooted in beside Phoebe. Tara followed me and Chad followed her. The prettiest women will have a hard time standing next to Phoebe -- she had it. She made a tremendous change from the urban wear she sported earlier. A soot asymmetrical neck, one shoulder martini dress clung to her shape like aloe lotion. Girlfriend was styling with her black and plum Costa Blanca pumps.

And she smelled gentle. "Bois D' Argent, three-point-four-ounce bottle."

"You have a nose for Christian."

"I'm fond of expensive fragrances." I said. "Where are we going for dinner?"

"Enjoy the ride." Phoebe inspected her nails. "How much is a meal and conversation worth?

Tara smiled.

"Half a million." I crossed my legs, getting more comfortable. "And if its nice as what I hear, I'll double that number next trip."

"Half way to the top will get you thirty kilos." Chad fond his tongue.

I did the math in my head and wasn't cool with the price for the money I'm spending. "Make it fifteen-five a package, we can do business. A lot of business.

I took note that we were driving in a semi-circle around about an eight block radius and were enroute towards the hotel. No she didn't. I know this chick didn't have me go out of my way getting all cut to joy ride. My sneaker and jeans would have been straight.

Phoebe gave Chad a nod than fanned her pretty aroma.

"At nine in the morning be at this address." Chad passed Tara a tan match book. "Park next to the black Yukon. Did you get the right briefcase?"

"Got it," Tara said. "The ten buck leather one from the dollar store."

I couldn't believe this, now they want us to stay another day. There's no way I'll be able...maybe I'll...I don't know what I'm going to tell Limbo. "All hundreds like you asked. I can't stay another night, we need to do this tonight."

We pulled under the hotel's awning.

Phoebe shifted her body toward me, I could feel the material of her dress against my leg. "In the morning, Rhapsody. Is it a deal or was this conversation a waste of my time?"

"I told -- "

Tara pinched me. "We'll be there."

I was furious and Tara was going to hear about it.

Tara sucked her teeth and avoided my gaze. "Chad, I know you're not going to leave your little cousin cooped in this hotel all night. Take us out, I didn't spend money on this dress for nothing. What are ya'll dressed up for, a limo ride?"

"No." I frowned at Tara. "We're okay, besides, Tara I have to call my husband."

Phoebe leaned forward, looking past me at Tara. "A friend of mine is having an album release party, I don't mind if you hang."

"Cool. Let me walk my girl in so I can use the ladies room. Be right back."

Tara's heels clicked up the walkway. As soon as we were inside the lobby, she grabbed my elbow and spent me to her. "What's up with all this Limbo my husband shit?" Hands on hips.

I was cornered, at least that's how I felt or tricked myself into believing. Our friendship had been tried and tested before, we've endured. We've done enough dirt together within the bureau that would get us both decades of prison time. She's trustworthy, it was a requirement of me membership to the clean up crew. I wanted to tell someone anyway, it's been eating at me.

"Well?" Hands still on hips.

I told her. Told her that I'm in love with Limbo. It wasn't supposed to happen like this, but my heart has a mind of its own. She just stared. I told her that I tried to tell my heart what to think, but it refused to listen.

Tara looked at me as if my feelings angered her. She came closer to keep our conversation private. "Save that soap opera drama, Jayme. Girlfriend, we're not angels by no means. We literally get away with murder. But you can't be falling in love with targets. You'll be forced to make a choice. Crooked cop or crook. You know too much dir." She released my elbow. "If you're not with us, then you're with him. The clean up crew won't let you walk away to join the other team with their secrets. They'll clean up their mess first." A pause. "We never had this conversation." She started to leave then stopped. "You sure you don't want to go out and have some fun?"

In the comforts of the quiet suite, I finally listened to my voice mail. Limbo's messages started out saying, "I love you, too. Stop at the video store and pick up that new DVD, Training Day." Then it went t. "I love you, too but you're starting to worry me. I hope don't nobody call me talking about ransom, the pussy good, but your ass is it. Get at me, Baby Girl." They ended by saying, "where the fuck at? After all this time, now you wanna bitch up on me. When did we get on game time? You got one hour to get your pink ass home or play off's begin."

After a much needed sigh, I dialed Limbo's cell phone.

CHAPTER THIRTY-SIX

Keri

"What you got in the box, Mayweather?" That awful cigar rested in Thurston's tar stained lips. He stood up to shut the blinds. SAC was too tall. He made me dizzy looking up at him from the seat I settled myself in.

"You have to help me save Jayme." I wiped my sweaty palms on my jeans. I needed my vitamins. "The Lamont Adams' case is too much for her. She's gotten herself emotionally involved and is planning on going renegade. She's in love, and is contemplating confessing to Adams that she's with the Bureau -- blow the whole case."

"What!" He banged his big fist against his precious desk. That God awful cigar fell to the floor. I mean just in that short time, sweat formed on his nose, even his brow wrinkled. "Bust a blood vessel after you see what's in the box. I went over this information for hors, it's enough incriminating evidence in here -- " I patted the cardboard lid. "To give Adams a life sentence -- then some. Only thing, though, there's nothing here about any money."

"Where did this stuff come from?" Thurston stood here like he was a raging bull ready to charge. The only thing left for him to do was snort and paw at the floor with his dress shoe.

"Followed Jayme yesterday morning, she's been hiding it in a storage unit in Richland. She's been lying to you."

"Time for clean up to arrange for her to have a little car accident."

"That won't be necessary, I have a plan. Jayme's been a part of this team from the beginning. She needs our help, not a mishap."

"Millions are riding on this. Johansson can be dangerous to all of us. If I don't have clean up, pay her a visit, what would you suggest I do?"

"Listen to her first." I took a mini cassette player from the box and rewound the tape. The first speaker is Limbo, Lamont, whatever you want to call him. The other voices I don't know who they belong to yet."

"Let me have it," he said."

I pressed play.

"...the way I figured it is we run a six month operation. Slam three hundred keys and be done with it. Everyone here will walk away from Johnstown rich men."

"What does that work out to be over the six months?"

"Fifty-two keys a month. Thirteen a week." The accent was Southern.

Limbo again. "As it stands, there's no real competition so we can walk right in and set up shop. Bricks go for forty, but we're gonna move them fast at twenty-eight on the weight

264

side. I get them from my connect, for fourteen thousand and four cent."

I fast forward the tape.

"...two point." The speaker paused. "That's a four way split, it's five of us in here."

"And what you mean by smashing niggahs the old fashion way?"

"I'm glad you volunteered -- "

" 'Cause niggah, you just got elected."

"Bang!

Thurston jumped at the sound of the gun blast.

"Ain't nothing like the back of the head. The old fashion way."

I shut the tape recorder off.

"We need to find that body." Thurston swiveled the chair. "We have Adams in a clear cut drug conspiracy and a murder that we can place him at the scent. I'd like to see him wiggle his way of this one. I'm having him arrested." He picked up the phone.

I put my finger on the button breaking the connection. "Let's think his out a minute. There's all kinds of material in this box. Pictures of automatic weapons, body armor, money, and numerous recorded conversations. Why must him when we can get these other guys that are in collusion with him and possibly the money, too. I want to help Jayme out of this. Limbo trusts me. I've been staying at his house with Jayme off and on for the last week."

"That doesn't mean he trusts you."

"When you're giving him and Jayme the unh unh un, it does."

"I don't need those details." He pulled a dildo from the box.

"It's where she hid the flash drives, look inside it."

"Never mind. Where do you want to go with this?"

"I'll take up for Jayme's slack and find the money." I touched the box. "Nothing in here suggests its whereabouts. Fifty-fifty split on any sum I find."

"Sixty-forty, the crew has to get paid." He offered me his huge hand.

"Deal," I said, as we shook on it. "First thing we have to do is get Jayme back on our team. I'm close to them, I'll get closer and find out who these other guys are."

"If Johanson's in love like you say, her allegiance is with her emotions. Nothing is stronger than love -- not even the threat of death. She wasn't planning on turning in none of this, so how are you planning to get Johansson to see things straight?"

"I'm going to turn Romeo against Juliet. He's been out of jail for two months, now we have four months to bring his operation its feet and get rich in the process. How about letting me make a phone call? I need a private line that Mr. Limbo can call me back on."

CHAPTER THIRTY-SEVEN

Limbo

My pager buzzed as I was headed out the door to cop my son's the mini-bikes that they had been at me about. The number was unfamiliar. Baby Girl didn't come home last night, all I could think of was Sadiq had her somewhere gagged and duct taped or worse. I jumped in my car and drove to a nearby gas station to use the phone there, didn't want my number registering in some bandit's caller ID.

I fed the hungry phone a case quarter and dialed the foreign number. "Who's this?"

"Hello, no-show," her voice was soft, its allure sexy. "I waited all night for you the other night. Is Rhapsody with you?"

"Nah, Keri, I haven't seen her since I left her with you. From my understanding, she was supposed to be kicking it with Tara yesterday. When's the last time you saw her? She has me worried."

"She was at you guy's house sleep yesterday morning when I finally decided to leave. Her, Tara, and I were supposed to do the hairdresser pampering thing yesterday, but we can't seem to catch up with her. I keep getting you guy's answering machine and her voice mail. That's why I decided on paging you."

A black Regal bumping A Piece of My Love pulled into the gas station's lot. The song reminded me of the first time Rhapsody voiced that she was loving me.

"Limbo, you there?"

"Yeah, Keri, hit me again if you hear from her. Let me know something."

"Can I tell you something, between me and you?"

"That's your call."

She was quiet for a few heart beats, just enough to raise the suspense.

"It's about your girl."

"Spiel it."

She clammed up on me again. Put me in the frame of mind of the movie Jaws we watched a few nights back.

Dun Da Dun Da. Dun Da Dun Da

"I'm only telling you this because it's evident that you're a good man. I wish you were mine   Excuse me, hold on a minute."

Dun Da Dun Da. Dun Da Dun Da

"Sorry about that," she said. "I'm just going to say it."

"Thanks for cutting the bullshit."

"You need a woman capable of complimenting you, which Rhapsody can't. She's cheating on you. I don't get it, she doesn't even have the decency to cheat with someone of your caliber or better. This moron she's seeing is named

David, he's jobless and lives in his mother's basement. I told her it's disrespectful to give him your money, but she told me to mind my business. I know she's with David if she's not with any of us. It's no secret Jayme's desire for sex is knocking at nymphomania's door."

"Who is Jayme?"

"I was thinking about my sister, her and Rhapsody are a lot alike."

I was listening, but something else caught my attention. I peeped that the Regal's plates were from Philadelphia as it blended into traffic. "Where does David live?" I have a trick for him and Rhapsody.

"Don't know." She keeps that a secret. The first time I met him was at your house. She got tired of spending long hours by herself.

"MY house!", I shouted in my head over and over. I was sick. "Keri, I gotta bounce."

"You're not going to mention this conversation are you? I don't want what the three of us share to change." She had beg in her tone. If she didn't want things to change, she would have kept her fucking mouth shut.

"I religiously believe in dying with my secrets. Religiously I despise anybody who hasn't died before they told their secrets. She'll never know about our little secret. Don't trip, you can still get some dick." I know that I made Keri feel like shit. Now there's another person who feels like I do.

The next time I see Rhapsody she'd better duck. I ain't prejudice towards who gets it. I fed the hungry phone again. Rhapsody's voice mail took the call. Love, by Musiq Soulchild played in my ear, then Rhapsody's recorded voice said, "Limbo, if this is you, I love you with all my heart. Everybody else leave a message."

Beep!

"Where the fuck you at?" After all this time you wanna

bitch up on me. When did we get on game time? You got one hour to get your pink ass home or the play off's begin."

When things are on my mind, there's one place I knew I could always to got talk, to get a verbal dose of Motrin -- Prospect Projects, to see Ms. Renea.

At first, Prospect community turned its nose up to me, especially the senior citizens. They use to point me out and whisper to their other Ben Gay buddies that I was a drug dealing menace. Within weeks of my initial arrival -- 1996 -- I painted another picture to manipulate their judgment. My homebody Twenty-One always told me, "Limbo, in order for you to be successful in the narcotics business, you have to have the community behind you."

"How am I supposed to pull that off?" Nobody wants a street pharmacist posted up in their hood." I would say.

"That's something you have to figure out on your own. I fuck with you because you're not afraid to think."

And I thought about it.

I arranged for van services to carry the elderly to bingo on Saturday and Sunday nights. The hood received Butterballs for Thanksgiving. Just as they now that I'm back. All single women and the elderly walk ways were shoveled and salted each snow fall. Me and Murdock arranged for Cocoa's Soul food to cater the monthly community meetings. Bear's little league baseball team had new outfits and equipment every season. I created a collection where all the hustlers who worked for me in whatever capacity, contributed a hundred dollars a month. The money was used to make up the difference on the elderly prescriptions that they struggled to pay each month. If there was anything left over, the community's chair would use the money in some other beneficial way. During the Christmas season every family in the projects received a fifty dollar gift certificate to the grocery store. Since, I've been back, the same programs and principles have been set in place -- enforced with an iron fist. No, when I slide through the hood, like today, I'm a superstar. Instead of the finger pointing and wishes of my downfall, it...

"How you doing today, Mr. Limbo? It's always a pleasure to see you."

I stepped out of the ride. "I'm good, Mrs. Jenkins, what about you?"

Mrs. Jenkins is an eight-something, 'it-ain't-too-much-I-ain't seen' woman. She used to look for reasons to call he cops on me. Now...she loves me and will put her right hand on the bible and commit perjury for me.

"I'm getting along just dandy for an old tired woman. It's hotter than the devil's breath." She wiped her wrinkled brow. "Ain't it?"

"Yes ma'am, but enjoy it. A nasty scrotum shrinking winter'll be here soon."

"Yeah, I know it -- hate a chill that shrinks my ball. You know I want to thank you for what you've done for that foolish boy of mines. Hershel put his life savings into that club of his. If it wasn't for you partnering up with him, the bank would have foreclosed. Hersh' be round here drunk somewhere."

I could see Mrs. Jenkins ten times a day, and each time she would than, me. "Don't mention it."

"Where you off to?" She eased onto her porch rocker, fanning herself with the Tribune Democrat.

I told her that I was about to holler at Ms. Renea after I stopped by Ms. Evans house to see if she needed anything.

"Ain't no use." She sat the morning new down. "Lilly May Evans got that Teddy Pendergrass pouring out them windows like she done lost the little mid she has left. Means one of two things she's so drunk she can't piss straight, or she's got this young man over there..."

Trigger ought be ashamed messing with a sixty-year-old woman.

"...they got one of those on again, off again things going for themselves. Every time he sneaks through her door some late nights. Think I don't be watching? Anyhow, every time they spend time together, she complains to me that she's afraid that young man is going to ruin her spinal cord."

We talked...no Mrs. Jenkins talked, a few minutes more, then I went to see my home girl, Ms. Renea.

I called Ms. Renea home girl or Mama depending what engine she was running on.

"Damn, homey, it smells like Flipper's ass in here."

She tied her housecoat and snuggled down in a worn Lazy Boy. "Don't you worry yourself about that. You smelling fresh fish. They had a special at the market today. I remember you said that when you wanna stick your hands in my pot."

Ms. Renea is a beautiful cocoa woman. To be an older woman, she gave younger females a run for their money when she strayed away from her everyday attire of slippers, housecoat, head scarf and a cup of cappuccino. She had a middle-twenties daughter that had her beauty had been passed down to, that wouldn't give me the time of day. Ms. Renea transformed from the life of the party to neighborhood mom. Her house, most days, is busier than the Grand Central Station. I enjoyed my time with her, she'd been the closet thing to a mom I'd known in over a decade.

"Go in the kitchen and pour me some more." She passed me her coffee cup.

While I was in the kitchen a little light skinned kid opened the buckled screen door and asked to borrow some sugar. I already knew where to find it.

Home girl called out from the comforts of her Lazy Boy to the kid. "Jujuan, tell your mother I wanna buy some food stamps tomorrow when she gets them."

"Okay," he said going out the door.

I grabbed the TV remote and sat down.

"Boy, now you know I don't like getting in business that ain't my own, but that European -- "

She was definitely running the Mama engine.

" -- I get a bad feeling all down in here." She pinched her lower abdomen with both hands. "Hell, I know how pretty they are to look at, subliminal messages screwed us all up. And I hear all 'bout their animal ways behind closed doors." Mama looked at me for the first time since I sat down. "Them European females been bringing great black men down, from the time they left the Caucasus Mountain and we taught them how to live civil. Lamont Adams, don't make me tell you I told you so. Keep messing with that girl and you're the next great man going down."

"Mama, I swear I done heard this same conversation in so may forms. Everybody is just judging Rhapsody because of their personal run-ins with crackers. I had her checked out a long time ago. She's good people for real, if you can look pass her skin." The way I felt right now, I don't know why I still wanted to defend her. "She's the only person who kicked the visiting room doors in for me. She made it easier for me to deal with the reality of my divorce. She held me down."

"Boy pay attention, everything that shine ain't worth nothing. One day you're gonna wish you had listened to somebody. Let me tell you something my Mama told me, 'if everyone keep telling you that you're an elephant, check your breath for peanuts. '" Mama threw her hands up and looked a the smoke-stained ceiling. "Lord, help take the spell off this boy's mind so he can think for himself. 'Cause this European he's laid up with is thinking for him.

Why is everybody hating on Rhapsody? It only made me want her even more. Then again, maybe I should take into consideration what everyone has said. They all can't be wrong, can they?

"And any chance you had with my daughter ain't a chance no more. That's one thing Andrea don't play is brothers messing with white girls."

"I never tried to holler at Andrea. Besides, she ain't never looked my way."

"You young men today think yins so game conscious…You got a lot to learn. She ain't never looked in your direction because she wanted you to notice her. Gimme a few dollars to buy some food stamps with. Have you seen Nina and Mocha? Their families are getting antsy, they haven't seen them children in a week."

"No, Mama, you know how those two are. They're liable to be anywhere."

Me and Mama talked for hours before I stepped outside. Kids scattered in every direction asking for dollars as the melody Billy Boy's ice cream truck drew nearer. It was flaming I decided I wanted something cold, too. I was standing in a thick know of kids when the ice cream truck stopped in front of us. Something urged me to turn around. There were two white boys, a white girl, and three black kids watching all the other children gathered around me laughing and waving their money. I know they didn't have any money because they had the "left out" look. A look, that was my best friend as a child. I called them over then addressed the whole group of kids. "Everybody put away ya'lls money. Save it for a rainy day or something. I'm treating."

"Word," a kid asked with ashy elbows said.

"You the man.", came from a girl with pig tails. I could tell she was going to be fast.

"Niggah, you faking", another kid said.

"Child, no he ain't." Pig trails rolled her eyes and sucked her teeth. "You was just all on his swipe talking 'bout how nice his ride is. Now you got the nerve to think he can't handle some small shit like ice cream. Damn, you be straight up lame sometimes."

274

I knew she was fast. There were a set of twins in the crowd. They made me think of my own triplets. Ya'll two first. Come up here."

They made their way to the front.

"What's ya'll names?"

One of them answered for the both. "I'm Rashad, this is Rasheed. If we're gonna be first our brother has to be first with us."

"Where's the little dude at?"

Rasheed turned and pointed to a kid with long braids. "Come on, Lil' Eric."

Little Eric walked up to me and gave me a pound. "What's up, big money." He was the oldest. "Me and my brother's want whatever cost the most since you got it like that. Let me hold something, too. Rasheed need a new bike tire."

Rasheed agreed.

I like these little dudes. "You got that if it's all right with your mother."

I drove away from Prospect Projects with my pockets two-hundred dollars lighter. By the time I was done, I was buying grown folks banana splits. I didn't mind, it took my thoughts away from Rhapsody.

Night caused the temperature ease up some. Me, Murdock, and C-Mack was in our safe house on the outskirts of town. Trigger was still laid up with Lily Mae Evans. Six money counting machines sang in a harmony that I loved to hear. Stacks of rubber banned bills were everywhere.

"Here go another fifty grand." C-Mack tossed me the bundle of money. I dropped it in a box with the others.

Murdock put a rubber band around another wad of bills. "I'll resurrect Jesus and nail him to a cross again about this green shit. What time is it? Niggah, I feel like Usher, 'cause I got a real pretty pretty little thang waiting on me." He didn't sound half bad singing the line.

"Ten after nine." My cell phone played its melody. "What's cracking?" I never bothered to check the caller ID.

"Hey, what are you doing?"

"What you mean what I'm doing? Where the fuck you at and why don't I know about it?"

Murdock pulled a hoody over a slug proof vest. "I told you to get rid of that hoe. You beat the brakes of the pussy, kick that pale bitch to the curb and go get your family back. I don't trust that hoe. Niggah, we peeps but Elixir my family, she come first."

"Stay the fuck out my business, Murdock -- "

"That was a very ignorant thing for him to say." Came from the other end of the phone.

"Shut the fuck up! Ain't nobody talking to you."

Rhapsody got quiet.

I sat the phone down. "You got something you wanna get off your chest. It's plenty room for you to do it in." I pushed the box of money aside with my foot.

"Dig this," C-Mack said. "Chill with that bullshit, we got business in here to take care of. Ya'll can settle that personal business on a later note."

"Mack, got out my motherfucking way before we all be in here knuckling it up." Murdock put his gun on the table. "So this what it comes to, Limbo? You swell your chest up at me 'cause I'm telling you something real?"

I sat my gun down. "I ain't got nothing to rap about. You wrong. You don't tell me what to do. The way you said that like it's been aching your tooth for awhile. You feel like you need to stand up for your cousin, then stand up, niggah. She left -- "

Murdock rushed at me, we fell through the table. Money and the counting machines scattered across the small room. C-Mack jumped out our way and let us thump. He had me pent.

It was hard for me to move with a slug proof strapped around my chest.

"You better hold on for dear life. I'm gonna beat your ass when I get up." I started rocking from one side to the other looking for the leverage I needed to reverse this situation.

He tried to knee me and I found my loophole. I hooked his leg around the back of his knee and threw my arm around his neck and used all the strength I had to lock my hands together, I came off my back like a cat. I could tell hat he wasn't trying to hurt me, because he hadn't swung. Picture me not.

"I ain't gonna rush you, get up." I stood and balanced myself to box. Murdock got up as quick as I did and I stole him. The blow connected with the side of his ear.

He staggered back.

I went in to get another one off, but he caught me flush on the mouth and rushed again. I used his weight against him, tossing Murdock into the wall. I ran behind him, grabbing him from the back with a sleeper hold that I had perfected as a kid. "I'm gonna show you how it feels to be choked out."

"Hold up, ain't nothing cracking." C-Mack approached. "I'm not about to sit here and watch you choke the homey. Limbo, you on some fuck shit about a broad." He started to pry my arms from Murdock's neck. "You tripping on the homey cause your hoe goy you in your feelings. Ain't nothing gangster about that."

"Fuck this niggah, Mack!" Murdock pulled away, stuffed his piece in his waist, and left.

C-Mack shook his head and began to pick up the mess. "Fool, you tripping, you need to get a grip, Cuz."

"I ain't trying to hear it." I picked the phone up. "Where you at?"

"What's going on, Big Daddy? Are you okay?"

"Don't as me nothing, answer my motherfucking question."

"I'm with Tara. Sorry I didn't return your calls, but Tara is really going through tough time, she needs -- "

"So you with Tara, huh? Keri told that her or Tara couldn't find Rhapsody.

"Yes."

"Oh, yeah. What the fuck she need with you that was important enough to neglect your obligations at home? You bet' not lie. I'm on the verge of cutting your ass slam off."

"Tara was raped yesterday, she's having a hard time coping with it. I'm just supporting my friend. I figured that you would be more understanding, more supportive of me."

My conversation with Keri played old and clear in my mind. Rhapsody had just shown me a side of her that I wasn't going to deal with. Liars are dangerous people, they'll trick you out of your life. I couldn't believe that she would burn bread on her best friend like that just to save her own ass. I couldn't believe that I had just swung on mine like he was a stranger. "Don't play on my intelligence. That's the worst thing a person can do to me. Rhapsody, stop fucking lying. You would've been better off coming clean, but you wanna shoot some bullshit under me like I can't tell that it stinks."

"I'm not lying! Why would I lie about something like that?"

I guess she was exercising the 'that's my story and I'm sticking to it'. "Something I wanna know. I'm done rapping about it. Just don't frown." It was then that I decide to stick my spoon in some of these other flavors of ice cream that I'd been dying to taste. Tally up the cash, then disappear just like she had. I Only I would never come back. Signs and symbols are for those that are conscious. She lied and cheated once, she'll do it twice.

STREET GAMES

"Big Daddy, don't be like that. I promise to be home tomorrow."

"I don't give a fuck what you do," before I hung up C-Mack yelled, "Bitch."

CHAPTER THIRTY-EIGHT

Rhapsody

The shopping markets lot was just starting to fill as Tara and I pulled away from the black Yukon. The exchange with Sprinkle and Jerico went well. "I don't trust Jerico." I blended in with traffic.

"He's mellow. I had the same feeling about him until I sat up in the hospital talking with him all night. For a drug dealer, he's okay, has a good conversation. Under that hard exterior there's a big teddy bear."

"You see why I didn't want to go out. You end up in somebody else's gun fight. You're lucky it was Phoebe who took one and not you."

"She was only grazed, Jayme."

"It's not the point. You shot somebody and fled like you're some criminal."

We took the drugs to a Pittsburgh's field office, secured them with a property officer and headed out to Johnstown. On the drive home I told Tara of my run-in with Limbo.

"You told him what? Why did you have to say it was me who was raped? I can't believe you would jinx me like that. Shit like that can come to pass." Tara watched the roadside blow by us.

"Don't get superstitious on me. I apologize. But it was the only thing valid I could think of at the spur of the moment." I thought about how Big Daddy accused me of being a liar. I didn't understand it. "For some reason he didn't believe me, even called me a liar."

"Bingo." Tara rolled her eyes at me.

"He would have no idea that it was a lie."

An hour and seventy miles had passed before I exited route 56 coming into Johnstown. My cell phone started to hum a lullaby. The whole time I was on the highway my phone hadn't rung once. Now that I am home, it was like somebody had a bug-Jayme-radar. After a glance at the caller ID, I knew that it was Thurston. Out of a world full of people, I'd prefer to be bothered by anyone other than Thurston. I connected the call. "Hi, Thurston."

"Congratulations are in order, Johanson."

"Thanks, but making a common buy doesn't warrant a personal congratulations."

I could tell from his sloppy speech pattern that he had a cigar wedged in his face.

"We're not on the same page, I'm talking about the amazing job you've done in the Lamont Adams case."

My heart dropped hearing that name.

Thurston went on. "This information you've collected is more than enough to make Adams a permanent fixture in the prison system. But I want to send his friends with him."

Tara shifted towards me being nosy -- a character flaw she's famous for. I shrugged. "Thurston, what are you talking about, what information?"

"The box you had Mayweather bring in here. I suggest looking into some workers disability if you forgot that fast."

None of this is real. Nope, it wasn't happening. It's a dream, I'm sure of it. There's no way --

"Jayme!" Tara snatched the steering wheel "Pay attention to the road. What are you trying to do, get us killed? She guided us out of oncoming traffic. I hadn't realized that I went blank. Not until a car with a blaring horn drove past with its driver giving us the birdie.

"Are you girls alright?"

"We're fine, Thurston, let me call you back. I'm just getting in, I'm at my wits end."

"Fine, Fine. Call me when you get it together. Johanson, one more thing before you go."

I couldn't take nothing else. "What is it?" I didn't mean to sound that way.

"Keep up the good work. I'm proud to have you on the team, and my team."

"Thanks." I straightened my posture and stared off into the open road. I dropped Tara off at her aunt's and went to my house -- the one Keri was staying in -- to confront her for putting me in the cross. She wasn't home and the recording on hr cell phone kept saying, "The wireless customer you're trying to reach is out the service area." I would have waited for her to show, but I had been away from Limbo long enough. I'd catch up with her later and when I do --

The phone rang.

I knew it couldn't be Keri. What reason did she have to call home and she was the only one living here. The number had a 410 area code. Who do I know in Harrisburg?

Bill collector.

I grabbed he phone next to my sofa and settled on its cushion. "Hello"

"Uh…yes, is Ms Keri Mayweather around by any chance? His voice had the tone of a bill collector."

"She not in and she won't be living here any longer."

"I hope I'm not too late, has she done something wrong?"

Wrong? Stabbing me in the back, endangering the existence of my love life isn't right. "Who am I speaking with?"

"Doctor Zimmerman, I'm a resident psychiatrist with the Harrisburg Mental Health Hospital, for the criminally insane. It's a very important matter that I speak with Keri or -- "

I could hear him shuffling some papers around.

" -- would you happen to know where I can reach Ms. Jayme Johanson?"

What a jerk. "I'm Jayme. What is this about?"

"Thank God." He honestly sounded relieved. "What a stroke of luck, I was able to contact you like this."

"Not a lot of luck involved when you dialed my house." I flipped my sandals off and tucked my feet under me.

"I assure you, Ms. Johanson, that I had no idea. This number is listed in Keri's file as her aunt's contact information. Have you by any chance seen Keri?"

Keri's file. "A couple days ago. Doctor Zimmerman, what is the nature of this call?"

"Keri is a patient of mine. I've been caring for her since the age of nine. There -- "

"Are we talking about the same Keri Mayweather? Keri's not seeing a psychiatrist."

"I assure you that she does from time-to-time. I monitor her scheduled prescription pick-ups. My computer is showing she hasn't filled her prescriptions since she left our in-patient program two ago. Keri is very unstable without her meds."

"Keri on medication…unstable, this is a joke right?"

"Not at all, Ms. Johanson, this is not a laughing matter. And if she's been more that four days without meds, I'd suggest that you call your local authorities. Keri is a threat to herself and you."

"Me?" The yellow hairs on my arms stood like pine needles.

"Yes, I take it you don't have the slightest idea of what you're dealing with?"

Silence.

My quietness must have been a good enough answer for him.

"Keri is on one milligrams of Risperidone and an equal dosage of Quatiapine. Without meds, she's deprived of reason."

"Are you really trying to convince me that Keri is literally crazy?"

"About you, yes, but to call a person like Keri crazy is modest. She's a psychotic, psychosexual cannibal."

I immediately remember when we were in training. Keri and I were in a BAU class (Behavioral Analysis Unit) discussing the dynamics of killers, more specifically pattern killer. He BAU teacher, Special Agent Cynthia Edwards, shut the projector off then addressed the class.

"Follow me. There was a funeral for a white man in his late thirties. His wife and niece are sitting a few feet away from the casket mourning their loss." Agent Edwards walked the length of the case room as she painted her picture. "One of the deceased coworker's is at the altar speaking of the good things he remembered about the bastard. The wife speaks next, followed by some other associates." Agent Edwards stopped in front of me, shifted her eyes between Keri and myself, then continued pacing. "The preacher is delivering a few words from the good book when the church doors swing open.

Everybody turns and looked at a handsomely dressed man as he enters the sanctuary and seats himself. After the service ended, the man, who came in late was gone." She scratched her neck then leaned on a conference table at the font of the room. "the niece asked her aunt who the man was." The aunt had no idea. She asked the preacher, coworkers, her uncle's best friend. No one had a clue who this mysterious man was." Agent Edwards took her spectacles off and wiped them clean with her blouse. "Two weeks later, the niece murdered her older sister." She pushed the spectacles back on her face. "Why did the niece kill her sister?"

Rawlings always had an answer, he blurted out, "because she caught her sister with her boyfriend."

Agent Edwards looked at Rawlings over her frames. "No."

Nester raised his pudgy hand. "She found out that her sister was responsible for the uncle's death "

"No." Agent Edwards stopped in form of me once again.'

I didn't have a clue why the girl murdered her sister. There wasn't enough information in the story for me to draw a logical conclusion. The only answer I could give was a shrug of my tired shoulders.

"That's easy," Keri said. "She murdered her sister so she could see the man who sat in the back of the church again."

"I've been a BAU teacher for eleven years and none of my students have ever answered that question correctly but you Mayweather."

Keri smiled, assuming she had scored a few points with Agent Edwards.

"I don't see the humor, Ms. Mayweather. Only serial killers and psychopaths can answer that question correct."

Sweat formed over my lip, I took the phone away from my ear and stared at the glowing numbers. Bullshit! "I've

286

heard enough. Doctor Zimmerman. Keri put you up to this nonsense. I'm hanging up, I'd appreciate it if you not call back."

"Why do you think I wanted to contact you?

What a jerk face. "I haven't a freaking clue, but I suppose you're going to tell me...I can't believe she would stoop to something this low."

"This is no game, Ms. Johanson. Do you have any idea of how obsessed Keri is with you?"

I could hear him shuffling through papers again.

"Here, let me read this to you." He said. "It's a statement she made in one of our counseling sessions. And I quote, 'I love Jayme as I love air. If she'd let me, I'll try her skin on. One day, she'll do something stupid to upset me and I will. That's Keri without the proper dosage of meds. She's a mental misfit, but with the proper meds, she's competent enough to mingle in any occupation and gain acceptance to any social gathering that suits her." He paused. I could hear him breathe, "Listen, Ms. Johanson, Keri has an exaggerated sense of well-being. She takes break from reality. Are you aware of what happened to her parents?"

"She never knew her father." I twirled the phone cord around my finger. "And her mother died giving birth to her. I can't believe I'm entertaining this conversation with God-only-knows-who. Keri has some issues, but this stuff you're saying is far fetched. I can't listen—"

"At nine, Keri's school teacher became concerned about her three day absence without receiving a call from her parents. The school had planned to look in to the matter until Keri showed up to school covered in dried blood."

I was pacing the small patch of carpet between the sofa and coffee table.

He went on. "The authorities found her parents slain in their home. Her father was found in front of a television set with his throat slit. Her mother was still in bed with a portion of her vagina and reproductive system eaten. Keri has taken on the identity of a lesbian because in her mind when she's performing oral sex, she thinks that she is reentering the womb."

"Why are you telling me this?

"Because you're dealing with an insanely clever person who hasn't picked up the medicine that will keep her on the reasonable side of the spectrum. Keri also has ungovernable desire to be you. Without those med, she's functioning from a deranged personality."

"Suppose what you saying is true -- "

"I'm Doctor Zimmerman. I work for Harrisburg Mental Health Hospital. My extension is 216, look me up in the directory and call me right back." He hung up.

I thought about all that he had said. In fact, I played the conversation back several times while staring at the phone. I pulled in a deep breath and stabbed 411 on the phone's key pad. An operator gave me the hospital's number. "May I have extension 216?" I almost choked, my stomach swan dived, my jaw bone dropped when Doctor Zimmerman answered. "So what do you suggest that I do?"

"If Keri isn't taking her meds, you need to call the authorities. To get what she wants there is no telling what she's capable of.

"What is it she wants?"

"You."

On the drive back to Limbo's and my honeycomb hide out, I rationalized with what I had learned about Keri. No way! She was up to her old tricks and I refused to be fooled any longer. I knew her nice-guy act was too-good-to-be-true. Boy, I could kick myself for being so stupid. If she was anything like the Doc' had suggested, the Fed would know about it. She would never have passed the psychological evaluation aptitude test, right? What about those vitamins she always pops in her mouth?

Limbo filed through the door a few minutes after me. His presence was marked with anger. The danger lurking behind his eyes made me uncomfortable. I tried to lighten the tension by asking, "You want to order out? I rented the movies you asked for."

"Go back and eat where you slept last night." He stood in the refrigerator door, drinking orange juice out of the carton. I hate it when he does that.

"Big Daddy. Lets be adults about this. I was with Tara. Why would I -- "

He grabbed me by the neck and forced me tot e kitchen table. My face was pressed against my car keys. He poured the orange juice over my head and I gasped for air like I was drowning. He tore my skirt off.

"Not like this, Limbo, please."

"Shut the fuck up." He squeezed my neck with such a force, I thought my head was going to pop off.

"Please, not this way."

He had his way with me. He pumped my butt so violently the table leg broke. It felt like he was ripping me. When he pulled out I had no control of my rectum. My bowels moved right there.

"Fuck you," he said with no emotion. "Clean my floor, and first thing in the morning, get your ass up and find a job. You're gonna need it. You think I don't know what's going on? I can see through smoke and spot the fire before it starts. If you got a problem with what I did or said pack your shit and beat your feet by the time I get back." He went upstairs, showered and left.

CHAPTER THIRTY-NINE

Limbo

C-Mack was lounging on the couch, lining the room, putting his southern charm on this project chick Stacy. Stacy is thick in the thighs with a tiny waist line. She is thick and tender in the trunk like a juice sirloin and her titties made mouths water. Her dark skin is pretty as a newborn, and that face of hers… Stacy made dog shit look delicious. Somebody needed to have a long talk with God about making Stacy so hard on the eye. I guess He showed her mercy by blessing her with an amazing body and crazy sex appeal.

"Mack, what do you from me, honestly?" Just hearing her you would think she a dime.

C-Mack rubbed her sirloin. "Some of this."

She giggled.

C-Mack polished off the rest of his cognac "I'm bouncing. I'll holler."

"Cuz, you stay smashing on ugly and fat broads." Trigger was feeling the alcohol. I could tell 'cause when he's tipsy, he doesn't care about other peoples feelings.

Stacy didn't seem offended by his comment.

"Every type, style, and size woman needs some loving." He winked at Stacy -- she was tickled. "See, Trigger, ya'll chase them pretty hoes, that's in high demand. Everybody done ran through them. That's why they're pussy holes this big." He made a big hole with two hands. "Don't nobody want women with great personalities but me." He showed Stacy his gold fronts. She showed him her pearly whites. "It's like I'm breaking in virgin pussy every time. Homey, all them broads that you think is ugly got pussy holes this small." He made a tiny hole with a thumb and a finger.

Trigger laughed. "You country as hell."

"The only thing country about C-Mack," I said, "is the Mason Dixon Line."

"Hit me up if ya'll need me. Call Murdock so you two sociopaths can kiss and make up." C-Mack threw his arms around Stacy like she was Miss America and heeded for the steps.

Stacy turned around and mad a tiny hole with her fingers.

Tight. I could only imagine.

"Yeah, Mack is right, you need to holler at Dock. Las time it took ya'll a month. Ya'll tow worse than brothers" Trigger drained his glass. "I'm getting ghost, too, Steph' waiting on me."

"McDaniel's?" I couldn't believe what I was hearing.

"Could be, could be not." Trigger made a b-line for he steps.

I sat there pretending to enjoy the club atmosphere. Cuties shaking their booties on he dance floor didn't even have it's usual effect on me. Multi-colored lights cut through layers of cigarette smoke. It always felt good to sit on top of y throne overlooking a club full of admires. But tonight I'm internally fucked about Rhapsody and my fallout with Murdock.

Yani cut across the dance floor and disappeared in the ladies room. What the hell. Rhapsody amended our relationship rules. I reached for the phone and punched in the numbers for the ladies room. Why couldn't someone other than Drama-Queen, Trina answer the phone.

I got right to the point. "Trina, let me hear one time that I called this bathroom and I'm gonna wire your mouth."

"What are you talking about?"

"Not right now. Stop while you're ahead. Put Yani on."

"What color is your panties?"

"What color is wet?"

"Who you leaving with?"

"Nobody."

"Don't make me ask you again."

"I'm leaving with you."

"My ride is out back meet me in five minutes."

CHAPTER FORTY

Keri

Limbo backed out the drive and faded into the night. Now it was time to work my magic. I slid my key into their front door. I expected to see Jayme with a bloody lip or if he was anything like me, he would've swollen her eye. But nothing like the sight before me. It angered me and I would make him pay, but it served Jayme right. She was laid sprawled out on the floor weeping. A piece of her skirt was in a kitchen chair, the other piece was on the floor beneath the toppled table. Her thong was gathered around one ankle. A rank smell that I had mistaken for spoiled broccoli hit when I came in, gut the misconception was cleared up when I got closer to Jayme and saw her feces on a tile next to her. Serves her right for thinking she can love a filthy, dirty rotten nigger. She'll learn that it's me who loves her, understands her.

"Oh, my God, Jayme! Look what he'd done to you. You're...Oh, gosh, you're bleeding." I kneeled beside her and rubbed her arm. "You're gonna be okay, I'm calling the paramedics."

"Don't touch me." She hurried to her feet, surveyed her mess then began to clean it. "You conniving bitch, Keri, how did you get in my house?"

"The door was open. You can't let him get away with this, he's a monster. Can't you see that? How could you call yourself in love with someone who'd treat you like this?"

She tied a plastic garbage bag and with no regards to her own partial nakedness. Sat the bag on the porch. "Why did you take the case reports and the evidence from nay storage unit? What gave you the right?"

I followed her to the bathroom. "What's with you? He violates you and you're on his side. I was looking for some of my belongings that I can't seem to find and I came across the evidence." I sat on the vanity chair. "I'm trying to stop you from making a big mistake. I'm a Federal Agent, what was I supposed to do?"

"Respect us, respect what I told you about Limbo and I." She stepped in the tub.

"It's never going to be you, me, and him. We belong to each other. I don't know why you can't get that through your fat skull. Once Limbo is arrested, you'll laugh at yourself for being naïve. Then things will go back to normal. I was born to eat pussy, Jayme. We can venture out once in a while, to satisfy your craving, but we're not going to make this a permanent arrangement. It started with just you and me, that's how it'll end."

Jayme had no expression on her face like she had just received a revelation from some distant place. She seemed to visually withdraw.

"I knew I should never have taken you back. You haven't changed, your whole act was phony from word go. Did you speak to Limbo while I was out of town?"

"No."

"I don't believe you."

"Jayme -- "

"Never mind. Don't have your friend or whoever he was call my house again with the foolishness. Who was he, someone with the Bureau?"

Friend call the house. "What friend? I don't have people that I consider friends."

She rolled her eyes at me and turned the bath water off with her foot. "You trying to scare me into being with you. I didn't think you would stoop to such levels."

"Jayme, I don't know what you're talking about."

"Play dumb for all I care. Too bad you don't, because you accomplished the exact opposite. I don't to be with you ever again. It's over, cherish the memories."

"You need help, this guy has got you all screwed up." I was trying to be cool about the situation, but I wasn't a minute away from ringing Jayme's skinny neck.

"We don't have nothing left to talk about unless you can fix what you did. I want you to move out of may house ASAP and don't ever come back here. You mad it impossible for me to keep Limbo out of jail, but you haven't stopped me from loving him. You stopped me from loving you -- you lose. She laid the rag on her chest and leaned back in the tub, "I don't even want to see your face. Make sure the door is closed behind you."

She started washing herself, blocking me out, humming a melody as if I wasn't there. Be cool, just be patient. When she calms down, come to her senses everything will be fine. If not I'll hurt her. "Listen"

"Just leave, Keri, That's real simple."

CHAPTER FORTY-ONE

Murdock leaned on the car horn doing a good job at disturbing the peace. C-Mack had plenty of time to be ready before Murdock arrived. It was early, but the August morning was already hot. Murdock could imagine what the temperature would be by noon. He fingered the door-panel buttons, causing the power windows to separate him from the extreme heat. He set the air-conditioner's climate e control, then text-messaged Ghetto. Murdock glanced at Stacy's front door and leaned on the horn again.

Ghetto read the text message then shoved the phone in his pant pocket. Ghetto had been appointed manager over operation Project Oakhurst. He sat on a bench at the basketball court smoking a blunt, while talking to MarTay, who was looking to find employment hustling for the team. The team consisted of several key players that only communicated through encrypted messages. The distributor held the bulk of the cocaine in a non-disclosed location, where he killed time with a Sony Play Station. The team's head pitcher, whose responsibilities were to oversee the project's crack house, and the street pitchers, made money drops to the money man--who made hourly rounds. This was Limbo's insurance policy that if operation Project Oakhurst experienced a raid or a pitcher was pinched, his money wouldn't go to jail, too. Then, according to Limbo's logic, there were the most important members of the team --the lookouts. They were stationed at every possible entry to Oakhurst. Unlike traditional drug rings, Limbo paid the lookouts the highest pay next to the manager. He stressed the fact that their job was invaluable, because their keen eyes kept the entire operation safe and open for business. All twelve members of this project's team answered to Ghetto. Ghetto answered to Murdock.

"You don't know how I need you to put me on." MarTay was slumped over watching a colony of worker ants building. "My girl is pregnant, the rent is behind, I'm doing bad."

Ghetto blew smoke through his nose and looked at the older MarTay with disdain. "This ain't one of those jobs if you fuck up, you get fired and collect your last pay. You fuck up here, you get fucked up and you work your mistake off." Ghetto watched a maintenance truck park two doors away from the distributors. "If you have any brush with po-po for any reason you're outcasted."

"I can understand that, so I'm down?"

"You haven't earned that. I'm gonna keep it gangster with you, I know you're a stand up dude, but I don't like you. You're soft, you advertise it in your eyes. But I'm not gonna let my personal feelings interfere with my business and you done gone and knocked my little cousin up so I'm gonna give you a chance to take care of your business." He realized that he had never saw the maintenance man unloading tools from the truck One thing he knew for sure was that the Housing Authority only hired once a year. He turned back to MarTay. "You're on for a week trial basis. Your numbers at the end of the week will decide if you can stay. Go to apartment 381, take the long way. There's a pack and a cell phone waiting on you. My people will show you how to work the phone so you and the rest of my team will straight in these streets. Don't leave that apartment until you understand the phone language."

"Thanks, Ghetto . I'mma hold it down."

"Don't thank me, Thank your girl."

MarTay started in the direction of apartment 381. Ghetto kept his eyes on the maintenance man.

Lump, the distributor, had been playing Resident Evil up until Ghetto's text message forced him to take a break. He positioned a bundle of cocaine on a digital scale. He adjusted the quantity until he was satisfied with the reading. He packaged the chalky substance, knocked on the living room wall, and removed a painting of the Boondocks.

Jazmyne was lounging on the couch watching a rerun of Jerry Springer, wishing that her shift would come to an end so she could go home to be with her lover. She knew that he wanted his hair braided tonight. A smoking kill commercial came on, she took the Kool away from her lips, and stubbed it out. She was pushing the deadly smoke from her lungs when a knock from next door rattled the living room wall. She lugged an oversized painting of the Keystone Cops off its hook and stood face-to-face with Lump.

"MarTay on his way down here for this pack." Lump passed Jazmyne a sandwich bag through the hole.

"Tiffany's MarTay, scary MarTay?"

"Yup." Everybody wants to be hustlers. Give him a phone, too. Jazmyne, when can we see each other? You know I'm feeling you."

"When everybody else on earth dies. I still might not fool with your sorry butt after the way you played me."

"We were in junior high. You still tripping on -- "

She hung the painting back on its hook then went back to her TV show, while waiting on MarTay.

C-Mack came out of Stacy's house fastening his button down.

"What took you so long?" Murdock shifted the Escaladé in drive.

"You know I got thick bone syndrome. I couldn't leave without tapping that ass again. Where we headed first?"

"We'll make a pick up in my projects first, then double back and make your rounds."

"Dig that." C-Mack rolled a blunt.

"Try putting some food in you before you stuff yourself with smoke."

"I can't eat if I don't start my day off with a fat one. Did you holler at Limbo last night?"

"Nah, I ain't tripping though, that's my niggah. We wouldn't be real if we didn't get into it. Rhapsody pussy whipped him, but if he feeling her like that, I shouldn't be force feeding my opinion about the bitch. I still don't think I said anything wrong."

"You didn't if she was just somebody he fucking, that niggah love that hoe. You see hoe he blew up on you. That love shit is for real."

"I feel you."

When they arrived in Oakhurst, C-Mack was good and high and hungry. Ghetto was informed, five minutes ago, by two of his six lookouts that Murdock was on the premises. Murdock made his first stop at the safe house to collect the graveyard shift's bankroll from Donut, the money man. When Murdock drove away, Donut made the next necessary text message in order for a successful drug delivery.

"What's for tonight?", Murdock asked as the car rolled to a stop in front of a phone booth with its glass broken and years of names burned into its plastic ceiling.

"Same ole same ole." C-Mack bit his McMuffin. "Make my rounds, get blinded all day, step up in Everyday People, and get blinded some more while I weigh my options."

Weigh your options?"

"Yeah, Cuz. It's a lot of hood boogers in there. I gotta wait 'till the Hennessy starts talking shit in my ear. C-Mack, that's the booger for you. Look at the way she's shaking that dump truck for us. Yeah, that's the one, that's who we fucking tonight.' The Henny got a hell of a mouth piece."

"Cuz, you bugged out, let me make this call real quick."

Murdock took a large Micky D's bag from the console and stepped inside the booth.

"Are you sure?" Jazmyne stood next to MarTay.

"Yup, I got it down pact." He stuffed the phone is his back pocket. "Twelve-twenty four close down and bring the work back. Four-twelve a raid is in progress. Five-eleven the money man is about to meet me. Four-eighteen -- "

"I'm convinced. Just don't forget them or the rest. Those codes will save you a trip to the county and your life. We work as a team, think as a team." Jazmyne's phone buzzed, delivering an encrypted text message.

"I'm gone, Jazmyne."

"Hold up, I'll walk with you. I need to get something to eat."

They walked to the end of the court yard together and parted company. MarTay went to start his first day of work, Jazmyne went on her way. When she made it to the corner, she crossed the narrow street and stopped in front of the phone booth. "Excuse me, are you going to be long?"

"Nah, little Mama, I'm getting off now." He was on the phone with Las Vegas getting the NBA line. Murdock left the phone booth and drove away.

Jazmyne pretended to use the phone for a moment. She put the receiver on its cradle, picked up the McDonald's bag, went to the apartment, and banged on the living room wall.

Murdock cruised over to the playground and powered the window down. "Ghetto, come bust it up with your homier."

Ghetto scanned the block, taking notice of the morning rush, before he pulled himself off the bench and bopped over to the car.

C-Mack flashed a fresh blunt. "Get in, young Cuz."

"What's on your niggahs minds this morning? Ghetto loved being in the presence of C-Mack and Murdock.

"Business," Murdock said. "What's up with this month's collection?"

"I snatched it up this morning when the shift began." Ghetto counted out twelve hundred dollars. "I hired a pitcher this morning, if things work out for he the pot will be sweeter next month."

Murdock reached over the seat for the money. "Mrs. G could use, it, there's a lot of things she wants to do in this community."

"Niggah, what you all quiet for?" Ghetto pushed the back of C-Mack's head.

"Don't make me fuck your frail ass up, Ghetto, fucking with my high, young Cuz."

Punk you've been threatening me since the first day I met you. Mack, you all talk" Ghetto climbed out the car.

"I did that little niggah." C-Mack was telling Murdock then he rolled the window down. "Ay, Ghetto."

He turned around.

"Get your weight up, young Cuz." C-Mack tossed him the blunt.

"It's that florescence green. That sticky icky, Cuz." C-Mack threw up their neighborhood as they eased away from the curb.

There was only one more stop that the duo had to make before they went to C-Mack's projects and repeated the same process.

Mrs. Gladyce was humming a heartfelt version of Swing Low, while scrubbing her breakfast dishes, then Murdock rapped on the screen door.

"Come in here, baby. I figured you would come by and visit with me today, Murdock". She never turned away from the sink.

"Good morning, Mrs. G. How'd you know it was me?"

"When God takes away your eyes, he blesses you with other senses."

"It smells good in here."

"You ten minutes, too late. But I can throw you something together if you hungry, baby."

Murdock dropped the twelve hundred dollars on the table.

Mrs. Gkladyce heard it when it connected with the surface.

"God bless you."

"I don't think that dude has too many blessings for me."

The way Mrs. Gladyce maneuvered around, Murdock always wondered if she could see.

"Sit down her, boy, and let me tell you something."

"I can't , Mack's in the car. I'll sit with next time."

"If I wasn't a good goddam Christian I'd curse your mothafucking ass out. Now you sit your tired ass down here before you make me bring these Sonny Listons out of retirement." She balled her fist. "This ain't gonna take but a minute of your damn time, boy. I swear you lucky I'm a Christian.

They both sat down. She took Murdock's hand in her vein ridden wrinkled hand. "Don't you ever let me hear you say no such thing again. God bestows blessings on everybody. He might not give you the blessings you want, but He gives you the one you need. You're just taking your blessings for granted, overlooking them because all you can notice is what you ain't getting. Is your mother healthy?"

"Yes, Mrs. G."

"How about your childings?"

"My daughter is fine." Murdock smiled as he poctured his little girl's smile.

"You sitting here talking to me so that means you got your life. Be thankful for what God has given you. Look a the seniors in this housing project that this money helps. That's a blessing for them, and you'll be blessed for giving somebody else a blessing no matrer what, even if you are doing some wrong."

"Thanks for setting me straight, Mrs. G," Murdock said, going to the doo4r.

"You know that bastard Bush is cutting Medicaid again. When he does that, I'll never be able to save up for those new swing sets. The children need them. After we pay for the prescription balance each month there's only twenty five dollars left, and half of that goes towards gas money." Mrs. Gladyce said a silent prayer.

Murdock peeled off some money. "Here's five hundred, the swing was my favorite when I was a little boy. Hook the kids up.

Mrs. Gkladyce stood in her screen door as Murdock went toward his car. "God bless you," she called, "and for God sakes pull them damn pants up on your butt, boy."

Murdock wondered if she could just a little.

306

CHAPTER FORTY-TWO

Keri

The house was calm, it had a family feel to it. A life-size portrait, hanging over the aquarium, gave me the impression as if Limbo and Jayme were keeping their eyes on me. All of a sudden, the portrait transformed right before my eyes. It took on the post of a vicious gate-keeper. Limbo growled and barked, foam formed at his mouth form the boundary of the oak frame. Jayme hissed and clawed at the canvas -- both of them threatening me to leave the privacy of their fortress. I looked away then shifted my gaze back at the nosy pointing. "You shouldn't make that ugly face Jayme. You got it all wrong. I love you, not him." I pointed to the flea bitten man and climbed the steps that led to their bedroom.

The sliding door moved with little or no effort along its tracks. I thought choosing outfits would prove difficult until I saw an abundance of cleaner's bags. Had to be the outfits he wears more than the others hanging there. One-by-One, I took my time sticking transparent listening devices to the bagged outfits.

Jayme will be so proud of me when this is allover with.

The dresser rested against a wall l like a tired factory worker who's worn out from holding the weighty jewelry sparsely scattered atop it. I shifted thought Limbo's watches, all which, I'd seen him wear on several occasions, and found places for devices there, too.

I wrapped my sweaty hand around the doorknob to the then paused -- a thoughtful pause. I faced the portrait again, wondering who this was showing me their fangs, Rhapsody or Jayme.

CHAPTER FORTY-THREE

Limbo

It was deep into October. Business was better than ever. Me and Murdock wasn't beefing, but we haven't spoken in over a month, well not directly. It had a lot to do with our overgrown egos and foolish pride. Neither of us wanted to be the first to apologize. I promised myself when my feet hit the floor this morning to end our silence the next time I was out. I would have called him, but face-to-face is better. I had just decided to give Rhapsody the time of day again, she had felt the wrath of my cruelty for days and some how found a way to smile. I told her, point blank, "You're a fucking liar." Since I had decided to put my skates on, I never questioned her about her two-day hiatus again. Things between us could never be the same, but I could swallow her for the time being.

She was snuggled up beside me with her feet under my butt. "How about we rent a new release and a triple X? I'll fix us some hot chocolate and we can get that heavy quilt from the closet and screw and watch movies until tomorrow."

I had a hand in my pants, the other clutched a TV remote.

"I'm not going out for the movies."

"My suggestion, I'll go."

"Handle that then."

She slipped into her leather, flipped her collar up to protect her from the cold. "Are we spending Thanksgiving together?, I'd be honored to meet your folks."

I looked away from the local new. My grandmother came to mind. She told me stories of how her great grandmother was raped the white men on a plantation. How her great grandfather was striped of his sanity because he could do nothing but watch and help with the babies when they were born.

Grandma always reminded me of my family's history by saying, "Boy, now that's the reason we high yellow." Then she would put her arm next to mine, showing me how close in color our skin is. Grandma told me that after her grandmother died on her hands and knees, scrubbing a white family's floor, she migrated to the north to give the new generation of our family a better chance at life. I can't take Rhapsody home. It would be the cause of my grandma's heart failure. And my mother…that's another story. But I bet she still thinks she can kick my ass.

"I'm chilling with my sons' on some personal time. We can do something together another time, Baby Girl." I shifted my attention to the new. "Why?"

"I just wanted to know if we were going to be together. Seeing that we're not, do you mind if I spend the holiday with Tara and her mother."

"Do what you do, Rhapsody."

"Why'd you say it like that?"

"Go and get the movies if you going, before I change my mind."

She formed her lips to say something but hesitated. A tear swelled in her right eye. "Limbo, Big Daddy, I'm sorry. I'm not sure of what, but I know Keri told you something. Whatever it was, she lied." She pushed the ear out with a blind." Keri will do or say anything to destroy what we have. I love you and it hurts me each day you act dry and distant towards me. It's been too long, we can't keep this up. I sleep beside you every night and I still find myself missing you." She dropped her head and sighed. "I did lie to you. Tara didn't get raped, but I was with her the entire two days. Just me and her. I needed some time to think. I never lived like this, seeing so much money at once. The expensive gifts, trips out the country for a day, guns, bullet proof vests. It was happening so fast, it scared me. You being a drug dealer and all."

I hit her with a don't-you-ever-let- me-hear-you-say-that again look.

"I...I, ah I just needed some time to slow down and think abut the consequences of what I've gotten my self into, about the effect your life could have on my career."

I had become curious. I'm always interested in knowing where a person's mind is at. "What did you come up with?"

She stuffed her hands in the coat pocket. "I want to be with you no matter what. Just because this life style is opposite of what I'm accustomed to doesn't mean I should be worried. No one has ever treated me like you have."

She was on the verge of more tears.

After a sip of air, she went on "Keri knew that I need some time to myself, to sort things out, because I told her. She volunteered to cover for me until I got it together. That's why I know you talked to her, whether you admit or not.

She reached for the door then turned back. Te4ars traveled the contours of her face. "One more thing, Big Daddy, ask yourself what was Keri's intentions behind telling you something so hateful. You know that she doesn't want us together. Keri wants it to be her and I -- exclusively."

Rhapsody walked out into the cold.

CHAPTER FORTY-FOUR
Rhapsody

The video store is two blocks away from my house so I decided to stoop, to give a Keri a deadline to move. To bring procrastination to an abrupt halt. Just as all the other times I've dropped by, Keri's car wasn't in the driveway. I figured I'd go in any way.

I froze at the door. I sensed the ultimate betrayal. A freight came over me, followed by pounding heart and a cold chill along my spine. The other day I returned to Limbo's and my house, after a yoga session the gym, and smelled an expensive perfume that wasn't my own. I couldn't call it by name either. Naturally, I checked Limbo's clothes for the scent of the other woman, but I found no traces of her. She only lingered in the air. The part that bothered me that day was Limbo was out of town buying equipment for his sports bar. Or maybe he wasn't. That same fragrance I smelled the other day perfumed the air here, too. I knew that Limbo was having sex with someone else...because a woman knows. But he would never bring a woman home unless...

It makes sense that Keri is the other woman, she had been to our house. "I'll kill her." My heart went humpty thump.

I never realized how much I'd miss my personal space. Now that I think of it, it's not that I missed it. I just didn't want Keri in it. The back stabbing cunt. I gave the hose a quick once over, fond the name of the mystery fragrance, and ended my visual with the kitchen. It's strange because I can't recall one time using the stove, but this is my favorite room. It's soft, pastel paints, I ran my hand across the flower-printed curtains. Then I noticed that my spice cabinet door was ajar. I went in to close it flush, but something hindered it from shutting. I opened it and found the problem. Keri's journal. I always wanted to know what she spent hours at a time writing in this thing. Or, so I thought.

My Jayme. In fleeting moments-erratic-like the random blinking in and out of an huntress' reality. I become her. How do I explain it? Do I squeal on myself or hint at the ritualistic festival of idol worship by pointing out the sacred verses carved into the contours of her pretty body? I am an idolater, I confessed. I pray to my Jayme. I dive into her --eyes open --in moments of insatiable passion tantrums, with the momentum of a lone hawk driven by hunger pangs. Eventually and elegantly having intercourse with" that", which is fortunate to be chosen from the lower level of the food chain. I can taste the emotional residue of her inner secrets when I lap at her pulsating sex organ. I savor Jayme's taste on my bumpy tongue. She reminds me of abstract art created through sanguinary desires. Something close to the stained face of a solitary panther after a hunt...after its kill, licking its satisfied lips omni presently so as to fully enjoy the rhapsodic embrace of oneness. Jayme is more to me than a fucking bloody stain around my lips. She is the make-up on my face that makes me

...beautiful. Soon she will give herself to me completely and expose her underbelly or die by the violence of my passion. She had yet to feel my explosive love -- when she does, she'll understand what my parents now understand. Love. Hate. Pain. Death.

My hand was clamped over my mouth, as I read from Keri's journal. I backed into the garbage pail and it toppled over. I read more of her sick entries from over the course of a two year period. I know that Doctor Zimmerman was right about Keri's mental unstableness when I read a 2000 entry that said "I'll consume her like I swallowed my dear mother."

CHAPTER FORTY-FIVE

Three men cruised the street in silence. The driver spotted the BMW and gave his partners a nod. One man dumped ashes out of the window, then loaded twelve rounds in a streetsweepers rotating chamber.

The driver smiled and parked under a blown street lamp. Pay-back is a bitch.

In the back seat, the youngest of the three men, shoved a hundred round magazine in a Mack 90, then passed a twelve gauge to the driver.

The men left the car armed, dangerous, and angry.

"Fuck!" Murdock stabbed the Play Station's reset button with a finger.

"Boy, would you sit still? Jazmyne sucked her teeth and pulled Murdock's head back in position, then continued to comb thorough his thick afro. "I don't know why you put me through this every three days. Making me wrestle with you to braid this nappy shit of your. If you sit still, I could've been done."

"Chill. If I didn't love sitting between your thighs, I wouldn't be over here so much turning a twenty minute job into an hour and half workout." He leaned his head back, resting it on her crotch.

Jazmyne popped him with the afro comb and smile. "You're too much." She leaned forward and kissed his nose. "We can finish this later, there's other things we could be doing."

"Only if you promise to respect me in -- "

Murdock's car alarm sounded off.

The man with the twelve-gauge pointed out Jazmyne's two-family house. Then he blended into the privacy of the darkness between her house and the neighbor's. The other two hit men squatted behind the BMW parked out the two-family.

"Let's make this shit happen," the darker one said.

The other man rammed his beefy shoulder into the car door causing its Viper to scream in the quiet night.

The shot gun toter observed as the BMW's external and internal lights blinked. A wandering stray came down the sidewalk, curious about the noisy car, he sniffed its tire then lifted his leg to take a piss.

Murdock took his .45 from under the couch cushion and went to the window. He saw the dog drain himself on the tire and trot away. He took his keys from his coat to deactivate the alarm.

"What is it?" Jazmyne beckoned him back to the seat between her legs with the wave of the comb. "Come on, let me finish."

"Some mutt decided to use my ride as the toilet."

Jazmyne laughed then started on the next braid. "Pick me up after tomorrow after I work my shift and I'll fix you a good meal"

"Girl, every time I come over here I leave her spent. What you trying to do kill me?"

Her devilish grin spoke loud and clear

"After next month, I won't need you to work the projects. I got something legal for you lined up. Me and Limbo been working on a little something."

"Ya'll talking again?"

"Nah, not yet. This ain't nothing new for us. It's cool though, that's my niggah."

"Well one yins need to be the bigger man and apologize. You never know what might happen. You don't know what it's like to live day-to-day wishing that you had something to someone and now you don't have the chance. It's been hell on me ever since my mother passed. There's so much I shoulda said."

"You right, bit it ain't that serious."

The man rammed the car again leaving a deep dent in the rear door.

I'm about to put a hole in this mutt. Save the dog pound the expense of feeding his ass." "Murdock went out on the porch with gun in hand. The street was quiet, no sign of the dog.

The men squatted behind Murdock's car watched him in the refection of a Honda window parked across from them. One winked at the other when Murdock made it to the steps. They raised their automatic weapons.

CHAPTER FORTY-SIX

Rhapsody

My stomach awoke me for the third night in a row. I barely made it to the bathroom before I puked. The news warned of a stomach virus going around, but I don't have a clue how I caught it. I brushed the sour taste from my mouth and washed my face. I navigated my way down our dark flight of stairs wishing Limbo was home. Feeling sick, not having anyone around to comfort me, makes my illness that much more unbearable. The refrigerator bulb brightened the kitchen as I surveyed its contents. The hum of its motor had a weird soothe to it. Frustrated because there was nothing on the shelves -- I wanted -- to calm an upset stomach, I pushed the door shut.

Our community's security lights cast a small beam through my kitchen window. I stood in the shine and penned Limbo a note and stuck it to the refrigerator. I pulled a coat over my pajamas, stepped into a pair of knock-around Reebok, and headed to the convenience store for a ginger-ale, Pepto, and soup. The low temperatures of the night had a mellow affect on my queasiness.

The ale felt like hocus pocus dripping down my throat into the pit of my stomach. I pulled away from the store's lot, figuring that I could catch up with Keri this time of night. With all the things I learned about Keri's mental vacations and the death threats made against me in her journal, I did not want to face her alone. I told Limbo in my note that I'd be back in ten minutes, another five wouldn't hurt. Keri couldn't dodge me tonight.

"As usual." I put the car in park. Her car wasn't here. I swear every time I come here she's not here. I took my gun from the trunk and went inside to pen her a formal eviction notice.

Now I had a name for the fragrance that tickled my senses when I went in -- Bond no. 9 Wall Street. Written on my foyer wall, in red lipstick were the words, "Good-bye for now!" The exclamation point made my hairs stand. I was okay with the goodbye -- ecstatic even. But for now, part frightened me, making my stomach upset again. I ran through the house like I was trying out for the fifty yard dash. The finish line was in the half-bath. I hugged the porcelain and puked some more. I didn't think there was anything left inside of me to come out.

All of Keri's belongings were gone. I made sure every window was locked then went to the spice cabinet to make sure her journal was gone, too. The door wasn't shut flush. My heart tap danced on my rib cage. I gulped in a breath before I opened the door.

My extra set of keys was the reason the door was partially open this time.

CHAPTER FORTY-SEVEN

The man anchored between the house was invisible to Murdock, from where he stood. He stuffed the gun in his waist band then pulled his keys out. He went to the top of the porch stairs and pointed the key ring at his car.

The gun men laid their weapons across Murdock's hood and trunk and then let loose. The first six bullets hit Murdock in the chest, bringing him to his knees. The next ten turned his thighs into spaghetti.

Murdock tumbled down eight steps, landing on his belly facing the neighbor's shrubbery that took on the form of an army of assassins.

Jazmyne hit the floor when the bullets rang out. Her picture window turned into shattered glass. She crawled across the room, unplugged the lamps, and dialed 911.

Murdock aimed the .456 at the malicious shrub. "That's all you lames got?" he squeezed the trigger until the barrel kicked back. "Punk motherfuckers can't hurt -- ", it was hard for him to breathe. His chest t felt like it had been flattened. He thought his legs were on fire. "--you can't hurt me." His words were only loud enough for him to hear. "I'm...a...mother...moth...rider." His vision blurred, useless trigger pulling again.

The two men stood to finish Murdock off. The shotgun toter waved them off as he climbed the banister, then he came down the porch stairs.

Blood stained Murdock's teeth."...rider...Cuz..."

He put the shotgun's barrel on Murdock's back, pulling the trigger three consecutive times. With each blast Murdock's body levitated off the concrete.

He stood over Murdock. "A life for a life, namean?"

The three men climbed in the black regal and drove away as the sirens drew near.

CHAPTER FORTY-EIGHT

Limbo

We rushed to through the emergency room's automatic doors. The place was filled to capacity with injured and sick people. A LPN had her head buried in a computer.

"Excuse me, Miss," I said with as much patience as possible.

She continued to type, never acknowledging our presence.

"Bitch, don't act like you don't hear me talking to you." I leaned across her cluttered desk. She looked into my bloodshot eyes then turned away.

C-Mack shut her computer off.

"I'm gonna try this again." All my patience was gone. "My friend, Murdock, was brought in an hour ago. He was shot. How is he?"

"She don't know nothing," Trigger said. "Get us somebody down here we can talk to."

She reached for the computer. C-Mack stopped her.

She pried her wrist out of strong grip. "I understand that you guys are upset, but if yins want some help the first thing I'll need is the use of my computer." She turned it back on. "Now what's the patient's name?"

"Murdock" Trigger said.

Keyboard typing. The blue screen went blank then it filled with information.

"Yes, multiple gun shot trauma. Your friend was rushed to surgery upon arrival. I'm showing that he's still in surgery. I'll notify the resident physician to let him know the patient's family is here. In the mean time I need one of you to follow the red line over there to Patient Intake and give the receptionist there any information you have on your friend, like his real name for starters. We need to locate his past medical records, it's imperative to his life.

The four hours we'd been waiting seemed like four hundred years. All of our nerves had blown fuses. Jayzmyne arrived carrying a camera a few moments after Rhapsody. Jayzmyne had been sobbing since the time she showed up. We all listened to her version of what happened then fell silent. I don't think two words were spoken between the five of us in over three hours. I patted Baby Girl's back. "Take Jazmyne out front for me for some air, she's stressing me out."

Rhapsody threw her arms around the emotionally traumatized woman and led her through the automatic doors.

C-Mack slid in the seat beside me. "It's gonna be hell to pay when I find out who done this."

A lump formed in my throat. "On my gangster, homey…somebody's gonna feel my pain. Why Jazmyne got a camera?"

Trigger flipped through a Don Diva magazine. "She's gonna take pictures everyday she said, so Murdock can see the progress of his recovery. To motivate him. You know how fragile and sensitive Jazmyne is about Dock."

The elevator door slid open. A group of doctors stepped out and went their separate way. One slim man dressed in green scrubs came over to see us. My heart tried to jump out of my chest.

"Are you all the family of Daryl Watson?" He looked over his rimless frames.

Trigger sat the magazine down and stood. "Yeah, how is her?"

Me and C-Mack were on our feet now, too. I didn't like the look on the Doc's face. He had one of those expressions that said, I'm exhausted and I don't know how to break the news.

Doc wiped his glasses with a handkerchief then shoved them back on his round face. "Mr. Watson is in critical condition. He's still recovering from general anesthesia at this time. The extend of his injuries are severe."

Rhapsody and Jazmyne came inside, Jazmyne burst out crying when she saw the doctor.

Doc looked at her. "It's been a long night for all of us. I understand that you all are worried and equally concerned, but the best thing for everybody is to go home and get some rest."

When Rhapsody, took my arm. I could hear Jazmyne behind me, to my left, sniveling. I focused on Doc. "I'm not going a damn place until I know what's up with my homeboy. That's my best friend you just got done cutting on. There's only two things you can do for me, give it to me raw, and lead the way to Murdock. That's the order I want it done in."

"ICU has strict visiting regulations. "At -- "

C-Mack grabbed the name tag hanging from the doc's scrubs. "Doctor Kevin Scott, you don't want no trouble. I don't want to be the cause of your troubles. Break the rules, it won't be your first time."

He took his time and looked at each one of us over he glasses. "Okay, okay, but only one person for a couple of minutes."

He hit the elevator's up button. The metal doors eased open.

Doctor Scott stepped into the mechanical box. So did me, Trigger, and C-Mack.

"What floor, Doc?" Trigger unfastened a button at his shirt collar.

He looked at us and sighed.

A SUV with government plates glided to a stop outside of Conemaugh. Thurston flicked cigar ashes out the window. "Stewart, you and Rawlings get the good cop bad cop part in the script."

Both agents in the back seat nodded.

Another nod from the passenger's seat.

"Nester, you follow my lead."

"Mr. Watson can point out the yellow brick road that'll lead us President Bush's bullet proofs."

"You mean missile proof." Rawlings tightened his shoe laces.

The ghetto is a breeding ground for killers. Gang bangers. We don't have no idea of the army forming against us right here in the United States. When those vest came up missing, even the CIA thought it was the work of international terrorists. It wouldn't surprise me none if the Crips and Bloods has nuclear weapons stashed basements of projects across the country."

Thurston slurped on the tip of his chewed cigar. Each agent weighed Rawlings' logic on the scale of their mind.

"You and your theories." Nester turned and eyed Rawlings.

"We're talking about your basic curb punks here. They're not smart enough to plot on that scope."

"My theories, " Nester said, half under his breath, half above it. "The size box you're stuck in amazes me. These same punks were smart enough to make each of us millionaires. We couldn't think of a way to do it ourselves so we use this badge-_" He flashed his government shield. "--to steal it. I respect these guys. They were intelligent enough to acquire vests that not even the CIA can get. Don't sleep on these punks."

"I don't totally agree either. Your argument has merits." Thurston shut the engine off. "But I don know that Adams has something to do with the stolen vest."

At the mention of Adams' name, Stewart came to life. "I've been wanting to come face-to-face with that bastard. If I can get away with it. I'd kill him over a period of ten days, for what he done to Curlew."

"I'd like to kick a crevice in his as myself." Rawlings stepped out the SUV and stretched.

CHAPTER FORTY-NINE
Limbo

Intensive Care Unit smelled heavy of industrial disinfectant. The dull hallway was cluttered with echoes of respirators and monitors that beeped every few seconds.

Doctor Scott stopped us in the middle of hall to prep us for we were about to see. "There is no good way for me to say this."

"Save the medical lingo, Doc," C-Mac said. "Give us the uncut version, in plain English."

Doc pushed his glasses further up the bridge of his nose. "I don't believe in God, only medicine and science. Mr. Watson's will to live is impressive. Even with medicine and medical facts, I didn't think he would survive through such a complicated surgery." Doc kneaded his temples. "Mr. Watson fooled me, which is difficult to do. We had to amputate his legs from the highs down."

I shed a tear for the first time since me and Murdock was little boys.

In Dr. Scott's field, he'd seen many tears. Mine were no different from his expression. He continued. "It's none of my business where Mr. Watson came across a presidential issued armored vest, but it saved what remains of his life. His complications stem from blunt force that tips that scale at about a thousand pounds per pressure. He was shot with three different weapons. Two of which, at an intermediate range. The muzzle velocity of those two weapons variants between thirty-five hundred to five thousand feet per second. The vest stopped the bullets, but it was no match for the impact."

Doctor Scott acknowledged a colleague with a thumb-up as she passed us. "Imagine an angry elephant stomping on your chest," he said, turning back to us. "The force broke Mr. Watson's ribs. The ones that weren't broken were fractured. His left lung was violently damaged from bone fragments. We had to perform a pneumorectomy."

"You did what?" C-Mack asked.

"We removed the lung." His tone had no feeling in it.

My voice trembled. "So you're saying that Murdock will need medical attention the rest of his life?"

"In my professional opinion, I think Mr. Watson's will to live will abandon him in less than twenty-four hours."

The straightforwardness of his words crashed into me like an out-of-control elephant.

Trigger clenched onto Doc's elbow. "The surgery was a success right? Right, Doc?"

Doctor Scott wiggled himself free." Those were the injuries sustained from two weapons. Mr. Watson was shot several times in his back at point-blank range. The fire pattern suggested a shotgun. Just as in the case of the other bullets, they never made it past the vest. However, the blunt force knocked his spinal cord to pieces, causing irreparable damage and internal hemorrhaging. With intensive spinal damage, Mr. Watson can no longer breathe on his own. He's breathing now with a ventilator.

Doc rubbed his temples again. I could see the fatigue in posture.

"You can't go inside Mr. Watson's room, but you all can see him from the observation window. If you will follow me, I'll let you see him now." Doc scratched his close-crop blond hair, rubbed the rattail at the nape of his neck and led the way.

Beneath a maze of tubes and wires, Murdock laid there with his eyes closed. I could tell he was in pain from the way his face was twisted. There was a change in the beep patterns dancing across his monitor.

Murdock knew we were here. I wanted him to know how sorry I was. That, if we could trade places, it would be me in his bed. I wanted to tell him that I was tripping when we got into it last month. I pressed my forehead on the window, while tears escaped me. "Is he suffering?"

Murdock's eyes opened.

M lips quivered.

His dancing beep went flat and cried a steady roar.

Doctor Scott ran to Murdock's bedside, Medical Assistants came from every direction.

C-Mack's fists were so tight his knuckles were white, Trigger was somewhere between oblivion and emptiness. My stomach knotted up like C-Mack's fist. I could feel my heart beating in the region of my feet.

The flat-line wouldn't dance again. After the third time Doctor Scott yelled out "clear" and stuck the paddles on Murdock's chest, C-Mack pulled me away from the window and led me to the elevator.

My cell phone rang. Now wasn't the time. I didn't want to be bothered, but I answered anyway, "Hello."

"Not only don't take threats lightly, my patience wears thin quick. It's taking you too long to visit the city of brotherly love. Your right-hand man for mine."

"We just got married. To death do us apart." I hung up and the last ear tumbled down my face.

The elevator opened and we were confronted by four men waving FBI badges.

CHAPTER FIFTY

Rhapsody's sneakers squeaked across the tiled floor. "If there is something I can say about this hospital, the cafeteria food is decent and its medical staff is the best in the state. Murdock will be fine."

"I don't know what I'd do if I lost him. He's my heart." Jazmyne smeared away a tear on a soaked napkin as they approached the counter.

"What would you like?" Rhapsody dug her wallet from her handbag.

"I...I'm too upset to eat anything, you go ahead."

Rhapsody put a hand on her cocked hip. "At least get something to drink. I know there's not much liquid left inside of here-", she poked Jazmyne. " -- you need to refill your tank if you expect to get some crying mileage."

Jayzmyne smiled, but she felt miserable.

They started their journey back to the lobby through a maze of spotless hallways. Rhapsody spooning mouthfuls of yogurt -- Jazmyne refilling her cry tank.

The tears started again. "It happened so fast. In one breath we were enjoying each others company, the next bullets were ripping my living room apart."

Rhapsody held her and prayed that she would never have to go through an experience like this. After being a witness to the opposite side of the coin, Rhapsody decided that she would never shoot anyone else.

"I just want to tell him that I'm sorry."

"It's not your fault, Jazmyne. Don't punish yourself."

Her eyes dripped like a leaky faucet. "I could of done something to help him. He wouldn't been hurt so bad if is did."

The squeaky sneaker's came to a stop. Rhapsody lifted Jazmyne's head and could feel the pain parading in her fragile face. "Don't beat yourself up. The people who did this to Murdock weren't rookies. If you had done anything else beside call the police, you'd be in the bed next to Murdock's or worse.

Girl, you have to stay strong not for yourself but for Murdock, too."

Jazmyne hugged Rhapsody and let it all out. "I can't lose him. There's so many things that I have to tell him. She sniveled. "I was going to tell him tonight that I'm pregnant."

"Congratulation, girl" Rhapsody gave their hug an extra squeeze and had a few silent thoughts.

"Every time, it never fails. It's my life story, every time something or someone good happens to me, something bad comes along and cannels it out."

They followed the green arrows directing them to the lobby. Rhapsody couldn't imagine being in Jazmyne's shoes. Not being able to say the things she needed to someone she loves. Blaming herself for a tragic misfortune. After settling in the comforts of the lobby's leather seats, both women entertained their private thoughts.

Thirty minutes had come and gone since Limbo and his crew followed the doctor into the elevator.

"What's taking them so long?" Jazmyne fiddled with her camera. Her face was swollen to a puff.

"I don't know, but I have an idea, you just have to promise you won't cry.

CHAPTER FIFTY-ONE

Limbo

"Freeze!" A guy wearing an FBI sweat shirt aimed his gun at us.

He three other drew their guns, too. "Turn around and place your hands on the wall," a huge guy, chewing in the end of a cigar said. He stood tall as C-Mack, but he was every bit of three hundred pounds.

I heard one of the agents call the big guy Thurston while they were frisking us. We were lined up beside a Pepsi machine. My hands were on the wall when Thurston whispered in my ear.

"I can't prove it, but I know you're responsible for Agent Curlew's death. I promise you'll pay for it in due time. For now, I wanna know how does a common street thug get his hands on armored vests made especially for the president?"

He dug in my pockets, took my money out and shoved it in his own. "All seven vests mysteriously d disappeared, last year. Just like I'm sure about Curlew. I'm sure you hoodlums have the other six jackets." Thurston put his massive thumb on a pressure point behind my ear. "Where are they?"

The pain was excruciating, but I refused to let him see weakness. I thought about how I just watched my fiend die and went numb allover.

"This is bullshit!" Trigger called out over his shoulder. "Arrest us or leave us the fuck alone."

Trigger's head crashed into the scattered gray wall. "Shut up, punk." The agent bowed Trigger in a kidney. Trigger went to his hands and knees. "You punks get a thrill out of killing agents. Curlew was my partner."

I could feel C-Macks' temperature go skyward. It was in his eyes.

"Easy, Mack. These lams fucked up. We can afford to hire Johnny Cochran for this civil suit."

The agent reared back and kicked Trigger with the whole house. "The next field goal is for your ass, Limbo."

C-Mack knotted his fist and spun around. "Fuck, Cochran. They ain't got no grounds to shoot. Let's thump, fuck that brutality shit."

Ding!

The elevator opened, and out came Rhapsody and Jazmyne.

Rhapsody stepped between me, C-Mack, and Thurston. "What the hell is going in here? Somebody show me a warrant."

The other agents holstered their guns. Jazmyne helped Trigger to his feet.

Thurston looked down on Rhapsody as if she had stolen his fifteen minutes of fame. He glared at her while he addressed me. "Remember what I told you, Adams. I never break a promise."

Rhapsody stood her ground. "We'll get a restraining order first thing in the morning. While my lawyer files a class action against the FBI--". She examined the United States Government's seal on the agents sweat shirt. " -- for racial profiling and anything else that'll stick."

A brilliant flash burst from Jazmyne's camera. It came in handy after all.

"Come on, Thurston." An agent wearing a worn-out shirt with a button missing at the collar nudged the bigger man. "Let's see what information we can squeeze from the gimp down the hall."

Before the four agents went through ICU entrance, Thurston said, "Adams, you can pick your money up at the Government building during banking hours. Please don't forget what I said."

Rhapsody cleared her throat. "Don't you forget what I said."

C-Mack threw an arm around Rhapsody's shoulder. "Thanks for saving me from catching a case."

"It's cool."

Jazmyne fell out in the elevator when I told her that Murdock died. Her anguish carried her beyond the range of known values.

CHAPTER FIFTY-TWO

Keri

Having my own place meant I no longer had to worry about someone violating my space, snooping through my cupboards. I sat my purse on the sofa and started towards the spare bedroom. From the entrance's threshold, I lingered on an array of torn photos collaged on the surface of the walls -- I had yet to cover the ceiling. This room became a shrine to my Jayme. Since I moved in tow weeks ago, the majority of my time is spent here watching her, listening closely to him. I shed every stitch of clothing in the doorway. I have to be natural, and pure to enter here. I went over to the eavesdropping equipment, powered it, and turned up the volume. Then I took my rightful place in the center of the room surrounded by thousands of images of Jayme. Sitting like a Buddhist Monk, I removed each item from the drugstore bag, placing them in front of me. Glue -- Elmer's, petroleum jelly, and a package with blue writing that read, 'Photos do not bend'.

Car tires rolled over gravel. A car door slammed shut. Seconds later, Limbo spoke to someone he addressed as Hershel.

I slowly turned my head towards the equipment. Its recording reels began to spin. Back to what I was doing. I dumped a hundred reprints before me. Limbo and Jayme were in the photos holding hands.

Static blurted from the equipment. Where every Limbo is, his location is interfering with the signal. Elevator. Tunnel. Any place like that.

I focused back on the reprints. Jayme and Limbo were happy together, smiling. The photo was oozing with love. Then it started to happen again. Limbo's crooked smile turned flat and unfriendly. His eyes aimed at me like a double-barrel shotgun. Then he started to cuss me. Threaten me. Hurt my feeling.

"Bitch, let me outta this picture. If I ever find a way outta here, I'm gonna kill you. I promise."

I clamped my eyes, covered my ears. His torment was muffled but I had a pretty good idea of what he was saying. After a long minute, he piped down. I racked one eye and moved my hands a little.

"Die a thousand deaths, you psychotic, bitch! Open your eyes, dammit. I know you can hear me. Stay away from my Rhapsody. Stay away from us."

Now I've had it. Her name is Jayme and she's mine. I ripped him off the photo,

"Don't you do that, let me outta of here."

I turned his face to the carpet --he hates that. I violently started to tear him away from the other ninety0nine. He had the nerve to insult me the whole time. I had only torn Limbo from thirty, maybe forty photos when the static cleared and voiced purred through the eavesdropping equipment. The reels had to be dizzy from spinning so fast.

"--you already know the business. Ride or die ain't just slick words to me. It's an all day, everyday demonstration. I'm with you wherever, however." That was the one the call C-Mack. I could tell from his southern babble.

Limbo: "This the last run. I don't want to put nobody else in my business at this late date. The balloon is out the question, the weather won't allow it. I say we stuff a smuggler, drive it here ourselves and be done with it. Or I can cut the checks now...done deal."

Trigger: "Cuz, if nothing else, I wanna finish this for Murdock. Hoe wouldn't want us to fall short of our prize. Only a week after Dock's funeral and you suggest that we quit. Riders don't quit, homey. To me the idea of that is like hitting the best pussy in the world and pulling out before you nut. Nah, homey, it don't go down like that. I want that prize just like I gotta have that nut."

Limbo: "One thing we all know is that Murdock wouldn't agree to muling or quitting." He laughed. "I can hear him now talking about 'we big boys, big boys make big boy moves. Pay somebody to bring the work in. We ain't got nothing to lose but our freedom to the Federal Sentencing Guidelines' then he would say, I ain't with that transporting shit."

Trigger: "You sound just like him. I'mma miss that niggah." A pause. "What would he say when it's all said and done, Cuz?"

Limbo: "He would say lets ride. This the move, me and Trigger will make the trip. C-Mack, you hold things down around here."

C-Mack: "When is it going down?"

Their conversation lasted another twenty minutes then I powered the eavesdropping equipment down. It finally served it's purpose. Thurston would be jubilant.

I popped the top off the jar and dug out a wad of petroleum. The ointment soother my tender skin as I smeared it over a portrait of Jayme tattooed to my breast. Sticky stuff in one hand, photos of Jayme in the other. I went to my artistic collage and began to paste. "This Thanksgiving will be the best ever. Smile if you agree, Jayme."

She stared at me from a thousand sets of dirty-green eyes.

"You have such a beautiful smile."

CHAPTER FIFTY-THREE
Limbo

"Hello." I held the phone between an ear and a shoulder while I secured my closet safe.

"May I speak with Ms. Rhapsody Parrish."

"She's away for the holiday. What's up though?"

"I'm Donna Troutman from PPH."

"PPH? I never heard of that," I said as I scratched the initials on paper.

"Planned Parenthood. I'm -- "

"And what is this concerning?"

"Patient information is not privy to others unless patients give prior consent. Could you have her call me at her earliest convenience?"

She gave me her contact information.

"I'll let her know you called."

"Thank you, happy holiday."

CHAPTER FIFTY-FOUR
Rhapsody

Tuesday, two days before Thanksgiving, the weather in Virginia was in the single digits. The heart inside this Ford isn't worth a damn.

Tara ended her phone call and turned to me. "Sprinkle said to pull in the warehouse, she's a few minutes away."

"Did you get that?" I aimed my words a t a brooch clasped to my blouse.

Agent Rawlings confirmed that he and the others had heard the information that Tara had just given, through my micro ear-piece. Then he went on to say, "You know, Johanson, you shook me some that night at the hospital. For a minute there, I was thoroughly convinced that you went Janus-faced on us."

Toe wiggle. "My parents didn't raise a two-faced child. This is a dirty, immoral job...sometimes you have to put on a good show. What I'm doing is working, if I had you fooled."

Agent Rawlings and I shared a few more fraudulent comments then I rubbed my hand together in front of the heat vent. "The air team and ground units are in place. It's up to us now."

"It'll be like give Similac to a greedy baby." Tara wheeled the Ford onto the industrial road that led to our meeting place -- an abandoned warehouse.

My ear piece came to life. "Johanson we have just established a visual on you.

We drove into the warehouse, I processed the room. Barren, no signs of foul play.

Rawlings spoke to me again. "Johanson, a Ford identical in color and make to your vehicle just entered the grounds."

I told Tara that Phoebe and Trent were in the vicinity.

She nodded.

I wasn't feeling this for the first time. I just wanted to get it over with and put this life behind me so that I could move on. I could smell the dampness and oil stains in the concrete floor inside our car. Lately my sense of smell was bionic. I could smell a full course mea a state away.

A navy Ford entered, parking three feet away from us. "The gangs all here."

"Yup." Tara and Trent shared a smile followed by a slight nod. "You ready?"

Boy was I ready to put this behind me. I whispered into my brooch, "Agent Shepard has exited the vehicle, move on my cue."

Trent kept staring at me while Phoebe and Tara talked, the made me uneasy. I put my hand o my Glock to calm my dancing nerves. From that point on, I watched him from our car, he watched me from theirs. I rolled the window down some and listened.

"--how do you know that we didn't short change if you don't count the money?"

"If I thought you were the type to short me, we wouldn't be doing business. But you could say I'm counting it." Phoebe placed the briefcase on the scale. "Every bill has a different weight. Hundreds weight one –point-two grams. A million in hundreds weighs what then?"

Tara looked at Phoebe in amazement. "Twenty-six point four pounds."

"Plus two pounds for the briefcase."

Tara shifter her gaze to the digital read out. "Twenty-eight, four."

"One million on the nose."

Trent watched me.

Phoebe opened her trunk. From what I could tell, I think she was peeling the carpet back.

"Sixty bricks of the best coke on this coast." I heard Phoebe say. They exchanged car keys then waved for Trent and I to come out of the cars.

We both walked up on the tail end of Tara and Phoebe conversation

"Call me when you're ready to do this again." Phoebe said.

Trent extended his hand to me. "We all can't keep meeting like this. It doesn't always have to be business."

"I prefer business." A breeze pushed through the room, fanning around the smell of oil. My stomach was starting to protest. "Hanging out with you guys is bad for your health."

Phoebe laughed and rubbed the shoulder she been shot in the night they went out together, or should I say attempted to go out?

"Chad told the truth about you," he said.

My heart stuttered. "And what truth did he tell?"

"All work, no play."

"I can do all the playing I want once I'm multi."

Phoebe put her arm around his waist. "Ambition is a turn on for him ain't that right, Trent?"

"It ranks with intelligence and sexy women." He penetrated me with his rusty color eyes.

I blushed. "Thanks, flattery will get you everywhere." I yanked out my Glock. "But where you're going flattery will make you somebody's bitch. You're under arrest."

The sound of helicopters hung overhead. SWAT crashed through surrounding windows. The ground units rushed in with their weapons drawn. With all the commotion going on, the only thing that registered was everyone shouting for Trent and Phoebe to "Get Down!"

Tara fell to the oil-stained floor unconscious when Phoebe snuffed her. I turned my gun on Phoebe. She wasn't frightened now, like she wasn't in the hotel room when we first met.

"Bitch, this the second time you pointed a gun at me. I gave you a break the first time."

"Don't do nothing stupid," I said, "these people will kill you."

"I don't give a fuck."

The look on her face told me that she was going to be gunned down. The other agents closed the distance with caution.

"Relax, Phoebe," Trent said, "this is entrapment, we'll be out by midnight." He slapped me so hard and quick, I never saw it coming. I'd never been hit like that. My spittle stretched around to my ear. My eyes watered. I could smell his sweaty palm stained in my face.

352

Tara was regaining consciousness while Phoebe was being cuffed. I found my sense, but I could tell that my thin face had been dented. Agent Rawlings moved in to apprehend Trent.

I shook as much of the blow off as I could. "I got him, Rawlings." I grabbed Rawlings' cuffs and kneed Jerico in the groin. He squirmed on the gritty floor. I dropped my knee on the center of his back, squeezing the cuffs around his wrist until they wouldn't click anymore.

"I'll hunt you down and pay you back, if -- "

"You have the right to remain silent." I banged his head against the ground. "You have the right to rot in prison." His head met the ground again and again. I took all my problems out on him. He should have kept his hand to himself. All I can remember is my face stinging and hearing Rawlings say, "Okay, Johanson, he's had enough."

My face was bruised, I shoved the mirror back in my purse and turned onto Tara's street. We had been quiet for several miles at a time during our long ride home. When the silence did break, it was polluted with Tara's complaining. "You should have shot her face off," she would say. I'd let her know that she should relax. A few months from now, we would be laughing about the one-hitter that Sprinkle put on her. Although, I didn't really mean we. My ties would be severed tonight.

"Fuck you, Rhapsody. I don't find that shit funny," she said more than once.

I parked in front of her high-rise. She got out and slammed the door without saying goodbye. That was the first time since we've known each other that we parted ways without wishing well. Everything around me is changing. From Tara's I drove to the post office in search of an all-night mail-drop. My trunk light shined in the night when I unlatched it. Staring into my cluttered trunk, I focused on a small box that seemed to be waiting on me. It was time -- long overdue.

My loquacious inner voice started nagging again. Don't do this to us, Jayme.

I placed my service revolver in the box first.

You're freaking screwing up everything we've worked for.

My badge.

Mom and Dad aren't going to be thrilled by this unthinkable decision. He's a nigger for Christ's Sake.

The security clearance card.

They're not going to let us go. Didn't you hear what Tara said? We know too much.

"Shut the hell up. I told you that I'm running things now."

"You talking to me?" A guy walking a dog -- a mean looking dog -- glared at me.

"No, excuse me. I was talking to myself."

"I didn't think so, ain't that right, Malice?" He rubbed the dog. It growled. "They got a place for bitches that talk to they self." He walked off.

The last item I put in the box was a video tape. The tape will allow me to die of old age and not someone's bullet. I wish I could package up the voice, too. Unfortunately, I'm stuck with it for the duration. I addressed the box to Thurston, then let it slide down the mail shoot. I picked up my order from the caterer's and went home.

Limbo looked at me when I walked through the door. He stopped feeding the Tiger sharks and stared at me as if I were intruding on a sacred feeding of his dangerous fish. "What are you doing here?"

"Once I got there, I was uncomfortable. Felt out of place, Tara had family coming from everywhere."

354

Limbo held a doomed mouse by its tail, taunting the hungry sharks.

I went on. "Seeing the spirit they was in made me want to be with my family -- you."

He dropped the poor mouse in the tank. I used to close my eyes, but I'd gotten used to the slayings. Men and their fetish to watch death. The mouse pumped its tiny legs in an attempt to swim nowhere. The three sharks attacked before the rodent could figure which way to go. Their upturned tails and pointy fins sloshed through the water as their triangular teeth shredded the vermin. Blood stained the water until the powerful filters sucked up the mess.

I could hear mice scratching at the side of their box prison sitting on my coffee table. "Since we're not actually going to spend Thanksgiving together, I made arrangements for us to have our own private dinner, right now."

He came down off the ladder. Planned Parenthood called for you yesterday." He watched for a reaction. He waited for a response.

My features were impassive. God, I wondered what the results were. Positive could be both good and bad. Negative could solve all my worries.

"What they want?" He picked up the box of mice.

"'I'm starting the pill. We go at it like teenagers."

He started up the ladder. I grabbed his belt loop. "No, wash your nasty hands, and come help me get this food out of the car."

"What the fuck happened to you?" He stepped down. He turned my head by my chin, examining my bruised face.

My toes began to tap inside my shoes. "Tara's obnoxious little nephew was playing with a soccer ball in the house. I swear he deliberately kicked that darn ball in my direction. I could have killed him."

"Looks like somebody slapped the shit outta you."

We had a wonderful dinner with all the Thanksgiving trimmings to go with it. Dessert was even better, we made love into the morning hours.

I awoke the next morning with my skin sticky from cranberry sauce. My patch of pubic hair was matted together with pumpkin pie. Last night was awesome. Limbo handled me with so much feeling and tenderness. I'll never forget the warmth of his voice when he confessed his love to me last night.

The shower was running and I could see Limbo's silhouette behind the stained-glass door from the bed. I climbed in the warm water with him. "What's gotten you up so early?"

He turned to face me, stopping the water from pelting me. I'm hitting the highway this morning.

I stiffened with disappointment. I'd planned a movie and leftovers for us. "The holiday isn't until tomorrow."

He moved, the water sprayed me. "That's why I'm bouncing today."

"I want to move away from here, Big Daddy."

"Thought about it myself." His locks clung to his sculpted body like wet mop strings.

"I don't think you understand me, let's leave the state...the country."

"The country is out of the question. I'll never go that far away from my sons. Rhapsody, where is all this coming from?"

I thought about what I wanted to say. "I want our life together to thrive off as many opportunities as possible. You're going legit, why not open your sports bars and publishing company in a yard you haven't took a dump in?" I took the wash rag and wiped away some soap he missed around his ears. "This place can't offer me a single job in the psychology field. It's like I went to school for nothing. We both need a big city to move and shake in."

CHAPTER FIFTY-FIVE

Limbo

"I'll be in there in a few, Cuz," I said.

"It's on." Trigger put me on hold.

I scratched my neck realizing that something was missing.

"Uh, Limbo, I was thinking, maybe -- "

"I'll call you back. I forgot something." I hung up and called home.

Rhapsody answered with her seductress voice. Her "Hello" was tender and colored with sex appeal.

"Baby Girl, I left my necklace. Go upstairs and get it, I'm turning around now."

"Which one do you want?"

"The one with the ankh charm."

minutes later I walked through my front door and
sody was wearing a checkered school-girl skirt.
oout those damn skirts that drives me mad. Maybe
ed innocence and mixture of naughtiness. She sat
on the couch with her feet propped on the glass surface of our
coffee table. She wasn't wearing any panties. My necklace
hung from her fingernail, the ankh strangled itself between her
legs.

"Is this what you want?"

Talk about the key to life.

I swallowed the lump growing in my throat. I felt light-
headed. It had to be because all the blood in my body broke
the sound barrier rushing to Big Daddy.

Rhapsody came to me. She eased the necklace over my
locks. The front door was still open. The morning light
shining in on us. She locked her eyes on mine and went to her
knees to swallow my other lump. I fell in love with Rhapsody
for the second time at this moment. She never used her hands.
She pulled my zipper down with her teeth. I don't know how
she did it, but she pulled Big Daddy from the confines of boxer
shorts, through the zipper hole with her mouth and took me
there.

With my creamy fluid gathered in the corners of her
mouth, she turned around and placed her palms on the third
step, leading to the second floor.

"Give me a little bit before you go. A quickie." She
wagged her white heat.

I looked through the screen window behind me. My
neighbor waved as she walked by carrying a bag of groceries. I
smiled returning the hello. She couldn't see Rhapsody because
the aluminum portion of the screen door shunned outsider's
views.

She wagged again. "Limbo."

Her peach was raised like it was swollen. All it took was for me to see the pink part.

I backed out the driveway shaking my head at Rhapsody waving at me from the porch. "Girl is something else." She had drained me in less than ten minutes.

CHAPTER FIFTY-SIX

Agent Nester applied pressure to the gas pedal. He switched his two-way radio to a secured channel, then spoke into the mic. "Limbo is now leaving the Richmond area, for the second time, in the vehicle matching the description and bearing the same registration as before."

"Run it again," Thurston said.

"Teal Chevrolet, Pennsylvania registration Xavier, Zebra, Bob, fifty-three, forty-four." Nester kept his distance from Limbo in the morning traffic.

"Stay with him," Thurston said, "We must confirm that Adams leaves the area."

One township on top of an abundance of minutes slipped by before Nester radioed Thurston again.

"Uh, Thurston, I've partially identified Thomas 'Trigger' Green entering the vehicle with Adams. Both occupants are traveling out of town -- west bound.

CHAPTER FIFTY-SEVEN

Limbo

Each time I cover this last stretch of highway, a deep case of nostalgia wrecks into the core of my soul when Downtown Cleveland's night lights come into view. Not the mere homesick of missing the place responsible for my grooming, but of being home and not being able to go to my Mama's home. It's been a long time, but tonight that would change.

I respected my Mama's call and it hurt me like hell to watch her and my sister from a distance. Like clockwork, 7:30 Monday through Friday Mama would come trudging down the street with my sister Erykah in tow. They would sit at the bus stop, Mama putting the finishing touches on Erika's hair while she swung her tiny legs from the bench. Erykah used to scrunch her face when Mama licked her thumb and wiped Erika's face. I hated it when she put spit on my face, calling herself cleaning it. I always wondered why Mama didn't at least buy a car with the money I religiously sent home every month. The years changed and Mama started leaving home alone in the mornings. Erika's legs had grown long enough for her feet to touch the concrete from the bus stop bench and she was off to school every morning with a group of friend.

I'll never forget when me and my little sister had our first conversation. The last interaction we had was me pushing some food in her mouth and she was wrapping her tiny hand around my finger. It was "96" Erykah was tender and ten and my heart. I'm cruising the block in my customized wagon, tinted windows rolled down about an inch. I parked a few feet away from her bus stop as I did every morning. I spotted her in my door mirror talking to another little girl, I learned was named Teede.

They walked by the car, both clenching books. Erykah was saying, "My Mama says if you don't get better grades, I can't be friends with you, Tee."

"Your ma be bugging."

"You just have to understand her. She demands excellence from me. Everybody that I'm allowed to be around has to compliment the way she's raising me. Mama refuses to settle for less from me or anyone dealing with me. Why you think she's hell on my teachers?"

Tee shrugged.

"The same reason she hit your mother with twenty moral-and-principle questions before I was even allowed to walk to he bus stop with you."

Tee straightened the back of Erika's collar. "Man, I'm glad she's your ma and not mine."

"Don't worry about that, Tee, just get your grades together. You're my friend and I don't want my Mama to separate us 'cause she will. She ain't joking."

I was bobbing my head to Bone, Thugs and Harmony's, First of the Month, which was only two days away.

A group of boys came towards me. I'd seen them around the game room during school hours.

Erykah squeezed her eyes shut. "Shoot, I don't feel like being bothered."

I turned the music off.

Tee looked at the boys. "Don't pay no attention. What does your ma want from you?"

My sister is too intelligent for her age. Keeping my eye on her over the years I learned that she was smart enough for older children to resent her and for her peers to be confused by her.

Erykah hit Tee with a look much too mature for a ten-year-old. "For me to be the best at whatever I choose to do."

There's no doubt about it that's my Mama's child, with my Mama's philosophy on life embedded deep.

"Miss School of the Arts. What's up with it, Erykah?", a kid with braids said. There were three of them, in all. Reminded me of me, Murdock, and some of our other homeys in our bus stop days.

"Hi, Jordan."

He circled my sister and Tee as if they were prey. Jordan was cocky. "Don't hi me. What's up with them digits? Teede, I want yours too." He was now in back of them.

"These stuck up hoes think they too good for us, 'cause they go to that smart school," came out a chubby kids mouth with a fucked up hair cut.

"Who you calling a hoe?" Erykah said, "I don't see your Mama standing out here."

Tee's eyes widened as the chubby kid's pride swoll up in his chest.

"He ain't stutter," Jordan was saying in my sister's ear. "Ya'll both hoes...any you my hoe." He put his hands up Erika's skirt and snatched her underwear down to her boney knee caps. Her books fell to the ground. Some note book paper tumbled away with the morning breeze.

What the fuck did he do that for? I would of let the name calling go. I rushed from my car. They were laughing and calling my sister and Tee hoes.

I punched Jordan like he was a grown man. Knocked his foolish ass unconscious. That wasn't enough for me, driven by pure rage. I picked the punk up and slammed him in the hedges lining the tree lawn. Fuck it, me and the homey's would be waiting on big brothers and daddies tomorrow. Chubby and the other boy tried run. Before he could get away, I kicked a plug in his fat ass. I started to let some shots off in the air, but I didn't want to scare my sister.

I asked Erykah if she was all right. Tee was gathering the scattered books.

Erykah was embarrassed. She nodded while hiking her underwear back in place. "Thank you."

Her voice stole my heart. Delicate. Dainty. Confident. Pure. I heard her voice many times before, but never directed to me. We looked so much alike, but she had my Mama's acorn-shaped eyes.

"It's cool." My breathing evening back out, pulse easing back to calm.

Jordan peeled himself from the hedges and stumbled away after Tee cracked him over the head with a book.

I shoved my hands in my pocket and turned to leave.

"That's what big brothers are for, right?"

That voice. Erika's precious voice. She knew who I was. I stopped in mid stride. I stiffened. My heart banged against my rib cage like Bone-Thugs-N -Harmony banged in my ride. It took everything in me to turn around and face her again.

I was ashamed. "You know who I am?" I couldn't make eye contact so I chose to stare at her shoes and flowery socks.

"Minus the dreads, you don't look that much different from the picture Mama has. I never said anything to Mama, but I know you see me off to school most days."

"Is Mama--" I stepped to her then hesitated.

"It's okay." She assured me then came into my arms.

I took her off the feet trying to hug for the years I'd missed. I miss you and Mama so much."

"Then come home. Mama doesn't say it but she misses you, too. I knew it from the time I found out she sleeps with your picture under her pillow. Been doing it for a long time."

"I can't yet. One day I'll be home." I put her down.

For the next two years, I carried her and Tee back and forth to school. Even when I left the city to put my thing down in Johnstown we secretly kept in touch.

I wheeled the car onto Kinsman Avenue. "Tell your peoples I said what up." I turned off Kinsman onto 93 and glided to stop in front of Trigger's place.

"It's on." Trigger stretched. His ball cap shaded his eyes. "What time we pulling out?"

"Tomorrow. Sometimes after dinner, I wanna catch the night traffic. I'll hit you up about nine. We'll bounce at ten."

"It's on." He gave me a pound. "Enjoy your Thanksgiving, Cuz."

"You do the same." I watched Trigger bop up the drive way and disappear into a side door.

I called my partner, Little Bill, and told him to meet me. I drove over to St. Clair, dropped the car off to get stuffed. It was only a ten minute wait before Little Bill drove up.

He reached over and unlocked the door for me. "What's cracking?" he asked s I climbed in.

"Ain't shit." I pounded my clenched fish on top of his. "I was thinking about your brother T-Bone the other night. How is he?"

"Terrance is cool, he's got an escort service in ATL. He's doing big things in the dirty south."

"Legalized pimping. I knew that boy would -- "

"I met with Erykah last Sunday. She's really growing up."

"That girl been grown. What was wrong, LB?"

"Nothing, it's cool, we met at Tower City for lunch. She just needed some ends for some books. Nothing big. You must have a loyal mechanic to work on your car over the holiday." He rested his elbow on he armrest. Me and LB go back further than Huffy bikes and Hide-and-go-get-it. He's the only person, besides Elixir, who can see the wheels turn in my head now that Murdock is gone.

There was no need to respond to LB's comment. I watched the roadside from my window as we caught up on some other things.

We pulled in front of my mama's decomposing house.

LB shut the engine down. "This is a beautiful thing you're about to do. It's long overdue, but you shouldn't be coming here until you leave the game alone."

I let out a breath. "It's over, LB."

"Now you think I'm a fool right? I ran with you my whole life.

Before me and Spencer got shot up on that job, we were all thick as Serena Williams, Mack, Dock -- all of us. What's left of us is still thick. I know how you ride. It ain't a wrap."

"It's the last run. I'm cleaning my hands."

"Every hustler I know and had known always says it's his last play. I hope you're the one with the strength to wash your hands. You and C-Mack is the last ones still in the streets from our original set, Cuz." I wanna see you make it -- with your life. I'd hate to lose another good man."

"I'm here for the long haul, homey."

"Hope so."

I watched LB's taillights until his right blinker stuttered. With my Mama's package under arm, I walked up the old, squeaky porch steps. I thought the wood would give from the way it strained under my weight.

Standing face-to-face with a large door whose paint peeled and curled from age, I traced over my name that I carved in this door with Murdock's Chinese star. I got my ass kicked every time my Mama thought about the twenty extra dollars a month rent she had to pay for my vandalism. She thumped my ass every time she paid it, too.

The last time I faced this door it seemed like a wooden giant. Now it isn't so big and intimidating. I'll never forget the last time. I had just turned fourteen, showing my first signs of a mustache. Erykah was a colicky baby, but today it was spasmodic gas that caused my sister pain. She strained her lungs and wet her eyes because she was hungry. Colored water wasn't cutting it, she wanted milk.

Mama was on the neighbor's phone stretched from next door. She was doing her best to be civil with our welfare caseworker. "I don't want to hear your fucking thoughts on affirmative action. You don't know a damn thing about being a disadvantaged Black -- a single Black woman. Ms. Gabert, my food stamps are over ten days late. Hold on a minute." Mama covered the phone and said to me, "Pick your sister up and quiet that child. Don't you see I'm talking business? Give her a bottle."

"She doesn't want it. She keeps throwing it. Can't you see she's hungry?" We were all frustrated.

"You better watch your damn lip when you speak to me. I clothe you, feed you, and keep a roof over your head even if it ain't much. I will kick your ass, do you understand me?"

"Yes, ma'am, I apologize." I picked Erykah up from her make shift play pen. She reached out to me as I approached.

"That's a good example of how your lips better sound from now on."

"Yes, ma'am." I carried Erykah to the kitchen. Her sobbing was chopped in intervals now. I could hear my Mama fussing on the phone again.

"They couldn't have been issued or I would have had my stamps last week. That means I wouldn't be talking to you this week."

I blocked Mama out. My sister straddled on my hip with her puffy pamper that I had to change, because I noticed it needed to be done. I pulled the refrigerator open like something had changed since the last time I opened it.

Still empty.

Arm & Hammer. A gallon milk jug with a coroner of water in it. Ketchup. A Miracle Whip jar with scrapings on the side. An empty glass, and the damn light bulb.

Erykah looked at me with her faded-brown eyes. I looked at her. She burst out crying again. Babies have no understanding of no food.

"Shh." I rocked her. "Big brother gonna make it better from now on. -- promise." I kissed a salty tear away and sat her on the middle of the table. "Don't move. I'm finna fix you a wish meal. Wish we had something better to eat."

There was one hot-dog bun left in the bag on top of the refrigerator. I tore the moldy part off the rubbed it on the sides of the Miracle jar.

Erykah watched with concern, or maybe it was disbelief.

I cracked the bun open and squeezed a line of ketchup in it, then took a small bite. "Erykah, you got to pretend it's what you like to eat. Taste like chicken to me.

My Mama was shouting at Ms. Gabert now…

"Goddammit! Last month was last month, I'm talking about right now. You know what, I'll be in the parking lot waiting on you when you get off. You drive the Nissan Maxima, the green one right?"

"Uh, oh! Mama don't play. Last month the electricity got cut off and everything in the fridge went bad, which why we're fucked now. It's hard to play catch up when you live hand-to-mouth. Government-check, to government check. Anyhow, our last caseworker put a restraining order on Mama after she threatened the lady's life for an emergency food voucher.

Mama was hot, I could hear it in her voice. "A threat, Ms. Gabert? You motherfucking right, it's a threat and a promise. If I'd sell pussy for mine, I'll beat your conservative-ass for them."

Erykah finished her wish meal. I took her back in the living room, changed her pamper. This time she accepted her colored-water bottle.

Mama was trying to call Ms. Gabert back. After a few failed attempts, she gave up. "I'mma make her wish she never took that job. Take the phone back next door, be careful with it the cord has a short in it and I ain't trying to pay for it."

When I came back Mama gave me a store list while pulling out a ten dollar bill from her bra. "This is the last money we have left in the world. Hold on to it real tight. You hurry down to Euclid Deli, and tell Mr. Williams want all the stuff on my list. This ain't enough money for everything, so tell him to put the balance on my bill.

CHAPTER FIFTY-EIGHT

He banged on the heavy door. He couldn't wait to trade what he had in his pocket for crack. All seemed quiet on the outside of the old clapboard house, but he knew it was an animal house on the inside. The thought of a mega blast excited him.

More banging.

A two inch slot slid open. "What?", came from the other side of the reinforced maple. "Kick rocks, Straight Shooter, I told you don't come back. Don't make me pay somebody to lump you up. Beat it."

"Pay me. I'll whoop my own ass."

Before the slot closed, Straight Shooter held up an envelope.

"Come on, Zackzon. Don't do me like this. I got something good and cheap for you."

The slot closed and the door eased open. "Get in here, niggah."

Addicts were freebasing in every corner. Two veteran crack prostitutes were coaching their curious tricks into smoking the pipe. It only takes one hit to ruin a life. Straight Shooter wanted to participate in the festivities with longing passion.

"Niggah, come on." Zackzon pushed him through the room to the kitchen. Zackzon hated dealing with crack head, but the money made him put up with them.

When Straight Shooter entered, one pit-bull growled, the other showed him her teeth.

Manny Cool pet her massive head. "Be cool, baby." Manny Cool was sitting at the table in front of a cookie sheet of crack. He and Zackzon wore surgical masks and plastic gloves. An attractive lady with a long braid down the center of her back stood naked over a cast-iron stove, cooking cocaine.

"Manny Cool, this is all I got." Straight Shooter reached his skinny arm across the table to give Manny Cool the envelope, but froze when both pit bulls stood on all fours, growling a death song.

Manny Cool laughed. "Give me the shit." He took the contents from the envelope. "Kathy Adams." He glanced from the food stamp voucher to Straight Shooter. "One day somebody is gonna catch you in they mailbox and crush you." He passed the voucher to Zackzon.

"You know who Kathy Adams is?"

"Nope."

The naked woman carried a laboratory beaker over to the sink. She was sexy, but Straight Shooter was only interested in the white substance she was handling.

Manny Cool cut a piece of crack from the cookie sheet. "This is all you can get. My people might not be able to bust these. How long you had them?"

376

Elixir was playing double dutch when I came down the street. I asked her where Murdock was.

She gave her friend the ropes to turn. "Around the corner shooting dice,"

I loved that girl from the very first day I met her at a school basketball game. We gave each other a hug. I promised to walk her to school tomorrow then I went and found Murdock. I told Murdock what I was up to, he didn't agree but he held me down. I never thought he wouldn't

We made it to my destination. As we climbed the steps, Straight Shooter rushed out the house with his hand gripped around something my Mama told me to hold on to her money. Murdock and Straight Shooter greeted each other with a nod. I've known Straight Shooter since I used to come through the hood on my big wheel, but today is the first time he went out of his way to avoid looking at me.

Strange.

Zackzon stared at us like we were in violation. "What ya'll little niggahs want? Limbo, I told you before that we'll get at you when we need you."

"So you saying you ain't gonna let me see Manny?"

"He'll be in the game room tomorrow morning. Holler at him then. Now roll out, we taking care of business. Both ya'll punks know that."

"Business is why I'm here." I stuck my little chest out. Zackzon always enjoyed a display of hardness.

He stepped off some, looked up and down the long block, then jerked a thumb toward the house. "You little punks get in here."

Manny Cool's face lit up when he saw me. That only lasted a second before it turned serious again. "You spent that money I gave you already?"

The dogs growled.

I had always heard about his killer pits, Crack and House. Heard the vicious stories about the things they had done to people. I squatted down, closest to the one near me.

The rumble in its chest grew louder.

"Crack will bite the life outta you. Leave him alone, Limbo." Manny waved me away, but I ignored him.

Murdock touched my shoulder. "Chill."

I looked Crack in his eyes and reached out to him real slow.

"You don't wanna bite me do you boy?"

More growling.

I touched his wet nose then stroked the length of his head. Crack's growl was replaced with a wagging tail that slapped against Manny Cool's chair. That was a sign that I was going to be a major player in the dope game. "Manny, you didn't give me nothing." I was petting Crack's solid body now. "I ran plays for that change. I still got it, but that ain't working for me. It's time for me to do my own thing. My Mama stressing, on the verge of catching a case, my baby sister need formula and ain't shit in my refrigerator."

Murdock was glued to the naked cook.

Manny stood and pulled out a .44 Bulldog.

I jumped back from Crack. "Whoa, what the fuck, Manny?"

Manny stood over Crack and frowned. He pointed the muzzle at the top of Crack's massive head.

I watched him pull the trigger with his lip turned up. The naked woman working her magic with Pyrex and beakers flinched when the gun blast. She went back to mixing her potion as if nothing happened.

"Damn, Manny," Murdock said, "why you do that for?"

"This game is serious. That's the price of betrayal, don't ever disrespect the code." He turned to me. "Limbo, come over here and rub my bitch, House." He pointed to the lone pit.

"Nah, I'm good. I don't want you to kill her."

"I respect that." Manny took his seat. "So you ready to spread your wings. Be careful where you drop your feathers, this is what I'll do for you." He took a piece of cocaine from the cookie sheet and eye-balled it in his palm. "Bring me back two hundred for this."

Zackzon came in the kitchen. "Twenty-one said he'll be here in a few."

Manny nodded.

I shook my head at the dead dog then looked at the rock. "Nah. What you're offering me is employment, homeboy. I'm trying to open my own business, no strings attached. My family is counting on me." I took my Mama's ten dollar bill from my pocket along with the thirty I made from him. "This all I'm working with. Put me on for this."

Manny Cool laughed. "You got crazy potential, Limbo." He tossed me the rock.

Zackzon took my forty dollars.

"A new star is born," Manny said. "I just ask that you keep the paper in the family."

"I can sleep at night dealing with family."

I was proud, it made me feel worthy, capable to do something that's considered bad to put food on my Mama's table. That's a good thing. From this day forward, I vowed to take up my absent father's slack, to be a financial influence on my family's situation.

No more ketchup sandwiches for my sister.

No more worries of where the next dollar is coming from for my Mama.

No more tears, no more no mores.

The neighborhood jitney driver helped me unload a car-full of groceries onto my front porch. Payment was the only thanks he wanted. Mama was rocking Erykah to sleep when I marched through the door.

"About time. What did you do, build the store?

It didn't make any sense to respond. I carried the first two bags in the kitchen.

"How much do I owe Mr. Williams?"

"Nothing." I went to the porch again for more groceries. When I came in with the next two bags, Mama's face tightened.

"Where did those come from?" She reached over the back of the couch and slid the sun-stained curtain to one side, seeing eight more bags, and a case of baby formula loitering on the porch.

I started to lie but I learned a long time ago that I wasn't good at it. "I bought them."

She laid my sister down and followed me into the kitchen. "Bought my ass, where did you get this from?" She went through the big bag closet to her. "Take it back, I'll owe out my whole check and some of next months for all of this. Lamont, have you lost your mind?"

No, I hadn't. I was fed-up of living fucked up. After today we would no longer be ranked wit the have-nots. I tried to avoid the question and continue what I was doing.

Mama stood in the kitchen entrance, blocking the only route to the porch. "Don't ignore me, Lamont Adams."

My full name is not a good sign, "We don't owe nobody nothing, Ma. I bought them."

"You don't have no money and no job. You ain't fit to buy nothing."

It was at this moment that I changed from a boy to a man. "I put my hustle down. We gonna be straight from now on." I looked my mother in her angry green eyes. "Ain't nobody looking out for us." I pulled the refrigerator door open

380

and a roach staggered out. He was probably dying of starvation, too. "Erykah don't have no understanding of nothing to eat. You said it ain't no such thing as God, because if there was a God then we wouldn't be living like this. But I kept praying to Him anyway, and He sent my cocaine as an answer to my prayers. We straight."

I felt years of penned-up frustration and the weight of my mother's anger when her calloused palm slapped my face. I staggered back, the whole left side of my body was on fire.

"You selling drugs?" I'm doing my best to keep you away from the streets.'

I pulled myself together and stood my ground. "I don't know what for, the streets bought us a house full of groceries. Doing right ain't did nothing but left these shelves empty." I pointed to the refrigerator. "I'm not convinced that the streets is bad, all I see is good thing happening in them. So I brang some of it home, cause this ain't good." I pushed the door shut.

"Lamont, baby, listen to me. Nothing good can ever come from doing something bad. Yeah, you'll get ahead for awhile, but the end results isn't worth it. Our situation will change because we are doing right. Baby, I know it may not seem so at first. But remember when they tore that old building down the street and set up a construction site? I remember how you was saying how ugly it was and what a mess they made. Now look at what became of that ugly mess -- a beautiful rec center." She wiped a tear away from her face. "It took hard work, time, and patience to turn that mess into something positive. The only thing that will come from drugs is death and jail. That's not what I want for you. I'm raising you to be the best you can be -- "

"And be the best at whatever I choose to do. This is the best thing I've ever done." I pulled out a knot of twenties, tens, and singles. "Hustling gave me results right now. Doing right gets me used tennis shoes from Goodwill. I want Nikes, too.

Mama, you deserve some new shi--, I mean stuff, too. I'm gonna get it for you. You said be the best at whatever I do. I'm gonna hustle. Death or jail isn't in my future. I got ambitions of getting rich. Rich enough to take care of all of us forever."

"Yeah, and I'll go back to church. That's enough, Lamont. Selling drugs is not the answer to your problems. We'll never have another conversation like this, you hear me? If you try to be slick I'll have you locked up myself."

"I'm not going to stop unless you can show me somewhere else I can make nine hundred dollars in three hours."

Mama's shoulder moved some. I ducked thinking she was going to take my head off.

"I'll be damned," Mama said. "I'll let you bring the streets home." She turned her back on me and stomped up the stairs.

I had gotten the bags off the porch and was putting the groceries away when Mama came down stairs with a suitcase.

"You think you grown enough to tell me what you're gonna do after I told you what you wasn't gonna do? I'll tell you this, I'm not going to put conditions on you being the best. But you're not going to be the best drug dealer, indulging in wrong behavior living under this roof. The streets can't offer you the life I want you to have, and I'm not gonna let you bring the streets in here and offer them to your sister." She sat the suitcase down. "I've always let you make your own choices, now you need to make the most important decision of your life." Mama pointed out the living room window. "The streets or us, Limbo."

That shocked me. How did Mama know that name? Why didn't she bring it to my attention long before today?

I stood on our front porch with the suitcase.

Mama towered over me from the doorway. She looked at me. "Lamont, you'll always have a home here, but you can never come here while you're hustling drugs." Tears traveled down her round face. She shut the door with a thud.

I think Mama thought that I would fall in live and would be pounding on the door in the middle of the night, talking like I had some sense. She had another thing coming, I had kingpin ambitions.

CHAPTER FIFTY-NINE

Limbo

It took fourteen years to realize my street dream. I traced my name carved in the wood once more then knocked.

I could hear someone moving around inside. My heart felt like it was trying to jump out of my chest. Next it was the squeaky floorboards straining under someone's weight.

"Who is it?"

"It's me, Mama."

I watched the door knob. It didn't turn. Nothing happened. Seconds felt like hours.

The door opened.

Mama stood there in her work uniform. She is beautiful 51-year old woman. Her round face has the radiance of a teenager. The only signs of Mama's age is the laugh lines and scattered strains of gray. Last time we faced one another off on this porch, Mama looked down on me. Now I towered over her. She looked at me so hard, I was ready to turn and leave. The hardness vanished, then she smiled and opened her arms. "Boy, come hug your mother."

"I'm...I'm home, Mama"

We held onto each other for a long moment.

"I brought you something." I could tell that she was going to cry. I was giving Mama the gift when Erykah came down the steps with a phone glued to her ear.

"Ma, who's at--", she dropped the phone and jumped in my arms. "Lamont, what are you doing here?" She glanced at Mama then zoomed in on me. "You're out the game? Say work."

"Yeah. I got some loose ends to tie up. But for the most part, I'm out." This was the best moment of his life, next to when my son's were born. "Let's go inside, if that's all right with you, ma?"

"Bring your handsome self in here."

Erykah led me in the living room by my hand. I glared at her so that she wouldn't let Mama see me too much familiarity between us.

Mama whipped her tears away and held her dress up. "What am I supposed to do with this. I don't go nowhere I can wear this expensive thing."

I sat down. Erykah sat beside me with a mile-wide smile.

"You don't remember what you said to me the day I chose to do my thing in the streets?"

She was holding the dress against her body, imagining how she would look in it -- like all woman do. "No, Lamont, not exactly. I try not to think of it much because of the pain that accompanies the thought."

I rubbed my sister's back. "I promise to never cause either one of you any hurt again. Ma, I hate to focus on that day, but you told me that you would go back to church if I made enough money to support our family." I shifted my sight to Erykah. "My children's kids are wealthy. Erykah, your kids are rich."

"I don't have any kids, boy, yours is enough."

"When you do have some, they'll be well taken care of."

Mama scrunched her face. "What do you mean by his enough?"

"You want something to drink, Lamont? Let me get you and Mama something." Erykah went to the kitchen.

Mama looked at her then at me. Damn, I knew she would fuck up.

"Ma, why haven't you moved away from here. I send you enough money every month for you to have bought you a nice house by now."

"I live within my means, this place is just fine. I saved every penny of that money. I figured if I didn't have to bury you with it, I'd use it to hire a few sharks in designer suits to get you out of a life sentence."

"You saved it all, ma?"

"Every cent." She headed for the stairs. "Come on, I'll show you."

I followed her into her bedroom. She kneeled down beside a tired dresser and tugged the carpet back. I sat on the bed and eased my hand under her pillow.

Nothing.

Mama pulled up three floorboards.

I checked under the other pillow and found a picture of me in my younger days, when I was bad as hell.

"All fourteen years of it." She brushed dust from her hands.

I eased the picture back then stood over here. "Ma, it's got to be at least a half million stashed here. This money shouldn't be here, anything could happen to us.

She used the dresser for leverage to stand up. "I don't know how much is there." She pointed. "Too much to count. I tried once but it gave me a headache."

Erykah walked in carrying drinks. "Good, God, Ma! Where did all that come from?"

"Your brother."

"Well, now, you can use it to furnish your new house." I took out a set of keys. "This one is for the house...and this one is for your car, Ma."

"What kind of car is it?" Erykah asked. "I know it's phat to death."

"You bought a house...for—"

"Ma, we need a family home, were all your grand kids can come to, like my grandma and grandpa's house."

I woke up aching from sleeping on Mama's run-down couch all night. We all got ourselves and took care of our particulars in the bathroom, then I took Mama and Erykah to see their Beachwood home.

Erykah ran through the house like a kid in an amusement park.

Mama walked the corridor leading to an indoor pool. "Lamont, this is too much. What am I going to do with this big-ass-house?"

"Enjoy it and relax in it. The only people who thinks something is too much are broke. We're a long way from it."

After we viewed the forty-one hundred square foot split level, we drove to Elixir's to spend the day as a family.

"Daddy!" All three of my boys attacked me when I came through the door. We rolled and wrestled and laughed in floor until Elixir came out of the kitchen and said, "Ya'll stop before something gets broke. Hey, Erykah, I didn't know you were coming, Girl, I thought you were going to watch these brats last week?

My Mama glared at me and Erykah. Elixir looked at us like who is this strange woman.

I got up from the floor. "Elixir, this is my mother."

Elixir's eyes widened.

"Little Lamont, Latrel, Lontrel", I said, "Ya'll come over her and meet your grandma."

Mama studied the expression on Elixir's face. "Don't worry about it, baby. They told on themselves last night."

Elixir wiped her hands on her apron then reached a hand. It's a pleasure t finally meet...you...Ms. Adams." She turned to me. "Lamont, baby you quit?"

CHAPTER SIXTY

The clean-up crew gathered in a U-Haul parking lot.

Thurston thumped the butt of his cigar. "There's only two ways Adams can get into town." He spread a map across the hood of Keri's car. "The county line, here on Route 403. He pointed. "And the county line here, on Route 56. He looked up at the Federal Agents. "We're splitting in two teams to set up surveillance at these locations. I'll head team one, and Agent Mayweather will lead team two. Nester, you and Rawlings head out with Mayweather. Stewart, you're with me."

Keri Mayweather pulled her hair into a ponytail. "Everyone remember, Limbo and Trigger are armed and murder at the blink of an eye. They must be treated as threats to your lives and nine times out of ten, they're wearing body armor. If with get into altercation with these guys, shoot to kill."

"Once we know that Adams is in route to Johnstown." Thurston said, "I'll add Johanson to my team."

"What are you trying to do, Thurston?" Keri scowled at him. "She'll warn him."

"Don't worry. I'm on top of it." He shifted his attention to Stewart. Where are we on the communications surveillance?"

Stewart stopped his pager from beeping. "Both cell phones linked to the Adams vehicle will be disconnected within the hour. The communications technicians are listening to Adams with their electronic ears, their giving me up dates every fifteen minutes. Right now he's eating dinner with his family."

CHAPTER SIXTY-ONE

The taxi cab driver leaned on the horn outside of Elixir's house like he was in a rush. My sons were all over me, like usual. Elixir did her thing in the kitchen, I was stuffed.

"Get me one like this, Daddy." Lontrel pulled my necklace out of my shirt.

"You like this thing?"

"Yeah, it's slick."

I put the necklace around his neck. "Now it's your slick piece."

The horn blew again.

I stood to leave. "Aw, Daddy, stay the night with us. Mommy don't care. Do you, mommy? Little Lamont put Elixir on the spot.

Everyone else stopped enjoying each others company to hear Elixir's response.

She looked at me with those powerful brown eyes. "That's something only your father can answer." Se was always and expert at shifting weight.

"Little Lamont, you and your brothers spend some time with your grandma and Aunty Erykah. I'll come get you soon and we can kick it at my house. Your mini-bikes will be there, too."

"Now that's what's up." Lontrel said.

"You little cats come give me a hug."

I gave all the women in the house hugs, too." While embraced with Elixir, she locked onto my eyes and said, "Be careful."

Elixir's embrace didn't have the magic it used to have. All we ever will be is parents, I will never get over her abandoning me.

"Keep the meter running, I'll only be about ten minutes."

"Pay me now and I'll wait." The taxi driver held out a hand. I strolled through a set of double doors into my home boy, Twenty-One's marble hall.

One of his women helped me out of my coat and hung it. "Twenty-One is waiting for you in the study."

He led me to the west wing of the mansion.

The study was magnificent. I admired it every time I'm here. Antique furniture well positioned through the room. Floor-to ceiling bookshelves covered each wall. There had to be over a thousand books here.

Twenty-One took a long draw from a blunt and pass it to Little Scarp.

"Players." I touched fists with Twenty-One then Little Scrap. "Look at you, I guess I shouldn't call you Little Scrap no more."

He had really outgrown since our Willow Arms days.

"Nah, Limbo, I'm big boying like you. You know?"

Twenty-One laced his fingers behind his bald head and leaned back on a leather davenport. "My girls fixed enough food to feed the projects, let me have one of them get you something."

"Homey, I can't eat another bite. Elixir did it up pretty big." I went to the bookcase. "I'm about to get down the highway anyway." I read a few titles from the spines of books: The Intelligent Investor, Obvious Absurdities, The Prince, The Spiral staircase.

Twenty-One nodded his head toward his library. "Don't just look at them, get you something to read. Give yourself credit to comprehend something you normally wouldn't relate to...think outside of the box -- and never let people or words overwhelm or overpower you."

I selected a book. "I'm feeling Sir Isaac Newton. I like the way he puts words together."

The Principle of Math, good choice." Twenty-One motioned for me to sit. "That's basically what I want to talk to you about -- math."

Scrap stood and stretched. "I'mma get out ya'lls way so ya'll can rap. He hit the blunt once more than gave it to Twenty-One.

"You bouncing?"

"Nah, I'mma go upstairs, get on the computer and check out the stock exchange so I can see my bread is doing." He gave me a slight hug. "It's good to see my niggah."

"The feelings mutual, Homeboy." I took his seat.

Twenty-One crossed his legs and stretched his arms across either side of the couch. "Limbo, the game ain't the same no more. My supplying days are over, I'm taking my winnings and let the savages do what they do. It's time for us to be professional sucker duckers."

"I feel you."

"No, I don't think you really do. Prince called it the 'Signs of The Time." He pointed a finger at me first, then at himself. "And that what we have to do, peep the signs and understand them for what they are and not the illusion in which they appear to be."

I was paying attention to him, while flipping through the book. Me and Twenty-One are both twenty-eight, but I could never measure his wisdom in numbers. Since the beginning of our business relationship, he always wanted to have sit-downs with me, to lace me with game and jewels to live by. Never once in over twelve years have I ever heard this unsettled tone in his voice.

He went on. "We've got niggahs talking about they ain't never going back to the joint, but out here in these streets doing the same shit." He paused. "With no intentions of building a bridge to get out. These niggahs is potential rats, homey."

"It ain't too many of us left that's gon' hold court in these streets, Twenty-One. We been knew that." I closed the book and looked at him.

"Yeah, but that don't matter. The whole personality of the game has changed. So either we must change our game or fall victim to the reconstruction of this game." He went to a mini-bar to fix himself a drink. "I'll use you for example. I stood outside looking in on your signs for quite some time now."

He threw me for a loop. What did he mean my signs? I watched him pace between his desk and a ten-foot statue of the first black billionaire, Reginald Lewis, chiseling out a block of stone.

"First you get jammed on some bullshit. Your wife leaves you. You lose your crib and the bulk of your paper. A rat niggah hooked you up with your main broad -- I'm not insinuating anything. Murdock took one for team. Now I'm stuffing bumpers with cocaine and you're the mule. What is the shit coming to?" He stood in front of me. "I always fucked with you for your ability to think, because I never thought you would be what you're becoming."

"Twenty--"

"Limbo, you're falling victim to the reconstruction. I'm just telling you to pay attention to the signs. It's time for a change of game. Math never lies. Ten plus eleven always equal Twenty-One." He pointed to the book in my hand. "And that's The Principles of Math."

CHAPTER SIXTY-TWO

"We're not getting anything but some children talking," Agent Stewart said. "Communications hasn't identified Limbo's voice in over an hour."

Thurston went to the rear-end of the SUV to take a leak. While he drained himself, he spoke to Stewart over his shoulder. "What time was Adams scheduled to leave Ohio?"

"Ten.'

Thurston shook himself, dry, then checked his watch 12:10 am. If he left on time, he'll cross one of these county lines in an hour forty-five minutes. Get Johanson on the line. I wanna see her sweat while we play the waiting game."

"Come on, Cuz." C-Mack threw his arm around Ghetto and they staggered out the club.

"I'm hungry as a motherfucker," Ghetto said. "That's the best smoke I had all year."

C-Mack unlocked the Hummer doors. "I got the munchies too."

"Let's grab some pizza from the deli, then go kick it with wild-ass Tink in Oakhurst."

"Sounds like a bet."

Ghetto was stuffing his mouth with an extra cheese and mushroom pizza when C-Mack turned onto the narrow road that would lead them into Oakhurst Housing Projects.

C-Mack steered the Hummer with his knees while he rolled a blunt.

Ghetto received a text message. He pressed send and the screen read: four-twelve. "Stop this motherfucker, it's a raid going down."

C-Mack slammed on the brakes. A Ziploc bag of marijuana spilled to the floor. He could see police lights flashing in his rearview. He whipped the car into he nearest driveway and pulled to the backyard until the police sped by.

"I hate fucking cops"

"Turn left here," Ghetto said, "I wanna peep something and stay off the main street at the same time."

They drove down the side street and that's when Ghetto witnessed. the maintenance man slapping a pair of cuffs on one of his look-outs.

"I knew something wasn't right with that dude."

"Which one?", C-Mack watched the arrest from the rearview.

"That cop was in the hood last month posing as maintenance."

C-Mack's cell phone chirped to life.

He stuck the phone to his ear. "What the fuck is cracking?"

"Mack, this is Spencer. I don't know to what extent, but Limbo's in trouble."

"Where are you going, Sugar?" Trenyce turned over to face her husband.

Spencer scooted himself out of bed into his wheel chair. "Can't sleep, that's all. I'm going to watch TV or something."

"Come back to bed, Spencer. You can play with your new computer mumble jumble in the morning."

"I won't be long, Trencye, I promise." He wheeled himself down the hall, into his office.

He heard his wife say, "whatever."

Spencer parked in front of his computer and examined the disc. He knew that the capabilities of this new program would bring his investigating firm more business. The new Tracker program gave him access to 79% more information than his old Tracker.

He loaded the computer and typed in the password.

"Good morning, Spencer," the computer said, "welcome to Tracker five-thousand." The screen saver vanished. "Please type in subjects name then click on one of the following choices.

Most recent information
1995-2000 information
1990-1995 information
1990 information to first data entry

Spencer pulled his desk drawer open to retrieve his record book of client information. He slid the drawer out too far, causing it and its contents to fall to the floor.

"Just damn great!" He looked down at the mess. This was the second time this week he had dumped the drawer on the floor. The record book was open to a page that had a yellow post-it stuck to it, with Limbo's name on it -- circled. Written under the name was Find skelton. White female,

Francine Rhapsody Parrish. Born 1976, Charlotte, North Carolina -- Portage, PA.

Spencer leaned over and picked the record book up with two fingers. He typed in Rhapsody's name then clicked on most recent information.

CHAPTER SIXTY-THREE

Rhapsody

I felt around in the dark for my cell phone. I found it on Limbo's empty side of the bed. "Hello." I was intoxicated with sleep, I had no idea what time it was.

"Suit up and boot up," Stewart said, "We're short handed with surveillance down here on Route 56."

"What time is it?"

"A little after one."

Thurston couldn't have gotten my video tape, yet. No way possible. So this call is legit. "Who's under surveillance?"

"A nickel dime hustler coming from Pittsburgh. Confidential informant gave us a tip that he'll be bringing in a quantity of heroin tonight. Get down here we need you."

"Where at on fifty-six?"

"The county line."

I couldn't wait until I was free from this madness. "Give me fifteen minutes." I swung feet around to the floor. "Stewart, how did you know I could get away?"

"For crying out loud, we know that Limbo is out of town."

I parked on the side of the highway behind Thurston's SUV. Cars zipped the highway going in both directions as I climbed in Thurston's back seat. I rolled the window down some to let thick cigar smoke escape.

"Glad you could join us, Johanson." Thurston positioned his weight on the armrest.

Stewart filled me in the man-power that was in the field tonight.

"This is a bit much for a petty hustler. Who is this guy?" I stuck my head between the seat and looked at them both.

Ashes fell from the tip of Thurston's cigar into his lap. "I wouldn't call Adams a petty hustler. Actually, I believe we're under manned tonight, dealing with a cop killer."

I was stuck with right there between the seats.

"You're going to need this." Stewart passed me a FBI jacket.

I rushed out the car and puked up leftovers. I got in my car and dialed Limbo's number. I had to stop him, tell him everything. I shook uncontrollable as his phone rang.

"The wireless customer you're trying to reach is out of the service area."

My eyes started to leak. I dialed back and got the same recording. I jumped. The heavy knock on my car window scared the shit out of me. Thurston was standing there with his cigar glowing in the dark.

He opened my door. "Who you trying to reach? No, let me guess -- Adams. Stop wasting your time, his phone is disconnected."

Stewart stood behind him.

He snatched me from the car. "I'm disappointed in you, Johanson. You really pissed me off." He took my weapon from my holster. "You betrayed our crew, and lied to -- "

"Thurston it's not -- "

He clamped his massive hand around my neck and penned me against the car. "Don't make me pop this fucking thing off your shoulders." He squeezed until he cut my air supply off. "You have one chance to redeem yourself and make us trust you again."

Stewart cocked his revolver and pointed it at my head.

I pawed at Thurston's vice grip around my neck. It didn't budge.

"When we stop Adams tonight, you're going to kill him. Make thing right by Curlew. But I'll settle for your life, right her, right now."

"What's it gonna be, Johanson?" Stewart put the muzzle on my temple.

The strength withered from my body. Io was desperate to taste air again. I knew that unconsciousness was seconds away. I looked into Thurston's eyes, he bared down harder.

I tapped his hand and nodded as best as I could.

He let go.

I dropped to the gravel and hugged the guardrail, sucking in as much air as I could. I'll never take air for granted again. "Okay...I'll do it."

"Bring your ass." Thurston grabbed me in his powerful grip and shoved me in the back seat of his SUV. "You're the best shot in the Bureau. What a tragedy it'll be for your mother and father if you miss." He slammed the door shut. He and Stewart climbed in the front seat.

The CB came alive.

"Thurston, a vehicle matching the description and registration of Limbo's car just entered the county."

The sound of Keri's voice unnerved me.

Thurston let out a cloud of smoke. "Mayweather, you know what to do." He turned the ignition.

Stewart pressed the indiglo button on his Times. "One, forty-five. He's on time like clockwork."

"I'm in route," Keri said, "but there's only one occupant in the vehicle, and we can't confirm if it's Limbo."

CHAPTER SIXTY-FOUR

Spencer stared at the computer screen in disbelief. He had no idea who Limbo's Rhapsody was. He trembled as he reached for the phone and stumbled through the digits. "Pick up, Limbo. Come on man, pick up."

"The wireless customer -- "

He hung up and stabbed in C-Mack's number.

"What the fuck is cracking?" C-Mack held the phone to his ear as he made a right on red.

"Mack, this is Spencer. I don't know to what extent, but Limbo's in trouble."

"It's trouble on this end, too. The cops hitting us up with a late night raid. What's the business, what kind of dilemma is the homey faced with?"

"Rhapsody isn't white, the real one is a Black girl. I'm sitting here looking at pictures of her now. Pictures of her at her parents funeral, ,high school graduation pictures. There's even one of an article dated this month in her college newspaper that got national attention of her protesting against abortion."

C-Mack tapped Ghetto. "Get Limbo on the phone." He focused back on Spencer. "Are you sure about this?"

"Unless they're twin sisters and Limbo has the albino one."

Ghetto shut his pone off. "I'm getting a recording."

C-Mack spinned the steering wheel left. "Try Trigger."

"I got the same thing."

"I got a recording, too", Spencer said. "I don't know what's going on, but if I had to take a guess, the Rhapsody Limbo's with is the police. I suggest that you lay low -- real low until we get in touch with Limbo. If she isn't the police, whoever she is, she went to great lengths to protect her real identity by stealing someone else's."

"Son of a motherfuck!" C-Mack drove by the projects he managed and saw the task force stuff the back of a patty wagon with four of his workers. "They're on to us, Spence. Get in touch with Elixir or Trigger, make sure Limbo doesn't get on the highway. Candy Shop closed. I'm headed out now."

"Let me see what I can do." Spencer browsed through the information on Rhapsody. "I'll touch bases with you when I have something solid." He hung up.

"This the end of the road, Ghetto." C-Mack pulled over. "What you gon' do? This here is a memory. I'm -- "

"Cuz, I'm rolling with you."

"Dig that, C-Mack eased away from the curb.

CHAPTER SIXTY-FIVE

Limbo

The highway was dark. I couldn't keep my eyes open. I reclined the passenger's seat, until the headrest touched the back seat. "The county line is about forty minutes from here."

Trigger gripped the steering wheel with one had, "Go on, catch you a few. I know the way from here. When are we gonna wear our welcome out in Philly?" I'm dreaming about some get-back." He looked at me from under the brim of his ballcap.

I closed my eyes. "Spence is doing some research for me now. It won't be long, Trigger." I couldn't get comfortable with Murdock on my mind. "Trust me , it won't be long before I give Sadiq the blues. Put your seat belt on...and take that cap off."

A voice in the distance tugged me from sleep.

"Limbo." Trigger shook me. "We got company."

I opened my eyes to see the Incline Plane light up the night. In the distance, it climbed the hillside at a snails pace.

Trigger tapped my knee. "We got cops behind us." He aimed his thumb towards the back seat.

I propped myself on an elbow and looked out the rear window. Three black SUV's with cherry warning lights, flashing from behind their windshields rushed towards us.

A u-turn was out the question. We wee separated from the opposite traffic by a concrete lane divider that ran for mile. I could see no further than the sharp curve in the road ahead of us would allow. I reached over and put my foot on top of Trigger's and pressed down hard. "Drive this motherfucker!"

Trigger yanked the car around the sharp corner and we were faced with a road block. Seventy yards in front of us were another three SUV's blocking the road surrounded by agents in blue windbreakers. The yellow FBI letters reflected off our headlights.

Trigger slowed the car to a stop. Nosey motorist eased by the stand-off on the other side of the concrete divider. A barricade in front of us, the SUV's came to a stop fifteen feet behind us, waiting on us to make the next move.

Trigger clenched both hands on the steering wheel and stared at me.

I lugged the two heavy 45's from under my seat. "Going to prison is not an option."

Trigger yanked a 9mm from his waist, then secured the Velcro on his slug proof vest. "You singing my song,' ride till we die." He pounded his fist on top of mine. "Limbo, you my niggah."

"Tell me that when we get outta this shit." I shoved an extra in my back pocket. "But if we just gotta die, let's make sure we take a whole bunch of these motherfuckers with us." I looked at the way the Feds had us boxed-in, again. Then I steered at a car lot to my left. "I got a plan." I punched in C-Mack's number on my cell.

"The moment of truth." Thurston stopped approximately twenty feet behind Limbo's Chevy. He butted his cigar.

Stewart unloaded all but two bullets from the shiny clip.

"Time to earn your keep." He passed Johanson her Glock.

Her hands trembled. How easy it would be to shoot them both. She was a dead woman for sure if she did that. She looked at the gun in her hand and thought of the day she committed to never pull the trigger again. She would break that promise tonight. She shifted her sight from the Glock to the Chevy's brake lights. A bulled smashed through the windshield and lodged in the seat inches away from her.

Thurston was too big to duck in the seat like Stewart had. Thurston kicked the SUV in reverse and stomped on the gas. Within seconds the scent became tense as a hail of bullets tore into each of the three vehicles backing away from Limbo's Chevy.

"Fuck!" I threw my cell phone to the floor. "Gimme yours." I tried C-Mack on Trigger's line but got the same response. A wireless customer message.

I said a silent prayer for my sons then opened the sun roof. "Plan B."

"And what's that?" Sweat was dripping from Trigger's forehead, soaking the cigarette hanging from his lips.

"I don't know, we'll make it up as we go." I stood in the seat and poked my body through the sun roof. I pointed one 45. at the barricade, the other at the SUV's behind me then finger fucked both triggers.

The guns sounded like cannons going off. The SUV's started to back up. I dropped down in the seat. "We stand a chance over there." I jerked my head towards the lot and grabbed the door handle.

Trigger stopped me. "Hold up, give me that book."

I watched the SUV's skid to a stop through the back window.

"This ain't no time -- "

"Just give it to me."

I tossed him The Principles of Math. He wedged it against the gas pedal. The engine whined. We stepped out and Trigger shifted the car in drive. As the tires smoked against the pavement, I started pumping slugs into the gas tank. Trigger followed my lead.

The car went up in flames a few feet away from us. As the fireball picked up speed and rushed toward the barricade it exploded. The night was brighter than a firework display on Independence Day.

Bullets rang out from behind us. The SUV's were approaching again -- fast. Guns were being fired from the windows. We ran toward the car lot. My leg gave out and I went down hard. "Son of...fuck!" Pain ripped through my leg.

"Get off your ass." Trigger grabbed me and drug me behind a row of cars.

When I saw off the blood, the pain got worse. "This wasn't a part of the plan." I could hear car tires screeching to a stop. Fire engines shouted in the distance.

Trigger was peeping through the car window we took shelter behind. "It don't look good for the home team. They got us cornered.

I forced myself on a knee. Sure enough, the Feds had made their stand. They were crouched down behind front ends and car doors with their weapons pointed in our direction.

It's too many guns against these." Trigger motioned to our weapons.

I eased back in the sitting position and took the clip from my pocket. "We can't stay here much longer. They'll surround us. If we can make it over there." I pointed the '45' to a wooded area behind the car lot. "We can give'em a good fi -- "

"God dammint, man! Limbo, we were set up from day one."

"Tell me. I need to stay off this leg while I can. It's a nice hump to those trees."

"You got to see this for yourself." He was breathing hard.

I balanced myself on a knee. The big bastard from the night at the hospital was shoving Rhapsody past the security of their vehicles

She had a bull horn and was wearing a fucking FBI jacket. Anger and hatred shook me with unimaginable force. I squeezed my eyes shut and heard a thousand voices trapped in my head.

...she must be the devil...

...I'm the one who bites...

...get rid of that white bitch, she's cancer...

...she'll bring him down, they've been doing it for centuries...

...it's bad enough you got on, but two is bound to be trouble...

...keep messing with that girl and you're the next great man going down...

Now it all made perfect sense. The way she handled a gun. Why I could only have a piece of her love.

Then I saw a red head peeping at me -- Keri.

Rhapsody out the bull to her mouth. "Limbo...I didn't plan for you to find out like this. I tried to save you from this, but Keri crossed me. I'm supposed to kill you tonight or they're going to kill me." She took her gun out and threw it to the street. "I don't feel the same as when I took this assignment. I really do love you."

"Fuck you, if you loved me you woulda put me up on game."

"I was going to. I quit the other night. I was tricked out here tonight." She looked back at the agents behind her. That when I made my move.

I stood up and raise my gun. "Fuck you." Before I could pull the trigger, Keri was already firing. If I love to tell about this, I'll never fail to mention the evil look in her eyes as sparks leapt from the front of her gun. A bulled slammed into my neck. I emptied my clip in Rhapsody's direction as I went down. I wanted to take her with me. "Pay attention to the signs." Twenty-one's words echoed.

CHAPTER SIXTY-SIX
Rhapsody

I turned back to Big Daddy and he was raising his gun. Shots went off behind me. I felt like I would die when I saw him stagger back. He started to return fire. I went to the ground and watched him fall to the ground as bullets few over my head. I could see a portion of his body under the car. Trigger sprung up like a trapped cat, throwing bullets at the police line. I reached in front of me and eased my gun toward me. I laid there with my head on the ground. I found Keri to my left and put the gun behind my back. I looked over my shoulder and sent two shots into the door she hid behind.

"Agent down!" I heard Rawlings yell out.

They all unloaded on Trigger. Windows fell out the car he stood behind. Then he went down beside Limbo.

I ran the fastest that I have in my life to Limbo. I could've died when I saw him laying in a pool of blood, shaking, staring at the stars. I wiped the finger prints from my gun and put it in Trigger's hand. I propped Limbo's head on my knee and dialed 911 on my cell.

"911m what's your emergency?"

"I'm federal agent Jayme Johanson. There's been a shooting.

"What's your location?"

"I'm on Broad Street in front of Andrient's car lot."

"Is the victim breathing?"

"He has a pulse, but he's not responding."

"There's a unit enroute."

I hung up and rubbed the sweat away from his forehead. My tears dripped onto his face. "They're coming to help you. Don't you die on us. You have to stick around to meet your baby."

He closed his eyes and the shaking stopped. I put my ear to his heart but didn't get anything because of his bullet proof vest. I tilted his head and squeezed his nose preparing the give him mouth-to-mouth and looked up into Thurston's angry eyes.

A Johnstown police officer ran up and holstered his service revolver. "Are you alright, Ma'am?"

I was sure glad to see someone on the right side of the law. "Yes, it's him, he needs some help." I wiped away the tears blurring my vision and rocked Limbo. Other members of the police department started to show up.

The officers kneeled beside me. "Who's in charge here?"

Thurston reached his huge hand out. "I'm Special Agent in Command, Marcus Thurston". He lit a cigar. "Good job, Johanson, I need a report on my desk first thing in the morning."

The paramedics parked between the rows of cars. The Emergency Response Team bolted from the ambulance carrying medical kits.

The officer looked at Limbo then turned to me. "Does he have a pulse?"

"It's weak." Now there can never be an 'us'. After tonight, all this will be stored in the past and I'll go somewhere far from here and enjoy what the future promises with my child -- Limbo's child. I kissed his lips then the Emergence Response Team took over. I read the officer's name tag. "Officer Floyd, could you take me somewhere?"

He studied my face with understanding eyes. "Yeah, where do you want to go?"

"Pittsburgh International Airport."

THE END
LOOK FOR THE SEQUEL TO "STREET GAMES" - COMING SOON!

BRAND NEW!
From BLACK PEARL BOOKS

"TRUE PLAYA FO REAL!"

"Gritty Urban Realism At Its Best!
....*Legit Baller* Is The Truth!"
- Lynne D. Johnson, VIBE MAGAZINE

LEGIT BALLER

A *Jerry Blackshear* Novel

ISBN: 0-9766007-2-2
www.BlackPearlBooks.com

"LEGIT BALLER" DESCRIPTION

Jay Bernard has been dedicated to his craft as a baler. That is, until his deeds land him a 14-year bid in the Federal Pen on drug-charges.

Kim, Jay's supposed 'Bonnie' to his 'Clyde' wastes no time in cutting ties after his sentencing by moving her game to the new Baller-Kint (Paris).

During Jay's incarceration, sexy Summer Foster, proves to be a better friend than anyone who'd benefited from Jay's life-style. Though from the same hood, Summer has managed to rise-up, earning a college degree and currently an M.B.A. student at Harvard.

After his early-release, Jay finds it hard to avoid the only life he knows, even with the love and encouragement from an old-friend (Summer) for him to go 'Legit' – Old habits, just seem to die hard!

The complete opposite of Jay's gangsta, Summer views him as much more than just hard-rock – but a true diamond-gem! However, Jay's past and the streets keep calling him.

Paris views himself as a street-rival of Jay's even before his stint in prison, and now feels threatened that Jay may want to re-claim everything back – his drug territory and his woman (Kim)!

When the inevitable confrontation arises between Jay and Paris, the next move could be the last!

"Gritty Urban Realism At Its Best!
... Legit Baller Is The Truth!"
Lynne D. Johnson, VIBE MAGAZINE

BRAND NEW!

From BLACK PEARL BOOKS

HUSTLERS

EVERY GAME...
HAS ITS PRICE!

"This Joint Is So Hot!... Ghetto-Fab!... Game Has To Be Recognized!"
-Terry Shropshire, ROLLING OUT MAGAZINE

RONALD QUINCY

ISBN: 0-9766007-3-0
www.BlackPearlBooks.com

"HUSTLERS" DESCRIPTION

Popcorn & Bay-Bay have been boyz for what seems like forever. Since they were 'shorties' growing up in Richmond-VA, as the crowned Street-Prince-boys to their OG-fathers who carried notorious reputations in VA's streets as true hustlers, nothing separated the two of them -- until both of their fathers fell victim to the hood.

After the deaths of their fathers, Bay-Bay's mother decides to relocate to Miami, Florida – temporarily ending their contact.

Several years later, Popcorn & Bay-Bay are all grown-up and reunite with plans of taking 'The Game' to the highest level – fulfilling their destiny as Street-Royalty.

Peaches, a hood-sophisticated dime-piece and Popcorn's wifey, is thoroughly satisfied with the kinky-work he's puttin'-down in the bedroom, but suspects that Popcorn is cheating on her with his life-long female friend (Yolanda) who he seems to always be around.

When Popcorn suddenly starts disappearing at night and begins flashing more cash than his 'lawn-business' could possibly provide, Peaches doesn't feel like she even knows who he really is.

As Popcorn seeks to gain revenge for his brother's murder, he wants to know if he can totally put his trust in Peaches? Is she just a dime? Or is she truly his 'to-the-grave' Ride-Or-Die chick?

Out for her own personal-revenge to satisfy her suspicions of Popcorn's indiscretions, Peaches makes a decision that will come back to haunt both of them.....maybe forever!

Money, Betrayal and the constant Struggle-for-Power are just the normal territory for Real Hustlers!

*"This Joint Is So Hot!....Ghetto-Fab!....
...Game Has To Be Recognized!"*
- Terry Shropshire, Rolling Out Magazine

BRAND NEW!

From BLACK PEARL BOOKS

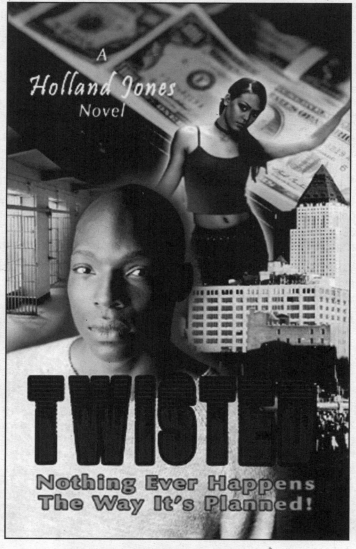

A *Holland Jones* Novel

TWISTED

Nothing Ever Happens The Way It's Planned!

ISBN: 0-9728005-7-3

www.BlackPearlBooks.com

"TWISTED" DESCRIPTION

Nadine, a sultry, ghetto-fine conniving gold-digger, will do whatever it takes to make sure that she is financially set for life -- even at the cost of breaking-up a family.

When Wayne, Nadine's man since high-school, is sentenced to two years in prison for a crime he did not commit, he's betrayed by the two people he trusted the most—his woman (Nadine) and his cousin (Bobo).

Asia, a curvaceous diva and designer-clothing boutique owner with a wilder-side sexual-preference becomes an unlikely confidant to her best-friend Nadine's man (Wayne) during his incarceration.

Meanwhile Bobo, one of VA's most notorious and most successful Street-Entreprenuers, manages to hustle his way into staring down a possible life sentence.

Now that the roles are reversed, it's Bobo who's now facing some serious prision time, as Nadine tries to do whatever it takes to keep her hands on the secret stash of cash hidden in a suitcase that Bobo left behind.

Money, greed and sex always have as a way of gettin' things **Twisted!**

"Daaaaayummmmmm! Holland Jones brings it! A hood-licious story that combines deceit, murder, freaky sex and mysterious-twists! You gotta get this one!"

-- Winston Chapman, Best-Selling Author of *Caught Up!* and *Wild Thangz*

BRAND NEW!

From BLACK PEARL BOOKS

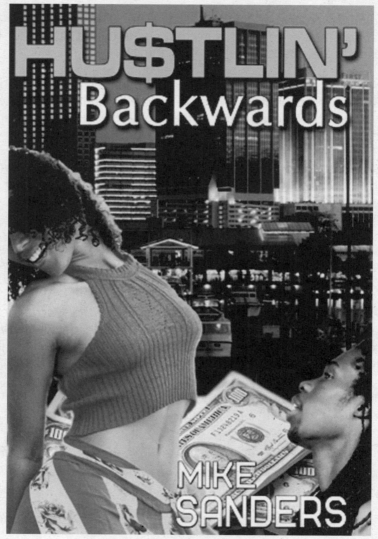

ISBN: 0-9728005-3-0

www.BlackPearlBooks.com

"Hustlin' Backwards"
DESCRIPTION

Capone and his life-long road dawgz, June and Vonzell are out for just one thing…. To get rich!….By any means necessary!

As these three partners in crime rise up the ranks from Project-Kids to Street-Dons, their sworn code of "Death Before Dishonor" gets tested by the Feds.

Though Capone's simple pursuit of forward progression as a Hustler gains him an enviable lifestyle of Fame, Fortune and all the women his libido can handle – It also comes with a price.

No matter the location – Miami, Charlotte, Connecticut or Puerto Rico – There's simply no rest for the wicked!

WARNING: HUSTLIN' BACKWARDS is not the typical street-novel. A Unique Plot, Complex Characters mixed with a Mega-dose of Sensuality makes this story enjoyable by all sorts of readers! A true Hustler himself, Mike Sanders knows the game, inside and out!

"Fast-Paced and Action-Packed! Hustlin' Backwards HAS IT ALL -- Sex, Money, Manipulation and Murder! Mike Sanders is one of the most talented and prolific urban authors of this era!"

BRAND NEW!

From BLACK PEARL BOOKS

NASTY

GAME TIGHT...
...EVERY NIGHT!

A
RAHSAAN ALI
URBAN JOINT

ISBN: 0-9766007-6-5
www.BlackPearlBooks.com

"NASTY"
DESCRIPTION

Life-long friends, Nate & Moe, are certified players! Both have used their jobs in the entertainment industry to their advantage with the women they meet.

Moe is a well-known radio DJ in New York, while Nate is doing his damage with a pen as a magazine writer in Baltimore.

When Nate loses his job in B-more and moves back to New York to freelance for one of the hottest urban magazines, a controversial article he writes about star music artists that are using drugs could lead to his permanent down-fall.

Moe warns Nate about releasing the article, but Nate's regaining of success has him feelin' himself too much – Now he's making big-cash and begins feeling like he's untouchable! Playing women may only get him slapped, but playing with the industry's hottest hardcore rappers that have millions to lose from the article could get Nate 'slumped'!

Kaneecha (Moe's girl), is a sexy-diva clothing model and nympho without a conscience. Kaneecha's always gotta have it, whenever, where-ever! But a horny-night decision may come back to haunt her.

Tierra is a blunt-smoking, hood drama queen from Queens, NY. Though she's known Nate for a long time, it wasn't until he resurfaced in New York years later that she recognized that she wants a piece of that! Later, she views Nate as the answer for her baby-daddy drama.

Janettea (Nate's 'main-girl') is an independent sophisticated-dime that's doing her own thing with interior designing, but can also cop an attitude with a quickness! And, she ain't above giving a beat-down to a hoochie she thinks is sexin' Nate.

All the dirt Nate's doing begins to catch-up with him. Having twice narrowly escaped the hardcore rapper's crew of henchmen seeking revenge against him – he might not be so lucky the next time! Doing the ultimate dirt to his boy Moe, has serious consequences of its own! And, his player-ways gets him played!

It's just the price you pay for being NASTY!

BRAND NEW!

From **BLACK PEARL BOOKS**

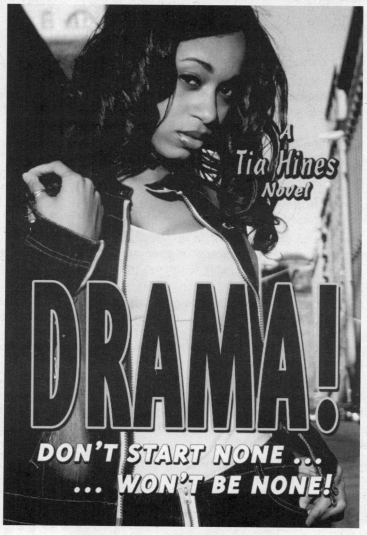

A Tia Hines Novel

DRAMA!

DON'T START NONE ...
... WON'T BE NONE!

ISBN: 0-9766007-5-7

www.BlackPearlBooks.com

"DRAMA!"
DESCRIPTION

Destiny Smith, a young sexy diva, is intent on living the wild-life – a path that puts her on a collision course with nothing good! Spoiled by her boyfriends and protective brother (Chicago), she feels like the world owes her and she'll settle for nothing less.

Sexin' a ball-player, fightin' hoochies, back-stabbin', lyin' and cheatin' are all fair game in the ordinary day of Destiny.

When Destiny's wild behavior catches-up with her and lands her in serious trouble with the law, it's up to her brother (Chicago) to again rescue her. Having no choice, Chicago accepts a favor from a rogue cop -- a favor that he'll soon regret taking – one that will cost much more than they're willing to pay!

Though Chicago takes it upon himself to look-out for his full-grown sister, especially after the broad-daylight murder of their mother – he's also struggling with his own personal-demons. On-and-off relationships with hoodish girlfriends, money problems, court battles, consistent drama-situations in Destiny's life and the rogue cop's increasing strong-arming of him – all of these things are beginning to wear him down to a breaking point.

Chicago tries his best to hold it together – keep from going gangsta, and solving problems in his normal way...with a gun! – But when the tables are turned on him and he smells a set-up that threatens his life, he's forced to take matters into his own hands!

And, when an unexpected event reveals the identity of his mother's killer, placing him face-to-face with them, it's definitely gonna be ON!....There's NO WAY and NOBODY that can stop the *DRAMA*!

BRAND NEW!

From BLACK PEARL BOOKS

DYME Hit List

EVERYONE'S A TARGET TO A TRUE PLAYA

CURTIS ALCUTT

ISBN: 0-9766007-1-4

www.BlackPearlBooks.com

"DYME HIT LIST"
DESCRIPTION

Rio Romero Clark, is an Oakland-bred brotha determined to remain a Playa-For-Life!

Taught by the best of Macks (his Uncle Lee, Father and Grandfather), Rio feels no woman can resist him. And he knows that his game is definitely tight, considering that he's as a third-generation Playa.

It is Rio's United-Nations-like appreciation for all types and races of women, from the Ghetto-Fab to the Professional, that leads him to the biggest challenge of his Mack-hood, Carmen Massey.

Carmen, a luscious southern-Dyme, at first sight, appears to be just another target on Rio's *Dyme Hit List!* Possessing a body that's bangin' enough to make most brothas beg, mixed with southern-charm that can cause even the best playa to hesitate, Carmen's got Rio in jeopardy of getting his Playa-Card revoked.

Burdened with the weight of potentially not living-up to the family Mack-legacy, Rio must choose between continuing to love his lifestyle or loving Carmen.

Unexpectedly tragedy strikes in Rio's life and a dark secret in Carmen's past ignites a fire that threatens to burn-up their relationship, permanently.

"*Dyme Hit List* is On-Fire with Sensuality! This story is pleasingly-filled with lotsa lip-folding scenes! Curtis Alcutt is a bright new star in fiction!"

-- Winston Chapman, Best-Selling Author of *"Wild Thangz"* and *"Caught Up!"*

BRAND NEW!

From BLACK PEARL BOOKS

NUBIAN JAMES

SHAKEDOWN

SECRETS ARE
THE HARDEST
THINGS TO KEEP

ISBN: 0-9728005-9-X
www.BlackPearlBooks.com

"SHAKEDOWN" DESCRIPTION

Paris Hightower, is a sexy young thang who falls in love with the man of her dreams, Tyree Dickerson, the son of very wealthy Real Estate tycoons. But there's a problem.... Tyree's mother (Mrs. Dickerson) thinks that her son is too good for Paris and is dead-set on destroying the relationship at all costs.

After Mrs. Dickerson reveals a long-kept secret to Paris about her mother (Ebony Hightower), a woman that abandoned Paris and her brother more than fifteen years ago when she was forced to flee and hide from police amidst Attempted-Murder charges for shooting Paris' father --- Paris is left in an impossible situation.

Even though the police have long given-up on the search for Ebony Hightower (Paris' mother), the bitter Mrs. Dickerson threatens to find her and turn her in to authorities as blackmail for Paris to end the relationship with her son.

Paris knows that Mrs. Dickerson means business – she has the time, interest and money to hunt down her mother. Left with the choices of pursuing her own happiness or protecting the freedom of her mother, a woman she barely knows, Paris is confused as to the right thing to do.

As the situation escalates to fireworks of private investigators, deception, financial sabotage and kidnapping, even Paris' life becomes in danger.

Just when Paris feels that all hope is lost, she's shocked when she receives unexpected help from an unlikely source.

"Be careful who you mess with, 'cause Payback is a ......! *Shakedown* combines high-drama and mega-suspense with the heart-felt struggle of the price some are willing to pay for love!" -- Winston Chapman, Best-Selling Author of *"Wild Thangz"* and *"Caught Up!"*

BRAND NEW!

From BLACK PEARL BOOKS

BUSTED

NEVER UNDERESTIMATE
A SISTA'S REVENGE!

RHONDA Swan

ISBN: 0-9766007-0-6
www.BlackPearlBooks.com

"BUSTED"
DESCRIPTION

Arianna, Nicole and Janelle each have met a charming man online at LoveMeBlack.com, a popular internet-dating website.

Arianna Singleton, a sassy reporter who moves to Philly to further her career as a journalist, finds herself lonely in the big 'City of Brotherly Love' as she seeks a brotha-to-love online. After several comical dates with duds, she thinks she's finally met a stud.

Nicole Harris, a sanctified Public Relations Executive residing in Maryland puts her salvation on-hold when she begins living with a man that she's met on-line. Stumbling across her new beau's e-mails, she realizes that his Internet pursuits didn't end just because they now share the same zip code.

Janelle Carter, a Virginia Hair Salon Owner spends her nights cruising the Web taking on personas of her sexy, confident clients. A business arrangement that she makes on-line brings her face-to-face with a man she thinks is her destiny.

The lives of Arianna, Nicole and Janelle collide in a drama, as they discover that they've all been dating the same man....Chauncey, a brother that makes a habit out of loving and leaving women that he's met thru LoveMeBlack.com.

The three of them plot to exact their revenge on the unsuspecting Chauncey, as an unforgettable way of letting him know that he's been *BUSTED*!

"Rhonda Swan 'brings it' in this comical story that's a warning to wanna-be players as to what can happen if they ever get *Busted*!"

-- Winston Chapman, Best-Selling Author of *"Wild Thangz"* and *"Caught Up!"*

BEST-SELLER!

From BLACK PEARL BOOKS

SLICK

NOBODY'S MAN
IS SAFE...
...NOT EVEN
YOUR MAN!

Brenda
HAMPTON

ISBN: 0-9728005-5-7

www.BlackPearlBooks.com

"Slick"
DESCRIPTION

Dana & Sylvia have been girlfriends for what seems like forever. They've never been afraid to share everything about their lives and definitely keep each other's secrets ... including hiding Dana's On-The-DL affair from her husband, Jonathan.

Though Sylvia is uncomfortable with her participation in the cover-up and despises the man Dana's creepin' with, she remains a loyal friend. That is, until she finds herself attracted to the very man her friend is deceiving.

As the lines of friendship and matrimonial territory erodes, all hell is about to break loose! Choices have to be made with serious repercussions at stake.

If loving you is wrong, I don't wanna be right!

"SLICK!!! .... Ain't That The Truth! Brenda Hampton's Tale Sizzles With Sensuality, Deception, Greed and So Much Drama – My Gurrll!"

- MYSTERIOUS LUVA, BEST-SELLING AUTHOR OF
SEX A BALLER

BEST-SELLER!

From BLACK PEARL BOOKS

AN ESSENCE® MAGAZINE BEST-SELLER

WILD THANGZ

Things Get HOT
Livin' In The
FAST LANE!

WINSTON CHAPMAN

ISBN: 0-9728005-2-2
www.BlackPearlBooks.com

"Wild Thangz"
DESCRIPTION

Jazmyn, Trina and Brea are definitely a trio of Drama-Magnets - the sista-girlz version of Charlie's Angels. Young & fine with bangin' bodies, the three of them feel like they can do no wrong – not even with each other.

No matter the location: Jamaica, Miami, NYC or the A-T-L, lust, greed and trouble is never far from these wanna-be divas.

Jazymn has secret dreams that if she pursues will cause her to have mega family problems. Though the most logical of the group, she can get her attitude on with the best of them when pushed.

Trina wasn't always the diva. Book-smarts used to be her calling-card. But, under the tutoring of her personal hoochie-professor, Brea, she's just now beginning to understand the power that she has in her traffic-stopping Badunkadunk.

Brea has the face of a princess, but is straight ghetto-fab -- without the slightest shame. As the wildest of the bunch, her personal credos of living life to the fullest and to use *what her mama gave her* to get ahead, is constantly creating drama for Jazymn and Trina.

When past skeleton-choices in Brea's closet places all three of them in an impossible life-and-death situation, they must take an action that has the most serious of consequences, in order to survive!

The very foundation of their friendship-bond gets tested, as each of them have the opportunity to sell-out the other! The question is, Will They?

Wild Parties, Wild Situations & Wild Nights are always present for these Wild Thangz!

Best-Selling Author of "Caught Up!", Winston Chapman weaves yet another suspenseful, sexy-drama tale that's a Must-Read!

"Wild Thangz is HOT! Winston Chapman shonuff brings the HEAT!"
-- Mysterious Luva, Essence Magazine Best-Selling Author of
"Sex A Baller"

BRAND NEW!
From BLACK PEARL BOOKS

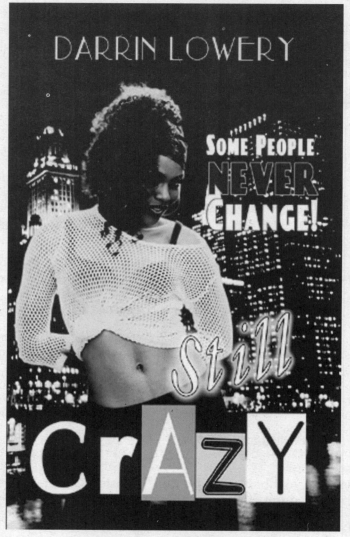

DARRIN LOWERY

SOME PEOPLE NEVER CHANGE!

Still CrAzY

ISBN: 0-9728005-8-1
www.BlackPearlBooks.com

"STILL CRAZY" DESCRIPTION

Kevin Allen, a rich, handsome author and self-reformed 'Mack', is now suffering from writer's block.

Desperately in need of a great story in order to renegotiate with his publisher to maintain his extravagant life-style, Kevin decides to go back to his hometown of Chicago for inspiration. While in Chi-town, he gets reacquainted with an ex-love (Yolanda) that he'd last seen during their stormy relationship that violently came to an end.

Unexpectedly, Yolanda appears at a book-event where Kevin is the star-attraction, looking every bit as stunningly beautiful as the picture he's had frozen in his head for years. She still has the looks of music video model and almost makes him forget as to the reason he'd ever broken off their relationship.

It's no secret, Yolanda had always been the jealous type. And, Kevin's explanation to his boyz, defending his decision for kicking a woman that fine to the curb was, "She's Crazy!".

The combination of Kevin's vulnerable state in his career, along with the tantalizing opportunity to hit *that* again, causes Kevin to contemplate renewing his expired Players-Card, one last time. What harm could one night of passion create?

Clouding his judgment even more is that Kevin feels like hooking-up with Yolanda might just be the rekindling needed to ignite the fire for his creativity in his writing career. But, there are just two problems. Kevin is married! ....And, Yolanda is *Still Crazy!*

"Darrin Lowery deliciously serves up.....Scandal & Sexy-Drama like no other! *STILL CRAZY* has all the goods readers are looking for!" -- *Brenda Hampton, Author of "Slick"*

BEST-SELLER!

From BLACK PEARL BOOKS

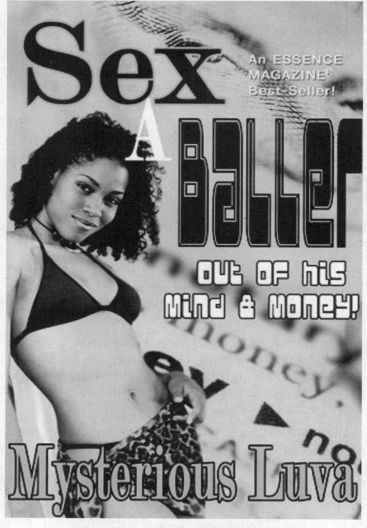

An ESSENCE MAGAZINE® Best-Seller!

ISBN: 0-9728005-1-4

www.BlackPearlBooks.com

"Sex A Baller"
DESCRIPTION

Mysterious Luva has sexed them all! Ball players, CEO's, Music Stars -- You name the baller, she's had them. And more importantly, she's made them all pay......

Sex A Baller is a poignant mix of a sexy tale of how Mysterious Luva has become one of the World's Best Baller Catchers and an Instructional Guide for the wanna-be Baller Catcher!

No details or secrets are spared, as she delivers her personal story along with the winning tips & secrets for daring women interested in catching a baller!

PLUS, A SPECIAL BONUS SECTION INCLUDED!

Baller Catching 101

- Top-20 Baller SEX POSITIONS (Photos!)
- Where To FIND A Baller
- Which Ballers Have The BIGGEST Penis
- SEDUCING A Baller
- Making A Baller Fall In Love
- Getting MONEY From A Baller
- What Kind Of SEX A Baller Likes
- The EASIEST Type of Baller To Catch
- Turning A Baller Out In Bed
- GAMES To Play On A Baller
- Getting Your Rent Paid & A Free Car
- Learn All The SECRETS!

BY THE END OF THIS BOOK, YOU'LL HAVE YOUR CERTIFIED BALLER-CATCHER'S DEGREE!

BEST-SELLER!

From BLACK PEARL BOOKS

"AN ESSENCE MAGAZINE® BEST-SELLER"

CAUGHT UP!

Dare to explore a world most have only heard about!

Peachtree S

WINSTON CHAPMAN

ISBN: 0-9728005-0-6

www.BlackPearlBooks.com

"CAUGHT UP!"
DESCRIPTION

When Raven Klein, a bi-racial woman from Iowa moves to Atlanta in hopes of finding a life she's secretly dreamed about, she finds more than she ever imagined.

Quickly lured and lost in a world of sex, money, power-struggles, betrayal & deceit, Raven doesn't know who she can really trust!

A chance meeting at a bus terminal leads to her delving into the seedy world of strip-clubs, big-ballers and shot-callers.

Now, Raven's shuffling through more men than a Vegas blackjack dealer does a deck of cards. And sex has even become mundane -- little more than a tool to get what she wants.

After a famous acquaintance winds-up dead -- On which shoulder will Raven lean? A wrong choice could cost her life!

There's a reason they call it HOTATLANTA!

BRAND NEW!
From BLACK PEARL BOOKS

HYPED

Sophisticated Game...
...is still just
as GHETTO!

A LUKE NOVEL

ISBN: 0-9728005-6-5
www.BlackPearlBooks.com

"HYPED"
DESCRIPTION

Maurice LaSalle is a player – of women and the saxophone. A gifted musician, he's the driving force behind MoJazz, a neo-soul group on the verge of their big break. Along with his partner in rhyme and crime, Jamal Grover, Maurice has more women than he can count. Though guided by his mentor Simon, Maurice knows Right but constantly does Wrong.

Then Ebony Stanford enters Maurice's world and he begins to play a new tune. Ebony, still reeling from a nasty divorce, has just about given up on men, but when Maurice hits the right notes (everywhere) she can't help but fall for his charms.

While Maurice and Ebony get closer, Jamal is busy putting so many notches on his headboard post after each female conquest, that the post looks more like a tooth-pick. When a stalker threatens his life, Maurices warns him to slow his roll, but Jamal's hyped behavior prevails over good sense.

Just as Maurice is contemplating turning in his player card for good, stupidity overrules his judgment and throws his harmonious relationship with Ebony into a tale-spin. When it appears that things couldn't get any worse, tragedy strikes and his life is changed forever!

A Powerfully-Written Sexy-Tale, *HYPED* is a unique blend of Mystery, Suspense, Intrigue and Glowing-Sensuality.

"Buckle Up! HYPED Will Test All Of Your Senses and Emotions! LUKE Is A Force To Be Reckoned With For Years To Come!" -- WINSTON CHAPMAN, ESSENCE MAGAZINE BEST-SELLING AUTHOR OF "CAUGHT UP!" AND "WILD THANGZ"

BRAND NEW!
From BLACK PEARL BOOKS

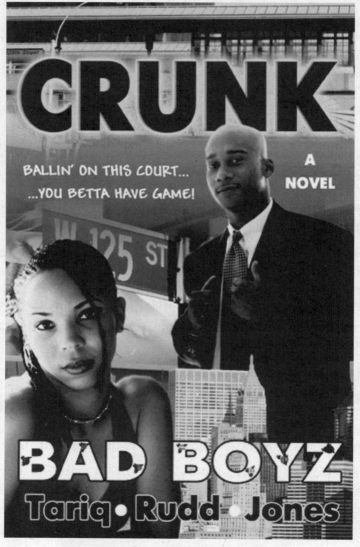

CRUNK

BALLIN' ON THIS COURT...
...YOU BETTA HAVE GAME!

A NOVEL

W 125 ST

BAD BOYZ

Tariq•Rudd•Jones

ISBN: 0-9728005-4-9
www.BlackPearlBooks.com

"CRUNK"
DESCRIPTION

Imagine a Thug-World divided by the Mason-Dixon Line……..

After the brutal murder of four NYC ganstas in Charlotte, the climate is set for an all-out Thug Civil War – North pitted against South!

Rah-Rah, leader of NYC's underworld and KoKo, head of one of the Durty South's most ferocious Crunk-crews are on a collision course to destruction. While Rah-Rah tries to rally his northern Thugdom (Philly, NJ & NY), KoKo attempts to saddle-up heads of the southern Hoodville (Atlanta, South Carolina & Charlotte).

Kendra and Janeen, a southern sister-duo of self-proclaimed baddest b*****'s, conduct a make-shift Thug Academy to prepare KoKo's VA-bred cousin (Shine) to infiltrate NYC's underground, as a secret weapon to the impending battle.

The US Government, well-aware of the upcoming war, takes a backseat role, not totally against the idea that a war of this magnitude might actual do what the Government has been unable to do with thousands of life sentences -- Rid society completely of the dangerous element associated with the Underground-World.

Suspensfully-Sexy, Erotically-Ghetto and Mysteriously-Raw. CRUNK will leave you saying, Hmmmm?

"Get Ready For A Wild & Sexy Ride! Twists & Turns Are Abundant! An Instant Urban Classic Thriller! Tariq, Rudd & Jones Are Definitely Some BAD BOYZ! Errr'body Gettin' CRUNK!"

Black Pearl Books

Get In The Mood!

WWW.BLACKPEARLBOOKS.COM

Your Best Source For HOT & SEXY URBAN STORIES!

JOIN THE E-MAIL LIST!

NEW RELEASES, SPECIALS & FREE GIVEAWAYS

ON-LINE ORDERING:
www.Amazon.com

AUTHORS:

INTERESTED IN BEING PUBLISHED BY BLACK PEARL BOOKS INC?

Send Synopsis Cover Letter
& (Non-Returnable)Full-Manuscript To:

BLACK PEARL BOOKS
3653-F FLAKES MILL ROAD ▪ PMB 306
ATLANTA, GEORGIA 30034
Review Process Takes About 3-4 weeks

BLACK PEARL BOOKS
PUBLISHING

Your Best Source For
Hot & Sexy Urban Stories

LOOK FOR THIS LOGO – For Quality Urban Books!

www.BlackPearlBooks.com

Join Our E-Mail List
For New Releases,
Specials & FREE
Giveaways!!

Black Pearl Books Publishing

Get In The Mood!

WWW.BLACKPEARLBOOKS.COM

Visit Eric Myrieckes' Website!

www.EricMyrieckesBooks.com

TO ORDER ADDITIONAL COPIES OF Black Pearl Books Titles:

ON-LINE ORDERING:
www.Amazon.com

AUTHORS:
INTERESTED IN BEING PUBLISHED BY BLACK PEARL BOOKS INC?

Send Synopsis Cover Letter
& (Non-Returnable) Manuscripts To:

BLACK PEARL BOOKS, INC.
ATTENTION: EDITOR
3653-F FLAKES MILL RD ▪ PMB 306
ATLANTA, GEORGIA 30034
* Review Process Takes About 3-4 weeks *

BLACK PEARL BOOKS INC.

ORDER FORM

Black Pearl Books Inc.
3653-F Flakes Mill Road- PMB 306
Atlanta, Georgia 30034
www. BlackPearlBooks. com

YES, We Ship Directly To Prisons & Correctional Facilities
INSTITUTIONAL CHECKS & MONEY ORDERS ONLY!

TITLE	Price	Quantity	TOTAL
"Caught Up!" by Winston Chapman	$ 14. 95		
"Sex A Baller" by Mysterious Luva	$ 12. 95		
"Wild Thangz" by Winston Chapman	$ 14. 95		
"Crunk" by Bad Boyz	$ 14. 95		
"Hustlin Backwards" by Mike Sanders	$ 14. 95		
"Still Crazy" by Darrin Lowery	$ 14. 95		
"Twisted" by Holland Jones	$ 14. 95		
"Slick" by Brenda Hampton	$ 14. 95		
"Hyped" by Luke	$ 14. 95		
"Dyme Hit List" by Curtis Alcutt	$ 14. 95		
"Busted" by Rhonda Swan	$ 14. 95		
"Shakedown" by Nubian James	$ 14. 95		
"Hustlers" by Ronald Quincy	$ 14. 95		
"Legit Baller" by Jerry Blackshear	$ 14. 95		
"Street Games" by Eric Myrieckes	$ 14. 95		
"Nasty" by Rahsaan Ali	$ 14. 95		
"Drama!" by Tia Hines	$ 14. 95		

Sub-Total	$	
SHIPPING: ___ # books x $ 3. 50 ea. **(Via US Priority Mail)**	$	
GRAND TOTAL	$	

SHIP TO:
Name: _____
Address: _____
Apt or Box #: _____
City: _____ **State:** _____ **Zip:** _____
Phone: _____ **E-mail:** _____